The Cornish Mermaid

The Cornish Ladies
Book One

Fil Reid

© Copyright 2024 by Fil Reid
Text by Fil Reid
Cover by Dar Albert

Dragonblade Publishing, Inc. is an imprint of Kathryn Le Veque Novels, Inc.
P.O. Box 23
Moreno Valley, CA 92556
ceo@dragonbladepublishing.com

Produced in the United States of America

First Edition June 2024
Print Edition

Reproduction of any kind except where it pertains to short quotes in relation to advertising or promotion is strictly prohibited.

All Rights Reserved.

The characters and events portrayed in this book are fictitious. Any similarity to real persons, living or dead, is purely coincidental and not intended by the author.

ARE YOU SIGNED UP FOR DRAGONBLADE'S BLOG?

You'll get the latest news and information on exclusive giveaways, exclusive excerpts, coming releases, sales, free books, cover reveals and more.

Check out our complete list of authors, too!

No spam, no junk. That's a promise!

Sign Up Here

www.dragonbladepublishing.com

Dearest Reader;

Thank you for your support of a small press. At Dragonblade Publishing, we strive to bring you the highest quality Historical Romance from some of the best authors in the business. Without your support, there is no 'us', so we sincerely hope you adore these stories and find some new favorite authors along the way.

Happy Reading!

CEO, Dragonblade Publishing

Additional Dragonblade books by Author Fil Reid

The Cornish Ladies Series
The Cornish Mermaid (Book 1)

Guinevere Series
The Dragon Ring (Book 1)
The Bear's Heart (Book 2)
The Sword (Book 3)
Warrior Queen (Book 4)
The Quest for Excalibur (Book 5)
The Road to Avalon (Book 6)

Chapter One

Morvoren: Cornish compound name meaning mermaid or sea-maiden
Morvoren n.f morvoronyon n.pl – mermaid

The Present Day

WHY, OH, WHY had she agreed to accompany Josh on this tourist sea fishing trip out from Penzance? What's more, to do it on the very last day of their holiday, when she could have been topping up her tan in the tiny garden of their holiday cottage with a good book. Not only was she feeling seasick, thanks to the little fishing boat's diesel fumes and the strong stench of fish, but her poor heart kept doing a wild lurch every time the vessel bucked on the waves. And on top of that, she hadn't been able to locate any lifejackets.

She'd turned to Josh on the quayside as he held his hand out to help her on board. "Where are the lifejackets? I want to be wearing one. You know how I feel about water."

He'd laughed in his irritating way, as though she were an idiot for wanting to feel safe. "They'll be stored down below. This is a fishing trip, not the Titanic's maiden voyage—you're not going to need one." After a week of being laughed at, Morvoren was beginning to think their relationship doomed. Dumping him once they were safely home was something she was looking forward to.

Impervious to her suffering, the captain of the little fishing boat nodded his grizzled head towards the line of towering cliffs in the distance. The eyes of every shorts-clad tourist on the boat followed his pointing finger. "We'll head inland, now. You often get small shoals of mackerel near the cliffs. It'll be a bit rocky with this swell, but it'll be worth it."

Would it? Morvoren doubted it very much.

She'd only agreed to this trip because Josh had begrudgingly come on that pony trek with her. "I went riding with you, didn't I?" he'd wheedled. "I put up with getting a sore bum on that flipping horse, just so you could live your dream and ride on a beach. You owe me big time."

Backed into a corner, she'd said yes in a moment of foolhardy gratitude, when what she should have said wasn't repeatable.

Not content with her agreement, he'd rubbed in his victory. "You need to face your fears, Morvoren. You'll really love fishing and won't even notice the water." And his crowning argument. "Your mother named you after a mermaid, after all, and you kind of look like one, being so pretty and with all that long blonde hair." Something he'd repeated several times already this morning as though flattery would get him places.

Ha, bloody ha.

For the hundredth time, Morvoren scanned the deck and wheelhouse, searching for a locker she could fish a lifejacket out of in an emergency. Like right now. The way the little fishing boat was heaving on the considerable swell smacked her as worthy of emergency measures. Although the other half-dozen fishing tourists, who'd joined them on board an hour ago, seemed oblivious to the imminent danger of sinking. And Josh was totally ignoring her, chatting to a big bloke in a floral shirt about how to attach their smelly bait to the hooks.

What would happen if the boat capsized and sank? She, for one, would drown, because she couldn't swim. And the reason she couldn't swim was because water had always terrified her. So much so that she never went farther into the surf than ankle deep and suspected all waves of either harboring sharks or threatening to wash her out to sea.

Josh caught her looking at him, where he was busy unhooking a wriggling mackerel from his line, and gave her a condescending grin. "See. I told you it'd be fine. You just had to face your fear to get over it. Like those people did in that TV program. You're missing out on the fun just sitting there at the back on your own. Why don't you come over here with us, and I'll bait you a line? I told you it'd be easy to get over your silly little fears."

Really? She'd like to have seen him have to face up to a genuine phobia.

She forced a smile onto her face. "No, thank you. I'm fine here." Where she could hang on tight.

The engine note changed down to a gentle hum as the captain let it idle. With his sea-booted mate, he emerged from the small wheelhouse, ready to help everyone set up their lines again. They already had a good few iridescent, silvery-blue mackerel flip-flopping in the locker down the center of the boat.

"See this here cove." He raised his deep, gravelly voice above the mingled sounds of the engine, the crashing of the waves at the cliffs' feet, and the screech of greedy gulls overhead, eager to partake of the catch. "There's a story about this cove. It's been called Smuggler's Cove for a good two hundred years, but before that, it were just Nanpean Cove." He had everyone's attention, even Josh's. For a moment.

"'Tis said it's haunted by the ghosts of the smugglers who was caught by the soldiers and revenue men an' hanged in Bodmin jail back in 1811. Some of them was even killed right there on that beach." He pointed at the thin crescent of silver sand. "It were part of a county-wide clamp down on what were known back then as 'free trade.' And this here were the biggest catch o' free traders the revenue men ever had around these parts, with a man from ev'ry family in Nanpean village involved. A man from ev'ry family hanged."

Only yesterday Morvoren had been in Penzance's little museum while Josh fished off the harbor wall, and seen a whole display about smuggling. Part of it had covered this particular story, so it was fresh in her mind. Hadn't it said twenty men had hanged and three or four were killed on the beach, with a copy of an old portrait of one of them? To take her mind off her fears, she concentrated on remembering the details.

Up close to the wheelhouse, Josh scowled in annoyance at the delay to his fishing. He hadn't been interested in going to the museum with her yesterday, and she'd realized early in their holiday that while he was near water, unless the talk was about fish, he had the attention span of one of their brethren—a goldfish.

The captain smacked his lips in relish at the tragedy of the story. "Local legend do say there were an informer amongst the smuggler's own ranks, and he were the only man not hanged. The local villagers rumbled him, though, and chucked him off that cliff up there on the right." He pointed a gnarled finger. "Folks around here have never forgot their dead, an' 'tis said the smugglers' ghosts do walk the path up from the beach onto the moor ev'ry moonless night, the sound of their ponies' muffled hooves an' their quiet whispers all you'll hear."

"Like anyone cares," Josh said, rather too audibly.

Ignoring his rudeness, Morvoren stared into the cove. How inviting that curve of sand looked, where it lay between the cliffs and the narrow valley up which those long-ago smugglers had been intending to lead their ponies. How quiet and peaceful. If only she were on that beach instead of here in this unstable fishing boat.

The story told, the captain and his mate turned their attention to their passengers, helping them bait their lines and cast. Not that Josh needed any help. He was busy showing off to the laughing tourists that he knew what he was doing.

Selfish git.

With everyone happily oblivious to her woes, and with their fishing rods poised to add more to the mackerel haul, all Morvoren could do was keep hanging onto the side. The only one not fishing and the only one sick and the only one who didn't like this one little bit.

As the idling fishing boat tossed on the swell, getting far too close to those threatening cliffs for comfort, a wave struck her sideways on, and a sheet of cold spray flew up, spattering one side of Morvoren's face. What a very bad idea this had been. The diesel stink of the engine fumes mingled unattractively with the strong stench of fish and seaweed. No wonder she was feeling so sick. Bloody Josh and his love of fishing.

An even bigger wave splashed up, as the boat, with no one at the helm, turned against the current. The seawater soaked the deck and all down one side of Morvoren's already damp T-shirt and jeans, wetting one foot and plastering her long hair to the side of her face. Some of it went in her mouth and eyes, so she screwed them shut and spat violently. Goodness knew where the local towns' sewage went—probably straight into the sea.

She was still wiping wet hair off her face and clinging onto the slippery wooden rail with only one hand, when a second, much larger wave hit the boat side-on.

A few excited squeals and some hysterical laughter exploded from the fishing tourists. The boat rose into the air on the increasing swell, and Morvoren's precarious, one-handed hold slipped. The deck reared under her, propelling her upwards as though she were on a trampoline, then dropped away and twisted beneath where her feet should have landed. When she came down, the boat wasn't there anymore. Instead, cold water rushed up to meet her and the bright blue of the sky vanished into a blur of green.

Water went up her nose as she sank like a stone, the sea swallowing her.

The shimmering sunlight at the surface vanished, the water enveloping her like a cold bath. The underside of the boat hung suspended above her, its bottom red-painted and fat as she plummeted away from it.

For a long moment, a curious calmness had her in its hold. This was it. The end. Every childhood nightmare had been a premonition of this moment.

No. What was she doing? She had to fight to save herself.

With a burst of energy born of terror, she thrashed out with arms and legs in a wild attempt to stop this sinking and battle back to the surface. People floated, didn't they? Or so every swimming instructor who'd ever tried to cure her of her fear had reassured her. You won't sink. You're safe. How wrong had they been?

But however hard she kicked out, she kept on sinking. Was a whirlpool sucking her into a vortex she'd never escape from? Was she caught in some deadly undercurrent that refused to let her back to the surface? Waves of pure terror surged through her body, icy in their tight hold, freezing her brain and numbing every thought process.

Her legs were losing strength, and something inexorable was pulling her down, dragging her to her death, determined to drown her. She peered through the murky gloom. Rope, or maybe an old fishing net, had snared her feet, perhaps snagged on a rock or a wreck, lurking below the water, waiting to catch itself a swimmer.

The urge to breathe, to open her mouth and let in that murderous seawater, was overwhelming. A dim awareness surfaced in her fuddled brain. The more she struggled, the faster she was using up what little oxygen remained in her lungs. No. She had to breathe. She just had to.

The world darkened, her vision blurred, and the urge to take that breath magnified. She couldn't keep her mouth and nose closed any longer or she'd explode, and then she'd be dead anyway. She had to breathe. If only she had gills like a fish…

She opened her mouth.

Water rushed in, not cold and wet but hot and burning. No life-giving oxygen to save her. For a brief moment that stretched into an eternity, she drifted. It must be true that when you were dying your life flashed before your eyes, because here it was, galloping past in a thousand brief flashes from her first day at nursery school and Mum explaining for the umpteenth time that, no, it wasn't Morwen or Morwenna, but Morvoren. Then, on to her first boyfriend and those furtive kisses behind the cricket pavilion on the school playing field, followed by university, the car crash that robbed her of her parents, and finally, meeting her best friend, Tina, and renting their little flat together.

But it was over in a moment that stretched on forever, and darkness descended, darkness and nothing. If this was death, then it wasn't as bad as she'd thought it would be.

Chapter Two

1811

KIT HAULED IN his net over the side of his little sailing boat, the *Rosenwyn*, with a frown of disappointment and the ache of hard work between his shoulder blades. Her brown sails flapped loose in the light summer breeze. Nothing, again, even though he'd sailed out a long way to cast his nets. He might as well head back to Nanpean Cove and home.

However, despite all indications that today was not a good day for fish, he possessed the fisherman's optimism that trying just once more would give him something to take back to Jenifry, Uncle Jago's housekeeper and long-term bed companion. She would clap him on the back in congratulation and fry the fish in butter for their supper that night with some of her delicious bread to mop their plates. Then they'd wash it down with a pint or two of his uncle's finest cider, and maybe afterwards take a glass of good contraband French brandy as they sat in front of the fire together.

Shrugging his shoulders, his mouth watering, Kit threw his net over the side one last time. He might get lucky. He sometimes did close by the cliffs.

The net sank into the gently undulating surface of the sea, down and down, floating out of sight. One turn of the boat to gather up whatever he'd caught, and he'd haul it in. He pulled on the tiller, and the wind caught the sails. No point spending too much time. He gave the net a tentative tug, feeling the weight of something caught in it. Felt like a lot of fish.

Heart banging in the anticipation only a fisherman could understand, he began to haul the net in. With every heave of his strong, callused hands, his excitement rose. Whatever nestled in weed at the bottom of his net was heavy.

For a moment, he hesitated as the catch came into view. Something large and definitely not fish shimmered through the water. Through the weed, wet blonde hair trailed across the pale, blue-tinged skin of a face. Where the legs should have been—was that a blue tail?

Oh God, he'd caught a mermaid.

He couldn't have. They didn't exist. And on top of that, fishermen who caught them, according to the tales, either went mad or ended up dead.

Or both.

He nearly pushed the net and the mermaid back into the water, but then common sense took over. Firstly, it wasn't his net but Uncle Jago's, who would no doubt be furious if he lost it, as nets were either expensive to buy or a trouble to make. And secondly, that wasn't a tail, but legs in breeches.

Oh God, again. He'd dredged up a corpse. Hardly any improvement on finding a mermaid. Not that they really existed. Did they? Although his mother, a firm believer in all things fae, would have had something to say about his denial.

The net hung heavily on the side of *Rosenwyn*, making her heel hard to starboard. Much as he didn't want to, he'd have to pull the corpse on board. He'd have to touch it. He'd rather have touched a mermaid than the body of a drowned girl. A drowned girl in breeches.

Kit's hold on the net slackened, and for a moment the body in the net sank beneath the water again, the girl's light-colored hair floating ethereally about her beautiful pale face like weed. Then, squaring his shoulders for the unwelcome task, he heaved net and body onto the deck of his little boat as the sails flapped in the breeze.

A girl indeed, and not long dead by the look of her.

Her long hair once more clung to her pale skin, giving her a look of the mythical sea creature he'd first thought her. Dark lashes brushed her cheeks, and her lips were blue-tinged. Much as he recoiled from the task, he'd better disentangle her from his net.

Letting the *Rosenwyn* drift on the gentle swell, he rolled back the net from around the girl's body with some difficulty and, hauling her forward, sent her flopping onto the bottom boards. Water trickled out of the corner of her mouth as he freed her limbs from the clutch of the weed she'd become entwined in. Rotten bits of old netting snagged her feet, both of which were clad in some strange white footwear the like of which he'd never seen before.

What on earth was he supposed to do with a dead body? Today, of all days, as well.

He received an answer to his question quickly enough. As she slumped forward, she coughed. More water cascaded from her mouth.

She wasn't a mermaid, and she wasn't dead, thank the Lord. A wave of immense relief washing over him, despite a quick misgiving that it might be harder to deal with a live young woman than a drowned one, Kit leapt into action.

With deft hands, he propped her on her side against the thwart and thumped her on the back until she coughed again, and more water spurted out. "That's it," he said. "Cough it all up and you'll feel better in a minute."

She didn't look up but took his advice to heart and kept on coughing and spluttering, hunched there on the deck of his boat like a piece of flotsam. By the look of her, he'd better get her to the beach and onto dry land. Fast.

But where on earth had she come from? He gave a quick scan of the horizon as he gathered in the trailing ropes for his sails. Nothing.

No sign of any boat, big or small, and definitely no larger ships. The horizon was empty. No boat but the *Rosenwyn* had been out fishing that day, and yet, he'd managed to catch a girl in his net.

A mystery.

Leaving the semi-conscious girl to cough her guts up, he took down the sails and slipped the oars into the rowlocks. Far quicker to row than to try to tack against the wind. With practiced skill and powerful pulls on the oars, he steered the little craft deeper into the cove.

As he drew closer, the sound of the waves rolling up the beach, magnified by the high, surrounding headlands, assaulted his ears—stronger surf than when he'd set out this morning, but he could do it.

He glanced down at the girl again. "Nearly at the beach. I'll have you on dry land before long."

No response.

Where the breakers began, he pulled in the oars and, grabbing the painter, jumped into chest high water to drag the boat behind him. By the time he had it pulled out on the sand above the high-water mark, he was soaked to the skin.

Lucky for the hot sun.

Now he could turn his attention to the girl lying crumpled on the wet boards. She couldn't stay there. And for the first time he paid a bit more attention to what she was wearing. He'd thought her legs a tail, and he could see why now. Her tight breeches were of a faded blue-grey color not unlike the skin of a dolphin. Or of a mermaid. How very odd. And what was more, they rather disconcertingly revealed her exact shape from the waist down, something no young lady should consider doing.

He glanced at her top half and had to take a step back. All she wore at the top was some kind of thin chemise—and being wet it was almost see-through, revealing something black shining through from underneath—something black and lacy.

For a girl who'd attired herself in a man's breeches, this black lacy thing seemed quite out of character, but what it actually was escaped Kit. Perhaps she'd lost the rest of her clothes in the water, and all of this was some sort of undergarment?

"I'm sorry, but I'm going to have to carry you. I apologize in advance for any impropriety—it's not intended." There, that should cover him.

Not quite sure where to put his hands on this very underdressed female, he bent into the boat and scooped her into his arms, her head lolling unresponsive against his chest. Then, with the sand hot under his bare feet, he strode up the sloping beach toward the narrow group of dunes. Laying her down, he knelt by her side.

Damn it. He really didn't need this. Not today.

What should he do now? She'd coughed up most of the water, but her skin still had a worryingly grey tinge and her body had felt icy cold in his arms. She hadn't opened her eyes, but at least she'd stopped coughing, although that might not be a good sign. He glanced about in indecision. No blanket, and his own clothes were so wet there was no point in offering her his shirt, which was all he had anyway.

He took her cold hand in his and chafed it. "Miss?" he tried. "Miss, are you all right?"

He felt a fool. She clearly wasn't all right at all.

The girl stirred a little and her eyes opened a crack, enabling him to see they were startlingly blue. The bright summer sunshine must have dazzled her though, because she closed them again in a hurry.

"Josh?" she whispered, her voice feathery and light.

Who was Josh? A wave of unexpected annoyance washed over Kit that her first words had been for someone other than himself. He'd rescued her, after all, and not this Josh, whoever he was. Wherever he was. He cast a quick glance back at the sea, but it still remained devoid of all craft. No Josh in sight.

He patted her hand in what he hoped, not being used to rescuing damsels from watery graves, was a comforting way. There was nothing for it. He'd have to take her up to the farm despite what Jago would say about tonight. "You're freezing. I need to get you somewhere warm. Do you think you can stand?"

Her eyes opened again, a little wider this time, enabling him to further appreciate their mesmerizing color. He'd never seen eyes of such an intense blue. She licked her lips. "I—I think so. If you can help me up."

This meant touching her again, and despite the fact he'd already done so, reticence washed over Kit. If only she were wearing more clothes. He steeled himself and put a wary arm around her shoulders, propping her up into a sitting position. The effort made her close her eyes again.

"I'm so sorry," she whispered. "I think I'm going to be sick." She leaned away from him and cast up her accounts on the sand—a mixture of seawater and what looked like bread. She wiped her mouth and spat a few times. "Gross," came her whisper. "Don't look."

Obedient to her wish, he averted his eyes and peered down the beach towards where Rosenwyn sat. Still not a single other boat marred the blue horizon.

"I feel better now," the girl whispered, after a minute. "I'll get up if you can give me your arm."

Kit scrambled to his feet and bent to help her to hers. Once upright, she stood swaying slightly, eyes closed, as though dizziness threatened to overcome her, or the urge to further cast up her accounts. He kept a steadying arm around her shoulders, acutely aware of the chill of her skin against his own warm body.

Should he carry her? A difficult job through the soft sand of the dunes even though she wasn't very heavy. He was about to offer when she spoke again.

"Where am I?"

At least she was showing some interest in her surroundings now.

"Nanpean Cove. I pulled you out of the sea. You nearly drowned."

She blinked up at him as though barely seeing him. "Where's Josh?"

Despite the sand now sticking to her wet hair and the pallor of her skin, he could see she was a pretty girl, made beautiful by those eyes. He shrugged. "I don't know, but I have to get you somewhere warm and into some dry clothes. Can you walk, do you think?"

She nodded. "I'll be okay now. Lead the way."

The quicker he got her in front of the warm fire in Jago's kitchen, the better.

He slid his arm down until it encompassed her slender waist, far too aware of the paucity of her clothing, but manners dictated that he couldn't let her walk unaided. Not after nearly drowning. That thin undergarment felt like the next best thing to bare skin. A hot flush radiated through his body at the thought of touching this girl, or any nicely brought up young lady in fact, in such a state of undress. Usually, they were protected by their very considerable upholstery.

Together, they slogged up the heavy going of the dunes until they reached the path that led inland from the beach. This was where Kit had left his boots that morning, having run barefoot down to find his boat, carrying his oars.

He lowered his charge onto a hummock of tussocky grass. "I just have to put my boots on. Will you be all right sitting here for a minute? The next bit's steep. Don't talk if you don't want to."

A shaky nod.

In a hurry to get back to her, he pulled on his top boots over bare, sandy feet, stuffing his stockings into his breeches' pockets. The girl didn't look up once, her shoulders rising and falling with the effort of the walk through the loose sand, and her hair falling in sandy rats' tails over her face. Perhaps he should have obeyed his first instinct and carried her.

"Can you go on?" he asked, and she managed a nod.

Once he had her on her feet again and they were on the sounder ground of the stony path, Kit was able to lessen his hold on her. A relief. He'd been becoming more and more aware of the rise and fall of her unprotected ribcage against his arm, and that hot glow of embarrassment he'd felt earlier had grown.

Why on earth was he feeling like a green boy? It wasn't as if he'd never touched a naked female form before. Annoyance at his own reaction only served to make him more awkwardly aware of the girl at his side.

The steep walk up the dunes had brought some color back to her cheeks, bestowing an altogether healthier shade to a skin that was surprisingly tanned, as though she spent a lot of her time out of doors. Just as he did. How strange in a young lady of obvious delicate birth. Experience had taught him that ladies of quality normally abhorred being outside in the sun without a parasol in case they developed freckles. Did she have any? He took a quick glance and saw that a few sprinkled her small nose and cheeks.

"Not much further now. I live just up here. Do you still feel able to walk?"

A nod.

Every twist of the path from the beach was as familiar to Kit as the back of his hand, but it had never felt so long, nor so steep as it did today. The warm air hung in the narrow valley, redolent with the scent of the heather, and the cry of gulls rose above the hot summery sound of gorse popping on the steep hillside.

They paused for a breather halfway up and he lowered her onto a large rock where she sat with her head down, chest heaving with the effort.

"I'm so sorry to be such a nuisance," she whispered, without looking up, her voice croaky.

Kit shrugged, even though she couldn't have seen him do so. "I'm just glad I was there to save you and you're not dead." Not much else he could say. He fidgeted awkwardly and shifted from one foot to the other, unsure what to do next. "There's a fire in the kitchen to get you dry, and I can make you something to drink. Brandy? Water?" Why was he gabbling like this?

The girl took away the necessity for any decision, though, by getting unsteadily to her feet. "I'm as okay now as I'm going to be. Let's keep going before my legs give up on me."

He put a cautious arm around her, and she leaned into him, her body warmer now than it had been. Awareness of her almost naked proximity cascaded over him again.

At last, the brambles and hawthorns to either side of the path fell back, allowing the path to widen and reveal Uncle Jago's farmhouse on the brow of the hill. Tall chimneys poked above the horizon like pointing fingers, and the silvery woodsmoke from the kitchen range twisted up into the clear blue sky.

Within a few short minutes Kit was supporting the girl up the cart track between drystone walls, his heart a heavy, foreboding weight in his chest. Jago was not going to be happy about their unwelcome visitor.

Chapter Three

MORVOREN

Hooray. Civilization. Morvoren's heartbeat quickened at the thought that this farmhouse would surely have a phone she could use, or maybe this kind young man who'd rescued her could drive her back to Penzance. She fixed her gaze on the squat bulk of the house and quickened her halting steps. With its grey slate roof, it could almost have grown there, out of a wound in the landscape, the way the bark of a tree grows over a severed limb to hide the scar.

She peeked sideways at the young man who'd rescued her from the watery grave for which she'd surely been destined. The memory of the cold water burning her lungs in the dark green depths pressed in, and she shivered. When she'd opened her eyes to find herself lying on hot sand with his dark shape silhouetted against the bright sunlight, for a moment, she'd thought she'd died and gone to heaven. Then the cold and need to vomit had overcome her. She'd had no chance since then, and no inclination, to look him over.

Now, after struggling all the way up the path with his strong arm supporting her but his face virtually unseen, instinct took over, and she stole a furtive glance at him.

For "brave rescuer," he seemed to fit the bill. Taller than Josh by several inches, the long lean body pressed enticingly close to hers felt hard and muscular. Dark hair clung in wet curls to a high forehead, touching skin more tanned from the sun than her own. His profile, which was all she could see, showed a long, slightly aquiline nose, a strong chin and firm mouth, and the shadow of dark stubble on his jawline.

Now she was out of the water and had got rid of most of what she'd inhaled or swallowed, to her surprise, she found she could see the humor in her situation. Either that or it was a hysterical reaction. The thing she'd always dreaded had almost happened. Josh had abandoned her to her fate, and here she was, leaning on a man whose profile promised to reveal handsome, if stern, good looks when she got a better view of him.

"This way, miss. Watch your footing on the stones. They're a bit uneven here." With gentle hands, her rescuer guided her up a path edged with hawthorns and brambles toward a wooden gate set between low farm buildings. With a tanned hand, he unhooked a frayed rope from around the gate post and pulled the gate open a foot or so to let them through. The bottom of the gate scraped on the uneven paving slabs.

"Welcome to Nanpean," her rescuer said. "This way."

A proper old-fashioned farm. How quaint. Had she stumbled into a historical recreation of a bygone age, or maybe one of those religious cults that spurned all things modern? She glanced at her escort in his knee-high boots and loose white shirt. He certainly looked as though he might have stepped out of a romance novel, never mind a cult's HQ. Very Colin Firth's Mr. Darcy, only considerably younger and better looking.

She'd think about that later. Right now, getting to a phone was top of her agenda. That, and getting warm and dry.

A few scrawny hens scuttled out of their way as her rescuer escorted her with gentle firmness across the yard toward the ramshackle front porch of the house. A narrow gate set into a low stone wall separated the porch from the yard.

"You'll be safe and warm here," her rescuer said, pushing open the gate.

He seized the large, cast-iron knob and, turning it, gave the door a hefty shove with his booted foot. It swung open and, his hand in the small of her back, he ushered her inside.

What a gloomy house. Just for a moment, Morvoren's wits returned. Was it wise to be going into a strange man's house in the middle of nowhere, even if he had made promises of safety? But then, a serial killer would say just the same. Then common sense took over. What option did she have? And if he tried it on, she had a few moves. She'd taken self-defense classes at university.

Heavy, ancient beams stretched across the low ceiling of a long, stone-flagged room. Halfway down the right-hand wall stood what could only be described as a kitchen range—the sort you saw in National Trust restoration projects. In fact, the whole room, with its enormous oak table and long low benches, its oak sideboard and two high-backed chairs sitting on a rag rug in front of the range, looked like something out of a museum set piece. Very quaint. Just like the old-fashioned farmyard.

Odder and odder. The feeling of being isolated with a strange man, even if he was very handsome, swarmed in around Morvoren again, and she shivered.

He must have mistaken her shiver of misgiving for a shiver of cold, because the firm hand in the small of her back propelled her gently toward the range. "Come and get warm. Please." A glow of heat exuded from it, so she didn't protest.

"Won't you sit down?"

She perched on one of the high-backed chairs, extending her hands to the warmth of the fire before remembering her manners. "Thank you."

He stood back, and she looked up at him, seeing him properly for the first time by the flickering flames in the firebox. What was it about his dark hair and somber face that looked so familiar?

His loose white shirt gaped to reveal the topmost dark hairs of an admirably muscled chest, and he was wearing trousers something akin to jodhpurs above the long boots she'd closely inspected on the way up from the beach. If she hadn't seen his little boat pulled up on the sand, she'd have guessed he'd just been out riding.

Her gaze fixed on his face. Those dark curls, drying now, clustered around a sun-tanned face out of which a pair of brown eyes, so dark as to be almost black, regarded her in open curiosity. The lack of even the smallest of smiles gave his face a look of austere severity that didn't suit him.

But oh, how familiar his face was. Could she have noticed him on the street in Penzance during her holiday?

In encouragement, she let her own mouth curve into a smile.

For a moment he studied her face back, as though intent on committing it to memory, and she thought he was going to allow his sensuous mouth to soften into a smile, but he didn't. With a huff of exhaled breath, he turned away and strode over to the table in the center, an air of frustrated resignation about him that she didn't understand, his boots clacking on the flagstones.

But my goodness, wasn't he handsome with his darkly brooding good looks, his Mr. Darcy outfit, and his wildly curling hair. Quite the romantic hero.

KIT

KIT STARED AT the girl sitting in his chair. The fact that her long blonde hair had dried in salty rats' tails did nothing to detract from the beauty of her bone structure as she smiled at him. He experienced an urge to smile back at her but withstood the temptation. Her being here was not a matter for smiling about.

He looked her up and down. Since he'd inherited Ormonde from his late father five years ago, he'd met numerous eligible girls. But none quite like this girl he'd seen come back from the dead. But there was no time for idle speculation, he had to make sure she was away from the farm before nightfall and preferably before Jago returned from wherever he'd gone.

He met her candid blue eyes and almost took a step back, which was most unlike him. How, when she was just sitting there shivering in front of the fire, was she making him feel like a green boy meeting a pretty girl for the very first time?

What was there about this girl? He gave himself a mental shake. What he needed to do was to pull himself together and get to the bottom of how she'd come to be in the sea. She probably had distraught relatives searching for her if she'd fallen overboard from some passing ship. Yes, that was certain. He needed to find out who they were then set about locating them.

Straightening his spine, he clicked his booted heels together and made a small bow. "Christopher Carlyon, at your service, Miss…?"

She gazed up at him as though taken aback by his formal greeting, the smile slipping from her face to be replaced by a puzzled frown. Those eyes really were the deepest blue he'd ever seen. He could drown in them if he wasn't careful. "Lucas," she said, almost a question in her voice. "Morvoren Lucas."

What? Morvoren? Was she truly a mermaid as he'd first thought? No, that was just fancy and all wrong. She couldn't be, or she wouldn't have been drowning. However, at the very least, he wanted to know why someone had named her "mermaid." As a Cornishman, Kit knew all the stories told by fishermen and sailors of the many mermaids around the Cornish coast—like the Mermaid of Zennor and the one from Padstow who'd cursed the harbor. But he'd never before met a girl whose parents had named her for one of them.

Her smile tiptoed back onto her face, as though she'd read his mind. "Yes. Mermaid. My parents named me for a mermaid, and I can't swim and am terrified of water. Ironic, isn't it?" Her voice sounded stronger and more confident, with a clear hint of refinement. This was a young lady of good breeding.

Kit gave her a small nod. "So, Miss Lucas, how did a young lady, who can't swim but is named after a mermaid, end up in the sea?"

A bit blunt, but he was curious.

She shivered again, whether at the memory of nearly drowning or from cold, he had no idea, but it reminded him of his duties as a host. He pushed the black kettle onto the hottest part of the range. "I'm sorry. Don't answer. I've been most remiss. You're still cold. I'll fetch you a blanket."

She opened her mouth to reply, but before she could say anything, he stepped to the corner where the door to the spiral staircase opened and ran up the steep stairs two at a time, feet thumping on the creaking boards. Grabbing two blankets from the chest in the box room, he galloped back down the stairs.

He'd half expected her to have vanished away like the mermaids in the stories, but she was still sitting there, the chair drawn closer to the heat and her hands held out to the firebox.

She looked up when he came in, her face breaking into a smile again. Beautiful enough to have been a real mermaid, although some of the old fishermen swore a genuine mermaid had a wickedly ugly face and scaly skin like a fish. Not this mermaid—her face, especially now that it was no longer blue-tinged, took his breath away, her drying sandy hair only giving credence to her possible otherworldly origin.

"Here, Miss Lucas." He handed her the blanket and retreated a step, puzzled by his own reaction. As she draped it around herself and pulled it close, he slung the other one around his own shoulders and took a seat in the empty chair—Jago's—waiting for the kettle to boil. "Are you feeling warmer now?" Bit of a stupid question.

Miss Lucas sighed. "Much better, thank you. Do you have a phone I could use, do you think?"

A what? He frowned, wanting to be able to give her what she'd asked for but not certain what she actually meant. A phone? What was that? Best to be honest. "I'm sorry. I don't have one."

Her turn to frown. "I must have lost mine in the sea." She patted her hip. "It must have fallen out of my pocket, but even so, it wouldn't have worked after a dunking."

The kettle began to sing.

Best to humor her. Whatever she'd lost from her pocket must be important and she thought he might have one himself. Maybe he did, and she'd used a foreign word for something he knew by another name. She'd patted her hip which was where he usually kept his hipflask. Maybe that was it. A phone must be a hipflask. Of course, she'd need a tot of something to warm her up. A hot toddy would be far better than the cup of tea he'd been intending to provide her with.

Relief that he could help flooded over him. "Of course. I must apologize for being remiss in my duties as your host." Now he was sounding more of an idiot than ever. Whatever had come over him? He'd be dropping things next.

Conscious of his burning cheeks, he rose with as much dignity as he could muster and went to the cupboard in the far corner where Jago kept his best contraband brandy. With nervous fingers, he poured two generous tots into a couple of pewter mugs, then came back to the range. Picking up the kettle's hot handle with a rag, he added boiling water to the mugs and handed one to Miss Lucas.

"This should warm you through."

She sniffed the contents of the mug with a wrinkled nose. "What is it?"

"A hot toddy. That was what you wanted, wasn't it?"

She opened her mouth, and for a moment he thought she was about to say no. Then she furrowed her brow, sniffed it again, and took a tentative sip. "I don't normally drink brandy, but maybe just this once."

He knocked back his own drink in one go, the fiery trail it left down his throat giving him confidence. He felt both warmer and wiser at the same time. "You haven't yet told me how you came to be in the sea."

Her eyebrows shot up. They were particularly lovely eyebrows, arching in a gentle and slender curve, almost as though they'd been drawn on, above those blue eyes. He had to stop being distracted by her looks.

"Not much to tell, I'm afraid. I was on one of those sea fishing trips they offer to tourists in Penzance and fell out of the boat when a big wave tossed us up in the air. I thought I was going to drown. The next thing I knew, I was with you on the beach."

Now Kit was really flummoxed. Tourists? Some of his old school friends had gone on the Grand Tour of Europe after Oxford and liked to call themselves tourists, but he'd never heard of any of them deciding part of their tour needed to encompass a trip in a Cornish fishing boat.

Surely, she hadn't been out on an actual fishing boat?

Kit narrowed his eyes, puzzled that she could have fallen off some passing boat he hadn't seen while he was out fishing. He needed to get to the bottom of this. "What was the name of your vessel?"

She gave an eloquent shrug of her shoulders, the blanket slipping to reveal her thin undergarment. "I can't remember its name, but it was one of those trip boats from Penzance. My boyfriend persuaded me to go with him." She snorted in a very unladylike way. "Against my better judgement. Today's the last day of our holiday, and he loves fishing. Like an idiot, I agreed to go. He's not going to be my boyfriend for much longer, I can tell you."

What? Kit's frown deepened. What was she talking about now? Holidays? Trip boats? Tourists? He fancied himself something of a man of the world, despite his mere twenty-seven years, but these were terms he'd almost never come across in daily speech. What on earth did she mean? Well, he knew what a holiday was, but a trip boat? And a boyfriend? He'd never heard that word before, although it was reasonably easy to infer its meaning. Could she mean she had a suitor who'd taken her out on a ship and then lost her overboard? Perhaps someone she was engaged to, who liked fishing?

The thought that anyone would take their gently bred, possibly affianced, lady friend out on a rough fishing boat from Penzance and then not leap in to save her when she fell in, shocked him to the core. The blanket slipped a little more as she shifted her position and her odd, breeches-clad legs protruded. A lady friend so inadequately dressed as well.

The thought that he might have rescued not a mermaid, but a young lady whose lot in life had forced her into a career as a woman of ill repute, surfaced. Kit swallowed. However, one look at her convinced him she couldn't be either. She was far too sweet faced—not that being sweet faced meant anything, really. He just refused to believe a girl as beautiful as this one could be anything other than what he wanted her to be—a highborn lady who'd been unlucky enough to fall off her ship unnoticed.

At that moment, the front door swung open with a bang, and a burly figure strode into the room. Damn it.

"Uncle Jago," said Kit.

Chapter Four
MORVOREN

THE MAN STANDING on the threshold of the kitchen, an overly generous word for this primitive room, filled the doorway with his bulk. Under a voluminous and ancient leather waistcoat, he wore a not-all-that-clean, collarless cream shirt, the sleeves rolled up over hammy and hairy forearms, and a loose red scarf was knotted about his neck. A faded black tricorn hat tipped forward over his eyes, and in his right hand he held a gun that might well have been a museum piece.

A vision indeed.

Morvoren closed her mouth, which had dropped open at the sight of him, with a snap, unable to drag her eyes away from this apparition. If she'd thought her rescuer oddly dressed, this man took the biscuit. Maybe the BBC were filming a period drama and this man was an extra. Or perhaps this was indeed one of those religious cults where everyone wore old fashioned clothes and didn't use modern gadgets—like the Amish or Plymouth Brethren.

Her rescuer had jumped out of his chair the moment the newcomer arrived, letting the blanket fall from pleasingly broad shoulders. Now, he stepped toward the man he'd called his uncle. "I wasn't expecting you back so soon."

"So I see." The man's voice was a gravelly rasp. "What's this, Kit?

Who be this young… lady?" The last word came out as though he doubted very much it applied to her. As though any woman who turned up soaking wet and wrapped in a blanket in his kitchen was to be scorned. As though he suspected Morvoren of being something she wasn't.

She bristled at his implication, but, with a wary eye to the gun he was carrying, kept her mouth firmly closed. No point in riling a strange, armed man when you were stuck in a remote farmhouse where quite definitely no one would hear if you screamed.

Instead, she clutched the blanket closer to conserve the warmth she was building up. It felt like a shield against the penetrating and accusatory gaze this Uncle Jago had fixed upon her.

"We have a guest," Kit said, his tone defensive.

The newcomer stepped further into the room. With his free hand, he took off the old tricorn hat, placing it on the table without taking his gaze from her.

Feeling bolder, Morvoren returned his stare.

Several days' growth of grey beard adorned a square jaw, and dark, hawklike eyes regarded her in open hostility. She swallowed her fear down, determined not to let him see how much he scared her.

"So I can see," he rumbled.

Some small familial resemblance to her rescuer clung to the newcomer. Grizzled curling hair, similar to his nephew's, had been confined with a thin black ribbon in a ponytail at the nape of his neck. But whereas Kit's face might have a smile lurking somewhere just out of sight, Jago looked as though no smile would dare touch his.

"A mermaid," Kit elaborated, with an unmistakably wry glance in Morvoren's direction. "I fished her out of the sea thinking she was drowned, but she very handily revived and spilled her seawater. And here she is, warming herself by our hearth."

"A mermaid?" growled Jago, going to the table, where he threw down a brace of large rabbits he'd had tucked inside his capacious waistcoat. He leaned the gun against the table and gave a snort. "Mermaids bring only bad luck." His voice was heavily accented Cornish, unlike Kit's more refined tones.

Kit shook his head. "She's not a real mermaid."

Morvoren stared at her rescuer. Was that a glint of amusement in his solemn dark eyes? Did he, despite his apparently serious demeanor, find her predicament amusing? She had a sudden urge to burst out laughing, despite her feelings of unease or maybe because of them. Bubbling hysteria, no doubt. The disapproving scowl on Jago's face kept her under control.

Kit moved closer to his uncle, dropping his voice but not so low she couldn't hear every word. "She must have fallen off a ship and been washed inshore to where I fished her out in my net. It was pure chance that I cast a final time before coming in. Otherwise, she'd be floating out there, dead." He shrugged his shoulders. "But, for just a moment, I thought I'd fished a real mermaid out, and strangely, her name means mermaid in Cornish."

He cleared his throat, glancing back at her. "Uncle, may I present Miss Morvoren Lucas." He turned back to her. "And, Miss Lucas, this is my favorite uncle, Jago Tremaine. My mother's brother."

Ignoring Morvoren, Jago gave another snort and stumped over to the liquor cupboard where he poured himself a generous tot of brandy. "Aye, and your only uncle now, boy." He shook his head. "D'you not think it strange she's turned up here today? That she might be a king's spy?"

A what?

Kit shrugged his shoulders again. "Miss Lucas is clearly a lady, Uncle, and not a king's spy. She's here by chance. As I already said, it was pure luck that I cast my net one last time and caught her in it. I don't think even the king's spies are so desperate they'd have young ladies doing their dirty work by lurking on the bottom of the sea on the off chance I might happen along and sweep one up."

What was he talking about? Dirty work? King's spies? Morvoren frowned. Why were they both talking in riddles? And how overly polite was it for Kit to persist in calling her Miss Lucas? "Please," she interrupted. "I'd prefer it if you would both call me Morvoren. Miss Lucas makes me feel like I'm about fifty. And I can assure you, I'm definitely not any kind of spy." She held up her hand, and the blanket slipped sideways to reveal her damp T-shirt and jeans.

Oops.

Jago's already angry eyes widened, and he spluttered into his brandy. "What in the name of God is she wearing? Did the waves strip her of her clothes?" His eyes travelled south to her jean-clad legs. "And what on earth does she have on her legs? Men's britches? I can see the girl's legs!"

Guilt swept over Morvoren, although not for a reason she understood, and her cheeks flamed. She snatched the treacherous blanket closer, conscious of the fact that the sight of her legs seemed to have mortally offended Kit's uncle in some inexplicable way. Shrinking down into the chair, in an effort to appear less noticeable and offensive, she tucked the blanket tighter over her knees. At least she wasn't cold anymore.

"She came out of the sea like that," Kit said, apology in his tone. "I think the current must have stolen her clothes."

Morvoren opened her mouth to explain, then shut it again. Best to keep quiet and listen.

"Well, she can't stay like that." Uncle Jago stomped to the stairs door and flung it open. Heaving a deep breath, he bellowed up the stairs. "Jenifry! Where are you, woman? Get down here now. I know you're a-kippin' on my bed instead o' workin'. You're needed."

A snort of laughter emerged from Kit, and to Morvoren's surprise his dark eyes danced. So, he could let that severe exterior slip. Once more, her not-far-from-the-surface hysteria prompted the urge to laugh, but her nerves kept her silent in this apparent madhouse.

From somewhere upstairs came a loud thud, then heavy footsteps sounded on the spiral staircase. A moment later a woman bustled through the door and halted on the threshold, staring.

Of middle age and less than average height, the newcomer made up for her small stature by her presence. An air of animal fecundity hung about her, as though she were some female equivalent of Bacchus, about to dish out horns of plenty in every direction.

She beamed a five-hundred-watt, irrepressible smile at the man who'd summoned her as though oblivious to his tone of voice. Curious, Morvoren took a sideways peep at Jago and caught his austere face softening for a moment in what must, for him, have been a rare smile in return.

"You wanted somethin', surr?" Jenifry asked, her vowels rolling and the R on the end of the sir stretching out. Her gaze flicked from Morvoren to Kit and back again. "What's this you've brought home wi' you today, me 'ansum? A maid, it do seem. An' a wet one at that."

A maid? Morvoren bristled. Did this woman think she was a servant?

For an instant, the shadow of a smile lit Kit's face, and she had that feeling again of having seen him somewhere recently. But, as the smile was replaced by a troubled frown, the elusive memory drifted away like a snatch of mist.

Anyway, what sort of a place had servants, nowadays? She dearly wanted to ask lots of questions, but caution kept her tongue in her head lest she put her foot in it. A feeling had been growing that there was a lot going on here that they didn't want her to know about. Saying the wrong thing might turn out to be more dangerous than she anticipated.

Kit's gaze returned to Morvoren, serious again. "A very lucky young lady. Not at all what I thought I'd catch in my net for you to fry for our dinner. A mermaid... of sorts. Miss Morvoren Lucas, of..." His voice trailed off and he raised a dark eyebrow at her.

For a moment Morvoren didn't realize what he wanted. Then understanding dawned. "Of... Reading," she said in a hurry.

Jenifry's brow furrowed. "Be that in Cornwall? If so, I've never heard mention of it."

Jago shook his head with a look of impatience. "O' course it ain't, Woman. She'll be from up country t'other side o' the Tamar, in England, I'll wager. A foreigner."

Jenifry scowled. "How'd she come to be called after a Cornish mermaid then?"

Before anyone could answer this question, Morvoren butted in. "My mother named me after her Cornish grandmother, if you must know. And I really wish she hadn't, because I've got a phobia about water." She paused. "And Reading is in Berkshire."

Surely, they'd know where that was.

"She don't look like no mermaid to me," Jenifry said, ignoring Morvoren's words and tilting her head to one side as though to better weigh up any claim to a watery origin. "She do have legs."

Jago banged his pewter mug down on the table. "'Nuff o' that now. Mermaid or not, she ain't rightly dressed for going back where she come from. To this Reading, wherever that might be. You tek her up they stairs and find her some o' my sister's old clothes from that chest in the box room. She do look about the same size as Elestren were when she wore 'em. Make her decent to be seen. Then we can send her on her way." He turned back, fixing Morvoren with a no-arguments stare. "And you, Missy, you'll hop up they stairs right smart now and let Jenifry dress you proper."

What? They were going to make her change her clothes? Well, they were still damp, so dry ones might be nice. Jeans and a sweatshirt, maybe, and some dry socks. But Jago's sister's old clothes? Ew. Did she want to wear someone's castoffs?

Deciding she'd rather stay damp, Morvoren gestured at her jeans and T-shirt. "It's quite all right. My own clothes are nearly dry now."

Not quite true, but getting there.

Jago threw her the briefest of glances, as though he couldn't bring himself to look at her for more than a fraction of a second. "She can't stay in them things," he grunted, still not talking directly to her. "T'aint proper."

That did it. Now she most certainly didn't want to put on any clothes they might provide. Who did they think they were? More to the point, who did this rather odious old man think he was, as Kit had shown no inclination to make her change until his uncle turned up.

"I'm fine in my own clothes," she tried, glancing at Kit in the hope support might lie in that direction, but to no avail.

"You are indeed much of a size with my mother when she was a girl," Kit said, ignoring her protest. "Going by the portrait of her when she first married my father, her clothes should fit you well enough, although I'm afraid they won't be very modish."

Morvoren's mouth opened and closed a few times, but no sound came out. What was she supposed to do now? Agree to this? Jenifry had returned to the stairs as though it was the most natural thing in the world to provide clothing for a perfectly adequately, if damply, dressed stranger. "This way, Miss Lucas," she said, standing back to let her go first.

For a moment, Morvoren hesitated, weighing up her options. She could let them dress her in these old clothes and escape, or she could argue the point and possibly not escape. Huh. No contest. The look of threatening disapproval on Jago's face had her abandoning her blanket and scurrying up the shadowy staircase in front of Jenifry.

At the top, three oak doors with sizeable iron latches opened off a narrow corridor—one at either end of its short run and one almost opposite the staircase. It was this third door that Jenifry pushed open, then stood back to allow Morvoren to enter first. "In here, Miss Lucas."

The room was small, with a single gable window in the far wall and a narrow bed tucked away in one corner. Apart from two wooden chests pushed back against the wall beside the bed, everything else lay covered in white dustsheets, as though this room hadn't been used in a long time. The musty smell of long neglect hung in the air, tickling Morvoren's sensitive nose. She sneezed.

"Bless you, my dear," Jenifry said as she followed her in. "We don't often come in here, so there be a lot o' dust."

How right she was. Morvoren's gaze flicked over the contents of the room and came to a halt on the right-hand wall where a dustsheet had partially slipped from a large oil painting. A small, dark-haired boy in an old-fashioned, navy-blue jacket and knee breeches sat astride a smart bay pony, a white-capped sea in the background. This sea? The cove she'd just struggled up from? Perhaps.

She took a step closer. The picture had been executed in an outdated, classical style. Could it be one of Kit's ancestors? How very like him the child was with his mass of dark curls. And now she was looking at the picture, a bell jangled in her head and she remembered another painting she'd seen recently. The painting at the smuggling exhibition. A painting of a young man with darkly curling hair... A young man who'd looked like a younger version of Kit. Could the child in this picture have grown up to be the young man in the painting at the museum? Maybe an ancestor of Kit's?

Jenifry, who'd opened the lid of the larger of the chests, glanced up. "That be Mr. Kit, when he were a nipper," she said. "Right 'ansum he were on that pony. Proud as punch the day his father give it him."

This was a painting of Kit? Not one of his ancestors? Really?

Morvoren took a step closer to the painting, peering more closely. Why on earth was he riding in fancy dress? His hair hung to his shoulders and a lace ruffle adorned his throat. Out on the sea behind him, a full rigged schooner sailed. The picture could easily have been painted a time long ago. Yet another odd thing to add to the list of odd things about this farm.

Jenifry had lost interest in the painting and was busy unloading garments from the chest, which seemed to have the properties of Doctor Who's Tardis. "Best get those breeches off o' ye right now, Missy. No maid should be seen in breeches. 'Tis improper an' outlandish."

Morvoren frowned. Here was that mention of her being a maid, again. Did this woman assume she'd come here to apply for a job within their strange old-fashioned cult? Humoring their eccentricities was one thing, but agreeing to become a servant was another. "I am not a maid," she said, as firmly as possible. Best to lay down the law from the start.

This provoked a far stronger reaction than she'd anticipated. "Not a maid?" Jenifry squawked, her voice rising in what could only be shock. "You're not a maid?" Then understanding, possibly, flitted across her face. "Oh, I'm that sorry. Best t'ignore me, ma'am, but I thought Mister Kit called you Miss Lucas. I do beg your pardon, Mrs. Lucas."

What?

"I'm not married," Morvoren tried, brain whirling as she became more and more confused. But this, too, turned out to be a bad thing to say.

In an instant, the shock returned to Jenifry's open face. "Not married and not a maid?" she squawked all over again. "And not afraid to tell anyone? Proud of it even? Whatever next? What be this house a-comin' to?"

Morvoren's eyes flew wide as realization dawned. Was this woman talking about virginity? Her virginity? "I mean," she gabbled, the words tumbling over themselves. "I'm not a servant. Not a maidservant. I'm a nurse. A veterinary nurse. And I don't want to be a servant."

Although technically, she wasn't the kind of maid Jenifry was meaning, either. Probably not a good idea to mention that. She needed to escape this odd cult as soon as possible, where the only normal one appeared to be Kit, despite his odd clothes and serious expression.

Better put on what Jenifry had got out for her, then, if it meant being able to make her getaway all the sooner. Even though the array of clothing before her was like nothing she'd ever seen before. No jeans or sweatshirts in sight.

With deep misgiving, Morvoren kicked off her wet trainers, peeled off her damp jeans and tugged her T-shirt over her head to reveal her matching black lacy bra and knickers. Another bad move.

A horrified gasp emitted from Jenifry akin to the noise the kettle had made when it boiled, and her hands went to her ample hips. "What are those when they're at home?"

The bra happened to be Morvoren's favorite underwire and had come from the Victoria's Secret shop in Reading. She'd chosen the knickers to match, pleased with the little red bows on both. Had this strange woman never seen a bra and knicker set before?

"My underwear."

Jenifry shook her head in a mix of wonder and horror. "I've decent underwear right here for you, Miss Lucas." Her tone brimmed with righteous disapproval. "I'm sure only a French hussy would wear underwear as scant as that. Here." And she held out a pair of long white knickers.

Morvoren stared at the proffered garment. Its main drawback appeared to be that the knickers, if you could call them that, were made in two separate legs with a decided gap in the center. A bit drafty.

She took the knickers. "You want me to wear these?" Her own voice rose in righteous indignation that perfectly matched Jenifry's. "They're not even finished. Look—someone's forgotten to sew them together." Another mistake.

"Together? Why would anyone want to do that? How would you...?" Jenifry hesitated, her cheeks flushed, and she lowered her voice to a conspiratorial hiss. "How would you use the chamber pot or the privy if you had your drawers sewn up?"

What? They were meant to be like that? Morvoren glanced furtively about the room, but dressed in only bra and panties there was no escape. She was stuck. With a deep sigh, she pulled the strange knickers on, over her own underwear, of course, and Jenifry fastened them around her waist—individually. They reached to below the knees, the edges of each leg finished in age-yellowed lace. Interesting.

A white slip, also discolored with age and its time spent in the chest, went on next. And then out came something that could only be a corset.

"I can't wear that," Morvoren declared, hands on hips. "For a start, the weather's far too hot. I'll die of heat exhaustion." Why on earth had Kit's mother worn these clothes? And a corset? Confusion whirled around in her head along with an ever-increasing urgency to get out of here as fast as possible and back to normality.

She might just as well have banged her head against a brick wall. "No lady goes out without her stays," Jenifry opined, levering her into them. "Now breathe in while I does them up, that's a good girl. We'll make a proper job o' you yet." Her critical gaze slid to Morvoren's jeans and T-shirt where they lay on the floor, as if to infer that they were anything but a "proper job."

The next thing that went on was stockings, secured just above her knees with garters. These were followed by several layers of petticoats, and finally, Jenifry held up a pink and white striped gown with a skirt of generous proportions. It was certainly pretty, but on top of all the other layers it seemed distinctly over the top. However, Jenifry probably wouldn't allow her to escape in just the petticoats.

Did women in this cult really go about dressed like this?

Despite her protests, the dress went over her head and was finally done up, tightly, over her stay-clad waist. Peering down at herself when it was done, she had to admit she looked nice. Very different from her normal appearance. She couldn't help but long for a full-length mirror to admire her reflection. How lovely this outfit would have been to wear for an evening fancy-dress ball when she was at university. It had the feel of authenticity about it, even though it was making her sweat.

"Shoes now," Jenifry said, bending over the chest and emerging with a pair of exquisitely lovely, but unforgiving-looking, high-heeled shoes. Only this was where she ground to a halt, as no matter how hard she tried, like Cinderella's Ugly Sisters, Morvoren couldn't fit her size six foot into any of the shoes Jenifry produced. Kit's mother, Jago's sister, despite matching her in height, must have much daintier feet. So, to Jenifry's horror, the soggy trainers went back on again, which was probably a good thing as none of those shoes looked as though they'd be comfortable for actual walking.

"There," Jenifry said, standing back to view her protégée with an air of pride. "Keep them feet tucked away an' this'll do just fine. Only your hair to do now. And you've an advantage there with it being such a pretty color."

With a hairbrush and a length of pink ribbon, Jenifry battled Morvoren's sandy, sea-salty hair into a low ponytail, leaving a few short curls clustered about her face, then stood back to further admire the effect. "Now that's a proper job this time. Best get you down these stairs to see'f you pass muster for the gen'lemen."

Morvoren forbore from remarking that the last thing she wished to be judged by was whether the gentlemen downstairs found her to their liking. However, she submitted to following Jenifry out into the corridor and back down the stairs, but only because complying seemed the easiest way to escape this madhouse. The descent of the stairs was not an easy task, as with such long, wide skirts, she had to hold them out of the way of her feet. As a consequence, she descended slowly, afraid that at any moment she'd catch the edge of a petticoat with her foot and go tumbling to the bottom. The last thing she wanted to be while wearing these dodgy open crotched knickers was upside down in a heap on the floor.

Chapter Five

KIT

THE MOMENT THE staircase door closed behind Morvoren and Jenifry, Jago rounded on Kit. "What were you thinking of bringing some stranger here? Haven't we got enough on our hands already? You have to get rid of her, boy. 'Tis too dangerous to have some outsider here a-lookin' at what we're about. She's got to go. Right now. Before tonight."

Kit bit his lip, anger rising. "What else could I have done with her? I caught her in my nets and thought she was dead. Even when she came back to life, she was icy cold. I had to get her warm."

"She'll fetch us bad luck, mark my words," his uncle growled. "T'would've been better if you'd left her where she b'longs, at the bottom of the sea. T'ain't natural to go scoopin' up women off the seabed."

Kit bristled. Did Jago really think he should have just released her from his net and left her in the water? However, a decision needed to be made. "You're right. She can't stay here. As soon as she's decently dressed, I'll take her to Penzance. I'll get Jowan to saddle the horses. You still have my mother's saddle, don't you?"

Jago grunted. "Aye, that I do, lad, but it won't fit my cob. She'll have to ride your fine horse. No. You stay here and wait for her. Don't want to give her the chance to poke about. I'll away into the stables and roust that lazy bugger up. He can find that saddle and get the horses ready." He slapped Kit on the shoulder and strode to the front door. It banged behind him as he disappeared into the yard.

Kit stood for a moment without moving, thinking about what his uncle had said. Yes, it was odd that he'd found her today, and yes, it was indeed a very bad day for having a stranger around the farm. An unfortunate state of affairs, but it couldn't be helped.

His own clothes were almost dry by now, but to ride to Penzance he'd need his coat. Ignoring the snug-fitting, tailored coat he'd had made at Weston's in Town, he shrugged his way into one of Jago's much roomier jackets. Not such fine cloth, and the sleeves were a tad short, but altogether more comfortable for a hot day.

He was just fishing through his uncle's pockets when the door at the bottom of the stairs swung open and Jenifry came back into the kitchen. From behind her, a vision of old-fashioned loveliness entered the room. Kit froze, one hand in a pocket, the other holding some bits of useful string he'd found in the other.

The mermaid had transformed. Yes, the gown she wore was a good thirty years out of date and something his mother would have worn as a girl when she'd first met his father, God rest his soul, but nevertheless, it gave Miss Lucas the look of the real lady he'd taken her to be. She was quite breathtaking from the top of her simply coiffed head to the peep of those odd shoes from under her skirts.

Jenifry, standing to one side of this apparition like a proud lion tamer presenting her charge at Astley's, pulled a sad face. "Her feet be too large for any o' your ma's old slippers."

The ex-mermaid also pulled a face, but rather a disgusted one, and twitched at her waist with her fingers as though in discomfort.

"Took a bit o' doin' to get her into they stays," Jenifry said. "She don't like stays one bit."

"She is right here listening to you," Miss Lucas said, exasperation coloring her tone.

Why she should be so put out puzzled Kit. Every woman he'd ever met wore stays, even those of loose morals he'd encountered during his time at Oxford. And what fun it was getting them out of them. No, he mustn't think of her like that. She was just an unwanted encumbrance to be returned to wherever she belonged—to whomever she belonged to. Now was not the time to start getting sentimental.

He pulled himself together. "I'm to escort you to Penzance, Miss Lucas, from whence you informed me you set off this morning. If that is your wish. We shall locate your accommodation and return you to your…" He hesitated, wary of the word he'd heard her use. "To your boyfriend. My uncle has gone to tell his man Jowan to prepare our horses. I trust you won't object to riding under my escort? I'm afraid we only possess two riding horses, so Jenifry cannot accompany us—which I'm sure you would have preferred for the sake of propriety."

Miss Lucas's eyes widened, yet again. In fact, she looked as though everything was a surprise. "You're right. I do want to get back to Penzance, but by horse? Won't that take a long time and be dangerous on the roads? With all the other traffic?"

Kit nodded, puzzled. What other way was there to go? Oh no. Perhaps she was one of those infernal women who'd never learned to ride. "You do ride, I trust?" he ventured.

She nodded. "I do, but not regularly for quite some time. I learned as a child." Her face brightened. "Although earlier this week I did ride along the beach at Marazion, which was wonderful."

That was a relief. At least he could do as Jago wanted now and return her to where she'd come from. A tiny, confusing ache formed in his heart that she wasn't to benefit from their hospitality any longer. Shoving that to one side, he mentally shook his head. That could never have been an option, as she had no abigail with her to give propriety to her stay in a household belonging to two single men. His gaze fell on Jenifry. Not that Jago was technically single.

As if Kit's thinking of his uncle had called him, Jago chose this moment to reappear, grim-faced still. However, his expression changed to one of relief when he saw Miss Lucas adorned in proper attire for a lady, although the frown that followed probably signified disapproval of Jenifry's choice of the pink and white silk for a stranger.

"Horses're ready," he huffed at Kit. "Jowan's holding onto 'em by the trough. Best get her off to Penzance. I need you back here sharpish."

Kit extended his arm to Morvoren. "If you'll come this way, Miss Lucas, I'll have you back in your lodgings within an hour or two. Penzance isn't more than eight miles, and we can ride across the moors and keep up a good pace."

Like a wary fawn, Miss Lucas took his arm, her wide blue eyes regarding him in what looked like open curiosity mingled with a touch of trepidation as he led her out into the farmyard. As soon as she saw the two horses being held by old Jowan, though, she stopped so suddenly she let go of his arm.

Morvoren

A SIDESADDLE. MORVOREN stared. They'd put a sidesaddle on the horse they intended her to ride. Okay, she'd ridden a lot as a child and teenager, but never on a sidesaddle. Who had? Who rode like that nowadays unless at a posh horse show? Who would even want to? Not her.

The squat little man holding the horses turned a baleful eye on her and spat copiously onto the flagstones. He made the nefarious Jago look like a benign old grandfather. Grey hair had been shorn as short as his stubbly beard, and his face had the appearance of the knobbliest old potato that had grown wizened and shrunken at the bottom of the sack. The only thing that was missing was a hunchback and he would have been Dr. Frankenstein's helper, Igor, to a tee.

Kit, unfazed by this vision out of a Hammer horror film, had stopped beside Morvoren. Now, he turned to look at her, confusion, and a touch of irritation, on his handsome face. "Is something wrong, Miss Lucas?"

She sighed. "Please call me Morvoren, not Miss Lucas, or I'll have to call you Mr. Carlyon." She jerked her head at the horse. "Do you really want me to ride sidesaddle? I've never done it before."

The confusion only worsened. "But you said you could ride," he protested, sounding a little affronted, as though he thought she might have lied.

"I can," Morvoren replied. "Just not like this. Astride. On a saddle like this one." She indicated his own saddle, although even that wasn't quite like the kind of forward-cut jumping saddle she'd had for her pony as a teenager. She looked back up at him. "Never on a sidesaddle. Don't you have a different one I could use?" Although even astride, riding eight miles in a voluminous frock and those dreadful knickers would not be comfortable.

Now his expression changed to one of horror and shock. "But I can't escort you into Penzance riding astride… in a dress. You're a lady."

Why the heck not? Was she going to have to comply with all these silly rules in order to get away from here? "Very well," she said, setting her jaw and resigning herself to having to humor him. "I'll give it a go." She glanced around. "But I'll need a hat."

The light of realization brightened Kit's face. He turned back to the still open farmhouse door, from where Jenifry was watching. "A hat for Miss Lucas."

Jenifry was not gone long, returning in a couple of minutes clutching something that did not look at all like a riding hat. In fact, it was a faded straw bonnet. With ribbons.

She held it out to Morvoren with an air of pride. "Lucky I did know where there was one. But you're right. You can't go riding into

Penzance without a bonnet on your head, Miss Lucas."

Morvoren took the hat—the bonnet—and stared down at it. No protection at all were she to fall off. Did they not know about riding hats and how dangerous it was to ride a horse without one? With extreme reluctance, she set the bonnet on her head and did up the ribbons under her chin, feeling like a medieval soldier going into battle without a shield.

"Now," said Kit, that hint of annoyance lurking in his tone. "Let me give you a leg up onto your horse."

The stone mounting block had caught Morvoren's eye. "I'm perfectly capable of getting on by myself, thank you," she said, before remembering she was wearing a long dress and a lot of petticoats.

Ignoring Kit's offered hand, she climbed, with some difficulty thanks to all those skirts, onto the stone block by herself, the bones of that dratted corset digging into her flesh. Stays. Corsets, or stays, whatever you wanted to call them, were not meant for active young ladies, that was for sure.

Jowan threw a sideways glance at Kit, who was tapping his boot on the flagstones, and led the horse in the sidesaddle over to the mounting block, his rheumy old eyes sparkling with something that could have been amusement. How dare he laugh at her?

Morvoren ignored him. Now, how to mount and end up sitting on the saddle in the correct position?

She gathered up the reins. There was indeed a stirrup, so she experimentally set her left foot in it, but after that, she was lost.

Kit stepped closer. "I think you'll need a leg up," he said in a low voice. "Take your foot out of the stirrup, come down off that mounting block, and I'll give you one. Ladies can't mount unaided."

Feeling like an idiot—again—Morvoren hitched up her skirts and managed to get down from the mounting block without his help and without ending up in a crumpled heap. Oh, the indignities being forced upon her.

Kit held out his hands linked together to make a step. "Other foot. Put it here. Up you go and hook it over the saddle horn."

She set her right foot in his cupped hands, and he gave her a strong boost up onto the saddle. Jowan released his hold on the reins, and she shortened them up to take control of her horse, who stepped sideways.

She stroked his neck with one hand. "What's this horse called?"

"Prinny," Kit said. "He's my horse, actually. Prince in public, Prinny in private. I've given you Prinny to ride because my mother's old saddle, that she had for her mare, only fits him, and he's far better schooled than my uncle's old nag." He nodded at the other horse, a sturdier beast by far, resembling the sort of animal that might be better suited to pulling a cart. Taking the reins from Jowan, Kit sprang into the saddle without recourse to his stirrups.

Bit of a showoff, then.

"Shall we go?" He indicated the open gate onto the track, an air of impatience about him that made Morvoren feel guilty for imposing on his time. Only for a moment, though, as they had made her wear these awful clothes and ride on a sidesaddle.

He clicked his tongue at the cob. "We can take it slowly to begin with, but if we walk all the way it'll take us forever. When you feel ready, let me know, and we can canter."

Prinny followed the cob through the gate and out onto the track Morvoren had not so long ago stumbled up from the beach. This time, they turned north, heading uphill as the little valley widened out and became more wooded.

Now she was out of the farmhouse and on her way to Penzance, Morvoren's spirits lifted, and even selfish Josh began to look like a reassuring prospect.

"You certainly live in a very beautiful location," she said, as the distant purple slopes of the higher moorland came into view and a chough flapped lazily across the cloudless blue sky.

Kit nodded, his handsome face almost slipping into a smile, and for a moment the wall he seemed intent on maintaining between them was allowed to drop. "That's why I love it here so much," he said, dark eyes suddenly alight. "I couldn't ever be away from here for too long."

Surprised that he'd bared his soul to her, Morvoren nodded. "I do know what you mean. I've been coming to Cornwall for years and it keeps pulling me back like a magnet."

The horses' hooves rattled over the stones in the rough track. "You do?" he said, with a shrug. "It's the way all the Cornish-born feel. It must be the Cornish blood in your veins. When I'm elsewhere, I feel I'm not really alive."

"My great-grandmother was from Fowey." She wriggled her back where the sweat was sticking the hot silk to any square of exposed skin it could. Not the right outfit for a day like this. And Kit's looked no better. Today was a day for shorts and T-shirts.

Kit nodded as though he understood, which was nice, as Josh never had. Probably she was imagining any rapport here, but it made a change to do that for a while.

Another ten minutes of riding brought them to a line of half a dozen dilapidated cottages running off to one side at right angles to the path. The row sloped away uphill from where a small ford had been lined with slabs of stone.

Here, a group of women in long skirts and shabby blouses appeared to be doing their washing. In the stream, of all places. At the far end of the row of houses, a gaggle of small, scruffy children were at play with a couple of dogs and a rope swing under a sweeping chestnut tree.

What on earth had she stumbled upon here? More weird cult members?

As they rode past the women, Kit raised his hand to wave, and every woman straightened up and waved back, friendly smiles on their homely faces.

"Who're they?" Morvoren asked, her curiosity more than piqued.

"Villagers. That's the edge of Nanpean village," Kit said. "Jowan's is the nearest cottage. The rest of the houses are up beyond the trees. Fishermen and laborers, mostly, now the mines are all closed."

The feeling of having made a none-too-soon escape from this strange place washed over Morvoren. Maybe as they were going uphill, she could try a canter. Anything to get away a bit more quickly.

"I think I can manage a short canter now, if that's all right?" she ventured.

Was that a gleam of relief in Kit's dark eyes? "Of course. Uphill will be easier for you to begin with."

He was right. Cantering uphill wasn't so bad as she'd expected. Once she got used to how to grip the pommels it wasn't vastly different to riding astride. Well, it was. She was just telling herself it wasn't to bolster her confidence.

At the head of the valley a wide vista of moorland opened up, dotted here and there with grazing sheep, small stone-walled fields, and a few farmhouses, all smaller and poorer looking than Jago's. To the south and west the sea spread out in a hazy blue vista she'd have thought beautiful if she hadn't been so keen to get away from Nanpean and its weird inhabitants. The rust colored sails of a few sailing boats dotted the blue, too far off to make out any details.

Wherever the land was favorable, Kit kept them to as fast a pace as Morvoren's limited ability to canter would allow, so there was little opportunity to talk. Not that she really wanted to, even though she had a lot of questions she'd have liked to ask. His rather dour demeanor was enough to put her off. The sooner she was away from him, the better.

However, despite all the cantering, it was only after two hours of moorland riding that Kit finally announced they were almost at their destination.

Morvoren's eyes widened. How could they be? On the entire ride they'd not crossed even one road, nor seen any sign of a vehicle in the distance. Plenty of farm tracks and narrow footpaths, but not a single metaled road. Kit must really know his way about the countryside.

However, she had to admit that riding on horseback, even on a sidesaddle, across this high moorland was a much preferable way to travel than driving in a car, and especially more so than traveling by boat had been. But still, they couldn't be at Penzance already—could they?

Morvoren followed Kit's pointing finger. "Where?"

Sure enough, ahead lay the familiar, hazy shape of St Michael's Mount at the far end of Mount's Bay, with its castle on the summit and the stony causeway clearly visible with the tide out. But nothing else seemed to match with the recent memories she had of Penzance.

Their road sloped downhill, revealing with startling clarity that what lay before her, almost like a vision from Google Earth, was nothing like the town she'd left behind that morning. Instead, a tiny fishing village with not a proper road in sight hugged the coast. No supermarkets, industry, or modern buildings. Just tiny cottages clustered around a small, muddy harbor empty of both water and fishing boats.

This couldn't be Penzance, so where on earth had Kit brought her?

Chapter Six

KIT

FOR THE LOVE of God, why had she stopped now?

"What's wrong?" Kit asked, pulling Jago's nag to a halt.

Morvoren, as she'd told him twice now that she wanted to be called, seemed to have weathered her first time on a sidesaddle remarkably well. Her wavy blonde hair had lost the ribbon Jenifry had used to confine it. Despite the bonnet, it now floated about her face in the most becoming fashion. Enough to be quite distracting if he didn't watch out. What a good thing he'd be returning her to the arms of her gentleman friend and, hopefully, as they were unwed, some stalwart matron of a duenna.

Until this moment, he'd thought that undertaking would be an easy one.

"You said you were staying in a cottage?" he tried, aware that her face had taken on the stricken expression of the well and truly lost. "Do you think you can find it?"

She turned her anguished gaze on him. "But this can't be Penzance. It's too small." She swiped a hand across her eyes, as though doing so might change the view, and muttered to herself, "But there's St Michael's Mount, all right. That's in the right place. Or is it? Can there be more than one of them? But where have all the roads gone, and the supermarket and… and everything else?"

With a sigh, he resisted the temptation to say that of course it was Penzance and where else could it be, and instead, went for her last remark. "What roads?"

"Why, all the main roads." Morvoren shook her head as though to clear it, then spoke more loudly, although her words still sounded like rhetorical questions. "How can all of that just have disappeared? This can't be Penzance, can it?"

What to say to this? He'd never had anyone, still less a beautiful young lady, assure him that the place they were seeing was not the place he'd told her it was. Very confusing. She looked confused. He was too, and time was getting on. "I can see the line of the main road from here," he tried. "Just there where the trees run along. Come on, we'll canter the last quarter mile."

Without giving her the chance to protest, he touched his heels to Jago's cob and, beside him, Prinny sprang forward into a canter at the same time. Within scarcely more than a minute, they were pulling the horses to a walk where the road he'd indicated ran down the hillside into the outskirts of Penzance.

She'd asked for a road, and he'd provided her with one. "Here we are," Kit said, with a flourish. "The Penzance road."

A gravelly track wound down through the trees to snake its way between the closely packed cottages. The potholes marring its rough surface here and there were to be avoided, but otherwise, it was a fine road of which the Cornish, and by default Kit himself, could be proud.

"That's not a road," Morvoren declared. "That's a track."

"Track, road, what does it matter?" Kit retorted, a little flustered by her tone of apparent disgust for what to him was a jolly good thoroughfare. "It'll get us to where we want to go."

Morvoren shot him a frown as they passed under the last of the trees and emerged onto the road. A strong aroma of seaweed and fish rose from the harbor to meet them, mingling with the normal strong odors native to any village. A smell Kit loved. However, not so

Morvoren, it seemed. Her small and decidedly attractive nose wrinkled.

She must indeed be a fine lady if these scents offended her. No time to think about that now, though. He had to get her back to her lodgings so he could return post haste to the farm and Jago, preferably long before night fell.

"Where is your accommodation situated?" he asked as the road levelled out.

"Um, I was staying in a cottage in Abbey Place, near the harbor," Morvoren said, her voice redolent with uncertainty. "Number four. The Lobster Pot. It's a little cul-de-sac just off New Street."

Kit gave her a sideways look. Poor girl. She sounded addlepated, as though her dip in the sea had completely thrown her. Maybe she'd banged her head when she fell in? Perhaps he should have offered to check her over for bumps. The thought of running his hands through that mop of wavy golden hair sent a disturbing tide of warmth through his body.

No, he mustn't think things like that. It was his duty as a gentleman to return her to this "boyfriend" she'd mentioned, who would doubtless be returning from his so-called fishing trip with the tide. He gave himself a shake and concentrated on what she'd said. "Abbey Place must be close to Abbey Street, just above the harbor. I believe New Street is just around the corner. We'll go there first."

As they wended their way through the narrow streets, the clatter of their horses' shod hooves echoed on the cobbles. Kit kept a weather eye on Morvoren. Her anxious gaze flicked from left to right as though she couldn't believe what she was seeing. As though, for some reason, nothing about Penzance met her expectations. The fact that there was a definite mystery about her intrigued him more than he liked to admit.

Outside the tavern he and Jago liked to frequent on their visits to Penzance, Kit halted his cob. "We'll leave our horses here and proceed on foot."

She made no protest and sat demurely on Prinny while he dismounted and handed his cob to the ostler who came hurrying out to take it. Then Kit turned to help her down, and, with another wrinkle of her pretty nose, she rather awkwardly unhooked her right leg and slid down into his arms. He caught her around the waist and set her lightly on the ground, very much aware of the feel of her body under his hands and how different it now was to the first time he'd taken her in his arms on the beach. The feel of stays under his touch was somehow reassuring. The world was the right way up again.

Her eyes, those beautiful blue eyes, met his, and her cheeks, which had long ago resumed a normal coloration, flushed a becoming pink. Did she feel the same shiver of electricity as he did, every time he touched her?

"Which way from here?" he asked, releasing his hold on her as though she were a hot coal, immediately cross with himself for having done so. Best to revert to bluff indifference until he'd seen her safely ensconced in her lodgings. This was a girl he had to forget as soon as he parted from her, no matter how much he didn't want to.

She took a step back, her bosom, mostly obscured by the lace fichu around her shoulders, rising and falling as though she were breathless. "It wasn't far from the corner of New Street," she gabbled. "This way, I think." She certainly looked as shaken by the contact as he was.

Kit followed her, as, with determination, she turned down New Street, where small fishermen's cottages packed both sides of the cobbled road and a strong stench of privies had attached itself to the gutter in the center.

Abbey Place lay less than fifty yards along the street, recognizable only because someone had nailed up a sliver of driftwood on which the name—*Abby Plais*—had been painted. It proved to be a small, grimy-looking close, with cottages clustering cheek-by-jowl on both sides of a narrow, cobbled alleyway. Small front gardens, fenced with driftwood pickets, were spread with drying nets, and gaudily painted wooden fishing floats.

Kit stared at the cottages in a mixture of horror and annoyance. None of them appeared to be the sort of place a lady of quality would have chosen to reside. Could she really be staying in this impoverished side street? Or might her "boyfriend" be some unsavory adventurer who perhaps had eloped with a lady of quality and brought her to this low ebb in her life? And not yet married her.

Kit glanced sideways at Morvoren again, taking in her pale face and lips parted as though about to speak. As though, perhaps, to protest.

"Which one is it?" he asked, hope in his heart that she'd misremembered her address, and they were in the wrong place, vying with the need for this to be the right place. Then he could say a quick goodbye to her and return to the farm before he became even more involved.

She turned eyes stretched wide with fear on him, tears sparkling and ready to fall. "It-it was the last one in the row on the right," she managed, extending a trembling finger. "Only it didn't look a bit like this." Her voice shook as it rose to a plaintive cry. "Where have you brought me to? This isn't where I was staying. This isn't my Penzance. It can't be."

She swayed where she stood, her eyes still on him, almost pleading. Against his better judgement, which was telling him to leave her here in comparative civilization and run, Kit put out a hand to take her elbow. "Miss Lucas. Morvoren, this is certainly Penzance, and this is Abbey Place. I believe this is the only Abbey Place in Penzance. Perhaps you have it a little wrong in your head and your accommodation is elsewhere? Perhaps you mistook the name?"

Her tongue darted out to lick her lips. "Mr. Carlyon. Kit. Could you please tell me what... what year this is?" Her voice emerged, small and faint, yet resolute, as though she were steeling herself for some terrible shock.

Puzzled, Kit bit his lip. "Why, it's 1811, of course," he said, pleased to be certain of one thing at least. She might deny this was Penzance, but she couldn't deny the year.

Scarcely were the words out of his mouth, than Morvoren crumpled sideways to the ground.

Morvoren

THE SOUND OF voices forced its way through Morvoren's clogged brain. Was she back on the fishing boat? Buoyed up by that hope, she forced open her eyes.

Not the fishing boat.

She was lying in a propped position on a lumpily upholstered chair, her cheek resting against a pile of prickly velvet cushions. Her bonnet had gone, but, oh yes, she still had on that awful constricting corset, those *stays*, digging into her tender flesh and making it hard to breathe.

The events of the last few hours rushed back at a gallop, crowding themselves into her spinning head. Penzance as she'd never seen it before, shrunken to a tenth of its correct size, and packed with the homes of what had to be poor fisherfolk. The cottage she and Josh had rented for the week looking as though a family of squatters had been inhabiting it for a very long time.

"You're awake." Kit loomed over her, his face full of relieved concern.

And Kit. Of course, Kit. No wonder she'd thought he looked like the painting she'd seen in the museum. He had to be that same young man, preserved forever in oils and incarcerated in a museum for everyone to stare at. Because he'd been involved, no, was going to be involved, in the smuggling operation and killed on the very beach on which he'd dragged her ashore to save her life. Never mind what had just happened, everything she'd seen and read in the museum came flooding back. Kit, this vitally alive young man, was going to die when one of the smugglers betrayed the rest. Oh. God.

Might this all be just a terrible nightmare?

"I thought you'd hurt yourself when you fainted." Unaware of the upheaval in Morvoren's head and heart, Kit gestured at the beamed ceiling overhead and the dark interior of wherever they were. "I carried you back to the tavern where we left the horses, I'm afraid. It was all I could think of to do. There was nowhere more respectable to take you."

Wait? She'd fainted? She'd never done that in her life before. It must have been the shock of being told this was 1811. Not to mention the heat of the day... and those stays.

Today was turning out to be one shock after another.

Determination seizing her, Morvoren pushed herself a little more upright in the chair, and removed her cheek from the cushions. A little dizziness remained, but her wits were returning. What must he think of her? That she was some sort of weak woman who fainted at the drop of a hat? Probably. This was 1811 after all, and she'd just fallen neatly into the stereotype of a delicate Regency lady.

Raising her eyes, Morvoren studied Kit's concerned face. That he was a kind and honorable young man seemed evident from the way he'd looked after her, but the fact that he was also a smuggler now forced its way into the front of her mind and wouldn't go away. And, of course, that he was going to die. Very soon. Well, sometime this year. Sometime in 1811.

Kit's enquiring eyes rested on her in kind concern. Those of a young man who could have no conception of where she'd come from. Oh God! Did they still burn witches in 1811? If she told him the truth, would he think her one? Or maybe even lock her in a madhouse?

Could she bring herself to confide in him that somehow, something extremely strange had happened to her when she fell off that boat? That she knew he was a smuggler and was going to die because of it? But when? If only she could remember the date quoted on the exhibition in the museum. She swallowed the rising lump in her throat, steeled herself, and opened her mouth to speak.

The landlord chose this moment to shoulder his way into the room carrying a tray loaded with food and drink.

The moment was lost.

"You need sustenance after your swoon," Kit said, as the landlord laid the tray on the table. "And then we need to decide what to do next. Your cottage appears not to be where you thought it was. Might you have been staying with… anybody else?"

Definite hesitation from him there.

He took a watch on a chain out of his waistcoat pocket and surveyed it. With a frown, he stowed the watch away again. "Could we perhaps search for… your companions? If you give me their names, then I can make enquiries while you rest here. I commanded a private parlor for you, so you won't be disturbed."

Of course. He had some pressing appointment with his uncle that night. Might it be to do with smuggling? Oh, God, might it be the night he was destined to die? Guilt washed over Morvoren at not having paid enough attention in the museum.

"I'm sorry, but I have no one," she said. Best not to mention Josh again. Best not to mention boyfriends at all, as it seemed an anachronistic word. "I was alone. I don't know anyone here, I'm afraid."

Which was not a lie. If this really was 1811, then she knew no one in the entire world.

Kit frowned again. "Then you should eat and put some color back into your cheeks, for you've gone quite pale again, and I fear it's my fault for not having insisted you ate something while you were at Jago's farm. It's now well after noon and high time for sustenance."

He unloaded the plates from the tray. "And perhaps we can decide how to contact your family and find you some help." He glanced around, a frown on his brow. "I don't think you can stay here though—it wouldn't be at all respectable for a lady to do so without a maid."

No one could keep this pretense up so well. The fact that he thought she needed a maid to make her acceptable was the nail in the coffin to Morvoren's ruminations. From now on, she had to assume she really was in 1811, mad as that sounded, and act accordingly, or everyone she met was going to think her very strange. She began by tucking her feet out of the way under the skirts of her dress. She couldn't go running around Regency England in a pair of trainers.

In fact, she couldn't go running around Regency England at all, unless she managed to get her hands on some money. And where, for instance, was she going to sleep tonight, dolled up like a dog's dinner as she was but without a penny to her name. A sobering thought.

But for now, she was famished, and the spread before her looked most appetizing. Breakfast in her old world had been a long time ago, further than she'd ever imagined it could get. She'd think about what she was going to do next, later.

"Thank you," she said meekly.

The food might have been plain, but it was very good. Slices of crusty bread, thick yellow butter, a large pie she recognized as a Cornish Pasty and some crumbly cheese.

The landlord had brought a tall jug of cider from which Kit filled two small pewter mugs. Thirsty, and forgetting her new resolution to meet the expectations of ladylike behavior suitable to 1811, Morvoren downed her first in several long gulps, making Kit's dark eyebrows shoot towards his hairline. However, he followed suit, then refilled the mugs. Perhaps he liked ladies who knocked back their alcohol in one, or, worse, perhaps he doubted she was a lady. Better be more circumspect.

"Daveth serves fine local cider," he said, wiping his mouth on his sleeve. "Which I see you appreciate."

Conscious of needing to behave more appropriately, Morvoren nodded and took a small nibble of her pie. Not that she was going to be able to squeeze a lot of food in while wearing stays. Did women in the past suffer from malnutrition, or did they eat in secret in their rooms without their stays on? That was definitely what she'd have to do, or she'd starve.

Kit didn't seem to have noticed her discomfort. "Now," he said. "You say you are from Reading. I happen to know that town a little. It lies on the coach road from London to Cornwall, on the bank of the River Thames. But unfortunately, without finding your accommodation, we can't reunite you with your baggage, and a lady travelling without baggage is considered worse than a lady without an abigail."

"An abigail?"

He nodded. "You must have a maid with you to travel on the mail coach back to Reading. We'll have to find you one. And I hope you'll allow me to presume to pay for your ticket and traveling expenses along the way. It's the least I can do as you've lost all your belongings and your accommodation."

Morvoren swallowed, her appetite vanishing. No one in Reading was going to be waiting to greet her, that was for sure, and she'd be in the same pickle she was here.

"I'm afraid I don't have anywhere to go," she gabbled, before her courage left her and she let him magic her an abigail from somewhere and put her, and this as yet unidentified female, on a coach to a town that would be as unrecognizable as Penzance. Then she'd be truly lost, and besides which, didn't she want a chance to save her rescuer from being killed? One good deed deserved another.

Kit set down his cider and leaned back in his seat, yet another frown darkening his brow. "Well," he said, slowly and thoughtfully as though weighing his words. "I suppose I could take you to my mother and sister at Ormonde. They'd likely know what to do about your predicament." He paused before continuing with more confidence in his voice. "Yes, that sounds the best idea. That would solve this problem at least for a while."

It would solve hers too, because if he wasn't down here taking part in the smuggling, he couldn't be killed on the beach in Smuggler's Cove—Nanpean Cove as it would be now.

Morvoren studied Kit's face. "Are you sure? You're not responsible for me, you know, even though you saved me from the sea." But inside, she was cheering.

He nodded with an air of having made a firm decision. "Of course I am. I pulled you out of the sea and, on that instant, you became my responsibility. I couldn't possibly just leave you here in Penzance with no friends or family, no maid, and no money." He looked her up and down. "And only the clothes you're standing up in, which do rather stand out. What sort of a gentleman would do that?"

Tears threatened to fall. Morvoren bit her lip to prevent them. "That—that would be amazing." The sheer relief of being offered sanctuary and shelter, not to mention satisfaction that she'd be taking him away from danger and in some way paying him back for his kindness, washed over her, bringing a lump to her throat. Was there no limit to the generosity of strangers, even if this one, although undeniably handsome, was a tad severe in his appearance? Not only had he saved her life and escorted her to where he thought she'd come from, but now he was offering the hospitality of his own family. She wasn't such a fool as to turn him down. Instead, she bestowed a radiant smile on him. "Thank you so much."

A flicker of amusement showed in his eyes for a moment. "My sister will be overjoyed if I bring someone like you to visit her. She complains all the time about how dull it is now Meliora is married and lives in Bath and has sprained her ankle and can't travel."

Morvoren's turn to be puzzled. "Sprained her ankle? Surely she'll recover quickly if she rests her foot?"

To her surprise, color rose up Kit's neck to his face. "Er, it's not really her ankle. She's in a... er... delicate situation. In that condition. You know. Increasing."

She couldn't hold in the chuckle at his discomfort. "You mean she's pregnant?"

His eyes widened as though she'd said something very vulgar.

She chuckled again. "Well, why ever not just say?"

Kit's shocked face twitched as though he were restraining himself from smiling. "I have to admit my sisters are always very evasive about that... condition," he said. "And so is every other society lady I've ever met. Not that many of them even talk about it at all, that is. I just assumed we weren't allowed to refer to it directly. But you may be right. So much easier to say she's in foal or something similar. No one would get the wrong end of the stick then."

Well, not quite the same.

"Now," he said, the embryonic smile vanishing entirely. "We shall need to purchase our coach tickets for tomorrow morning first. Then collect our horses and ride back to the farm for the night, I'm afraid. The journey to Ormonde is a long one, and if I'm to travel with you, we must definitely engage a maid for the sake of propriety, and equip you sufficiently from my mother's old clothes, unfashionable as they might be. So, Jago is going to have to swallow down his ire and put up with having a visitor."

Lovely. Back to where Morvoren thought she'd escaped from.

Chapter Seven
MORVOREN

On the way back to the farm, a place Morvoren was not keen to revisit, Kit called a halt at the little row of cottages they'd passed on their way out. The women had finished their washing and it now lay spread over the bushes, drying in the sun.

Kit pulled the cob, who must have known he was nearly home, to an unwilling halt. "I'll just be a minute here at Jowan's cottage." He dismounted, looped the cob's reins over a rickety gate post, and strode up the front path of the nearest cottage, the neatest and tidiest in the row.

He knocked smartly on the door and, after a moment or two, this door, better painted than the rest in the row, creaked open. A rotund, red-headed, apple-cheeked woman who might have been somewhere about forty, emerged, bobbing a curtsey as she came.

From where she sat on Prinny by the ford, Morvoren could only see Kit's back and hear nothing of the low conversation he was having, but the woman's excitable reaction spoke volumes.

This was the woman Kit had picked out to be the maid who would give respectability to Morvoren and enable her to spend the night in the farmhouse with two single men—Loveday Curnow.

"Jowan's daughter," Kit had explained on the long ride back from Penzance. "She used to be lady's maid to my mother before she set up house with a fisherman from Nanpean village. You'll be relieved to hear she's a better worker than her father. Sadly for her, her fisherman's boat was lost in a storm last winter and she's been back here keeping house for her father ever since. I'm hoping she'll remember some of the skills she had in her youth, if you're lucky."

Not that Morvoren had any idea what those skills might be.

She watched Loveday in curiosity. Perhaps she was the one responsible for the neatly painted front door and the curtains hanging in the windows that made this house stand out as better than the rest. Somehow, from what she'd seen of Jowan, she couldn't imagine he'd be the sort to bother with such things.

From the eager smile on Loveday's face, it seemed Kit's persuasive powers were working. Either that, or being Morvoren's maid was a better alternative to being her father's. Beaming, Loveday vanished back inside her cottage and Kit strolled back to the horses.

"She's very pleased to be offered the job," he said, his eyes more troubled than Morvoren would have expected after this success in finding a maid and thus rendering her "respectable." Maybe he was thinking about how he would explain Morvoren's continued presence to his uncle.

Loveday emerged five minutes later with a bobbed curtsey and a "G'day to you, Miss Lucas," that Morvoren returned with a "Hello, Loveday." Then, with Morvoren still on Prinny, and Kit and Loveday on foot, the three of them continued down the track to Nanpean Farm.

Jago was much worse than Kit had been at hiding his annoyance at having to play host again. As the horses turned into the farmyard and he spotted Morvoren and Loveday, he sent a glowering look at Kit and stomped off into the house with his head down, his fury hanging over him in a black cloud.

It turned out that the full extent of Kit's hospitality involved him giving up his bedroom at one end of the house for Morvoren. He was to sleep on the small camp bed affair in the box room along with the dusty shrouded furniture and the chests of blankets and clothes. He seemed unperturbed by this prospect. "I've slept in worse places than this," being his only comment.

After an awkwardly silent dinner, and with Morvoren's offer to dry the dishes refused, Jenifry took her upstairs with Loveday. Back in the little box room, the two servants rummaged through the clothes chest a second time.

"I'll just put these things to air a bit," Jenifry said, fishing shapeless garments out. "There should be more than enough for you at Ormonde."

"You'll be needin' underwear an' stockin's, too," Loveday declared, piling these items up. "Good thing Miss Elestren had all new when she married Mr. Thomas."

"An' a good thing I hung onto all of 'em like this," Jenifry said. "Though I did think as 'twere a cryin' shame they didn't fit me."

"Like Jago'd've let you wear 'em," Loveday scoffed. "You might be warmin' his bed for him, but he ain't likely to tek you to wife, no matter what you thinks."

For a moment they looked as though they might come to blows, so Morvoren reached out and picked up a prettily embroidered shift. "This is beautiful. Did one of you make it?" Their argument was somewhat defused as Jenifry was forced to tell her Miss Elestren herself had stitched it as a girl. However, this distraction didn't stop the two women exchanging dark looks as the pile of chosen clothing mounted.

Best to ignore their bristling rivalry.

"Do you know where Kit's mother and sister live?" she ventured, instead.

"Ormonde," Loveday and Jenifry said in unison, clearly competing to be the one to answer.

Morvoren was none the wiser. "But where exactly is that?"

"T'other side o' the Tamar," Jenifry got in first. "A long way off."

"England," Loveday elaborated.

Not much help, as the Tamar marked the boundary between Cornwall and the rest of England even in Morvoren's world. Ormonde could be anywhere east of it. She left them to it and, hitching up her skirts, descended to a kitchen empty of Kit and Jago. Peace and quiet. She sat down by the range and stretched out her trainer-clad feet. If she didn't get these dreadful stays off soon, she was going to scream.

By the time Loveday and Jenifry had sorted out all the required garments and returned downstairs, still with a certain amount of bickering, evening was falling rapidly in the narrow valley. Neither Kit nor Jago had returned, the latter to Morvoren's relief. And it was high time to go to bed and leave them all to their smuggling. No doubt Jago and Kit were avoiding her and counting the minutes until they could be rid of her presence.

So, with Loveday hovering in attendance, Morvoren bid Jenifry goodnight. Refusing to be offended by the relieved expression on both women's faces, she trod the creaky spiral up to Kit's loaned bedroom. The moment she'd gone, the front door banged open, and the murmur of voices rose as the men returned.

Kit's bedroom occupied one gable end of the house, with a window onto the yard, and a second in the end wall giving a view down toward the cove. A large bed occupied most of the room, along with an old oak chest of drawers and a chair. All was scrupulously tidy, and the bed looked most inviting.

The relief of at last getting out of her tight-fitting gown was almost as great as getting out of her stays. How women in the past ate and breathed at the same time was beyond Morvoren, but she couldn't say this to Loveday for fear of being thought mad. She had to maintain the illusion of being a nicely brought up young lady who'd been wearing stays for years.

She decided on a different tack. One headed towards being more comfortable. "Could I possibly have my corset laced a little less tightly tomorrow, as I have a long journey to make?"

Loveday's apple cheeks swelled in a smile. "Lordy, Miss Lucas, 'tis only they Frenchies what wears corsets. Though I do hear that when she were just Miss Tremaine, Mr. Kit's mother called her stays her corset. On account of her mother being a French lady. Well, a Breton lady if we're to call a spade a spade. A lady from across the sea in that there Brittany. But they do speak French mostly there, so I hear, so I ses they're French as much as the rest o' Boney's lot." She laid the pink and white dress out on the chest of drawers and smoothed its generous skirts. "But tomorrow, I'll find you a travelin' dress what's a bit more generous in the fit. Can't have you a-faintin' away afore you reaches Exeter."

Heat swarmed its way up Morvoren's neck to her cheeks. Kit must have told Loveday about today.

"Lordy, don't you go a blushin' that you swooned, Miss Lucas. Fine ladies swoon all the time. 'Tis a mark o' their gentility. I'll see if I can find you Miss Elestren's old vinaigrette for you to put in your reticule."

Deciding that swooning must be more a mark of too tight stays than gentility, and that asking about a reticule was for later, Morvoren focused on what Loveday had said about Kit's mother. So, her mother, and therefore Jago's mother too, had been French—or Breton, whichever way you wanted to classify her. Interesting. Perhaps Loveday, who seemed to like chattering away, could provide some information about Kit.

"Do you have no idea at all where Ormonde is?" she tried.

She frowned as she folded the many petticoats and shrugged. "Not in Cornwall, like I said earlier. I don't rightly know where it be, but you an' me're goin' to find out, it seems." She smoothed the soft fabric as though it were a cat. "Miss Elestren did used to live right here until twenty year back. Not here at Nanpean, o' course, but wi' Mr.

Thomas at Carlyon Court, which be only a stone's throw from here."

She crossed herself quickly before continuing. "Right up until Mr. Thomas's older brother, Mr. William, God rest his soul, died in foreign parts, that was. Then Mr. Thomas had to move the whole family up to Ormonde because he were the new heir."

She tutted her tongue. "You see, like his pa, Mr. Thomas were a second son, not expected to inherit, so he'd been livin' at Carlyon Court all his life up till then. He were *our* Mr. Thomas." She shook her head. "Father, he were near an age wi' Mr. Thomas an' Mr. Robert—twins, they was, God rest their souls. Father were right good friends wi' them when they were all nobbut bad lads." She paused, a faraway look in her eyes. "I were right sad when Mr. Thomas did die."

Morvoren frowned, confused about who was related to whom. "Am I right in thinking Mr. Thomas was Kit's father?" she ventured. "And that he had a twin brother but both of them are now dead?"

Loveday picked up a high-necked and decidedly prim linen nightgown, liberally festooned with lace. "You has it right, Miss Lucas. Tooken sudden, Mr. Thomas were, five year ago now. Mr. Kit, who's his only son, he were still at Oxford when it happened. Father did tell me it were an apoplexy. Mr. Thomas, he'd got very big, jus' like his brother Mr. Robert did afore he died, an' they do say as how big folks're more likely to suffer an apoplexy. He did linger on a few days, I heard, in time for Mr. Kit to get to Ormonde an' see him, but there weren't nothin' the physician could do. 'Twere right sad."

That answered one question. Kit's mother and sister would be alone when Morvoren arrived uninvited to stay with them, with no possibility of a threatening male presence such as Jago's.

"Do you know what happened to the oldest brother? To the one called William?" she asked, as Loveday slipped the nightdress on over her head. She'd given the lacy knickers a raised eyebrow, but either Jenifry had warned her in advance, or she was of a more accepting nature, for she'd not said a word.

"Why, he were a good seven year older than the twins, I b'lieve and the heir to Ormonde. A proper trial to his old father." Loveday chuckled to herself. "All o' they lads were a handful, thass for sure. But Mr. William, he had the devil in him. Even when he were up at Eton. 'Tis said his ma and pa were right glad when he took hisself off to the colonies as a young man. Jamaica, I heard, to do some kind of work over there. I don't rightly know all the details, but my ma were a one for the gossip and she did collect it like lint to a pair o' moleskins."

Inwardly, Morvoren blessed Loveday's mother, whose knowledge was proving very useful. "So, let me get this straight," she said, busily organizing some sort of family tree in her mind of the people she was going to see. "There were three brothers who lived at Carlyon Court, which isn't far from here, and Kit's father was one of twins. The oldest brother died—without children, I'm presuming—in Jamaica or somewhere like that, and Kit's father became the heir, then inherited Ormonde? And that's where Kit's mother and sister live, but the father is now dead?"

Loveday nodded with a beaming smile. "You have it right there, Miss. Twins, they might have been, but with Mr. Thomas bein' the older by just a few minutes, he were the heir after Mr. William's death. And now," she turned back the covers on Kit's bed, "you hop in here nice'n'quick and snuggle down on this here feather bed, and in no time at all you'll be fast asleep. But jest in case, I'll pop down the kitchen and fetch you a nice glass o' warm milk to drink, laced wi' a tot o' the best brandy. Oh, an' if you need it, there's a chamber pot tucked under the bed."

Less than five minutes later, Loveday returned bearing a tall glass of hot milk smelling strongly of brandy and with a sprinkle of brown sugar decorating its frothy surface. As Morvoren was already in bed, Loveday stood the glass on the low bedside table and went to pull the curtains more tightly closed. "You drink up, Miss, an' keep they curtains tight shut. Don't want to see no hants on a night like this."

"Hants?"

"Ghosties. There be a lot o' ghosties hereabouts. You stay tucked in your bed no matter what you hear of a night. Best place ter be." And with that enigmatic remark, Loveday left Morvoren to herself.

She picked up the milk and sniffed it. Perhaps not. She didn't want to wake up with a hangover and it smelled strong enough that she might. She set the glass back down again and snuggled into the blankets and counterpane. This certainly was a very comfortable bed.

She woke to cloying darkness and silence. Only it wasn't true silence. From down in the cove came the distant rumble of surf, but from nearer at hand came a different noise. She rolled onto her back and stared up at the dim outline of the dark beams on the arching bedroom ceiling. What was that strange sound, like many slippers shuffling across a floor?

The muffled sound of hooves, that was what.

Many hooves pattering lightly on the track up from the beach. Hants? Did she believe in them? No. So impossible. Much more likely to be the smugglers they didn't want her to see. Casting aside Loveday's words of caution, Morvoren slid out of bed and crossed the smoothly worn floorboards to the end window. Drawing aside the curtain, she peered into the gloom of a dark and moonless night.

At first, despite her eyes being accustomed to the dark, all she could see was the shadowy bulk of the far side of the valley where the moors began, looming high over the little farm. Behind the moors rose the blue-black of a clear, star-spangled night sky.

Then her eyes caught movement. What was that? With no moon to illuminate the view, it took a long minute to make out the shadowy string of ponies trudging up the track from the cove, but there they were, all heavily laden with lumpish shapes that might have been large packages or barrels. Smugglers. The lead pony, the vague form of a man at its head, was just passing beyond view around the far side of the farm buildings.

The sound of the gate scraping across the flagstones carried through the still night air. She'd have a better view from the front window.

This time, proper caution raised its head, and she tiptoed across the creaky floorboards. With nervous fingers, she drew back the curtain at one corner to peer out more warily than before. A thrill of excitement sizzled at the prospect of watching real, nineteenth-century smugglers at work, that history was enacting itself before her eyes.

The yard was filling fast with shuffling ponies and men, whose heavy, hobnailed boots made far more noise than their ponies' muffled hooves. Where were Jago and Kit? With them or merely awaiting their arrival?

The low rumble of a gravelly voice came from by the front porch. "Keep it hushed now, all o' you gen'lemen, as Kit warned. We've got ourselves a guest upstairs, and we don't want her wakin' up an' seein' this." A low chuckle. "Though she shouldn't be wakin', not after the dose o' brandy Loveday give her."

A murmur of agreement susurrated around the farmyard, and the light laughter of at least two women. Loveday and Jenifry, of course. Smuggling must be as much a woman's thing as a man's.

"Well done, lads," Jago continued. "You can unload my brandy into the end shed. I've four barrels, I hear. And Kit'll have those two bolts of silk for Miss Elestren. You can give him those now." There was a scuffle as the men hurried to do as they'd been bidden.

"Where d'ye want the baccy, Jago?" called an overly loud voice.

A chorus of others joined in with low voices admonishing the speaker.

"Shush Clemo!"

"You deaf old fart."

"Keep it down."

If only they knew that she'd already worked out what they were up to and had no interest in giving them away.

Vague shapes milled about the yard as the unloading went on. Morvoren strained to see better. Was that figure near the porch familiar in its height and build, taller by far than the surrounding men?

Even as those thoughts crossed her mind, the man in question turned to glance up at the front of the house, perhaps seeking out her window. Perhaps afraid she might be looking out at the scene in the yard, despite Jago's assurances that she'd had her milk spiked.

Morvoren dropped the curtain and stepped back into the comparative safety of the dark room. The man had been Kit, dressed all in black and with an old tricorn hat jammed onto his head. Had he seen her?

She sat down on the bed, heart hammering. No denying they were smugglers. Kit and his uncle must be in league with the locals, or even organizing them.

Her excitement died, extinguished by harsh reality. Smugglers weren't just the romantic figures in books like *Moonfleet*; they were desperate criminals who wouldn't think twice about silencing someone they thought had been spying on them. Especially not when the spy in question had no relatives or friends in the world. How easy would it be to erase her from history with one crack of the neck? She could almost feel Jago's strong hands on her throat...

Downstairs, the front door banged. She jumped back into bed and pulled the covers up to her nose, closing her eyes and trying to steady her frantic breathing. Footsteps creaked on the spiral staircase, paused for a moment, then padded down the short landing to her door. Outside, they halted.

She fought to quieten her breathing, her whole body shaking. Was it Jago or Kit? Would Jago kill her in her bed if he knew she'd seen the pack ponies laden with contraband, or would Kit, unwillingly, she liked to think, do his bidding for him? Would she never get the chance to warn him there was a traitor in their midst?

The door creaked open.

She lay still.

Nothing. Whoever occupied the doorway didn't come into the bedroom but stood there for a long minute. Oh please, let it be Kit, not Jago. Perhaps she'd better shift a little. She made a sleepy noise and stretched her legs out. Would that convince him? Unless of course he'd seen her as clearly as she'd seen him.

The door creaked closed.

Was he inside the room, still watching, perhaps holding his cravat in his hands, about to strangle the life out of her? On Jago's orders. Were smugglers that ruthless? Was Kit that ruthless?

Nothing. She made another sleepy movement.

Still nothing.

Outside, the ponies' padded hooves shuffled across the cobbles and out of the yard. The gate creaked shut behind them. Someone would have looped that rope over the gatepost to make the yard secure.

She lay motionless, ears straining in the darkness, the sweat of fear sticking the borrowed nightdress to her back.

Muffled voices out in the yard. Male voices.

"Better lock the shed." Jago's deep, gruff grumble.

Kit's lighter, more refined tones. "She won't go poking around. We're taking the morning coach, so she won't have time."

A third voice. A woman's this time. It had to be Jenifry. "I don't think she be the type to snitch."

"Me neither. See yer all in the mornin'." Loveday's voice.

As she'd suspected, they were all in on this.

Jago's growl. "You can't tell jest by lookin'. An' she be a woman, an' 'tis well known that they doan know how to hold their tongues like a man do."

Jenifry's voice again. "You sayin' I can't keep quiet, Jago me 'an-sum? If you want more'n a pot o' hot flannel this night you'd best be mindin' what you ses to me."

Jago's voice, with an unaccustomed chuckle. "You knows I doan mean you, woman."

The front door banged as they came inside, and their voices died to nothing more than a general mumble. They didn't sound as though they thought they'd been seen. But Morvoren lay awake for a long time, ears still straining, picturing what would happen if Kit told his uncle he'd seen her face at the window, spying on their smuggling activities.

Eventually, they all came clumping up the stairs. Morvoren held her breath until Kit went into the box room and closed the door. Jago and Jenifry stomped into the bedroom at the far end of the landing with a giggle and a squeal from her as though she'd been goosed.

Only then did Morvoren feel safe enough to go back to sleep. An uneasy sleep, troubled by dreams of being on the bottom of the sea, of her legs tangled tight in a net, and being carried up from the cove slung over a pack pony with a pair of brandy barrels attached to her feet, and a loud voice telling Kit to go put her back in the sea.

Chapter Eight

MORVOREN

A TENTATIVE TAP on the bedroom door disturbed Morvoren's sleep. She rolled over in bed to discover early morning sunshine peeking in around the edges of the heavy curtains. Last night's experience came rolling back in a tidal wave, and she jerked wide awake in an instant. The tap on the door sounded again, more demandingly, so she sat up and pulled the covers up to her chest, despite the Victorian-modesty of her nightgown. "Come in."

Loveday bustled into the room carrying another glass of milk. Her eyes went to the full one by the side of the bed, now boasting an unattractively thick skin on its surface, and a frown furrowed her brow for a brief moment. "I did bring you some more warm milk, Miss Lucas."

A hint of disapproval marred her voice as she set down the new glass and retrieved the old. "Mr. Kit did ax me to tell you that breakfast'll be in ten minutes. He ses as he do want to get to the coach stop in good time."

As it turned out, neither Kit nor Jago were in the kitchen. Jenifry, a not-very-clean apron tied about her ample middle, looked none the worse for her nocturnal activities as she bid Morvoren a cheery good morning. Bustling from stove to table, she served up a plate of sizzling bacon, two fried eggs and some hot potato cakes, along with a far-too-dainty cup of strong black coffee. Wiping her hands on her apron, she sat down with her own hefty mug. From above, echoing through the old house like a drum, came the sound of movement, as Loveday took care of the packing.

Morvoren ate in silence for a while, all too aware that Jenifry was as much a smuggler as Kit and his uncle and that she should give nothing away.

Eventually, Jenifry set her coffee mug down on the table and wiped her mouth on the back of her hand. "Sleep well, did you, Miss Lucas?"

A loaded question if ever there was one.

Morvoren schooled her face into passive neutrality and looked up, meeting sharply intelligent grey eyes. "Yes, thank you. I've never slept on a feather bed before, and it was very comfortable." She paused before deciding to elaborate. "I slept like a log." There. She'd effectively denied having seen or heard anything.

Challenge that one if you can.

Jenifry's moon face broke into a broad smile. "That's good to hear. I did worry to meself as you might not have slept so well, bein' in a strange bed, an' all." She wiped her hands on her apron front. "Now, finish up your food because it'll be a while afore the coach stops for vittles and you've a long journey ahead o' you. I'm off to see if they've got the horse between the shafts yet."

Mindful of Jenifry's warning about the time until the next meal, Morvoren polished off the last of her breakfast and poured a second cup of coffee from the jug on the stove. Just in time to hear the thump on the stairs of Loveday dragging down the trunk she'd been packing. She appeared through the door at the bottom, her rosy cheeks a shade rosier and her breath coming fast. The object she was dragging was a much smaller trunk than the ones in the box room, but nevertheless, it appeared to be a weighty object. How much did one woman need in 1811?

Morvoren set down her empty coffee cup and hurried over. "Here. Let me help."

Loveday batted an admonishing hand. "No, no, no, Miss Lucas. I c'n manage right well, and it ain't for a lady to help the maid. I'll jest set it here and Mr. Kit or Father can carry it out to the cart in a moment." She plumped herself down on top of it, still puffing, and fanning her hot face with her hand. "And in a minute, when I've me breath back, I'll fetch your bonnet and gloves for the journey. An' a shawl lest it turn cold up country." She frowned. "You never can tell wi' foreign parts."

Voices carried from outside and the front door swung open. Kit came in, this morning dressed much more smartly. Even his unruly hair had been slicked into some sort of order.

He made Morvoren a brief bow and held out his hand. "The cart awaits you."

Morvoren hesitated.

He didn't drop his hand, though, and to leave him standing there holding it out seemed rude. She touched her fingers lightly to his, resolutely ignoring the frisson of electricity as it ran between them, and let him lead her out into the farmyard.

KIT

A SINGLE WOODEN fingerpost on the crossroads of two tracks marked the stopping place for the Exeter coach. Kit halted the cob and applied the brake. "Here we are. Time to get down." He looped the reins around the cart's brake handle and jumped down to walk round and help Miss Lucas dismount.

After a brief hesitation, she took his offered hand in her gloved one. Then, setting her foot on the step, she gave a little hop to land lightly on the ground, her strange shoes making a momentary disturbing reappearance. Something needed to be done about those.

Loveday climbed out of the back, and Jowan, with manifest ill will, lifted down the two trunks and his daughter's bag to dump them unceremoniously beside the fingerpost. Wasting no time, he clambered back onto the driving seat of the cart and let off the brake.

"Glad to see the back o' her," he grunted, jerking an ill-mannered thumb at Miss Lucas. "Be seein' yer." And with that surly farewell, he set off down the farm track, back hunched and shapeless hat jammed down over his eyes.

"Doan be wishin' me farewell, will ye?" Loveday shouted after him, hands on ample hips. "I might be decidin' to stay at Ormonde. Then you'll not be seein' me agin."

For answer, the old man hunched over even further, his head sinking between his shoulders. Hard to imagine him ever having been a carefree boy running wild with Kit's late father and his Uncle Robert.

Kit, Miss Lucas, and Loveday stood silent for a few seconds watching him go, until the hill hid his progress. Then, with a sigh, Kit took his pocket watch out and studied its pale face. "The coach should be here very soon."

He was right.

Within five minutes of standing in the rapidly warming morning sunshine, the coach appeared over the rise in the west. Four sturdy bay horses trundled along at a steady trot over the less than perfect road surface, the whole vehicle rattling fit to break apart. Already, luggage piled the roof, and a few passengers clung precariously to the outside seats. Nevertheless, the driver pulled his horses to a halt when he saw he had three would-be passengers standing by the side of the road.

"Three for inside?" he called down to them from his lofty perch at the front, his dusty, booted feet resting squarely on the footboard at Kit's eye level.

"Three for Exeter to join the Quicksilver tonight," Kit said, as the guard jumped down from beside the driver to open the doors and let down the step.

Two people already occupied seats inside the coach. In one corner a cadaverous man sat hunched as though desperate to keep his distance from his fellow passengers. And a fat matron occupied the seat opposite him, clutching a wicker basket from which came the unmistakable plaintive meowing of a disgruntled cat.

Morvoren took a seat by the window on the same side as the matron and Kit settled himself opposite. A moment later, Loveday clambered up to join them and wedged her ample bulk into the small space between Morvoren and the cat lady, and the guard folded up the step and closed the door.

They were off.

Kit glanced at Morvoren, who was staring about with the puzzled air of someone who'd never been in a coach before, her eyes flitting between the faded upholstery and the small sliding windows in each door. Her forehead glistened with a sheen of sweat that matched his own. This was going to be a long, hot day.

The indignant meowing from the basket on the fat lady's lap increased.

"There, there, Princess," the cat's owner cooed as though she were soothing a baby, but thankfully she didn't open the lid. Kit was not overly fond of cats, especially not in confined spaces.

He leaned back in his corner against the dusty upholstery and closed his eyes, determined to get some rest. After all, he'd had a very disturbed night.

The lady with the cat got out at Launceston, which was a blessing as the cat had clearly been in dire need at one point of the privy and the resulting odor of cat urine had become quite overpowering in the confined space of the coach. The cadaverous gentleman wrinkled up his nose and brought out a vinaigrette to sniff, and Kit sorely wished he had one as well, as the smell of cat lingered for some while after its owner had departed.

At last, after many stops to change horses and with darkness falling, the coach, with a blast on the post horn to let everyone know of their arrival, rumbled over Exeter's fine stone bridge and up New Bridge Street. It ground to a halt outside Thomson's Inn, opposite the cathedral.

"Exeter," Kit said. "We have an hour to spare before the mail coach leaves. We should go into Thomson's and procure some supper." He held out his arm for Miss Lucas to take. "Loveday can go to the kitchens, and we shall dine in the parlor."

Several other people were already in residence in the inn's parlor, presumably also waiting for the mail coach, but it was a spacious room. Kit steered Miss Lucas to seats at a small table in a corner away from the others and waited for the landlord to send in the meal he'd ordered.

For the first time that day he had her to himself. Yet again, she was staring around in wonder at the candlelit room and the log fire blazing in the hearth. She had the air about her of someone visiting Astley's to view animals she'd never seen before, and that he, Kit, was one of the exhibits. Very puzzling.

"The best coaching inn Exeter has to offer," he said, after scrabbling in his head for something to say. "The dinner they serve should at least be palatable."

She managed a tight smile as she took her seat. Her cheeks had flushed a becoming pink, possibly from the heat, but her eyes gave away her exhaustion, with dark rings starting to show beneath them. Clearly, unlike him, she hadn't managed to sleep on their long journey.

He cleared his throat. "I'm sorry. Should I have commanded rooms so you could rest? I'm not used to making allowances for ladies of gentle birth, unless you count my sisters, and two of them have been married for some while now, so only Ysella remains at home." He gave her a tired smile. "And I've never had to make allowances for that chit."

She shook her head. "Not at all. I'm perfectly fine and I don't want allowances being made for me. I'm stronger than I look." And this time her smile reached her eyes. "I managed a little sleep in the coach, although I have to say it's not the most comfortable of vehicles and the constant stopping for fresh horses doesn't allow for much peace."

That was reassuring. However, something about Miss Lucas that he didn't understand shouted to him that she was different, although he couldn't quite see how she could be. A girl was a girl, after all.

"I hope, in that case, that you don't mind us travelling on straight away?" he said, unable to take his eyes from her face. Damn it. What was it about her? He couldn't allow himself to show an interest, not with his dangerous responsibilities at Nanpean.

A gap-toothed serving girl in a grubby apron set bowls of brown soup before them on the table.

"Whatever you think is best," Miss Lucas said, stifling a yawn and dropping her gaze to her bowl. She gave a tentative sniff. "What do you think is in this?"

Kit sniffed as well, glad to be able to talk about the food. "Difficult to be certain. Thickened bone broth perhaps? It's hot, at least. If we don't eat it up quick, we won't get the roast, though, so best sup up."

There was indeed a taste of meat about the soup. Faint, but present, but as to what else was in it—that was anyone's guess. He'd heard enough cautionary tales about the food served in posting inns, even the best ones. Better, on the whole, not to know what you were eating.

"I'm sorry the journey is tiring you," he tried.

Miss Lucas raised her eyes to consider him, something going on behind them that he couldn't work out. "Having to use horse drawn transport does rather make the country feel large."

What an odd thing to say. As if there were any alternative. "It is large. Although not so big as the Americas, so I'm told." How inane was this conversation? What he really wanted to ask her was who Josh was, and what a boyfriend was, and why her accommodation had just vanished off the face of the earth. A lot of other things as well, but manners prevented him from reeling his questions off like an interrogation. A gentleman didn't demand things of a lady. And now he'd left Cornwall behind, he was back to being a gentleman. Damn it.

With their soup bowls emptied, the same girl brought out slices of still bloody beef, potatoes and a rather mushy concoction of cabbage and walnuts. Kit washed this down with several glasses of a claret of dubious origins but better taste than he'd expected. Miss Lucas, however, only sipped her wine.

Now or never. "Will your parents not be awaiting your return?"

Those blue eyes widened. "My parents are dead."

Of course. She'd said she had nobody. "But surely you don't live alone?"

She shook her head. "I live with a friend." She paused. "Another… young lady. Christina Armstrong."

This was getting somewhere. "Will she not miss you?"

Morvoren shook her head, her eyes darting sideways giving her the appearance of a frightened deer. "She's… not there at the moment, I'm afraid."

Progress at last. "She didn't accompany you to Cornwall, then?"

Morvoren picked at her food. "No. She didn't." Her words came out with a finality that had him stumped. As though she'd just closed a door in his face and shot the bolts across.

No time for anything else, though, as a shout of, "All's ready," rang through the inn.

Kit laid his napkin aside and rose to his feet. "That's us he's calling. We'd best make haste as they're not known here for their patience. If we're not careful they'll leave without us, but with our baggage." He held out his arm.

She stood up and took it with a smile. Perhaps she was glad the questioning was over. Her light fingers rested just in the crook of his elbow, as though she were getting more used to this action, the tingle of her touch most disturbing.

Outside, darkness had fallen, and the lamplighter had been round. The golden glow of the flickering streetlights spilled across the square, illuminating not just the large, smartly painted, red, black, and yellow mail coach drawn up outside the inn, but also the looming bulk of the cathedral across the square. Already, the passengers' baggage was strapped securely onto the coach's roof, and a guard, uniformed in a scarlet coat with blue lapels and gold braid, stood waiting to mount up and take his place beside the strong box of mail fastened to the back of the coach.

He'd already let down the step, and Kit handed Miss Lucas into the gloomy interior where a single small oil lamp now added to the fug. She cast it a suspicious glance, as though fearing it might ignite a fire inside the coach, which was, of course, possible, then settled down beside Loveday and arranged the skirts of her brown dress to demurely cover her strange footwear.

Taking his seat opposite the two women, Kit regarded Loveday with a jaundiced eye. How much easier would it be to continue to engage Miss Lucas in conversation if Loveday were not here with her flapping ears. Perhaps he should have bought her an outside ticket.

He was going to have to wait until they reached Ormonde to question Miss Lucas further. He had a lot more he wanted to ask her when she wasn't so tired, and the list was only growing the more time he spent with her.

Chapter Nine

MORVOREN

THE JOURNEY SEEMED to take forever. The mail coach, a much smarter vehicle than the one that had transported them to Exeter, bowled along the bumpiest roads in England at what felt like breakneck speed, but was really only a snail's pace when compared with a car. It rattled and banged and jolted Morvoren about so much, she couldn't sleep. She kept her eyes closed as much as possible, but every time she managed to nod off, the coach hit a sizeable rut, and a sudden lurch would bang her head against the side and wake her up. This must be why coach interiors were kitted out like padded cells.

Her sleepless situation was not helped by the fact that the guard blew his post horn very loudly as he approached each tollgate, every time making her start in alarm.

"That's so they can have the tollgates open," Kit explained when she threw him a shocked look the first time it happened. "The mail coach gets free passage through all the tollgates."

The fourth time the coach halted for a change of horses, another passenger arrived to join them.

He was waiting outside the inn when the coach arrived, dressed in a rather stylish long cape and with a smart top hat set at a jaunty angle on a head of carefully arranged chestnut curls. In one hand he held a silver handled walking stick, and in the other a pair of immaculate pale gloves.

As Kit helped Morvoren down from the coach to stretch her legs, he turned to greet them, a smile of studied charm on a face that would have been classically handsome had it not been for his thin lips. Heavily lidded eyes favored Kit with only a slight flicker of greeting before they fixed on Morvoren, cold appraisal emanating from them.

Heat flared on her cheeks. The stranger's gimlet gaze made her want to drape a cloak about herself, only she didn't have one. All she could do was draw her shawl closer around her shoulders.

She had the distinct impression this man was taking in not just her figure but also the state of her old-fashioned clothing. After a moment that felt as though it lasted forever, he raised an exquisite eyebrow in what might have been disdain. Anger bubbling at the cheek of him, Morvoren edged sideways, closer to the comforting safety Loveday represented.

Kit's whole body had stiffened, his hands forming fists by his sides.

"Well," drawled the newcomer in a deep voice. "If it isn't young Kit. Fancy coming upon you here."

"Fitzwilliam," Kit said, his own voice short and sharp. "What a surprise to meet you here, too. I didn't know you were in this part of the country."

The newcomer, Fitzwilliam, smiled, a rather condescending smile Morvoren didn't like. "Why would you? I was, er… engaged in visiting a friend."

Kit frowned. "Really?" He could be as condescending as the next man, it seemed. Morvoren suppressed the urge to chuckle as the two of them faced off against one another like a pair of farmyard cockerels.

After a long pause, Fitzwilliam spoke. "Aren't you going to introduce me to your lovely travelling companion?"

From her position behind Kit, Morvoren had a view of a once more archly raised eyebrow. Why did she get the impression he was implying something improper between Kit and her? A shiver of distaste ran down her spine, making her toes curl. Hopefully, whoever this Fitzwilliam was, he wasn't a close friend of Kit's.

"Fitzwilliam," Kit said, his voice stiff with barely hidden dislike. "May I present Miss Morvoren Lucas. She's travelling to visit my mother and sister at Ormonde, and I am escorting her... and her maidservant." He paused. "She's a friend of my sister's."

Morvoren made a rather awkward curtsey, assuming that was expected of her, wobbling a little at the lowest point.

"Miss Lucas, may I present Captain Fitzwilliam Carlyon," Kit said, as she rose. "My cousin."

Captain Carlyon held out a pale hand. "Charmed."

In a fluster about what to do, Morvoren could find no excuse not to let him take her hand.

He bared his teeth in a vulpine smile. "Quite charmed."

For a far too long moment he kept hold of Morvoren's hand, and it was all she could do to prevent herself from snatching it back.

Luckily, the coach driver was growing impatient. He leaned down from his lofty position. "Are you lot gettin' on or not? I've got to go or we're goin' to be late at the next stop."

Captain Carlyon released Morvoren's hand and stood back, with another smile, to allow her into the coach in front of him.

Conscious of not wanting to trip over in front of this man, Morvoren hitched her skirts up a little and managed to climb back into the coach without showing herself up.

The captain climbed in next, shrugged off his cape, and, to Morvoren's horror, took the seat beside her. Kit handed Loveday up then climbed in himself, and the guard folded up the step and closed the doors as Kit and Loveday took the seats opposite.

As the coach rumbled out of the inn yard, Morvoren settled as far into her corner as she could, leaving as big a space as possible between herself and Captain Carlyon. Which was just as well, as, typically of the sort of man he seemed to be, he spread his legs and sprawled across the seat as though no one else were trying to occupy it. Horrible.

Without a glance at Kit, whose anger pulsed through the coach, she leaned her head on the cushioned wall and closed her eyes, shutting everything out in the hopes of some sleep. The last thing she wanted to have to do was to talk to this odious man.

Kit

DAMN IT. THAT his cousin, of all people, should be here, in the middle of nowhere and getting into the same coach as they were. And sitting next to Miss Lucas, who did not, thank goodness, look at all pleased by his decision to occupy the seat beside her. A woman of good sense.

Kit handed Loveday in and climbed in behind her. The only remaining seat was the one opposite Miss Lucas, so he took it. Fitzwilliam had stretched his long, muscular legs out across the coach, and Loveday was having to keep her feet well tucked against her seat. Although she was only a servant and not one he even knew well, Kit's anger rose. Her ticket had cost the same as Fitzwilliam's, and she had the same right to foot space as he had, and yet somehow Fitzwilliam saw himself as more important than her.

Kit bit his lip, manners keeping his tongue in his head. He didn't want to cause trouble in front of Miss Lucas, tempting though it was. It had been just like that at school. Fitzwilliam had been four years ahead of Kit, and bullying had been his forte. Unfortunately, Kit had been a boy slow to grow into his height, and thus, from the day he first arrived as a scrawny nine-year-old, he'd been an ideal target for a bully like Fitzwilliam, for whom blood ties had meant nothing more than to provide a better target. Fitzwilliam had left school and joined the army before Kit had grown big enough to exact any kind of revenge.

Plus, Kit's position as the mere son of a younger son had done him no favors with boys like Fitzwilliam for whom status was the most important thing. And Fitzwilliam's mother was the daughter of a duke. What Kit hadn't known at the time, and only found out later from his older sister, was that Fitzwilliam's father, his own uncle, had been a rake of the worst kind and had seduced the Lady Elizabeth Kirkpatrick and dishonored her. Thus, the marriage had been at the end of a gun barrel. Ten years later, the Lady Elizabeth had come running back to her father's grand house, Denby Castle, bringing with her two small children but no husband.

Too late for Kit to have used this snippet of gossip at school, not that he would have. He fancied himself as not cut from the same cloth as Fitzwilliam. But he'd never been so happy as when Fitzwilliam's grandfather had bought him a commission in the army and he hadn't gone on to Oxford, as Kit had been planning to do.

Leaning back in the corner of the rattling coach, Kit regarded his ex-tormentor with the eyes of a boy who has become a man. Although Fitzwilliam had a good twenty pounds on him, he could take him now if he tried. Boxing, or swords, if necessary, but planting him a facer would be the most attractive prospect. Right on the nose. Oh, how he longed to do that, to pay him back for all the torment he'd suffered at his hands.

Fitzwilliam looked up from stowing his exquisite kid gloves in his hat. "Will you be staying at Ormonde for long?" he asked, making it sound as though Kit were visiting someone's tiny cottage, not his ancestral home.

Unwilling to supply Fitzwilliam with any information at all, Kit shrugged. "I cannot tell. I may or may not. I have only to deliver Miss Lucas to my sister and they will be content."

Fitzwilliam smirked, glancing across at Miss Lucas, who appeared to be sleeping. "With the temptations of your beautiful, but somewhat out-modishly caparisoned companion, I should imagine you'll be staying a while." He paused, upper lip curling suggestively. "I certainly would be."

Kit dug his nails into the palms of his hands. It was the way the man spoke, as though implying he thought Kit would be staying just to try to seduce Miss Lucas and for no other reason. Clearly that was what Fitzwilliam himself would do if he had the chance, despite his scarcely veiled sneer at Miss Lucas's clothing. Like father like son certainly applied to him. Kit had never liked Uncle Robert, and neither had his sisters.

An overwhelming urge to protect Miss Lucas from the Fitzwilliams of the world washed over Kit. Instead of reaching out and throttling Fitzwilliam, though, he said, "It will very much depend on my mother and sister, whom I've not seen for a number of weeks."

Fitzwilliam smiled. Never had a man so neatly fitted the description of a rake. "And my lovely cousin, Ysella, how is she? It's so long since I saw her. She was scarcely out of the school room then. She must be what? Eighteen now and ready for her first season? And if she's as lovely as your mother, then she'll be a rare beauty."

How was it the man could make Kit so angry with everything he said? That by mentioning Ysella and his mother he had somehow besmirched their names?

"My sister does well," he said, keeping his voice level, and determined not to give anything away. "But what about you? I heard you were still in the army, yet here you are?"

Fitzwilliam's cold eyes slid sideways to rest on the apparently sleeping Miss Lucas for a moment. "The army and I have not yet parted company," he said, a sardonic smile curling his lips. He tapped his thigh. "Sent back to England with a musket ball in my leg, but I'm quite recovered now. I'm to join a detachment of soldiers in the west country next week, to rout out the nests of free traders who seem able to run the gauntlet of the revenue men down there with far too much ease. Quite dull work for me, but a necessary duty." He looked back at Kit. "I am at this moment on my way to visit my grandfather at Denby before heading west to my posting."

It was good to have the heads up on the arrival of soldiers in Cornwall, although they might not be going anywhere near Nanpean, but Kit's heart sank, nevertheless. Denby Castle lay a scant ten miles from Ormonde Abbey, which was how his long dead uncle had managed to seduce the young and impressionable Lady Elizabeth so easily. To think of his cousin, with his bad reputation with women, no, with everything, staying so close to not just Miss Lucas but Ysella as well, curdled Kit's blood.

Fitzwilliam stretched himself out even further, seemingly oblivious to the reaction he'd caused in Kit. "If it's all the same with you, old man, I'll snatch a bit of shut eye for a while." He smiled again. "I'll be getting off the coach in Marlborough in the morning. Perhaps we should share a carriage?"

And with that, he closed his eyes and forestalled any reply Kit might have been about to make.

Chapter Ten

MORVOREN

WITH THE SUMMER sun already climbing the sky, the coach at last rolled down Marlborough's wide high street. Now here was somewhere Morvoren could recognize—to a degree—as she'd been here before as a teenager.

Kit, who had woken up a few minutes earlier, slid the coach window down and Morvoren peered out, brimming with curiosity as to how this town would look two hundred years before she'd last seen it.

Down the center of the street, a busy market was already mostly up and running. The stalls thronged with people in a variety of styles of dress from borderline smart to rough and ready. And the smells and calls of all manner of farm animals—pigs, geese, sheep, cows, and horses being the ones she could see—filled the air.

The coach rattled its way down the road on the right-hand side of the long marketplace to take a turn east along what would one day be the A4 trunk road. As the coach took the bend, and the road sloped downhill, the wise coachman slowed his horses to a walk on the slippery cobbles. Thank goodness.

In her corner, Loveday, who seemed to possess a cat's uncanny ability to sleep anywhere and with any kind of noise going on, snorted and stirred. "Be we there?"

"We are indeed," Kit answered, rubbing a hand over a chin much in need of a razor. "The Lamb at Marlborough. Another change of horses, but we will not be going on with the coach."

Captain Carlyon, also somewhat bristly chinned, straightened his cravat and began putting on his gloves, so, presuming it the thing to do, Morvoren slipped hers on again as well.

Gloom descended momentarily as the coach squeezed its way under the inn's low archway and into the large, flagstone yard. A moment later, the guard had the coach doors open and the step down.

Kit got down first and held his hand out to Morvoren. Having had little to eat and drink now for nearly twenty-four hours, she was beginning to feel a trifle wobbly, but she didn't want him to know that.

Loveday followed, then the captain, and the guard busied himself in unfastening the straps holding the baggage in place. Down came the two trunks and Loveday's rather threadbare bag, as well as Captain Carlyon's smart trunk. And all the while this was happening, ostlers were unhitching the spent horses and fetching out their fresh replacements.

Now what? Did Kit's mother and sister live somewhere in the town? Morvoren glanced at him for guidance, but he was studying his pocket watch with a frown on his face.

Captain Carlyon approached, his traveling cloak over his arm and his smart hat in one hand. He managed to look, despite the dark stubble on his chin, as though he'd come freshly from a comfortable night's sleep. "Miss Lucas, perhaps you and Lord Ormonde would care to take breakfast with me?"

What? Who? Lord Ormonde? Did he mean Kit? Morvoren couldn't help the questioning sidelong glance she sent Kit, and the sardonic smile returned to Captain Carlyon's face. Although whether it was due to her confusion, or to getting one over on Kit, she had no idea. He held out his arm, an expectant look on his saturnine face. "Allow me to escort you inside."

For a moment, she hesitated. She could take the proffered arm and let him lead her inside the inn with Kit left to trail in their wake. Or she could stand up to this over-confident young man who seemed to think he was God's gift to women.

However, she was a twenty-first-century girl. "No, thank you," she said, with as much cold force as she could. "I believe Lord Ormonde is pressed for time and we'll be traveling on immediately."

The Captain's dark face darkened still further. Morvoren had the distinct impression he was a man people rarely said no to. Ha. A warm glow suffused her body. Good. That'd teach him. She took a step closer to Kit and laid her hand on his arm. "Come," she said, feeling more and more like a character out of a Jane Austen TV adaptation. "Let us hasten to your mother's. I can't wait to greet dear Elyssa."

Good thing she'd remembered his sister's name.

"Ysella," Kit hissed under his breath, turning a bland expression on his cousin. With a small snort, that could have been of amusement, he laid his hand in a most proprietorial fashion over hers. "Indeed, we must do so at once, Miss Lucas. I fear this journey has fatigued you." He turned to the ostlers who were hanging about looking hopeful as though expecting a tip. "I left my phaeton here when I departed for the west country. Harness two horses to it, if you please. For Ormonde Abbey. I'll have one of the grooms return the beasts to you later today."

What kind of vehicle might a phaeton be?

KIT

WELL, THAT WAS neatly done. Fitzwilliam put in his place and satisfyingly annoyed. He couldn't have done it better himself. Kit kept a straight face as no one, not even a properly put down bully, liked to be laughed at. The last thing he wanted was his own cousin calling him out. That would be very inconvenient. Not that he was afraid to fight Fitzwilliam. Not now. In fact, he'd love to, although with fists, not in a duel. However, delightful as that prospect was, he had to control himself. A fight of any kind would interfere with the plans he had for his stay at Ormonde and no doubt upset Miss Lucas.

While the ostlers prepared two horses and harnessed them to his phaeton, Kit steered her to a low wooden bench out of the bright sun and she sat down, tucking those strange shoes out of sight under her gown. Fitzwilliam, his arrogant face a little flushed, had departed into the interior of the inn, no doubt to see about his own breakfast, and Loveday, a smug grin on her face, had wandered over to the archway to peer out into the street in curiosity.

Miss Lucas looked up at Kit. "I'm so sorry. I had to say we weren't going to have breakfast because the last thing I wanted to do was spend time with that odious man." She paused, her gaze intense. "I do hope you don't mind having to do without food. I'm hungry myself, but the thought of having to make polite conversation…" Her voice trailed off.

Kit allowed his lips to twitch in the vestige of a smile. "That's quite all right, Miss Lucas. You only said what I was longing to say but manners didn't allow. And it suits me to head back to Ormonde as quickly as possible. They'll have my phaeton ready in a moment and we'll set off. It's less than five miles, so we should be home within the hour. As long as we get decent horses." His gaze went to where the ostlers were putting the finishing touches to harnessing two beasts of mediocre quality to his phaeton.

He sighed. "Not quite what I would've liked. But… they'll have to do, I'm afraid. Come, let me help you up. Loveday, we're leaving."

Loveday, recalled to her proper duties, hurried over, face flushed with excitement. "They do have paved roads and houses four stories high," she exclaimed, picking up her bag and tossing it into the back of the phaeton as though it were a feather weight.

One ostler kept hold of the horses' heads, although they were not overly eager to be off, and the second lifted up the trunks and stowed them with Loveday and her bag. Then Kit helped Miss Lucas onto the front seat, climbed up himself and took the reins. He clicked his tongue and tickled the horses' rumps with the end of the whip, and the finely sprung vehicle glided out over the flagstones and into the street.

Here, he turned left, heading east along the main road, the wheels bouncing over cobbles that turned into a graveled roadway as they reached the edge of the town. A curious sense of elation at being home swept over Kit, although Wiltshire had never quite felt like home in the same way Cornwall did, and never would. But this was where his mother was, and that minx Ysella as well.

And on top of that, it was a beautiful morning, with dew still sparkling on the grass at the sides of the road, and a pretty girl beside him. Not to mention two bolts of silk residing in his trunk as presents for his mother and Ysella.

Very soon, they left the last of the straggling Marlborough cottages behind and were rolling through verdant countryside—past estate farms in the care of his own tenants, through leafy woodland and ever closer to Ormonde. How could he be anything but happy now he'd left behind the dangers that had threatened Miss Lucas in Cornwall? His own part in what went on down there he enjoyed immensely for many reasons, but exposing her to it was not something he wished to do. Hopefully she'd seen nothing, and if she had, would be wise enough not to mention it.

Kit waved a hand at the woodland. "Savernake Forest. Belongs to the Earl of Cardigan and his family. But they're never at Tottenham Park. Our nearest neighbor down here happens to be my cousin's grandfather, the Duke of Denby, of Denby Castle, but that's another ten miles beyond Ormonde and they're not always there."

"This seems to be a very well-to-do neighborhood," Miss Lucas said.

He glanced sideways. This time, with the well-sprung phaeton gliding over the rough road, she wasn't holding on so tightly to the seat rails, and a small smile played about her lips as though at last she might be enjoying herself. Good. He clicked to the horses again, and they increased their trot.

"Not really. At least no more so than any other area, I'd say." He frowned. "More so than Cornwall, though."

Perhaps now was the time, with Loveday otherwise engaged being dumbstruck by her surroundings, to ask Miss Lucas one or two of the questions that had been building in his mind ever since he'd pulled her out of the sea.

He cleared his throat. "Miss Lucas?"

She turned her head, her blue eyes bright with excitement despite the shadows beneath them. "Mr. Carlyon." Her face broke into a smile. "Or should I call you Lord Ormonde?"

Ah, that was something that needed explaining. "Please call me Kit, as all my friends do," he said. "But you are correct, and my title is Lord Ormonde. But I confess, it's something I try not to use when I'm in Cornwall. Lords are not popular down there amongst the fishermen and miners. To them I've always just been Kit, and always will be."

She pressed her lips together for a moment before speaking again. "What sort of a lord are you, if you don't mind me asking?" Her eyes twinkled in a suggestion of mockery, as though a lord might be something to poke fun at.

"A lowly viscount, I'm afraid. Nothing exalted."

She tilted her head to one side as though reassessing his appearance. "I've never met a lord of any kind before. This is all quite new to me." She dimpled. "But I promise that I'll call you Kit, and not something so stuffy as Your Lordship."

How hard it was not to smile back, but he had to be careful. This was a young lady he still knew very little about, and his mother, despite her humble Cornish origins, would not be impressed were he to entangle himself with Miss Lucas, nor anyone like her. He frowned as he remembered the last time he'd been at Ormonde and how his mother had virtually thrown Miss Caroline Fairfield, the daughter of her dear friend and neighbor, at him, all because Miss Fairfield happened to be the only child of rich parents.

Time for him to put a few questions. "Miss Lucas, I must admit to having a certain amount of curiosity about you. Perhaps you could provide me with your address in Reading?" A good place to start.

Miss Lucas's tongue darted out to wet her lips and her eyes for a moment took on a hunted look. Was she deciding what to tell him? Would it, perish the thought, be an untruth? She had the air of having something she wished, or perhaps needed, to hide.

"I was generalizing a little when I said I lived in Reading," she said. "In fact, the apartment I share with my friend… Miss Armstrong… is just outside Reading. In Caversham."

He inclined his head. This sounded like the truth. "And your friend? You said she was away. When might she be expected back?"

The hunted look returned, but she recovered her composure swiftly. "I'm afraid my friend, Ti-, Miss Christina Armstrong, has gone to stay with friends in the country indefinitely. The apartment will be closed up."

He pressed his lips together in thought. Again, this had the ring of truth about it, and yet, instinct told him she was not telling him the whole truth. Why would she feel the need to lie? She must live somewhere. Everyone did, even the poorest man. Might she be some kind of adventuress? The idea didn't shock him as much as it could have, and the corners of his lips curled in amusement.

Perhaps, as Jago wouldn't need him for a while, he would remain at Ormonde for a week or so in order to disentangle the mystery surrounding this singularly attractive young lady. Which made him think of his mother. That she would have something to say about his arrival with a young lady in tow, even one with a maid for respectability, was definite. That she would be outspoken about it was certain. The twitch of his lips became more pronounced, and he fought to control it. This was going to be interesting.

He straightened his face as the horses turned between the tall, granite, Cornish-dolphin-topped pillars of the main entrance to the park, and into the long carriage drive up to the house.

"Good morning, Mrs. Lennox," he called out to the woman standing outside the gatehouse, who bobbed a curtsey as they passed. "The head gardener's wife," he explained to Miss Lucas's raised eyebrows. "Drat it. The news that I've turned up with a young lady and her maid in tow will be all over the estate in next to no time." And this time his mouth really did manage a rueful smile. "The tongues of the local gossips will be wagging."

Miss Lucas appeared not to have taken in his words. She was too busy gazing around at Ormonde's extensive, rolling parklands.

The drive curled through ornamental woodland in a loop nearly half a mile long, then headed along an avenue lined with great lime trees on both sides. Beyond them, lay the deer park and, down in the dip, the lake that had been laid out by Capability Brown for Kit's great-grandfather.

As the drive swung around the top of the lake, Ormonde Abbey came into view, the house haphazardly tacked on to the remains of the old abbey that had stood abandoned for nearly a century after the Reformation. Successive wings had been added to the house by each generation of Carlyons, and now it sprawled across the landscape at the top of a slight slope, surrounded by ancient beeches and cedars of Lebanon, spreading their wide arms across the lawns.

Kit looked across at Miss Lucas. Her mouth had fallen open.

Chapter Eleven

MORVOREN

MORVOREN SHUT HER mouth with such a clack her teeth jarred. The house that had come into view at the end of the long avenue of limes was the most beautiful place she'd ever seen. It sprawled like a National Trust stately home, its ancient stone-built beauty in its own way as much a part of the landscape as Jago's humble farm.

Of course. Ormonde Abbey. She knew her history. Which of Kit's ancestors had won favor with a king in order to take over the abbey lands, and when? A feeling of participating in history as it unfolded coiled in her apprehensive stomach.

In the back of the carriage, Loveday was clearly having the same reaction as Morvoren, to judge from her gasps of surprise and an "Oh Lordy Lord!" that came squeaking out.

Morvoren turned to look at Kit. "This is where you live?"

He nodded with a slight smile. "Welcome to Ormonde, Miss Lucas." He tapped the horses lightly with the end of his whip and their trot sped up.

She couldn't stop staring. If he lived here, in this beautiful house set in what looked like a lot of land, why on earth had he been down in Cornwall taking part in dangerous smuggling activities with his not-at-all respectable uncle? Was he short of money? It didn't look like it, although she knew, this time from reading historical romance novels in her teens, that often large estates like this were no indication of great riches. A lord could be land rich but cash poor, so maybe that was it, especially if he, or his predecessor had a gambling addiction. That was it. Kit must be an impoverished member of the aristocracy.

Kit brought the phaeton to a halt in front of the central tower, which had a flight of wide stone steps leading up to huge double doors. As the wheels crunched to a standstill, one half of this door opened, and what could only be a butler emerged. The very fact that she was accepting there'd be servants in this house came as a surprise. Was she getting used to being in 1811 and assuming it would be like the books she'd read as a teenager? For the first time, the thought that this might be fun crossed her mind.

The butler, his solemn face devoid of curiosity, made a low bow and stepped up to hold the horses' heads while Kit looped the reins around the brake and jumped down from the carriage. With quick steps, he walked around to Morvoren's side and offered her his hand. "Miss Lucas."

Well, no going back now. She put her hand in his, and, holding the skirts she was beginning to get used to out of the way with her spare hand, stepped down onto the gravel. Kit turned to the butler, if that was what he was. "Roberts, can you take Miss Lucas's maid around to the servants' quarters and see she's looked after? And send our luggage up. Miss Lucas will be staying in the blue bedroom."

And with that, they abandoned poor Loveday to the butler's ministrations, and Kit, drawing Morvoren's hand through his arm, escorted her up the steps and in through the open front door.

After the bright sunshine of the day, it took Morvoren a moment or two to become accustomed to the somewhat gloomy interior of the house. She blinked a few times and stared around. She was in a stone-flagged hallway, with a door ahead and a substantial flight of stairs rising to the right, up to a shadowy half-landing.

"This way." Still in possession of Morvoren's hand, Kit led her through the next door and into a large, wood-paneled hall. A stone fireplace stood at one end, surrounded by upholstered sofas. Toward the other end, a row of silver candlesticks decorated an enormous dark oak table with a large number of matching chairs tucked in around it.

But the thing that struck Morvoren most was the paintings, and one in particular. Above the fireplace hung a very large picture of a man in a silvery wig and tricorn hat astride a prancing grey horse. To the right of this painting hung another. A portrait. Of Kit.

The one from the museum.

If she'd had any doubts about her foreknowledge, this rid her of them.

Before she had the opportunity to ask any questions, though, a footman materialized from nowhere, or so it seemed.

"Ah, Albert," Kit said. "Where will I find my mother and sister?"

The footman executed a formal bow. "Lady Ormonde and Miss Ysella are both in the library, my lord." As he rose from the bow, his eyes rested for a moment on Morvoren, as impassive and incurious as the butler's had been.

"Thank you, Albert," Kit said, and, keeping a firm hold on Morvoren's hand, he marched her across the hall toward a door on the far side.

She went with him, mainly because she had no alternative, but inside, her heart beat a thunderous tattoo and despite the constraints of her stays, her breath came fast and furious. What would Kit's mother and sister think of him bringing a strange young woman of dubious origins into their home? Of asking them to take in a waif and stray off the streets, which was in truth what he was doing. A waif wearing his mother's old clothes. Morvoren couldn't have felt more waiflike if she'd been a workhouse inmate in Oliver Twist.

Kit pushed open the door and ushered her through.

The library occupied a long, high-ceilinged room and fully lived up to its name. Shelves of books adorned every square inch of wall space, save for where four long windows let in the morning sunshine. At one end of the room, around the necessary fireplace, happily empty of a fire right now, a cluster of high-backed, upholstered chairs had been assembled. Seated in two of the chairs were two women.

Towing Morvoren in his wake, Kit strode up the room toward them.

The older of the two women could not have been in more than her late forties, her barely greying hair elegantly arranged in a tumble of dark curls that peeped from the constraints of a lacy mob cap. A hint of Kit clung to her features, but nothing of her brother Jago, thank goodness. However, something about her suggested she might be a country girl at heart. Maybe it was the laughter lines around her lively eyes or the sprinkling of freckles that decorated her small nose, but she looked as though she scoffed at staying out of the sun.

The other woman was clearly her daughter. A smaller, daintier version of her mother with the clear complexion of the very young and the same dark eyes as her brother, Miss Ysella Carlyon was undeniably a beauty.

Ysella leapt to her feet, dropping the sewing from her lap, and ran to her brother, throwing her arms around him. "Kit! Oh Kit! You're back. I'm so pleased. I thought you'd be in Cornwall for weeks yet, as you usually are!" On tiptoe, she planted a resounding kiss on both his cheeks then stood back from him, her eyes going to Morvoren, appraising and curious, and thankfully also full of cheerful excitement and welcome. "But who is this lovely creature?"

Lady Ormonde rose more slowly to her feet, her expression not matching her daughter's rapturous one. Instead, a stern frown had settled on her brow as she looked from Kit to Morvoren. No doubt she recognized one of her old dresses. As the mother of what must be a very eligible son, she was probably jumping to all the wrong conclusions at this very moment.

A hot blush rose up Morvoren's cheeks. What she needed right now was for the wooden floorboards to open and swallow her whole.

Kit released her hand. "Mother, Ysella, allow me to introduce you to Miss Morvoren Lucas, an acquaintance of mine from Cornwall. We had the pleasure of traveling up from Exeter together on the mail coach, and I have prevailed upon her to stay here with us for a while."

No mention of him having fished her out of the sea and thinking her a mermaid. That would most likely have been a hard story to get even his adoring sister to accept.

Lady Ormonde's gaze lingered on Morvoren's clothing. "I think there is a little more to this than you are telling us, Kit," she said, her voice icily cold, in stark contrast to her bubbly daughter.

"Mother!" Ysella scolded. "Don't be so mean." She turned back to Morvoren. "Miss Lucas, I'm so very pleased to meet you. It was becoming quite dull here without Kit, and now that he's back and has brought you for my entertainment, I'm sure we'll have much more fun."

"Ysella. Be quiet," her mother said. "I wish a better explanation from your brother." She fixed Kit with a stony stare.

What a formidable woman she was turning out to be. As bad, or worse due to her station in life, than her brother Jago. But what must it be like to be the mother of a son many gold-digging young women might be after? Just to snare themselves a title. Morvoren knew her Georgette Heyer. She'd probably be reacting in the same way if she'd been in Lady Ormonde's shoes.

Kit's mother fixed him with a hard stare. "Well?" When he didn't answer, she went on. "I'm neither blind nor stupid, my boy. Why is Miss Lucas dressed in one of my old gowns which is now thirty years out of date?" She raised a delicate eyebrow. "Does she possess no clothing of her own?"

Ysella's eyes flew wide. "Your old gown, Mama? I thought perhaps that in Cornwall they're behind the times with the styles."

"Yes. My gown." Lady Ormonde's cold gaze continued to survey Morvoren from head to foot.

Self-consciously, Morvoren tried to make certain her feet were tucked out of sight under her skirts, which of course drew Lady Ormonde's attention.

Her delicately arched eyebrows rose once more, and she returned her gaze to her son.

Kit heaved a sigh. "All right. I'll tell you. If you must know, Miss Lucas was lost overboard from a ship, and I rescued her. She… lost most of her belongings in the sea and we can't find any of her relations to come to her aid. Perhaps they've all sailed on to whatever destination her ship was headed to. I felt responsible for her, as I fished her from the water in my net, so I thought bringing her here, with a maid, of course, the best plan of action. I couldn't abandon her without even a gown to wear and nowhere to stay." He paused and gave his mother hard look for hard look. "Thinking that my mother and sister would welcome her."

A long silence ensued.

His mother broke it. "Am I to understand that when you rescued Miss Lucas, she was… naked?"

Best to keep out of this exchange.

Kit shook his head in a hurry. "Nothing of the sort, Mother, but her clothes were damaged, and she needed to borrow some clothing to retain her respectability."

"How romantic," Ysella gasped. "And you found her Mama's clothes. How clever of you, Kit, as she seems to fit them perfectly, although they're sadly not at all fashionable now." She turned a bright smile on Morvoren. "But I think you are much the same size as I am, and I should be delighted to provide you with some dresses that won't look so fusty and old-fashioned." She had an infectious smile. "It will be like having a sister again. My own sisters are so drearily taken up with their children and much older than I." She clapped a hand to her mouth. "And I'm not at all supposed to mention that Meliora is increasing, of course. What could be more dull than getting so fat?"

"Ysella," her mother said. "Enough. Perhaps you will take Miss Lucas upstairs to wherever it is your brother has decreed she is to stay. I'd like to have a word with him in private." She returned her gaze to Morvoren. "And do please find her something to wear that doesn't remind me of my girlhood."

"The blue room," Kit managed to interject.

Ysella took Morvoren's arm. "Dear Miss Lucas, do please come with me. I have a gown in mind that will suit your coloring to perfection." And with that, she whirled Morvoren out of the room.

KIT

NO SOONER HAD the door closed behind Ysella and Miss Lucas than Kit's mother turned on him. "Who is this girl?" she demanded. "And why have you brought her here? She must have family somewhere who can take responsibility for her, surely?"

Kit bristled. "She has no one, Mother, and I feel responsible for her myself having pulled her from the water and thought her dead. I could think of nowhere safer to bring her but here." He scowled at his mother. "You would have done the same yourself had you been at Nanpean with Jago. And as you can see, Ysella is already very taken with her."

His mother matched him scowl for scowl. "What I would have done is immaterial as I was not at Nanpean. I can't imagine Jago was very pleased. How do we know she is a respectable young lady who should be consorting with your impressionable sister? Surely, she has someone she can turn to apart from us?"

Kit marched to the fireplace to give himself time to think. Trust his mother to batten on to the one thing he couldn't prove. "She just is respectable," he said, annoyed at his feeble argument. "I know she is. One look at her is enough to tell you she's a lady of good breeding."

His mother joined him at the fireplace. "A lady of breeding can quite easily fall into bad company and lose her reputation. And what about her maid? Did you fish her also from the seabed?"

Kit huffed. "Of course I didn't. I've brought Loveday Curnow with me as her maid."

His mother's lips twitched. "I doubt very much she'll remember the few skills she had from her days at Carlyon Court. But it will please me to see her again." Her brows furrowed. "Do not seek to distract me, Kit. Your Miss Lucas must be from somewhere, surely? And you must ascertain where and return her there immediately. A young lady with no background to speak of is not to be trusted."

"Mother!" Kit exclaimed, his anger rising. "I would have thought that you of all people would be sensitive to her predicament."

His mother bridled. "Do not bring my origins into this, Kit, or you will feel my wrath."

What did he care for her wrath? He was the master here, and since the death of his father, this had been his house. "No, mother, your origins are pertinent to my argument, so I will use them." He caught her hand. "You came from nowhere to marry my father, against the wishes of my grandfather. Yes, he was a younger son of a younger son then, with no thought of inheriting the Ormonde title, but nevertheless, you were not from my father's social circle. And my father's family accepted you when they came to know you. So do not ride your high horse when I bring a young lady here whose pedigree you don't know. Have you become such a snob that you'd turn her out because you've not heard of her father?" His lips curled. "Although I seem to remember my grandfather certainly knew of your father—renowned as he was for his smuggling activities."

His mother's scowl softened a little. "But Kit, she's a nobody."

"As were you, once."

She pressed her lips together. "You say she has Loveday for a maid?"

He nodded. "I couldn't bring her here without one. It wouldn't have been seemly or proper to allow her to travel with me on the mail coach unattended."

"Well," she said. "Loveday was ever a lively abigail and no doubt will suit your Miss Lucas with her look of being somewhat… different." She paused, considering. "And you say her given name is Morvoren? That sounds like a good Cornish name. How appropriate that you pulled a mermaid from the sea." She shook her head. "I don't think I've ever come across the name Morvoren used before, but if ever it suited a girl, it's this one. With that hair she almost looks as though she could be one."

Kit let his lips twitch in the semblance of a smile. "So, she'll stay, Mother, and you'll make her welcome?"

His mother nodded. "I will, although I confess that at first, I feared you had brought your light-o-love here to us."

Now Kit did chuckle. "As if I would. What do you think of me, Mother, that you suspect I would dishonor you by doing that? I have no interest whatsoever in Miss Lucas other than to see her settled safely here, where I know she will be looked after."

Although that wasn't strictly true.

Chapter Twelve

MORVOREN

Ysella, bubbling with girlish excitement, led Morvoren across the imposing hall and back to the stairs. "This way," she said, tugging her hand. "We'll go to my room and find you a gown. I expect my brother has given you the blue room because it's our finest guest accommodation. But my own is nearly as beautiful, as you'll see. He allowed me to choose the colors and decorations myself as a present for my birthday." She swelled with pride. "Now that I'm eighteen."

At the top of the stairs, an oak floored landing festooned with rugs stretched away in both directions. Down one side ran a row of impressively large doors and down the other, long windows with wooden shutters folded back to either side. A fleeting glimpse of formal gardens showed through them, of hedges and gravel pathways and flowerbeds full of roses. Oblivious to her new friend's curiosity, Ysella pushed open the second door and pulled Morvoren in after her.

A four-poster bed dominated her bedroom. Was there likely to be one in the blue room? Morvoren hoped so. She'd wanted to sleep in a four-poster ever since she'd seen one at Hampton Court as a child. She surveyed the rest of the room. Ysella's choice of decorations was vivid, with deep pink walls, curling gold-leafed plasterwork, and a lot of antique furniture.

"Do sit down," Ysella said, practically pushing Morvoren onto a chaise longue by the window. "And take off your bonnet so I can see how pretty your hair is."

Feeling more than a bit bulldozed by all this enthusiasm, Morvoren undid the ribbons of her bonnet and took it off. That was better. She tugged off her gloves as well and stowed them inside the bonnet.

"Your hair is beautiful," Ysella enthused. "So very blonde and so fashionable. How lucky you are. Mine is just a boring brown."

Little did she know that Morvoren's had been highlighted just the week before her holiday so was looking at its best, even though in dire need of a wash. Loveday had confined it in a low bun, but after twenty-four hours of traveling, that had started to come loose, and the breeze had fluffed her hair out around her face.

Ysella's own hair was not the boring brown she'd claimed but a rich chestnut, a few shades lighter than her brother's. "Nonsense," Morvoren said. "You have the most gorgeous curls. Mine tends to frizziness if I'm not careful. I'd love to have hair like yours." Ysella's hair had been piled up on her head and bound with a gold silk scarf, leaving small curls clustering about her forehead and ears. Very Jane Austen.

Ysella patted her hair and beamed but without a trace of vanity. "My abigail, Martha, is very good with hair and needs only to see a style to be able to reproduce it for me. When I go to London for my debut next year, I shall be taking her with me. I can ask her to show your maid how to do your hair if you like."

Her debut? Of course, young ladies in the past had to "come out" and be presented in society when they reached marriageable age, in order to catch themselves a suitable husband. How very different this world was from Morvoren's own, where you just met boys in school or at university or at the pub and fell into relationships with them.

Morvoren smiled and nodded to the offer. "Thank you."

"Now," Ysella said, already moving on and forgetting about hairstyles. "We shall need you out of this dress and all those petticoats.

How Mother ever wore those things I do not know. I'll call Martha and she can help us." She went to the door where a tasseled rope hung and gave it a tug. Nothing happened, but presumably somewhere within the house Martha had heard her summons.

Within two minutes, Martha arrived with Loveday in tow. The latter had put on a clean apron over her traveling dress and swapped her straw bonnet for a lacy mob cap. Her eyes were round with wonder and her cheeks glowed even more rosily than normal.

"Now, Martha," Ysella declared, eyes sparkling. "We have a job to do here, and it is to turn Miss Lucas into a fashionable young lady." She was very much entering into the spirit of *Pygmalion*. "To start with, we need these dreadful old clothes off her, and I think the blue sprigged muslin will set off her eyes to perfection." She encompassed Loveday with her zeal. "And you, Loveday, will learn from Martha how to dress your mistress's hair so it cuts the mustard." She gave an infectious giggle. "This is going to be so much fun."

Feeling as though Ysella thought her a giant doll to dress up, Morvoren let them divest her of her many layers with great relief. Surely, beneath Ysella's floaty, high-waisted muslin gown there couldn't be as much upholstering as her mother's old dress had required?

Once she was down to those gappy knickers, Morvoren's three dressers decided that what she needed after so long on the dusty road up from Cornwall must be a bath. This she couldn't argue with, nor did she want to, but what she hadn't counted on was the fact that they wanted to be present while she took it.

Two footmen carried a large metal bath into the bedroom, hot water arrived, in buckets, and at last Martha declared the bath ready.

The footmen had set up a fancy painted wooden screen around the bathtub and, throwing caution and modesty to the wind, Morvoren stripped naked and got in. What utter bliss the hot water was.

Some time later, Morvoren emerged, glowing and clean, and a

delighted Ysella supervised her dressing from the ground up.

"I said this would be fun, didn't I? And I was right." she declared gleefully as Martha fetched out various different garments and laid them out for inspection while Loveday looked on, wide-eyed and open-mouthed.

To Morvoren's surprise, more stays were involved, but this time shorter, far gentler, and less intrusive ones, akin to a modern bustier. She'd have preferred to do without them altogether, but, as words of protest would have been ignored, she stayed silent. If she was stuck here in 1811 for a while, then she'd have to conform, at least until she found her feet. And besides which, even the most modest of busts needed control. She didn't want to go bouncing out of a low-cut dress like Ysella's at an inopportune moment.

"Now for the blue sprigged muslin," Ysella declared, as Martha fetched it from an enormous wardrobe.

It was indeed a lovely dress with a high waist and delicate puff sleeves. Morvoren smiled in pleasure as she looked down at herself in it. "I have to admit this is a lot more comfortable than your mother's old dress. I can almost forget I have stays on."

"Of course you can," Ysella rejoined. "I never notice mine at all. Now for some perfume, just here behind your ears and a dab on each wrist I think. Mama says you should apply it on, what was it, pulse points. I've no idea why but she's always correct."

Martha, with an air of smug superiority, showed Loveday how to pile Morvoren's hair up and secure it in position with a blue silk scarf. Ysella, who appeared unable to keep her hands to herself, tweaked a few curls about her forehead, and Morvoren's new look was complete.

"There," Ysella declared with satisfaction, standing back to admire her work. "That's so much better. I have plenty of clothes I can lend you while you're here with us, and we can visit my dressmaker and have her take your measurements for more gowns. Although you seem to fit in my clothes perfectly well, and I have plenty, so she might not need to. Come and admire yourself in my cheval glass."

The cheval glass turned out to be a mirror set in a wooden frame on some kind of swivel. Unlike a modern mirror, the reflected image was a little watery and darker than Morvoren was used to. However, it showed her a girl from the pages of *Sense and Sensibility* or *Pride and Prejudice*, with her hair as prettily styled as any Jane Austen heroine. She had truly been transformed, and if she dared admit it, felt quite pleased with the result.

"But what about her shoes?" Martha asked, indicating Morvoren's now stockinged feet with a curl of her upper lip. "She can't go putting those big ugly things back on. It'll spoil the picture she makes." Wrinkling her nose, she held up the trainers.

Loveday, who'd been a little overawed throughout the process of transformation, joined in with enthusiasm. "Her feet was too big for Miss Elestren's old shoes an' boots, so we had to let her keep those things on."

Morvoren eyed her trainers, now almost the sole reminder of her own world. She didn't want to lose them. "They're for running. And they may look odd to you, but I can assure you that they're very comfortable."

Martha gave one of them a tentative sniff. "Bit smelly. I haven't ever seen any lady wearing shoes for running." She paused. "Fact is, I ain't never seen a lady running."

Ysella laughed. "Although I daresay a few could do with being able to." She extended her own daintily clad foot and put it beside one of the trainers. "I wonder if my shoes might fit dear Miss Lucas. My feet are larger than Mother's. If not, I fear we'll have to raid the wardrobe of one of the maids. I'm sure at least one of them has big feet—they certainly sound like they do first thing in the morning when I'm still in bed and they're going about their chores." She turned to Martha. "The soft kid ones I think, as they're most likely to stretch and not rub Miss Lucas's toes."

As Martha hurried to find a spare pair of Ysella's shoes, Morvoren turned to her hostess, determined to set something straight. "I wish you would call me Morvoren. Miss Lucas makes me feel like an old lady of fifty."

Ysella's smile widened. "Why of course. And you shall call me Ysella, although Kit calls me Yzzie when he's not being quite as starchy as he's been today."

Martha brought the shoes, which to Morvoren's relief were only a tiny bit tight. She put them on and stood up, feeling every inch the Regency lady.

She was just admiring her newly upthrust breasts, when a sudden thought struck her. Never having mixed with the nobility before, she had no idea what she should call any of them. She needed to know before she put her foot in it. "Would you mind telling me how I should address your mother?"

Ysella frowned. "Why, Lady Ormonde will do nicely. That is what my dear friend Caroline Fairfield calls Mama when she visits." She giggled. "I daresay you will get to meet Caroline. I'm sure Mama will be inviting her to Ormonde as she still harbors the hope of making a match between her and Kit. Caroline's mama is great friends with my mama, and they've had a fancy to pair Kit and Caro off since Caro was in the cradle."

"Goodness," was all Morvoren could find to say in response to that gush of information. So, Kit was as good as engaged in his mother's eyes. No wonder she'd seemed unhappy when he'd turned up with a strange young lady in tow.

"And now," Ysella said, "we shall descend to the library again and from there go in to breakfast. It must be at least ten o'clock and high time for something to eat. I, for one, am famished."

She took hold of Morvoren's hand and propelled her out onto the corridor.

KIT

THE DOOR OF the library opened and Ysella came in, hand in hand with someone Kit scarcely recognized, so much of a change had been wrought upon her appearance. Her fluffy hair had been teased into golden curls and arranged on top of her head, supported in place by just the sort of silk bandeau his sister liked to wear. And gone was the outmoded dress of yesteryear to be replaced by the most becoming blue sprigged muslin gown, and elegant calf-skin slippers instead of those infernally ugly shoes.

And yet, something still marked her as different. Perhaps in the way she wore her new clothes and hairstyle, as though she were at a masque and this a costume only, and she a player. In fact, now he came to think about it, Miss Lucas had about her the air of someone totally out of place, as though she didn't fit into her surroundings at all, as though, perhaps, she wasn't even meant to be here.

Kit made a smart bow. "Miss Lucas, you look more charming than ever."

Miss Lucas opened her mouth to speak, but Ysella interrupted. "Oh Kit, do cease to call my dear Morvoren Miss Lucas. She has asked me to use her Christian name and so should you." She twinkled up at him with her usual effervescence. "Indeed, she tells me she has at least twice asked you to do so."

Kit frowned at his sister, wise to her ways. "It would not have been seemly for me to have appeared too familiar with Miss Lucas by using her Christian name whilst we were traveling," he said, aware that beside his open-natured sister he sounded pompous and stilted as soon as he opened his mouth but unable to stop himself. "However, if Miss Lucas still wishes it, I shall call her Morvoren while we are here at Ormonde."

Morvoren's slightly worried expression softened into a slight smile.

"I would like that, especially as you've already told me I should call you Kit."

He glanced at his mother, determined that she should accept her visitor—his visitor. "And Mother, I am sure you would like to call Miss Lucas Morvoren as well, wouldn't you?"

His mother, who had resumed her seat by the fireplace after their altercation, rose to her feet, her sewing gripped rather too tightly in her slender hands, her dark eyes veiled so he couldn't tell what she was thinking. "I feel it a trifle impolite to assume to be on first name terms on so short an acquaintance," she said.

How bloody irritating women could be, and how high his mother had climbed upon her horse since she'd been a farmer's, and a smuggler's, daughter living in a small farmhouse in Cornwall. The urge to take her by the shoulders and give her a shake was almost overwhelming.

Ysella, apparently immune to the hostility emanating from their mother, laughed, a happy, tinkling sound. "But Mama, Morvoren is to be my friend, and calling her Miss Lucas all the time will sound as if we are talking about a casual acquaintance and not someone who is staying with us in our own home. I insist that we all call her Morvoren. It is such a pretty name."

Kit would have burst out laughing at his mother's expression had he not been in full control of himself. Ysella, as usual, had his mother stumped, the chit.

Lady Ormonde, superbly conscious of her own role in his house, made a slight inclination of her head. "Very well," she conceded. "Morvoren it is." A slight smile lit her face, but not a totally convincing one. "It will serve to remind me of my childhood at Nanpean."

That would have to do. What a woman she was. However, thank goodness for Ysella, who could always wind their mother around her little finger, and indeed had also been able to do that with their father, when he'd been alive.

When she went up to London for her season next spring, she was going to be a handful with her rather too vivacious ways and her innocent view that everyone had the same honest outlook on life as she did.

Morvoren lowered herself into a rather wobbly curtsey to his mother. "I shall be honored if you will call me Morvoren, Lady Ormonde."

Chapter Thirteen

MORVOREN

ORMONDE ABBEY WAS like something out of a film or a television drama, and here Morvoren was, a part of it, in a kind of dream existence, yet everything was real. Somehow, she'd found herself living the sort of life some people, although not her, dreamed of. But for now, while it was still a novelty, she determined to find it in her to enjoy all these new experiences and push thoughts of what she'd left behind in her own world to the back of her mind. As well as everything about Jago Tremaine, the Mr. Big of Cornish smuggling.

Everything about this new, or should it have been old, world astonished her: the sprawling decadence of the house, the sumptuous bedrooms with their four-poster beds, the gorgeous clothes provided to her by a girl who seemed needily intent on becoming her best friend, the beautifully laid out gardens and the wide stretch of deer park beyond, the retinue of servants to fetch and carry for all of them… and Kit.

Behind everything, there was Kit, an enigma of a man who apparently divided his life between that of lord of the manor here at Ormonde and being a desperate smuggler in league with his dodgy uncle in Cornwall.

Now that they were away from Jago's farm, Morvoren was going to have time to relax and make the most of her surroundings. But that first day, at Kit's insistence, she spent the entire afternoon sleeping in her room.

Ysella protested. "But why does Morvoren need to rest? I'd much rather she and I could get to know one another better."

Kit frowned and shook his head. "Morvoren has had more than twenty-four hours of traveling, Ysella, and must be exhausted. It's impossible to get much rest in a mail coach, as you know."

Ysella pouted. "I'm sure I don't know. I never get to go anywhere, certainly not in a mail coach, and probably never will."

Kit's frown became a scowl all too easily. "And if you're not careful your words will come true. Now, allow Morvoren the afternoon to rest, something you might find beneficial yourself."

Whether Kit also retired to rest in his room, Morvoren had no idea, but the moment she wriggled out of her gown and stays, and her head hit the silk pillows on her borrowed bed, she was asleep.

Loveday woke her for dinner in the late afternoon. "Miss Ysella's sent a dress for you to wear for dinner."

Morvoren's eyes widened. "What? Another one? Shouldn't I just keep the blue one on?"

Loveday gave a solemn shake of the head. "Proper ladies and honorables, like Miss Ysella and her ma, they always change for dinner. I learned that when I worked at Carlyon Court, Miss Morvoren. 'Tisn't done to wear the same dress all day long. An' this one she's sent is right pretty. An' Martha's given me another lesson on how to do your hair."

Morvoren finally escaped Loveday's primping and emerged onto the wide corridor to find Ysella hopping up and down with scarcely concealed impatience outside her door.

"Did you sleep well?" She tucked her arm through Morvoren's. "Mama used to try to make me take a nap of an afternoon—so tiresome when there's so much to do. I like to make the most of my days. I do hope you'll enjoy dinner. Mama asked Cook to prepare Kit's favorite, as usual. Cook is so clever—last year for Kit's birthday she made real ice cream for him. We have an icehouse, of course, so it's easy for Cook. Quite delicious, but she doesn't do it very often. I believe I'll ask Cook if she can make us some while you're here. Kit will love it."

Her constant rattle of conversation left Morvoren, not a girl of many words, stunned, even a little shell-shocked. It hadn't taken her long to work out that Ysella was a young woman badly in need of someone to talk to other than her mother or her maid. However, despite the afternoon of sleep, or perhaps because of it, Morvoren was still very tired. She'd probably be able to cope with Ysella's boundless enthusiasm better after a good night's sleep. Hopefully, dinner would be over quickly, and she could return to bed.

Unfortunately, dinner in the great hall turned out to be a protracted affair of many courses, most of which Morvoren recognized but few she could do more than nibble, exhausted as she still was. To her relief, though, every time Lady Ormonde tried to engage her in conversation, Kit interrupted and headed his mother off in a different direction. Either he realized Morvoren's persistent exhaustion, or he didn't want his mother prying her financially destitute state out of her. For whatever reason, it enabled Morvoren to listen rather than talk, as Ysella chattered on and on to her mother and brother about horses, people she knew, and a musical recital her mother had taken her to in Marlborough last week.

A good hour and a half passed before they were all able to retire to the drawing room. Taking Morvoren's arm, Ysella pulled her to sit beside her on one of the prickly, over-stuffed, sofas, while Lady Ormonde took a second for herself and Kit stood stiffly by the fireplace. He had the borderline haunted look about him of a man who didn't want to be confined in a drawing room with three women, two of whom didn't seem to like one another. What a good thing Ysella was so friendly.

While Kit made conversation about the parkland and farms with his mother, Ysella kept up her wall of chatter, most of which washed over Morvoren's head. She couldn't muster the concentration to listen, and sat there, held stiff and upright thanks to her stays, trying to stifle her yawns behind her hand and prevent her eyelids from drooping.

At last, Kit must have noticed her futile attempts to disguise her extreme tiredness because he approached the sofa, a contrite expression on his face that might have been genuine. "I must apologize, Morvoren. I see you're still fatigued from your journey." The slightest of commisatory smiles graced his handsome face. "I fear we're keeping you from your bed. Perhaps you'll allow me to escort you up to your room?"

Morvoren threw him a grateful look and didn't argue. Taking the arm he offered, she bid good night to Ysella and her mother and let him lead her out of the drawing room and up the stairs. They walked in silence, Morvoren because she was so tired, and him probably for the same reason.

At her bedroom door, Kit halted. The walk had revived Morvoren a little, and now she looked up into his somber face and felt a longing to see that ghost of a smile transform his expression again. He was far too serious for so young a man. For a fearless smuggler. If asked, seriousness would not have been on the list of characteristics she'd have expected of smugglers. But how handsome he was. She couldn't help but wonder what it would be like to be kissed by him, the thought bringing heat to her cheeks.

"I don't think your mother likes me very much," she said, keeping her voice low even though nobody was about. In a house like this, servants might lurk around every corner, and she didn't want them gossiping about her any more than was necessary.

The frown she was so used to returned. "Nonsense, she was just taken by surprise by your arrival."

Morvoren managed a smile, aware of heat washing over her whole body as it reacted to his close proximity. "I take it you don't usually turn up here with young ladies you've pulled out of the sea and had to provide with clothes and a place to sleep?"

The frown dissipated and his eyes crinkled at the corners, as though he were fighting the urge to smile. "No. You're right. This is a first for me."

Was that a twitch of the lips as well? With only the light from the candles set in wall sconces, she couldn't be sure.

She gazed into his eyes. He was really very handsome when he wasn't frowning. Well, very handsome when he was, as well. Handsome in a rugged, devil-may-care way that set her pulse galloping. She tried another smile. "I hope I'm not inconveniencing your mother too much."

He shook his head. "Not at all. This is my house. My mother will do as I say."

This was clearly a man used to having the women in his life obey him. Probably like most men of his time. Hmmm. Now she was feeling less shocked by her arrival two hundred years in the past, her confidence was returning. A good night's sleep would be a great restorative. She needed her wits about her in this world.

She smiled again and was rewarded by another twitch of his lips. "Goodnight, Kit." And she went into her bedroom.

KIT

WELL, THAT HAD gone off without too many problems and his mother might even be softening toward their new house guest. And now he'd got her away from Nanpean, Kit had undergone a distinct softening of his own. Morvoren was such a pretty girl when she smiled… now she was properly dressed. Although she'd been most alluring in just those strange breeches.

He shook his head to clear it of that all too revealing image. No, he needed to concentrate on other things, not how she'd looked when almost naked... how her body had felt when he'd carried her up from his boat... how his own body was reacting at the mere thought of her in that semi-undress. Most distracting. Any softening in his mother would be completely undone were he to show an interest in Miss Lucas—Morvoren—other than as a gentleman helping a lady in distress. He'd make sure and leave her in his sister's more than capable hands tomorrow and go and pay Sam Beauchamp, his estate manager, a visit in his office. Sam always had things that needed discussing. Anything to keep out of the disturbing Miss Morvoren Lucas's way.

He walked along the corridor to the top of the stairs. Should he go back down to join his mother and sister? The hour was early as yet, but he'd had as tiring a couple of days as Morvoren, and not benefited from an afternoon of sleep. If only mail coaches were more comfortable vehicles and didn't blow those blasted posthorns so loudly every few miles.

Ysella forestalled any decision by coming running up the stairs. "Mama said I should go to bed myself to get some beauty sleep," she called out to him when she was only halfway up. "I didn't argue because I wanted to talk to you. She's taking coffee in the drawing room. Can we go into your bedroom?"

Heaving a sigh, Kit nodded, and with his sister scurrying by his side retraced his footsteps along the corridor to the far end. Ysella opened the door and skipped inside, not in the least resembling a girl who needed either her bed or her beauty sleep.

Kit sat down on one of the upholstered chairs beside his cold fireplace, and Ysella plumped herself down on the other, leaning toward him with the air of someone who intended to extract every last grain of information. "Do tell," she said. "Is she a real mermaid?"

Back to that again. Kit shook his head. "I know her name means mermaid, but I hate to disappoint you, Yzzie. She has legs. Did you not notice whilst you were primping her in your room?"

And didn't he know she had legs.

No.

He had to shut that image out of his head even though it kept shouldering its way back inside.

Ysella made a moue. "It's well known that once mermaids are on land their tails become legs. And you did fish her out of the sea, after all. Then there's her name. Although, if I were a mermaid, I'd give myself a non-mermaidy name so that landlubbers wouldn't suspect me." She tilted her head to one side. "Tell me everything. She's such a delightful creature with such lovely hair, and so pretty. I want to know everything about her."

Kit shrugged, instinct warning him not to give too much away. Yzzie was an empty-headed prattler at times and could not be trusted with a secret. "Not an awful lot to tell, I'm afraid. Just that I pulled her out of the sea in my net. Once she'd recovered, I took her to Penzance, where she told me she'd been staying, only we couldn't find the house she remembered anywhere. So, as she was alone in the world, I employed Loveday as her maid and thought it best to bring her here." He huffed. "Although I should have guessed Mother would object."

"A mystery!" Ysella clapped her hands together, ignoring the criticism of their mother. Trust her to fasten on the romance of the story. "A romantic mystery. Just like in Mrs. Radcliffe's *The Mystery of Udolpho!*"

Kit frowned. What had she been up to while he was away? "Have you been filling your head with romantic nonsense again? How did you get your hands on that book?"

Ysella bridled but didn't manage to look very contrite. "Caroline gave it to me." Her eyes twinkled with mischief. "And it is the most exciting story. So frightening." She paused. "If you were to read it yourself, then you'd know."

Kit shook his head. "I have no wish to read gothic mysteries, thank you, Yzzie. I can't imagine that Mother would approve this as suitable reading material, can you? If I ask her, will she be aware you've been reading it?"

Ysella's close study of her hands where they lay clasped in her lap gave him the answer to that.

"She doesn't know, does she?"

Ysella shook her head. "And it's too late, anyway," she retorted in a so-there tone of voice. "Because I've read it now and returned it to Caro."

"And you think Caro's mother will be happy that she has read it and loaned it to you?" Kit snapped. "Mrs. Fairfield is likely to be as angry as Mother if she finds out."

Ysella peeped up at him from beneath her long lashes. "Well, neither of them are likely to find out unless you very meanly tell them." Her lips formed the sweetest of smiles.

He sighed. How was he supposed to stay angry with her when she looked at him like that? She'd known how to twist their father around her little finger and now she was doing it with him. Every time he tried to tell her off, she bounced back as resiliently as ever, supremely confident that her beloved brother couldn't truly be cross.

She knew she'd won. "But tell me, Kit dearest," she said, a naughty dimple appearing in her cheek. "Don't you think Morvoren quite the prettiest girl you've ever seen?"

Now she'd put him on the spot. For a moment, he was lost for words. Of course he thought her pretty. How could he not? She was indeed the prettiest, no, the most beautiful girl he'd ever laid eyes on, but he wasn't about to say so to his sister or he'd have no peace and she'd be bound to let something slip to Morvoren. "She is tolerably attractive," he said, then could have kicked himself for sounding so pompous.

Ysella was clearly of the same opinion. "Oh, fustian!" she exclaimed. "How old are you, Kit? Twenty-seven or sixty-seven? You sound like one of the old dukes and earls in White's puffing on their cheroots and supping their port while they compare their gouty old feet."

Kit snorted with laughter, even though he knew he shouldn't have. "And what does a chit like you know of White's?"

Ysella tapped her nose. "More than you'd think. Caro's father is a member and she's overheard him talking about it. A lot. You know how her father can talk. Mother says he could talk the hind leg off a donkey."

"And Mother won't like you repeating that," Kit scolded. "It's a very rude thing to say."

"Mother said it."

"I can't imagine she said it in your company, though. You've been eavesdropping again. You know what they say about eavesdroppers—they end up hearing bad things about themselves."

Ysella giggled. "No one says bad things about me."

Kit shook his head. "You mean you've never heard anyone say anything bad. For all you know, nobody likes you."

She made a moue again. "Now you're being nasty, and I know you don't mean it." But she couldn't pretend a sulk for long. "I don't care what you say, Kit, I've made up my mind. I've seen the way Morvoren looks at you, and the way you keep taking sly looks at her when you think no one's paying attention. But you can't fool your sister. I think you and she will make an excellently good match."

Kit opened his mouth to protest, aware of heat creeping up his face, but Ysella was too fast for him. "I know Caro won't mind one bit. She doesn't want to marry you anyway. She's in love with a soldier. I can't remember his name, but she already told me that whatever Mama and her mother arrange, she's not marrying you. Even though you are a viscount."

Kit's embarrassment, that he hoped she hadn't noticed in the dimly lit bedroom, was replaced by amusement. "Well, all I can say is, that's good to know, as I too have no intention of marrying her."

Undaunted, Ysella nodded vigorously. "When I marry," she declared, "it will be for love. And I would like you to do the same, Kit. I would like to see you as happy as I intend to be."

Kit shook his head. "I have no intention of marrying anyone for quite some time, Yzzie, so you can call a halt to your matchmaking plans."

For answer, Ysella tapped her nose again and got to her feet. "I'm going to bed now, so I can be up early in the morning for a ride in the park before breakfast." She leaned forward and kissed her brother on the cheek. "Goodnight, darling Kit."

Chapter Fourteen

MORVOREN

THE NEXT MORNING, Morvoren woke early, probably thanks to the extra sleep she'd had the previous afternoon, which was just as well, as Ysella came bouncing into her room dressed in a rust-red riding habit and carrying another over her arm.

"Good morning, good morning, good morning," she gushed with the over enthusiasm of one who habitually rises early and expects everyone else to be happy to do the same. "I've brought you my old riding habit to try on, as I thought we should go for a ride around the park before breakfast." She tossed the habit, which was of a deep royal blue, down onto the bed and continued her bouncing passage to the windows, where she threw open the curtains.

Morvoren rolled over in bed, rubbed her eyes at the bright sunlight streaming in, and yawned. It did look like a glorious morning and a ride would be fun, even if it had to be on a sidesaddle again. At least she'd now had practice so shouldn't show herself up too badly.

"I've called your maid," Ysella went on. "So now I'll run downstairs and organize some hot chocolate and toast for us. We can't ride on empty stomachs, can we?"

The chocolate and toast, served in the breakfast room, went down well, although not quite the sort of hot chocolate Morvoren was used to, being less sweet and not made with milk but merely hot water with cream added. Ysella poured it herself from a tall chocolate pot into narrow cups, and they sipped the scalding liquid as they nibbled their toast. It filled a hole.

Then it was out to the front of the house where two grooms stood holding a pair of horses easily as fine as Kit's Prinny, and one more workaday beast. At least this time Morvoren knew the etiquette was to have a leg up onto the sidesaddle, this provided by the groom holding her horse, a pretty, dapple-grey mare.

She settled onto the saddle and gathered up her reins, much more comfortable in a riding habit than she had been in Lady Ormonde's old dress, and the groom stepped back with a small bow. The one who'd been holding Ysella's horse sprang into the saddle of the third horse and bobbed his head in respect. It seemed young ladies couldn't go riding even in their own parkland without some sort of male escort.

Ysella clicked her tongue and her own horse, a rangy chestnut, broke into a long-strided walk, hooves crunching on the gravel.

Morvoren tapped her grey's sides with the one foot able to do so, and touched the other side with the end of her whip. If only she'd had her phone, she could have Googled sidesaddle technique, but that must be on the bottom of the sea. Her mare fell in beside the chestnut and the groom took his place a discreet distance behind.

Ysella hadn't stopped talking since breakfast and being on a horse didn't slow her flow any. "Your horse is Sweetlip, a name that suits her perfectly as she's the sweetest mare we own. Mama's horse, of course. She trained Sweetlip herself. And mine is Lochinvar. Kit gave him to me for my birthday, this spring." She patted Lochinvar's gleaming coppery neck with pride. "Until then I only had my old pony, who I adored, of course, but he was just a pony, so not a lady's mount. Kit said a lady needs a suitable steed." She laughed, the sound echoing through the early morning, lovely to hear. What a happy girl she was. And how devoted to Kit. "My nephew Thomas has my old pony now. He's my sister Derwa's little boy. They live in Hampshire."

"Lucky Thomas," Morvoren responded, as a reply to this torrent of information seemed appropriate, but her eyes were absorbing the spectacle of Ormonde's extensive parklands. She'd been so nervous yesterday she'd not really taken it all in. And it was beautiful. A gentle slope led down toward the lake. On the far side, thick woodland covered a steeper hillside, and where the lake curved to the north it narrowed, and a five-arched, stone bridge bestrode it.

Morvoren was glad to have been given Sweetlip, who had a very well-balanced stride and carried her head and neck well. If Lady Ormonde had schooled her, then she must be an accomplished horsewoman indeed.

As they reached the level ground beside the lake, Ysella urged Lochinvar into a gentle canter and Morvoren let Sweetlip follow along the wide green sward that followed this side of the lake. At the bridge, Ysella slowed to a walk again and their horses' hooves clattered over the stonework. On the far side another wide green path skirted the lake and a second led uphill into the woods.

"Do you hunt?" Ysella asked. "Kit has had some obstacles built along the tracks in the woods, and they're such fun to tackle. I persuaded him to have them erected because when I follow hounds it's no fun to be the one having to take to the roads with a groom. I like to keep up with the huntsman and his hounds."

Did she mean fox hunting? In Morvoren's other life she'd been very much against any sort of field sports but no doubt two hundred years ago it was considered a normal country pursuit. Better not air her views. She shook her head. "Never, but I have done some jumping, just never sidesaddle."

Ysella's brown eyes widened. "Do you mean to tell me you've ridden astride?" she exclaimed, her face alight with what could only be described as glee. "You lucky thing. I so want Kit to let me try it, but he always refuses. He says it's not at all ladylike. How did you persuade your papa to allow you to do so?"

They were riding uphill now, under the sweeping branches of mature oaks and ashes. Morvoren bit her lip. Now she'd put her foot in it. Her response had just popped out before she thought about it. As a farmer's daughter, she'd had a pony as a child, much like Ysella, but she'd taken hers to countless small horse shows and done a lot of jumping competitions. Astride, of course. So jumping was something she was used to.

"Where I come from..." she said, with caution, as she wasn't at all sure how much she should give away. "Where I come from, young ladies learn to ride astride as we think it's more natural."

This shut Ysella up for a moment. But not for long. After a long pause, she spoke again. "You do? Well, I've often said this to Kit, and when my father was alive, I said it to him, and he said I was nothing but a hoyden." She giggled. "But now I have you to cite as an example, perhaps I can prevail upon Kit to allow me to ride astride."

Hopefully she wasn't putting too much store on that. Kit didn't seem the sort of man who would give in too easily on something like this, even to the pleading of his sister.

They came to a long ride slanting gradually uphill along which lay three low jumps—a kind of brush fence, a post and rail and log pile. Almost like the cross-country fences Morvoren had been used to riding over with her pony, Pippin. Her heart did a little flip. Sidesaddle? How did you stay on over even low fences like these when you were virtually sitting on a chair on top of a horse? Well, she'd have to give it a try, although not wearing a hard hat worried her considerably.

"I'll go first," Ysella said. "Sweetlip will just follow me over, but hold her back a little so you're not right on Lochinvar's heels." She glanced back at her groom. "Eliott will ride down the side and not jump."

Well, at least if she fell off, there'd be no danger of being trampled.

Ysella urged Lochinvar into a steady canter toward the jumps. The well-schooled Sweetlip was keen to follow but obeyed Morvoren's firm hold on her reins. When Ysella had enough of a head start, Morvoren muttered a quick prayer and slackened her reins a little as her legs gripped the pommel. Eager to catch up with her friend, Sweetlip bounded forward into a springy canter.

Ahead, Ysella took the first jump, sitting well back in the saddle as she did so, and Morvoren remembered with a start that until the twentieth century everyone had ridden over jumps like that. It was called the backward seat as opposed to the forward jumping seat she was used to. Would it make a difference to Sweetlip if she folded forward as she'd been taught as a child? Only one way to find out.

The first jump felt awkwardly like a cat jump, but she folded forward surprisingly easily, despite the pommels being in the way, and bobbed up again ready for the second fence. Sweetlip clearly had found the different style confusing, even though Morvoren had given with her hands to allow her to stretch her neck forward. However, the little mare sensed her freedom of movement over the second fence, and it was altogether more comfortable and less of a cat jump. And by the third fence she'd realized her rider wasn't going to be interfering with her mouth and soared over it beautifully.

Ysella had glanced back over her shoulder after each of her jumps, and as soon as Sweetlip landed after the third fence she urged Lochinvar into a gallop, flying up the track. Confidence brimming after her success over the fences, Morvoren let Sweetlip have her head and galloped after her.

To her relief, when the track took a turn downhill again, Ysella slowed to a walk, and the horses fell in side by side, flanks heaving. Behind, the groom brought his horse to a walk a polite ten yards back.

"Goodness," Ysella said. "Who taught you to ride? I've never seen anyone jump like that before. Didn't it unseat you?"

Morvoren shook her head. "Not at all. It's a far more natural way of jumping. It helps the horse's balance."

Ysella's face lit up. "Do tell."

As they rode down the track toward the far end of the lake, Morvoren gave Ysella a lecture about the forward seat, centers of gravity for the horse and rider, and how much better it was for the horse to allow it to stretch its head and neck and how much bigger jumps could be tackled if you did so. By the time they reached the lake, Morvoren had a convert on her hands who wanted her to teach her how to jump in the forward position, "Astride, of course!"

They swung around the head of the lake, where a small sluice gate sat beside a mill, then headed back along the other bank toward the house, woodland to the right and the lake to the left.

Which was when their friendly conversation was interrupted.

From a path through the woodland came the sound of galloping hooves, and out of the trees a rider emerged, hauling hard on the mouth of his horse to steady its pace. Morvoren was beginning not to be surprised by the clothes everyone wore, but this gentleman's immaculate garb so drew her attention she didn't recognize him for a moment.

He wore elegant, tight-fitting buff trousers topped with a blue tailcoat that fitted his muscular form like a glove. Top boots had been polished to the sort of sheen you'd be able to see your face in, and when he halted his horse and took his hat off, his hair appeared to have been artistically styled into a very Grecian look with lots of curls that couldn't possibly have got that way naturally.

As he returned his hat to his head, Morvoren realized this was Captain Carlyon from the coach journey. The journey that already felt a lifetime ago.

"Why, Miss Lucas and cousin Ysella," he said, laying on the lazy charm with a shovel. "I could hardly have hoped to be so lucky as to meet you two this morning when I took my constitutional before breakfast."

Ysella dimpled at him in pleasure. "Why cousin Fitz..." she began, eyes twinkling invitingly. "It's so long since we've seen you here at

Ormonde, I quite thought you'd forgot all about us. It's been so dull without you around. Are you staying with your grandfather again, or have you arrived to visit us?" She laughed. "I'm sure Kit will be pleased to see you."

Pretty unlikely.

"I'm staying with my grandfather," the captain said with a grin. "He's always most gratified to see me, as you might imagine, with me being his only male heir." He laughed in an offhand, rather smug tone that set Morvoren's hackles bristling. How could Kit and he, two cousins, be so different in every aspect? But Ysella seemed to like him, so best to be polite.

His heavy-lidded and rather insolent gaze moved on. "And Miss Lucas, what a pleasure it is to meet you again so soon." His eyes slid over her riding attire. "And so becomingly outfitted… this time."

Ysella turned questioning eyes as Morvoren forced a smile she didn't feel. "Captain Carlyon and I met on the mail coach, when I was otherwise attired."

Ysella chuckled. "Well, in that case you must be old friends and will need no introduction." Her eyes went to her cousin's face. "And I'm sure you will agree that this habit is much more becoming on dear Morvoren, with her eyes and complexion, than it was on me last year. How lucky it is that Morvoren is much my size, even down to her feet. Such bad luck to be shipwrecked the way she was without any of her trousseau."

Morvoren would have pinched Ysella's arm had she been close enough, but probably she wouldn't have had the sense to recognize it as a warning to stop talking. Knowing her luck, she'd have asked why she was pinching her. Morvoren groaned inwardly. Now the captain was privy to some of her story. Why couldn't Ysella have kept her mouth shut? Morvoren plastered on her sweetest smile, but it was too late.

The captain benefitted her with a curious stare. "Your story sounds most fascinating, Miss Lucas. I had no idea you'd undergone such adventures. Perhaps you might be happy to tell the tale yourself, now we are better acquainted?"

Damn this interminable polite conversation you had to stick to. "No, thank you," Morvoren said, hoping he'd take the hint. "It was so traumatic I'd rather not talk about it."

"So romantic," Ysella said, on a gushy breath. "Like a heroine in a book." She batted her eyelashes at her cousin in a way one could only describe as coquettish. It was all too easy to fall into the Regency way of thinking.

"Very much so," came the captain's reply. Perhaps Morvoren was reading too much into it, but she had a distinct sense of him wanting to find out more, and not for a good reason.

"For how long are you staying with your grandfather this time?" Ysella asked, as her chestnut laid its ears back at the captain's horse. Something Morvoren would have quite liked to do to its rider.

He smiled, a charming smile but a villainous one. Or maybe Morvoren was just biased. "For a week, at the most. I have a new posting to Cornwall that I must take up shortly. I've been visiting friends in Devon, and should be able to visit them again from time to time." He laughed. "They have a very pretty daughter and I'm anxious to further my acquaintance with her."

Ysella pouted. "Prettier than me, Cuz?"

This time his laugh was genuine. "How could any girl be prettier than you, little minx. But this young lady has a fortune to her name, and as, despite my place as only male grandson at the moment, I'm certain my uncle will produce a boy before too long, I need to marry into money. So her fortune does much to increase her beauty in my eyes."

Ysella gave a snort of laughter. "Always so open with your intentions, Cuz. And I love you for it. I should like to meet this young lady one day, if you have your wish and she becomes your wife."

He laughed in return. "And so you shall, so you shall. But not yet. She has no idea of my intentions, so after a brief sojourn with my grandfather, to make sure he hasn't forgotten my existence, I'll be off west again to take up my new post from where I should be able to continue our acquaintance and hopefully to press my suit."

Ysella reached out a hand and patted his arm. "I'm sure she'll have no trouble in falling for your charms."

How sorry Morvoren felt for this unknown girl whose possible wealth had rendered her attractive to such a cad as Captain Carlyon, for cad she felt certain he was. The fact that Kit so plainly disapproved of him was no doubt coloring her opinion.

"We're riding back for breakfast now," Ysella said, as the horses jogtrotted along the grassy track and a flight of ducks took off from the lake's mirrored surface. "Perhaps you'd care to return with us and take breakfast?" More batting of her long lashes. Of course, Morvoren was used to the ways of teenage girls in her own world, having not so long ago been one herself. However, she had a strong feeling that it wasn't the way Miss Ysella Carlyon, sister of a viscount, should be behaving with any man, not even her cousin. She had far too inviting an air about her.

Time to take a stand. "I'm sure Captain Carlyon has his own breakfast awaiting him at Denby," Morvoren said, with as much authority as she could muster. She was, after all, a good five years older than Ysella and had a lot more experience with men than she did.

They had come to where the track ran up the gentle rise toward the house, and here, thank goodness, as she didn't think Kit would be amused if they were to bring the captain back to breakfast, their unwanted escort declared he had to return to Denby.

"I shall be back to call upon you tomorrow afternoon," he promised, tipping his hat at them, but mainly at Ysella, who was, after all, his cousin. Then he looked straight at Morvoren, one sardonic eyebrow raised. "I shall certainly look forward to furthering my acquaintance with you, Miss Lucas."

Ysella favored him with the sweetest of smiles. Anyone who could withstand that would have to possess a hard heart indeed. "We shall look forward enormously to your visit, Cuz. I'm sure my brother will be delighted to see you again."

The captain turned his horse toward the woodland, pausing as he reached the edge to glance back over his shoulder.

"Humph," Morvoren said, turning back to Ysella. "That is a man with a high opinion of himself."

Ysella giggled. "I believe most young men are the same, or so my brother says." She shrugged. "But Kit is such a killjoy at times I know he must be exaggerating. He never wants me to have any fun but to end up like my sister Derwa, married to a stuffy old baronet and with two children already in her nursery. Or like my sister Meliora, married to a banker and already increasing. Pft. Their lives must be so dull." She twisted in the saddle to peer back toward where the Captain had disappeared. "I want something more interesting for myself, and I think, now that you're here, I shall begin with riding astride and you teaching me how to jump in the forward seat. That will be splendidly exciting."

Morvoren swallowed. Being friends with Ysella was going to be difficult.

Chapter Fifteen

KIT

KIT FOUND HIS mother taking tea and toast in bed, a shawl about her shoulders and a most becoming frilly nightcap on her head. He'd known he'd catch her like this, as she never rose nowadays until just before breakfast at ten. She looked up and smiled as he came in, fully dressed in top boots and a smart coat despite the early hour, his cravat immaculately knotted.

"Kit darling, come, sit down." She patted the edge of her bed.

Hers was a bedroom given over to extreme femininity, unlike Kit's father's bedroom that lay beyond the connecting doors. On inheriting the title and property as a boy of barely twenty-two, Kit had felt an overwhelming compunction to leave his father's room unoccupied and keep to the room he'd had for most of his youth. Perhaps one day he'd take over his father's room, but not while his mother was alive and kicking and in possession of the chatelaine's apartment next door. Although there was the unoccupied dower house…

He sat down on the bed and took a piece of her toast. "I trust you are well, Mother."

She set her teacup down on the tray, a raised affair with ornate, gilded legs. "Of course I am. You know very well I experience the rudest of health." Her eyes twinkled at him, so like those of her youngest child. "I believe my childhood by the coast and my peasant roots have provided me with exceptional vigor." She tutted her tongue at him as she'd been wont to do when he'd been up to mischief as a boy. "But I'm not so far into my dotage not to know you are merely trading pleasantries when in truth you have something else you wish to say to me."

Kit chuckled, his whole demeanor softening. "You have it right, as usual, Mother." The hand holding the toast dropped into his lap, only one bite taken. "I've come here to beg you to be kind to Morvoren."

His mother snorted in a most unladylike way, reminding him of how Morvoren had done just the same. "And what makes you think I shall not be kind?"

"Because I know you." He heaved a sigh. "You think her an adventuress who has hooked her claws into your only son."

His mother leaned back against her ample pillows and regarded him out of clever dark eyes—Ysella's eyes, and his, had he but realized it. "And has she not?"

Kit shook his head. "Of course not. I brought her here only because she has nowhere else to go, and I thought, perhaps mistakenly, that as my mother was herself once a lonely visitor here at Ormonde, that she might take Morvoren under her wing. And be kind."

His mother pursed her lips, which furthered her resemblance to her youngest daughter. "You play an underhand game, my Kitto. I admire your wish to help a young lady in distress, but I have to ask myself what it is you know of her? And will she be a good influence on your sister, who is already far too flighty and romantically inclined?"

Kit put his stolen toast back on her tray. "I will tell you the truth, Mother, because I have never lied to you. I do have an interest in Morvoren, I'll admit it, but I believe it's merely because she's a mystery. Yes, she's a pretty little thing, but as I told you last summer when you pressed the unfortunate Caroline Fairfield on me, I'm not ready for marriage. And Morvoren's well-bred, so it would be marriage with her or nothing. I've no wish for a country dalliance that could go nowhere."

But was he being honest? Did he even know what he wanted? Well, what he wanted was to be back at Nanpean where being a viscount was of no importance, and all that mattered was distributing the profit from the contraband and thus helping his people. He longed for the excitement of the midnight rendezvous, the passage of the muffle-hooved ponies and the taste of brandy that had paid no duty. So much more fun than being here at Ormonde or at his townhouse in London and having to dance attendance on vapid young ladies who held no interest for him whatsoever. Young ladies whose shallowness he abhorred.

So, if Nanpean was all he wanted, why was the image of Morvoren so ever present in his head? Why, last night, had he slept so badly, the vision of her when she'd walked in to dinner dressed in one of Ysella's gowns, not to mention of her in those tight blue breeches, plaguing his dreams and waking hours. And why did he long to buy her dresses of her own, furs and furbelows, fans and jewelry that would make her beauty even more captivating?

Or would it? Had she not been at her most alluring when he'd pulled her out of his net, and she'd spewed up the seawater on the deck of his little boat? And he'd thought her a mermaid.

He found his mother was watching him far too closely. Pulling himself out of the reverie he'd sunk into, he bestowed one of his rare smiles on her. "As I said, I would like to find out more about Morvoren and the mystery that surrounds her arrival in my fishing net, but for now, I have other things to occupy my time. Sam Beauchamp has business matters to discuss and requires me to ride out to visit our tenants, some of whom are in need of assistance. Morvoren and her mystery will have to wait."

His mother's gaze intensified, as though she knew he'd dodged the subject and hidden something from her. He might not have lied, but he'd been cagey with the truth. And she knew it. Drat the woman.

She'd always been able to discern his innermost secrets from his earliest boyhood. Impossible to keep anything from her.

Her brows knit for a moment then cleared, and the sun came out. "Off you go then, sweet Kitto, for I think I shall rise now and write some letters before breakfast. Do you know where your sister has gone this morning?"

Kit got to his feet, smoothing toast crumbs from his immaculate breeches. "Riding, I should imagine. She seems to live in the saddle since I gave her Lochinvar."

"She lived in the saddle before that as well," his mother said. "I sometimes wonder if she's some kind of centaur."

Kit smiled. "If she is, then it's because she takes after you."

His mother waved a hand at him. "Be off, you flattering rascal, and see if she's returned. Now she has that enormous horse, I sometimes fear for her when she goes careering over those obstacles you had constructed."

Kit did as she bid and closed the door behind him. On light feet he strode down the corridor to the stairs then ran down them two at a time, arriving at the front door just as Albert the footman was opening it. Three riders had at that exact minute arrived on the gravel, and the groom had dismounted to take the reins of the other two horses.

So, Ysella had prevailed upon Morvoren to go for a morning ride with her, and what was more had provided her with their mother's own horse to ride. Her audacity knew no bounds.

Kit walked down the steps and approached the horses.

"Kit!" Without even asking, Ysella jumped from the saddle into his arms. He caught her around her slender waist and swung her down, then turned to Morvoren, having to fight back the absurd and uncharacteristic diffidence he felt at having to touch her again, and held out his arms.

Matching hesitation troubled her eyes. Perhaps she'd prefer it if a servant were to help her down. But no, she released her reins and gave him a slight nod of thanks, then unhooked her leg from the pommel and slid down her horse's side. His hands touched her waist only enough to steady her, but in that instant a hot wave of awareness shot through his body, stronger than anything he'd felt so far, perhaps as a consequence of his disturbed night. Had she felt it as well? Was that the same shock flitting across her face?

He took a hasty step back, turning away in an attempt to hide his discomfiture, and the groom led the horses away.

Ysella, careless as ever, picked up her excess riding habit in one hand and ran up the steps to the front door in front of him, calling over her shoulder. "Come, Morvoren. We need to change for breakfast, although why we can't eat it in our riding habits, I have no idea. I so hate convention, but Mama will be shocked if we arrive looking like this and smelling slightly of horses. Come along."

Morvoren glanced up at Kit, a puzzled frown furrowing her forehead, and hurried after his sister. Had she noticed the color in his cheeks? Damn it. Why did she affect him so? Unused as he was to any woman, even any of the ones he'd been intimate with in the past, having such a profound effect upon his senses, all he could feel right now was annoyance. Perhaps he would forego breakfast and go straight to search out Sam Beauchamp.

Giving himself a mental shake, he strode off around the side of the house in order to approach the estate office via the stable yard.

Morvoren

Captain Carlyon returned on the following afternoon, as he had promised, or should that be threatened. In the intervening time, Morvoren's dislike of him had grown, perhaps nurtured by Ysella talking almost nonstop about him when they were together. If Morvoren hadn't known better, she'd have taken him to be a paragon.

Was Ysella's delightful cousin not handsome? And a soldier too, so obviously a hero. Did Morvoren not think so? And hadn't he shown an interest in her dear friend? Was she not lucky to have ensnared so handsome and well-connected an admirer?

Ugh. No thank you.

During the course of the intervening twenty-four hours, Morvoren learned a great deal about Captain Fitzwilliam Carlyon, or at least as much as Ysella knew, which was probably only a tenth of the truth. Instinct, and a certain amount of experience, told Morvoren that a man like that would have plenty he wanted to keep secret from young ladies, even those he was related to.

The captain's father and Ysella's had been twins, as Morvoren already knew, the elder by twelve minutes having been Thomas, the previous viscount, and the younger, Robert, a bit of a tearaway. "But of course," Ysella whispered. "When he was older, he became a terrible rake, although I'm not even supposed to know what one of them is." She giggled. "Mama thinks I know nothing. I'm not such an insipid miss as to not know all about rakes. I read the most fascinating book which my dear friend Caro lent to me. A book with a rake in it. So exciting and romantic."

The fact that she didn't know why the oldest brother, William, who had also been an "utter rake," had been packed off to Jamaica irked her very much.

"If it were only that he got a servant girl with child," she reasoned, "then the girl and her family could have been paid off. And yet Martha told me no one was. She had it from her mother, you see. Even if it were a girl of the *ton*, some lady or another, then a marriage would have been forced. But that didn't happen either. Instead, when my own dear Papa and Uncle Robert came home from Eton for the holidays, my mysterious Uncle William was gone, never to return. A mystery."

"Very much so," Morvoren murmured, as some comment on this

story seemed necessary.

"When Uncle William died in Jamaica, Papa was still living at Carlyon Court in Cornwall," Ysella confided. "As the older of the twins he became Grandpapa's heir. I never met poor Grandpapa though, for he died the year I was born. I think, from looking at his picture where it hangs upstairs, I would have liked him." She dimpled. "And papa used to tell me he would have liked me."

Morvoren made a mental note to look for this portrait.

"Papa met Mama in Cornwall, of course," Ysella went on, more dimples peeping and her eyes sparkling at the romance of her story. "There was quite an uproar about that, as you might imagine, as Mama was just a farmer's daughter." They were sitting in the rose arbor in the center of the formal gardens, the splash of a fountain to their right and the lazy buzz of bees heavy in the afternoon air.

"Dear Papa had been given Carlyon Court after Grandpapa inherited the title and moved to Ormonde. Uncle Robert was in the army, so he didn't need anywhere of his own, so Papa told me. And one day Papa met Mama, while he was out walking along the cliffs." She chuckled. "To see her now, you'd never guess her origins. She has quite the air of the aristocracy, just as she should. Papa taught her well. And she has taught me." She sighed a little as though learning to be a member of the aristocracy wasn't quite her cup of tea.

Morvoren listened in fascination. Miss Elestren Tremaine, younger sister of Jago and from a smuggling family, had married her fancy lord and been set up at Carlyon Court a few miles from the farm where she'd grown up. Ysella knew little of how her grandparents had felt about the addition of a farmer's daughter to the family. Easy to imagine though. Morvoren was having to do a fair amount of imagining as Ysella's knowledge was somewhat limited and confined to what she'd discovered through the backstairs gossip of her maid… and her maid's gossipy mother.

Robert had run off while still only a second lieutenant in the army with the daughter of their illustrious neighbor, the Duke of Denby.

"Of course, it didn't last," Ysella said. "The daughter of a duke couldn't be expected to live on the pay of a second lieutenant, but she did stick to her guns for quite a long time." She chuckled. "Long enough, at least, to have two children."

Trailing these two children with her, the younger of whom was Captain Carlyon, Lady Elizabeth had returned, her metaphorical tail between her legs, to the comfort of her father's bosom, or rather, his enormous stately home and its associated luxuries. "I'm sure she was very glad to be home again at Denby Castle." Ysella snorted with ill-concealed laughter. "But I don't think she can have truly loved Uncle Robert, or she would have put up with poverty for him."

"If Captain Carlyon is one of her children," Morvoren asked. "Who is the other?"

"Cousin Marianne. She's older even than my sister Derwa. Positively ancient." Questioning revealed her true age to be thirty-five.

Cousin Marianne, it seemed, had been married for some years to Lord William Fortescue, and Ysella vaguely knew their only daughter, Miss Charlotte Fortescue. "Mama sent me to school for a while, but it didn't take. Or I didn't take. I met Charlotte before they packed me off home. She's younger than me and such a bluestocking. So dull to talk to."

Marianne's younger brother, the captain, was of an age with Ysella and Kit's oldest sister, Derwa, now Lady Monckton, and had been in and out of the house throughout her childhood. Which was how she knew him so well and it seemed had developed a bit of a schoolgirl crush on him when he turned up in his smart regimentals.

"I do know he can be a bit of a rake himself at times," she said, on a chuckle. "But that's probably what makes him such fun to have around. Especially with Kit away so often. But I haven't seen Fitz for almost a year, thanks to him having been posted off somewhere on the continent with his regiment, fighting Boney. I'm glad he's left soldiering in foreign parts behind, for now."

She sighed and shook her head as though over a naughty child. "Kit's so often down in Cornwall at Carlyon Court I need someone to amuse me. I have my dear friend Caro, but she's quite straitlaced and proper, and whenever I want to have fun, she finds a reason why I shouldn't." She sighed again, even more deeply. "I sometimes wish I could go with Kit to Cornwall. I've asked him to take me. I don't remember it at all, as we moved up here to Ormonde when I was a baby after Grandpapa died. But he always tells me no. He can be so vexing."

Vexing or not, Kit was preferable any day to the captain. However, Morvoren had to push him out of her head. She was a mere visitor here, at least she hoped she was. Surely at some point she'd be able to find a way back to her own time, hopefully not by the watery doorway she'd arrived through. In the meantime, however attractive she found Kit, and however much his touch sent delicious electricity shooting through her, she had to restrain herself and keep aloof. It wouldn't do at all to become embroiled in a love affair nearly two hundred years before she was born. Who knew what repercussions that might have.

Just then, a footman arrived. He bowed smartly. "Captain Carlyon is waiting in the drawing room, Miss Ysella. Lady Ormonde requests your presence."

Ysella let out a squeak of excitement and jumped to her feet. "Dear Fitz is here, just as he promised. Come along. We must hurry to greet him." She tugged Morvoren to her feet.

Morvoren hastened in her new friend's wake, a feeling of foreboding heavy in her heart. If Ysella had been a twenty-first century teenage girl, she'd have already had her share of boyfriends and known how to behave with young men. But here she'd led a protected life and Morvoren guessed she'd scarcely laid eyes on an eligible man at all. Probably no romantic attachment existed between her and her cousin, and nor would there be on his part as he'd already said he needed to marry an heiress, but that didn't stop Morvoren feeling matronly disapproval of Ysella's delight at seeing him again.

Ysella slowed her pace in the hallway, in front of a mirror, of course, and patted her curls into place then did the same for Morvoren. With a look that said, "compose yourself," she pushed open the drawing room door and they glided elegantly through it.

Lady Ormonde was sitting very upright on one of the sofas, an expression of cool indifference on her lovely face, enough to intimidate the most ardent of beaux. But not this one. She was his aunt, so presumably he knew her of old, and also of her origins. He'd so far given the impression that he'd look down his rather long nose at anyone who'd begun life as a farmer's daughter. Morvoren bit her lip. Best not to mention her own agricultural origins.

The captain rose to his feet and swept a deep bow, to which both girls returned a suitably demure curtsey. Morvoren had been practicing hers with both Loveday and Ysella's aid, having explained that where she came from curtseying was not a normal greeting. Ysella had been very taken with this idea, so she'd had to hastily reassure her that she was keen to learn to behave correctly and not to persuade her new friend to adopt her own incorrect manners.

Rising from his bow, the captain favored them both with a sardonic smile, and waves of excitement emanated from Ysella as she and Morvoren took their places side by side on an over-stuffed couch.

"As I promised," the captain said, raising an arched brow at them, or rather at Morvoren. "I have called to make my presence at Denby known to Lady Ormonde."

Morvoren had the distinct feeling that Lady Ormonde was not at all susceptible to flattery. She had an air of practicality about her, and a stubborn set to her jaw. It made a nice change seeing her disapproval of someone else.

Lady Ormonde nodded to the footman waiting in the corner, and he pulled on the bell rope beside him. She then turned to the captain.

"And pray tell me, how is your grandfather the duke? I have heard that he's suffering badly from the gout."

While the captain politely engaged in conversation with Lady Ormonde about his grandfather's many ailments, Ysella and Morvoren sat straight-backed, thanks to their stays. No doubt sitting and listening was what young ladies were meant to do, but it made for a boring afternoon. Hopefully the captain wouldn't stay too long.

After five very long minutes, according to the slowly ticking clock on the mantlepiece, a second footman arrived carrying a tray containing a fancy teapot, dainty cups and saucers, and plates of bread and butter and small cakes.

"I hear that you have been away soldiering," Lady Ormonde said as the footman poured the tea, her tone even more supercilious than it had been with Morvoren. Good.

The captain bowed his head. "That is true, but I'm glad to be back. I was in Spain with Wellington but took a musket ball in the leg and was invalided home. I've been recuperating in London at my club, and now I'm heading to Cornwall to join a new unit. But it's been some while now since I was at Denby, and I wanted to visit my grandfather. He can no longer get up to London."

Morvoren could feel Ysella almost bouncing next to her in her longing to join the conversation. She put out a hand, took one of hers and squeezed it hard.

Lady Ormonde pressed her lips together as the footman passed cups to Ysella and Morvoren, her gaze still fixed on their visitor. "And was the marquess pleased to have you back at Denby?"

Morvoren's ears pricked. Who was the marquess?

The captain's sharp eyebrows met in a frown before he had his face under control. "My uncle is away in London at the moment, at Denby House."

Aha. The pieces fell into place. Clearly no love lost there. So, his uncle, the one with no sons, was a marquess, and presumably the son of the duke. The heir. The one he'd been so disparaging about the other day. If only she knew a little more about aristocratic titles.

The captain had recovered himself by then and his smile had returned. He smiled a sight too much. Kit's lack of smiles seemed so much more natural. A smile from him would have real meaning. No. Stop it. She had to stop thinking about Kit.

The captain was talking again. "One of the reasons I rode over here today was to deliver an invitation to you all to come to a ball at Denby in exactly a week's time." He paused, and his eyes went to Ysella's excited face. Did she fancy her cousin? Wasn't that a teeny bit incestuous? This girl wore her heart far too openly on her sleeve.

His eyes glinted. "I've persuaded my grandfather, who has always cherished me as his favorite grandson, that a ball would be a fitting welcome home to me after my time away from Denby in the service of the King."

Why did Morvoren doubt his claim to being the favorite grandson? Because he wouldn't be her favorite anything. Although perhaps he was the only grandson, and took the place by default. The thought made her lips twitch in a smile.

Loveday was able to fill her in later, as she'd had all the gossip from Martha, who of course had grown up here and, like all servants, so Loveday declared, knew everything about not just this household but all the neighboring ones as well. Having a gossip as a mother helped.

"The duke be right old," she said with glee, as she prepared Morvoren for dinner. "He did have three sons and a daughter, and that captain, he's the son o' the daughter who were her father's fav'rite child." The scandal of the daughter running off with a neighbor's younger son, a lowly lieutenant in a foot regiment, with no hope of a title, came tumbling out, possibly with more detail than Ysella had been given. She hadn't known, for instance that the shock had been enough to cause the duke to have a nasty turn, from which he'd taken a while to recover. Possibly a heart attack or even a stroke.

"She did come back right soon though," Loveday went on. "Got fed up livin' the life of a soldier's wife. Brung the children back with her she did, only not the father—Mr. Kit's wicked uncle." She gave a snort of derision as she patted Morvoren's hair into place. "Of the three sons, there be but one left now, as the other two died as children. The heir be that captain's uncle, the Marquess of Flint."

"Does he have sons?" Morvoren asked, knowing full well he didn't, but wanting to hear the servants' view. She slipped her feet into the dainty slippers Ysella had given her.

Loveday shook her head. "He don't, and he be in London lookin' for a new bride since his first wife died, and the baby she were birthin' with her. A boy. 'Tis said the marquess were mighty upset about the baby but not so much about the wife, as all she'd given him so far were girls." She chuckled. "Six healthy girls likely to cost him a lot in dowries. The talk o' the servants' hall is that he's thinkin' of convertin' to bein' a Papist so's he can put them all in convents to be nuns and save hisself some money."

Six girls. Morvoren had never before considered the importance for a man to have a son to not only carry on his name but also to inherit his title. Never having mixed with titled or even rich people before, she'd never come across this necessity. But even in her own time, a lord couldn't pass his title on to a girl, unless under exceptional circumstances.

She rose to her feet, ready to go downstairs to dinner. She'd think about all of this later.

Chapter Sixteen

KIT

"YOU DID WHAT?" Kit stormed, marching over to the fireplace and leaning against it. "You told him we'd go?"

His mother regarded him out of complacent eyes. "I did indeed. I had no idea I wasn't allowed to accept invitations to balls without your permission."

Kit scowled. "You know that isn't what I mean." He shook his head. "Ordinarily, I would be happy to accept, but not when it's in honor of Fitzwilliam."

His mother pulled her earlobe, where a large diamond earring hung, thoughtfully. "You know how much Ysella likes him. It would have been churlish of me to cry off, and besides which, he brought the invitation in person so it would have been rude to have turned him down." She smiled. "And he is your cousin, even though he's Denby's grandson. Being in Denby's family doesn't oust him from ours."

Kit scowled some more, refusing to be mollified by his mother's attempt at persuasion. "The fellow's a rake and I don't like him."

His mother smiled a smile not unlike her youngest daughter's. "And that's what makes him so attractive, Kit dear. Every nice girl loves a rake. They're so… interesting. You know how Ysella craves excitement."

Damn the woman. Now she was making him feel like a killjoy.

Like a fusty old man in his sixties complaining about the younger generation, when in truth, if only she knew it, he was embroiled in activities every bit as exciting as Fitz. Not that he wanted her to know. How did she always manage to do this to him when he wanted to put his foot down about something?

"Morvoren doesn't have anything to wear to a ball," he tried, knowing this was a losing battle already. "I doubt the Misses Sedgewick will have time to make her a suitable gown."

His mother's eyes lit up. "They will if I ask them to," she pronounced, and turned to the footman in the corner. "Albert. Go and ask Miss Ysella and Miss Morvoren to come here at once. I have something to tell them."

Kit sighed inwardly. Knowing his mother, she could indeed persuade the Misses Sedgewick to drop all other commissions in their Marlborough dress shop and set to work on a ballgown for Morvoren. But would she want to go? She'd been so awed by Ormonde, how would she manage at Denby Castle?

The girls arrived, pretty as a picture in their sprigged muslin day gowns, Ysella full of giggles, as usual, and excitement at the prospect of a ball, but Morvoren more restrained and serious. Good. He liked a girl not overly given to silly laughter and chatter the way his youngest sister was.

"Kit will take you girls into Marlborough in the barouche," his mother announced no sooner had the door had closed behind them. "You are to go straight to the Misses Sedgewick and have Morvoren measured for a ballgown. She can hardly go to the ball at Denby Castle in borrowed clothing."

Ysella danced across the room to her mother and threw herself down on the sofa beside her. "Does that mean I am to go as well?" Her dark eyes sparkled with excitement. "I hardly dared hope that you'd let me." She glanced up at Kit, cheeks glowing pink.

"As it's a country affair," Lady Ormonde said, jumping in before

Kit could offer a denial, which he'd been going to do. "You may accompany Morvoren and Kit." She paused. "And myself."

Ysella seized her mother's hands in hers. "Oh, thank you Mama! Thank you! Does that mean that I too shall have a new gown? The one I had last year for when we had our own ball here will be out of fashion and probably won't fit me any longer, now I've grown so tall."

The minx. If Kit had been able to have his way, she'd have been staying safely ensconced here at Ormonde until she'd had her coming out next season. But last year his mother had prevailed upon him to hold an autumn ball during one of his infrequent visits home, and of course, Ysella, at seventeen, had clamored to be allowed to attend. She'd worn him down, telling him that she'd spend the entire time with her dear Caro and not dance with anyone at all. This had been a lie, as her card had filled up amazingly quickly and he'd spotted her dancing with a different ardent young man for each dance. And now she was determined to outwit him and attend her first proper ball when he didn't want her to.

His mother huffed. "I suppose you'd better."

Kit tapped his foot on the hearth, but no one looked at him except Morvoren, an expression of compassion on her face. Did she know what he was thinking? Was she a mind reader?

"Oh, Kit, thank you so much!" Ysella gushed. "Come, Morvoren. Let us go and find our things and we can leave immediately if Kit will be kind enough to send for the barouche." She jumped up from her seat beside her mother and threw her arms around him in a bear hug. For a moment he didn't respond, before half-heartedly hugging her in return. She'd bamboozled him into getting her own way yet again. Heaven help whoever she married, because if her own brother couldn't curtail her, no one could.

He resigned himself to having the barouche brought round to the front of the house. In fact, he wouldn't send Albert, he'd walk round to the stables himself and set things in motion. He had no desire to stay talking to his mother a moment longer than he had to, for fear she might extol his cousin's virtues, if he had any.

MORVOREN

YSELLA DRAGGED MORVOREN up the stairs to her room where she threw open her wardrobe and rifled through the racks of dresses and coats to produce two very short jackets—one in a deep red that she put on, and one in an almost royal blue that she gave to Morvoren. "We must both go out in our spencers," she said. "In case the weather becomes inclement. Mama would be very pleased I thought of that." She waved an airy hand at the cloudless blue sky. "It might well rain before we're home again."

Martha, on being called, produced two fetching bonnets decorated with flowers to match the spencers, then, wearing gloves, and with Ysella clutching a purse that turned out to be what a reticule was, they descended the stairs with a lot more decorum than they'd ascended.

The barouche, a four wheeled vehicle drawn by two matching bay horses, had a collapsible hood, down at the moment due to the warmth of the day. A liveried driver sat perched at the front, high above where his passengers were to sit, and a footman stood waiting beside the already let-down step.

Not waiting for Kit's help, Ysella hitched up her skirts and hopped in, to take a seat facing the front.

Kit held out his hand to Morvoren, so she took it, feeling that exciting frisson of electricity run up her arm at his touch again. Compressing her lips, and controlling the urge to snatch her hand back, she let him hand her into the carriage. She took her place beside Ysella, and Kit took the opposite seat, his back to the driver.

The drive to Marlborough was uneventful. Ysella kept up a steady stream of chatter that Morvoren felt she only had to acknowledge from time to time, and the views were very pleasing. She had more leisure this time to take them in, as they passed through several small villages.

Marlborough was less busy than the first time she'd seen it. Their driver drew the barouche to a halt outside a smartly painted shop front where a few pretty hats sat in the window along with a fur cape that was never going to be fake. Above the window, a white sign on a blue background proclaimed, Misses H and L. Sedgewick, Dressmakers.

Kit climbed down from the carriage and handed both girls out onto the pavement without even a glance toward the driver, as though that worthy would know exactly what to do without being told.

Ysella pushed open the shop door and they stepped inside.

It was not like any shop Morvoren had ever been into. A room wider than the shop front stretched back into an interior lined with racks of wooden drawers from floor to nearly the ceiling. A wooden desk in the shape of a squared-off U ran around the edge and it was behind this that three plainly dressed young girls, none as old as Ysella, sat with their heads bent, busily working in what couldn't be good light.

Two angular, black-clad women, rather like a pair of crows, set down their own work and rose from behind the nearest section of the long desk. They swept low curtseys before approaching, ingratiating but rather superior smiles on their narrow faces. Both had their greying hair scraped back in tight buns with very small lace caps balanced on the tops of their heads.

"Lord Ormonde," gushed the taller of the two. "What a pleasure it is to see you in our humble shop. And Miss Carlyon too. Pray, do be seated."

Three seats were magicked out of thin air, it seemed, and Kit, Ysella and Morvoren sat in a row facing the Misses H and L Sedgewick.

Kit took off his gloves and nodded his head to them. "Good day to you both, Miss Honoria and Miss Lucinda. My sister's friend, Miss Lucas, is in need of a gown for the ball that's to take place in a week's time at Denby. My sister, also. I trust you can produce two gowns in so short a time? My mother was confident you could." He left his words hanging in the air with the implicit suggestion that if they couldn't, he'd have to go elsewhere.

They clasped their bony hands in unison. "Of course, of course. Our girls will stop all other work and begin your gowns immediately," said the smaller one.

She turned toward her work force. "Girls," she snapped, in a tone quite unlike the one with which she'd addressed Kit. "Finish off the seams you are working on and put away those garments. Lord Ormonde is ordering two ballgowns that need to be completed in a matter of days."

The girls, without lifting their heads, suddenly sewed all the faster. Morvoren narrowed her eyes and took a better look at them: small, undernourished looking creatures with their hair confined in tight braids down their backs. One was sewing a long seam, another attaching some sort of fancy brocade to a bodice, and a third, a row of pins held in her mouth, appeared to be tacking two pieces of fabric together with small, neat stitches.

Kit got to his feet and made a small bow to the sisters. "I have a few small errands of my own to pursue." He drew out his pocket watch. "It's nearly three, I see. I shall be back to collect you ladies in an hour." He fixed Ysella with a stern glare. "See that you have made your selections by then, so we may promptly return to Ormonde. I don't have the time to delay in Marlborough too long." And with that he beat what looked like a hasty retreat.

Ysella giggled. "He is such a bossy-boots today. We have so many things to choose we can't possibly have it done in a scant hour." She frowned. "But I suppose we can try."

The taller sister produced a tape measure and within a few

minutes Ysella and Morvoren were both being measured—on top of their clothes of course, and swatches of fabric were being brought out and unrolled before their eyes. Morvoren had very little input in this, as clearly Ysella had an eye for color and fashion and a very good idea of what she wanted not just for herself but for her new friend as well.

"This pale blue silk will reflect your eyes to perfection, Morvoren dearest," Ysella exclaimed as the Misses Sedgewick, in unison, unrolled a bolt of fabric on one of the work benches. She leaned in close in order to giggle and whisper, "Kit will love to see you in this."

Annoyed at the hot blush that rose to her cheeks, Morvoren went with the flow. "It's very pretty." So that was settled and, in the end, Ysella selected the blue for Morvoren and a shimmering gold for herself that would perfectly set off her dark hair and eyes.

"You will be the belles of the ball," one of the sisters said. "The dark and the fair goddesses. Athena and Aphrodite. Opposite extremes in blue and gold. The gentlemen will be awestruck when they see you."

Miss Honoria and Miss Lucinda, as their seamstresses addressed them when adding to the pile of necessaries needed to create a gown, brought out some sketches that Ysella pored over.

"This one here, with the small, puffed sleeves and the train in gauzy stuff," Ysella said, her dainty finger resting on the drawing of an elegant lady with tiny, pointed feet and the most gorgeous gown. "This one I see in the blue for Miss Lucas. And this," her finger moved on to a low-cut gown with no sleeves at all but merely a smidgen of material running over the shoulders, "for me."

"A perfect choice," one of the sisters cooed. "Aphrodite in blue, Athena in gold. And do you need gloves? Shoes? Shawls? We have it all here, and if you don't see what you want, we can get it for you. We pride ourselves in being able to offer a complete ensemble in one place."

Ysella nodded with enthusiasm. "Yes, fetch everything out."

Morvoren's gown was to be covered with a diaphanous silk chiffon as an overskirt that would make a train, something that filled her with a mixture of excitement and dread. It was bad enough trying to cope with the long skirts of her day dress without the possibility of something that trailed on the ground behind her, waiting to trip her up. "Couldn't I just have a dress without a train?" she pleaded, but Ysella overruled her.

"Nonsense, this is a ball we're going to and we have to look our most elegant." She giggled. "It'll be such fun. I'm so glad we'll be going together."

Quite by chance rather than design, they were just finishing their shopping when Kit returned, something over an hour later. A slight aroma of alcohol hung about him as he cast his eyes over the mound of things Ysella had selected. No doubt he'd been to the local inn for his "few small errands."

However, he gave the pile no more than a cursory glance. "Add these things to my account, if you please."

Miss Honoria and Miss Lucinda curtsied again, and Kit swept Morvoren and Ysella out of the shop, leaving those poor little half-starved looking sewing girls to begin working on the dresses. Not without Morvoren feeling guilt creeping up on her, though. If only she had money of her own, she'd have given them some, but she didn't, so there was nothing she could do. But Kit could.

She accosted him as soon as they were back in the barouche.

"Those girls who were working for the Misses Sedgewick," she began, catching his attention. "How old do you think they were?"

Kit raised a supercilious eyebrow. "What girls?"

Had he not noticed them? Were they so far below him that he didn't even know they existed? Although he had only been inside the shop for a very short length of time.

"They had three little girls working behind that counter, at the back of the shop in the gloom. All of them looked a lot younger than

Ysella."

Ysella nodded. "Yes, I've seen them there before when I've been to order something with Mama. They're excellent seamstresses. Such tiny stitches."

Morvoren gazed from one well-to-do aristocrat to the other and immediately understood why the French Revolution had taken place. "But they're hardly more than children, and they're being made to sit hunched over and stitching in dreadful light. They're not even fully grown yet."

Kit frowned. "They're lucky to have work. Many do not."

Ysella tilted her head to one side. "They must be at least fourteen, I would think. Any younger than that and their stitchwork wouldn't be good enough for the Sedgewicks' shop. So they're not really children."

Good heavens. She was still such a child herself at eighteen, and in one sentence she'd condemned fourteen-year-olds from a different walk of life to drudgery. Morvoren bristled but held herself under control. With difficulty. "Did you not see their thin little arms and pinched faces? None of them looked as though they'd had a good meal in months."

Kit frowned some more. "They'll be apprenticed to the Sedgewicks, learning their trade, so they won't be being paid much as yet. But I'm sure their parents will be feeding them." He shook his head. "You can't get decent work out of poorly fed staff. But they're nothing to do with Ormonde. I have no power over how the Sedgewicks treat their staff."

How to make them see that this was wrong, even if these badly treated children weren't from Ormonde? "Could we not send them some food?"

Ysella's face brightened. She clapped her hands together. "Yes. What a good idea. We could send them some sweetmeats and fancies as a reward for stitching our gowns at such short notice. We can get Cook to prepare a hamper for them."

Not being quite sure what she meant by "sweetmeats and fancies," Morvoren hesitated. But a hamper as a reward was a good idea. She needed to be more precise about what should go in it, though. "Sweetmeats and flowers perhaps for the Sedgewicks," she said, picking her words carefully. "But for those three girls I would suggest something more substantial that they can take home to their families. A large joint of meat, bread, fruit, perhaps some tonic wine? Foodstuffs that provide good nutrition. That would be more appropriate in their circumstances, don't you think?"

Two sets of surprised brown eyes regarded her.

Kit spoke first. "Ye-es. You have it right there. Even if they don't live in one of my properties, I suppose their want still concerns me because I use their employers' shop. That would be a suitable reward that would help their families as well as them, whereas sweetmeats, nice as they are, have little value for a child." His eyes twinkled. "Why, Morvoren, you have a fine sense of what is right." He paused, suddenly serious. "And it's only what I've done for the poor miners and fishermen in Cornwall in the past."

She sat back against the upholstered seat of the barouche, content at having improved the lot of those three little seamstresses, but most intrigued by his remark about the poor people of Cornwall. Could that have something to do with his reasons for smuggling?

Chapter Seventeen

MORVOREN

"WE SHALL GET up early tomorrow morning and you can teach me how to ride astride," Ysella said as she and Morvoren climbed the stairs to their rooms that evening, hands protecting their guttering candle flames. "I can wait no longer."

This didn't sound like a particularly good idea. "What if someone catches us?"

"Nonsense. We won't be caught if we get up at six. Mama stays in bed until nearly ten, and Kit will be busy in the estate office with Sam Beauchamp. I heard them talking this afternoon. Sam wants Kit to go over the estate books with him, and I heard Kit asking if there were any more families in want. When he's here, he does like to enquire into the welfare of our tenants. If I know Sam, he'll keep Kit occupied all morning, not even stopping for breakfast." She beamed. "Which means we can go down to the stables and make sure our horses have the right saddles for riding astride. No one will ever know."

The flaw in her plan seemed to be that the grooms would all know and probably gossip about it in the servants' hall, but Morvoren resisted saying so. After all, she did want to ride astride on that pretty little grey mare and feel the wind in her hair again in a gallop through the grounds of the estate. And jump those obstacles properly. Temptation was a fickle thing.

"What are we going to wear?" she asked, glancing down at her dress and fancy slippers. "We can't ride astride in riding habits. We need trousers. Where will you get breeches for us?"

Ysella tapped the side of her nose. "Come with me and I'll show you. Kit's and my old clothes are stored in our old school room. Since I abandoned it last year, it's been used for storage. No doubt it will stay like that until Kit decides to grace us all with a bride and some children, but for now, there are some very useful trunks of his old clothes in there that I've made use of before. He wasn't always as tall as he is now, you know."

Morvoren followed Ysella along the corridor to a door at the end, opposite Kit's own room. As he was even now downstairs enjoying a glass of port with Sam Beauchamp, who'd come up to the house after dinner, it was safe to investigate the school room.

The light of the two candles flickered over a room festooned with white dust covers that reminded Morvoren of the box room at Jago's farm, only a lot larger. Sure enough, as Ysella had said, to one side four large wooden chests stood uncovered. Ysella set down her candle and dived into the first one with unholy glee, rummaging through shirts, breeches, and jackets, and making an untidy mess all around her.

Eventually, she tossed several pairs of different colored knee breeches to the floor by Morvoren's feet and said, "Better try them on. I've noticed boys are not quite the same shape as we young ladies. Smaller bottoms for a start. And I've grown a bit since I last availed myself of these clothes."

Entering into the spirit of the game, Morvoren kicked off her slippers and pulled a pair of navy breeches on over her underwear. The flap at the front had her foxed for a moment, but she soon had the buttons fastened. She wrinkled her nose. "They don't feel terribly secure around the waist. Walking far in them might be embarrassing."

Ysella clearly had found the same problem. "There are laces at the back," she said, twisting around to peer at her rear view, while also holding most of her petticoat and gown out of the way. "Could you take a look, do you think? And tighten them for me?"

Morvoren examined Ysella's pert rear view by the inadequate candlelight. Yes, there were ties. She pulled them as tight as she could and did them up. "Is that better?"

She nodded. "Let's see if I can do the same for you."

She could and did. The breeches felt a sight more secure, although Morvoren couldn't help but think braces would have been useful.

"Now for shirts and shoes," Ysella said with determination, letting her skirts drop down over her breeches. "Our own stockings will be fine. And maybe coats?"

Coats turned out to be the biggest problem, as Kit had clearly been a slender boy and none of his coats seemed made for a womanly shape. No surprise, really. Morvoren fished a plain brown waistcoat out of the chest and held it up. "Will this do? We could wear waistcoats unbuttoned over shirts."

Ysella had found some shirts. "And these are nicely baggy so will hide our somewhat differently shaped top halves." She giggled. "Have you ever done this before? It's such fun to have the freedom of breeches after always having to wear a gown. No wonder men don't want us to discover it for ourselves."

Morvoren bit her lip, not quite sure how far she should share her own experiences. Well, why not throw caution to the wind? "I grew up on a farm," she confided. "And I practically lived in trousers for most of my life. It was just much more practical. No one thought it odd."

Ysella sat back on her heels, a natty red neckerchief in her hands. "Really? You're so lucky. I can't imagine what Mama would say if she could see us now. I don't believe she ever did anything exciting in her whole life. Your parents must have been very unusual." She paused, a small frown wrinkling her brow. "Where are they now?"

Morvoren sucked in her lips. "They died. About four years ago now, while I was at university."

Ysella's eyes widened, glittering with the reflected flame of her candle. "I'm so sorry." She laid a comforting hand on Morvoren's arm. "But you said university? How have you been to university? Aren't only men allowed to go?"

Uh oh. Big mistake. Morvoren floundered for a moment. "Just a slip of the tongue," she managed, annoyed with herself for having mentioned it. "I meant that I was still at school. Of course girls can't go to university. What would the world be coming to if we could? We'd be able to do the sorts of jobs men can do." She laughed, aware of how false she sounded and wishing she hadn't had to lie. How easy it was to make mistakes in Ysella's relaxed company. She needed to be more careful what she said.

Moving on to the second chest provided a collection of Kit's old footwear, some of it so small it must have belonged to him as a young child. Morvoren had to conquer an irrepressible, and downright silly, urge to take one of the small shoes back to her room to put under her pillow. She pulled herself together and, after trying on a few pairs, selected some stout buckle shoes that possessed the heels necessary to make riding safe. How odd, though, to be wearing Kit's old clothes. A warm glow had settled on her since she'd slid into the breeches, and now, complete in his shoes as well and with one of his waistcoats on over her pretty gown, it wouldn't go away. Good thing Ysella couldn't see her warm cheeks by this light.

"We'd best hurry," Ysella said, glancing over her shoulder at the slightly ajar door. "Lest Kit should choose to come to bed and notice a light in here. He's so very nosy. If he catches us, he'll be bound to put a stop to what we have in mind. He's become such a spoilsport since he inherited Papa's title."

Hurriedly, they stuffed everything they didn't want back into the chests, then, still wearing their borrowed breeches under their skirts and carrying the rest of their loot, hastened to their respective rooms.

Loveday was waiting in Morvoren's. There was no way of avoiding embroiling her in this escapade. Morvoren dropped the shoes, shirt and waistcoat on the bed and rounded on her, determined she wasn't going to get a chance to blab.

"No. Don't speak until you've heard me out." Morvoren lifted the hem of her dress to reveal the navy breeches she'd purloined. "You're not to tell anyone I've got these clothes or I shall have to ask Kit to send you back to Nanpean on the next cart going west." She reeled in shock at how easily she'd slipped into the role of entitled Regency lady and nearly spoiled the effect by apologizing.

A mixture of emotions flitted across Loveday's face—surprise and irritation, but both swiftly followed by curiosity. "What be you wantin' those boy's clothes for then?" she asked, not bothering to even acknowledge the threat.

Morvoren dropped the hem of her dress. "It's best you don't know. Can you unfasten my gown for me? I have to be up early tomorrow with Ysella." She turned her back on Loveday. No way could she get out of this dress by herself. What it was to be a Regency young lady and unable even to get ready for bed on your own.

Loveday began undoing the ties that held the back of the dress together from neckline to waist. "You be up to some mischief, I'll be bound, with that Miss Ysella. I've heard about her from Martha. She's not happy unless she's up to somethin'. You want to watch she doan get you into trouble, Miss Morvoren."

As Loveday was right in her surmise, Morvoren remained silent until her gown had been removed. A sudden realization dawned. She'd need her stays in the morning, drat it. She'd have to rope Loveday in as she couldn't put them on by herself.

She swung round, now only wearing her light shift. "All right. I'll tell you. I'm to teach Ysella how to ride her horse astride, but we can't let anyone know, as people..." and by this she meant Kit and his mother and probably all the servants, "... don't think riding astride is ladylike. But it is. It's how I've always ridden. So, we'll be riding really early, and I'll need your help to put on my stays."

Loveday pursed her lips and narrowed her eyes. "An' if I helps you, you'll be sure an' not let Mr. Kit send me back to Nanpean when he finds out what you done?"

Morvoren nodded. "Of course. You're *my* maid now, not his. And if you help me, you'll be my friend forever." Probably bribery would work better than threats.

Loveday remained silent for a minute, possibly considering whether Morvoren had enough power to force Kit not to send her back if he found she'd helped. Then she nodded. "All righty. What time d'you want me here by?"

Morvoren smiled. "Six, please. Ysella says Kit will be working all morning with Samuel Beauchamp in the estate office, so we should have a good three hours before Lady Ormonde gets up and we need to be in and changed for breakfast. That should be plenty of time."

Loveday's eyes twinkled somewhat conspiratorially. "I'll be here for six then," she said, with a grin. "To wake you up. But if anyone asks me where you is, I'll be sayin' you said not to be disturbed until after nine because you was tired."

Morvoren nodded as Loveday slipped her night gown over her head. "Good plan."

LOVEDAY DIDN'T NEED to wake Morvoren. She was already up and putting on her stockings when her maid arrived, the curtains of her room wide open, and bright early morning sunlight streaming in like an invitation to be up and about. Loveday had brought hot chocolate and cold toast, but Morvoren didn't mind and devoured it all, despite the bubbling excitement in her stomach.

Once Loveday had laced up her stays, Morvoren pulled on Kit's old shirt and wriggled into the breeches. And after Loveday had tightened the back ties, Morvoren fastened the buttons around her knees. Then his old shoes went on, a little dull from their long incarceration, but the leather still supple to the touch. She finished her ensemble off with a waistcoat and tied her long hair out of the way with a black velvet ribbon.

Loveday pushed the cheval glass forward, and Morvoren was just admiring herself in it and deciding she made a creditable boy, when her bedroom door opened and Ysella came in. She too made a creditable, if extremely pretty, boy.

"I did wonder if you might have overslept," she said. "But I see Loveday is privy to our adventure. I, too, had to take Martha into my confidence and swear her to secrecy." She skipped across the room and stood beside Morvoren. "Do we not look like brothers?"

Morvoren smiled, Ysella's boundless enthusiasm infectious. "We do indeed."

Leaving Loveday to tidy the bedroom, they tiptoed down the wooden staircase, treading only at the edges where Ysella vowed they would make no telltale creaks. She led the way across the great hall and through a small side door toward the back of the house, into the area where the servants lived and worked.

Of course, they were all up. Ysella hadn't taken into account that servants rise long before their masters to carry out all the chores the aristocracy don't even know go on. So their secret plan was rumbled from the start. The servants all saw them, from Cook in her clean white apron down to the footmen sitting polishing boots and the maids with their baskets of kindling and coal they were carrying upstairs to light the fires, even though it was summer.

Ysella put her finger to her lips and winked at them, and to Morvoren's surprise, she received conspiratorial winks in return. Perhaps they knew her of old, and she'd gone out through the kitchens in the early hours dressed as a boy before. They might not have been so forgiving if they'd known what unladylike activities she had in mind this time.

They made it to the stable yard at the back of the house unhindered. On the left, several wide doors stood open on various shiny horse drawn vehicles, while to the right, a pair of double-doors revealed interior looseboxes. And there were a lot of horses.

"Our carriage horses, Kit's driving pair, the pony who pulls the mower, the kitchen cob, the hackney for the governess cart," Ysella listed as they passed them.

Lochinvar and Sweetlip's looseboxes were next to each other at one end, but Ysella passed them by, heading for a closed door just beyond. The tack room.

And of course, it was occupied. A groom was sitting cleaning tack at a table in the center. The coachman who'd driven them into Marlborough, now out of his dress uniform and just in mufti and shirt sleeves.

He jumped up and sketched a hurried bow, while tugging his tow-colored forelock at the same time. "Miss Ysella. Miss Lucas." Despite their boy's clothing, he clearly had no difficulty in recognizing them.

"Good morning, James," Ysella said, her gaze going past him to the racks of saddles occupying the only harness-free wall. The sidesaddles they'd used up until now occupied two low-down racks.

"Shall I saddle your horses for you?" James asked, a little diffidently, his eyes roaming furtively over their breech-clad legs. Probably trying to work out how they planned to ride sidesaddle in these clothes.

Ysella nodded. "Yes please. But ordinary saddles. *Men's* saddles." She flashed a wide smile at Morvoren. "Miss Lucas is going to teach me to ride astride."

Poor James. He was, after all, in the employ of Ysella's brother, and not her, and was probably wondering how much trouble he was going to get into if Kit found out he'd aided and abetted this mischief.

But Ysella could be very persuasive and, by the look in the young man's eyes, she was winning. How could any man resist her charm?

"I tell you what," Morvoren said, feeling sorry for him. "You just show me which saddles to use, and we'll put them on ourselves. You can pretend you didn't even see us this morning. How would that be?"

Ysella grabbed her arm. "Morvoren! I don't know how to put a saddle on. We need James to do it for us."

Morvoren shook her off. "You might not know how, but I do. Let James go off so he won't get into any trouble. I'll show you how to saddle and bridle your horse—it's time you learned if you own one." High time. The thought that she'd reached eighteen without ever having had the necessity to tack up a horse by herself came as a shock.

Ysella's eyes flashed with excitement. "What an excellent idea. Off you go James. Perhaps you should polish the barouche in the coach house where you can't possibly hear us when we ride out."

With a look of relief, and after having briefly touched the two sets of tack that were needed, James scuttled away, hopefully not off to tell Kit what they were up to.

Morvoren took her set of tack and proceeded to demonstrate on Sweetlip how to saddle a horse. Then they fetched Ysella's tack, and Morvoren supervised while she rather ham-fistedly tacked up Lochinvar. But once she'd done it, she beamed with satisfaction. "I should do this every time I ride him. It's such fun. Why should our grooms have all the fun?"

Out in the stable yard, they made good use of the mounting block and in a moment or two were both sitting astride their horses, nearly ready to go. After a bit of stirrup adjustment and tightening of girths, Morvoren rode out of the stable yard into the welcoming early morning beside Ysella, who had a satisfied grin plastered to her face. This was going to be fun.

KIT

KIT STIFLED A yawn and tried to concentrate on what Sam Beauchamp was saying about the projected harvests on the various tenant farms. He knew he needed all this information, but it was too nice a morning to be looking at account books.

It was his own fault Sam was going into so much detail. He'd asked him which of the tenants in his many farms and cottages were suffering the most with the downturn in the rural economy, and Sam had taken him at his word and launched into an impassioned speech.

Sam was an affable young man approaching his thirtieth birthday, probably too affable to make a really good land agent as that required ruthlessness, but Kit didn't want ruthlessness in his agent. He wanted compassion. At Kit's own instigation, Sam had been handing out food parcels already this year to some of the elderly people who couldn't make ends meet. And now, it seemed, some of his other tenants might need help as well.

That Morvoren had assumed he wouldn't want to help the little seamstresses had annoyed him. He could have told her right then that he had enough to do with helping his own tenants, but he'd held his tongue. If she wanted to help those girls in thanks for making her a gown, then let her, even if it *was* he who ended up doing the helping. Perhaps she would teach Ysella some sense of responsibility.

Sam stopped talking and a grin spread over his homely face. "Sorry, Kit. Am I boring you?"

Kit flashed him a wry grin. Sam was someone with whom he felt entirely at home, as they'd almost grown up together here at Ormonde. When Kit had arrived from Cornwall as a rebellious nine-year-old determined not to be snatched from his ancestral county, Sam had been the only person he'd found to befriend.

Sam's father, Frederick Beauchamp, who now occupied one of the estate cottages and was all but retired, but who on occasion could be relied upon to give his son and his employer his advice, had been a land agent before Sam. On Kit's inheriting the estate and title five years ago, old Fred had declared that with a new lord, there needed to also be a new agent more similar to him in age. So, Sam had inherited his father's position much as Kit had inherited Ormonde. Since then, they'd rubbed along very well and the fact that Sam was a friend as much as an employee had never soured their relationship.

"Seeing it all on paper somehow doesn't make it real," Kit said with a sigh, thinking of the beautiful morning. "Why don't we ride out together, and you can show me what you've been doing?"

Sam closed the ledger book. "You've never had a better idea. It's too lovely a day to be shut inside. Let's go."

Together, they walked out to the stables where they found a distinct lack of grooms. "Probably at breakfast," Kit said. "Let's tack them up ourselves."

He and Sam went into the tack room and collected their saddles then walked down the row of stables. Sweetlip and Lochinvar were both missing, so the girls must be out riding. Hadn't he seen their saddles were still in the tack room, though? He must have been mistaken.

Once the horses were saddled, both young men mounted up and clattered out of the stable yard into the surrounding park land.

"Where should we go first?" Kit asked.

"The cottages near the mill," Sam replied. "Old Betsy Lockhart's been struggling with her arthritic fingers and can't make her lace anymore. And without the income from the lace, she's been finding it hard to pay the rent and buy food. I've told her not to worry about her rent, and I've had a hamper sent down to her from the kitchens once a week. We could start there first. She'll be pleased to see you."

Kit nodded. "Good idea. Betsy was always kind to me." He smiled in remembrance. "I well remember the honey cakes she always had ready, whenever I rode down there, as if she knew I was coming. I'm glad to be able to ease her old age."

They trotted their horses down the drive toward the woodland, Kit intent on turning this mission of mercy into a pleasurable promenade. The sun beat down on their backs and the water on the lake reflected back the blue sky and the few fluffy clouds. What could be better?

A flash of movement between the trees on the other side of the lake caught Kit's eye. What was that? He strained his eyes. It did *not* look like his sister and Morvoren.

"Sam," he called to his friend, whose horse had got ahead. "There's someone over on the far side of the lake. Looks like two boys on horseback."

Sam reined in and shaded his eyes to look. "You're right. And those horses look like *your* horses. I'm sure that's your mother's grey, Sweetlip. And that looks like Ysella's Lochinvar in the front. I noticed they'd both gone from their boxes, but I just assumed the young ladies must be out riding."

"Those are *not* young ladies," Kit said, anger rising. "Some local lads must have sneaked into the stables this morning and stolen the horses." Might they even now be making off with them to sell? "If so, they've a brazen cheek to try this in broad daylight. And where the hell were my grooms while this was going on?"

Sam set his heels to his horse's sides. "If we ride toward the mill, we should be able to head the thieves off. This way."

Both horses sprang forward into a canter, hooves thundering down the grassy track.

Chapter Eighteen

MORVOREN

Ysella and Morvoren had ridden over the jumps a good ten times, with Ysella's seat improving until she could have passed for a budding modern showjumper. Both Lochinvar and Sweetlip seemed much happier now their riders were giving with their hands and allowing them to stretch their necks as they took each fence.

"This is so much better than riding sidesaddle," Ysella said as they paused for breath after the last gallop up the track. "I shall have to ask Kit to put more jumps up. I feel so much more in rhythm with Lochinvar, and he feels as though he's taking off like a bird as he stretches over the jumps. It's so helped by being astride. Why on earth do men keep this method of riding to themselves? How selfish they are not to want us women to ride like this."

"I'm sure one day it'll become the normal thing for ladies to ride astride," Morvoren said, thinking of the fun she'd had with her pony as a child and teenager. "But probably not in your lifetime." Probably not for another hundred years, but she wasn't going to say that.

Ysella nodded as though satisfied and turned Lochinvar downhill toward the mill at the end of the lake.

Relieved she'd dropped the subject, Morvoren let Sweetlip fall in behind her as they rode between the trees, just a hint of the reflected glory of the lake showing between the leafy branches.

They'd nearly reached the edge of the woodland where the ground levelled out at the lake's edge when a shout sounded from up ahead. "Hey, you two. Stop right there!"

Two riders were coming past the mill in a canter, and one of them was waving his arm. Oh no. Kit and Sam Beauchamp who were clearly not up to their eyes in paperwork in the estate office as Ysella had vowed they would be.

"Oh, bugger it." The unladylike words popped out of Ysella's mouth before she had time to think, and she clapped one hand over her mouth as though to hold them in. Too late. Wherever had she learned to swear like that?

They stood still. There wasn't really much else they could do, under the circumstances. Kit and Mr. Beauchamp rode up, both slightly red in the face and angry.

"My God, Ysella," Kit shouted, his eyes flashing in fury. "What are you two doing out here dressed like this? And *astride* your horses? How unladylike can you get? We took you for a pair of horse thieves."

His eyes went to Morvoren. "And Miss Lucas. To say I am shocked that you've encouraged my sister in such hoydenish behavior is an underestimation in the extreme. I thought better of you, I have to say, even though I did not of Ysella."

Lochinvar curvetted as Ysella's hold on his reins tightened. "I made Morvoren do it," she burst out. "You cannot blame her for this. It was all my idea and I forced her into it so she could show me how to ride astride and teach me to jump in the forward position." Her eyes flashed as angrily as her brother's. "And I can tell you, Kitto, that if you took the trouble to let her teach the forward position to you as well, you would have far more fun out hunting and your horse would go more willingly over obstacles."

Morvoren stayed silent. Best not to interrupt the two angry siblings.

Sam Beauchamp moved his solid chestnut closer to Sweetlip. "Miss

Lucas, I presume. I haven't had the pleasure of your acquaintance yet. Samuel Beauchamp at your service." His gaze fixed on Morvoren's face, possibly trying hard to avoid looking at what she was wearing.

"You can both ride home with us immediately," Kit snapped. "Before any of our tenants or staff see you."

Ysella lowered her head but not because she was contrite. The naughty girl was trying hard not to laugh.

Kit sighed. "You've already been observed, haven't you?"

"Only the downstairs servants in the kitchen, and they didn't see us on our horses."

"You are incorrigible." Kit's eyes blazed. "I despair of you ever becoming enough of a lady for Mama to take you to London for the season."

"Maybe I don't want to go to London for the season," Ysella retorted, whipping Lochinvar around so he was facing the long green track along the side of the lake. "And maybe I don't want to do as you say. You're only my brother, not my father." She dug her heels into her horse's sides and he leapt forward from a standstill into a fast canter. She slapped her reins back and forth against his neck to drive him ever faster as she disappeared along the lakeside track as fast as she could go.

The other horses skittered on the spot in their eagerness to join in. "Bloody girl," Kit said, turning to Sam. "I'll have to go after her. Can you escort Miss Lucas back to the house at a more decorous pace and make sure she goes straight upstairs to change? I'll see you back there."

And with that, he spurred his own horse after his sister, leaving Morvoren alone with Sam.

They stood in a shocked silence for a moment or two before Sam looked across and smiled warily, concern in his grey eyes. "I must apologize, Miss Lucas, for having to escort you back under guard." The concern was replaced with a twinkle. He seemed a very stolid, dependable sort.

Morvoren smiled. "That's quite all right, Mr. Beauchamp. It will be a pleasure to ride in your company."

They rode back far more sedately than Kit and Ysella had done along the edge of the lake. A pair of beautiful swans glided in tranquil calm across the mirrored surface at one end, and at the other, lilies were just opening their porcelain flowers to the morning sun. Very idyllic. And no sign of either of the two Carlyons.

No sign of them in the stable yard either, where two young lads, eyes carefully averted, came running forward to take the horses as Morvoren slid from Sweetlip's saddle.

"It's quite all right," she said to Sam. "I can find my way back to my room by myself. And don't worry, my maid will be waiting to make sure I'm quite the girl again before you see me next."

He clicked his heels together smartly and bowed. "I shall return to the Estate Office in that case and get on with my work." He paused. "I trust you will give Miss Ysella my regards, and…" He paused again and licked his lips. "Compliment her from me on her excellent seat at a gallop."

Morvoren met his gaze and found his grey eyes dancing with amusement. "Thank you, Mr. Beauchamp. I will pass on your message."

Kit

Girls. Why were they so infernally difficult to manage and why did they always want to do something you would have expressly forbidden if they'd asked you? Kit threw his horse's reins to a stable lad and stomped into the house in pursuit of his sister. There being no sign of her meant she must have arrived a good minute or two before him. That'd teach him for buying her such a good horse.

In the servants' hall, every single one of them kept their heads down, not wanting him to accuse them of complicity in Ysella's misbehavior, presumably.

She wasn't in the great hall, thank goodness, so he hurried through it and strode up the stairs two at a time. The long landing their bedrooms opened off lay empty. He approached her door and hesitated. She might well be in the process of removing the offending garments. He knocked.

No answer.

He knocked again.

Nothing.

"Ysella, are you in there?"

Still nothing.

"Ysella, I'm coming in. I hope you're decent."

Still nothing. Be it on her own head. He turned the handle and pushed the door open, holding himself ready to beat a hasty retreat.

Ysella was lying face down on her bed, still in her boy's clothes, her feet, in a pair of his own scuffed old buckle shoes, hanging off the end. She didn't look at him.

He closed the door, walked with as much determination as he could over to the bed and sat down on the far-too pink upholstered chair beside it.

She still didn't look at him.

"Ysella," he tried, intending to begin with admonition, but his determination was rapidly failing and the humor of the situation was replacing it. A chuckle escaped him.

Her head whipped round. Her red and swollen eyes told him she'd been crying.

He shook his head in exasperation. What was there about his youngest sister that she could always swing him around to her way of thinking without so much as a lift of her finger, and his best attempts at discipline always went awry? It boded ill for any husband she managed to snare—she'd run rings around the poor sap.

"You do know that it is most unbecoming for a young lady to be seen by anyone whilst wearing breeches?" he tried, but couldn't keep a straight face. Her woebegone expression was far too comical.

She pushed herself upright and a matching chuckle escaped her. "But it was such fun, Kitto. And it's so much nicer to ride astride than on a silly sidesaddle in a habit with flappy skirts. So much more natural. I can quite see why you men so selfishly have kept it to yourselves all this time. Afraid we women would show you up if we got to ride the same way as you. We're bound to be better at it than you."

Kit sighed. Her argument had reason behind it. He wouldn't like to have to ride on a sidesaddle in a dress, so he could see why she didn't want to. But there was no getting around the fact that social etiquette insisted a girl should ride in a manner befitting a young lady, and riding astride did not fit that category. "I do understand," he said, all his anger floating away. "And I do commiserate with you and Morvoren and wish that it were different. But unfortunately, it's not, and you should ride the way all other young ladies ride or risk the approbation of society."

Her eyes narrowed, but her good humor didn't leave her. "But what if we were to ride like this only in the early mornings, when no one else is about? Could we? Please?"

He pressed his lips together, fighting the appeal in her wide brown eyes. Drat the girl. "Well," he said, regretting the words as they left his lips. "Well, perhaps just once a week. And at the crack of dawn. And not the two of you alone. You'll have to ride with me so I can make certain you're safe."

Or was this just an excuse to ride out with Morvoren, who'd looked so becoming in his blue breeches and that cream shirt?

Ysella launched herself off the bed and into his arms before he had time to dwell on that thought. "Oh, thank you, thank you, thank you, Kitto! You are the best of brothers. And perhaps Morvoren can teach you the forward seat over our jumps." She frowned. "And now that jumping is so much easier, can you not send the gardeners out to build some more for me? All over the estate? I so love jumping, as you know, and it's even better while astride."

Trying to disentangle himself from her limpet-like hold, Kit opened his mouth to reply but was interrupted by a tentative knocking on the door.

"Come in," Ysella cried, all trace of pique gone.

Morvoren came in, still strangely alluring in her breeches and shirt, and reminding Kit disturbingly of when he'd fished her from the sea in a state of semi-undress. He shifted uncomfortably at the memory, aware of heat rising up his neck to his cheeks. Why did her presence so often do this to him? Not even when he'd been a boy at Eton, testing out the fleshpots of Windsor, had he felt so absurdly aware of a woman. Most discomfiting.

Her cornflower blue eyes went from Ysella's happy face to his and she hesitated a moment, hand on the still open door, clearly unsure of herself.

"Do not vex yourself. It's all turned out perfectly," Ysella exclaimed, separating herself from Kit. "We are to ride out once a week in Kit's company—in breeches! And you are to teach him the forward seat and the gardeners will build us some more jumps. What could be better?"

"Young ladies who know their place and wear dresses," Kit said, lowering his eyes from Morvoren's frankly curious gaze. Was she wondering at how easily Ysella had got the better of him? He rose to his feet and brushed imaginary dust from his own trousers. "I think perhaps you girls had best get yourselves changed for breakfast before Mother gets wind of your escapades. You should also hope none of the servants let slip what they've seen."

"Pft," Ysella exclaimed, waving an airy hand at him. "I've worn your old clothes many times before and they've not told Mama. They won't tell her this time."

"They might if they find out you've been riding in them," Kit said. "Servants have a stronger sense of propriety than their betters. I'll speak to them, I think, and give them warning to be silent. But only if you two promise to behave yourselves. If you don't, Ysella, I shall renege upon my promise to let you go to the ball at Denby."

Morvoren's brows knit as she glanced at his sister, but she stayed silent. She seemed very good at holding her opinion in check.

"I promise," Ysella gushed. "We both do, don't we, Morvoren? So long as you don't forget your own promise, Kitto."

Morvoren nodded. "I promise as well."

Was that laughter playing at the corners of her pretty mouth? Was she, heaven forbid, laughing at him for having been so easily gulled by his chit of a sister?

He turned toward the door. "One other thing, brother," Ysella said. "You and I are going to have to teach Morvoren how to dance before Saturday night as she tells me she has never been to a ball and never learned to dance."

Kit stopped but didn't turn around. Teach her to dance? She was a girl who couldn't dance? Surely all girls learned to dance while in the school room. Everything about Morvoren Lucas only continued to become more and more mysterious. She knew how to ride astride but not how to dance. When he had composed himself, he turned around. "Very well. But with only the three of us, it won't be easy."

"I already have an idea for that," Ysella said. "Sam Beauchamp can join us as well and we shall make two couples. He's a good dancer. That will make things far easier. As for the rest, we'll have to imagine the other dancers."

"And the music," Kit said with a wry smile, and left the room before his hot color betrayed him.

Chapter Nineteen

MORVOREN

THE FIRST DANCING lesson was organized for the day after the debacle of the early morning ride. Morvoren and Ysella rose early for another ride but confined themselves to riding sidesaddle, like proper young ladies, under the escort of one of the grooms. From the amused look on his face, it was evident this young man knew all about their adventure of the previous day.

After breakfast at ten, Kit informed them he planned to spend the morning with Sam Beauchamp again, but that after a light mid-day repast, he and Sam would be at Ysella and Morvoren's service for the better part of the afternoon.

Morvoren had a few doubts about this. Did she want to spend time in Kit's company when he made her feel so... so what? She couldn't put her finger on the fluttering that disturbed her stomach whenever she caught him looking at her, and when he so pointedly looked away. Could it be desire? Did she fancy him? Could she be falling in love with someone who'd died two hundred years before she was born? Was that even possible? He was undeniably good looking, after all, and she liked him. But why was she feeling this way about someone who didn't seem to like her back very much, probably found her an infernal nuisance, and was likely ruing the day he'd offered his help.

From an upstairs window, Morvoren watched Kit and Sam ride

out to visit some of the estate tenants, whom, he'd informed her and Ysella, were in need of the sort of help they'd so very kindly donated to the young seamstresses and their families—at his own expense. Had there been a glint of wry humor in his dark eyes as he said this?

He sat his horse well, riding with a loose ease that Sam Beauchamp, an altogether more solid young man, didn't possess. As though, perhaps, he'd been born in the saddle, which he well might have been as his mother was so experienced a horsewoman. The way he rode, even though now only at a jog trot, reminded Morvoren of Ysella's style—relaxed and natural with a hint of recklessness to any possible injury.

She continued to watch the two very different young men until the track they were following reached the woodland and the trees swallowed them.

Now what? Ysella had informed her at breakfast that her mother wished them both to join her in the morning room, so it was with nervous steps that Morvoren now made her way there.

Ysella was already seated with some needlework in her lap and a faraway expression on her face, and Lady Ormonde, too, was engaged in some kind of sewing related activity. Unfortunately, sewing had never been Morvoren's thing. When you could buy clothes ready made for very little money and wear them a few times before you threw them away, what was the point of learning to sew?

She made an elegant curtsey to Lady Ormonde and her apologies for being late, then sat down beside Ysella, peering at what she was stitching. No way could she sew with such neat, tiny stitches. No way could she sew. Full stop.

"It's a bonnet for my sister Meliora's baby," Ysella explained. "Mama is embroidering the gown, and I am to work the bonnet for the child."

Aha. For the sister who was pregnant. Morvoren kept her mouth shut about that though, as no doubt her knowledge and choice of words would more than shock Lady Ormonde.

"Perhaps you would like to embroider a kerchief," Lady Ormonde said, holding out a square of white muslin. "It should not overtax you."

What? Was she a mind reader?

Better to be honest. "I'm afraid," Morvoren said, choosing her words carefully, "that you would not like my stitching as it's never been something I've practiced. In short, I don't know how to sew."

"Lucky you," Ysella whispered.

Lady Ormonde looked nonplussed, as well she might. Presumably, sewing was a thing all girls did in this time period. To occupy their time. Although the added bonus of providing new clothes for babies must be useful too.

"Perhaps you paint, or play the piano?"

There was a solid no coming on those two pastimes as well. Morvoren tried a winning and apologetic smile. "I'm afraid not. My skill at drawing is similar to that of a six-year-old, I'm afraid, and I've never learned to paint. Art was not a subject I studied while at school. And I'm afraid I'm tone deaf and unable to play any instrument." She paused. "I do admit it's one of the things I would change about myself if I could—I'd love to be able to sing in tune, and be just a little bit musical."

Lady Ormonde's brown eyes, so like Kit's and Ysella's, widened. "Tell me, Morvoren, what *did* you learn at school then?" Her tone of reprimand had gone and pure curiosity had taken its place, as though she were genuinely interested.

Morvoren's parents had sent her to a fee-paying school where she'd had an excellent all-round education—for the twenty-first century, but maybe not for the early nineteenth. "I'm afraid I learned a lot of things you might not find all that useful. I studied maths, which was my favorite subject, along with English and biology." Those had been her A level choices, but explaining that to someone in 1811 lay beyond her.

Lady Ormonde fastened on the one she presumably knew the best. "English, as in reading books, or perhaps how to keep a journal?"

Not quite, but Morvoren nodded, glad she'd found something to approve. "I am very fond of reading."

Lady Ormonde smiled back quite kindly. "Then perhaps you would care to read aloud while Ysella and I sew, as that is always a pleasant accompaniment to industry." She didn't wait for an answer. "Ysella, perhaps you will run to the library and select a *suitable* book."

Ysella dropped her sewing with alacrity and hurried off. In a few minutes she was back, armed with a leather-bound volume. *Belinda*, by Maria Edgeworth. Not something Morvoren had ever heard of. She'd been half-hoping for a Jane Austen, but maybe 1811 was a little early for something of hers.

She opened the book, cleared her throat, and began to read. "Mrs. Stanhope, a well-bred woman, accomplished in that branch of knowledge which is called the art of rising in the world, had, with but a small fortune, contrived to live in the highest company."

And so, until the promised light repast at lunchtime, she sat and read aloud to Ysella and her mother as they busily stitched at the baby garments, with all the while the rather interesting prospect of learning to dance with Kit looming for the afternoon's entertainment.

KIT

How had he got himself entangled with Ysella's plans to teach Morvoren to dance? And how had poor Sam been roped into them as well? Kit and Sam were riding back up the slope toward the house after a busy morning visiting some of his oldest tenants, checking roofs were watertight and finding out which of the inhabitants were in financial straits. He was returning with his purse a sight emptier than it had been when he set off, but at least he had some satisfied and grateful tenants.

As usual, it had troubled him to see that despite the apparent wealth that surrounded him at Ormonde, there were others for whom life was never easy, and perhaps a constant struggle.

He'd lived at Carlyon Court, a scant few miles from Nanpean, until his tenth year, when his father had inherited Ormonde and they'd had to remove to live in Wiltshire. But long before that, he'd found a friend in his mother's rascally older brother, Jago, and that friendship had never been allowed to dwindle. Whenever his father made his infrequent visits to Carlyon Court, usually for a few weeks each summer, Kit had begged to accompany him, and the two of them had seen the house opened up and brought back to dusty life.

Not that Kit had wanted to spend his time in the house. No, his goal every summer had been to spend time with Jago at Nanpean.

For Kit had early on discovered, to his delight, that Jago was a smuggler. With the romantic heart of a boy, he'd embraced it wholeheartedly, throwing himself into the adventure of what he saw as his uncle's exciting escapades. As he grew older, so he'd come to spend every summer at Nanpean with his uncle.

They sailed and fished together, lit lanterns to guide the little boats inshore so they could be unloaded on the beach at Nanpean, tied old sacking around the ponies' hooves, and trekked inland along the ancient hidden trackways to distribute their newfound wealth.

While the gentry quaffed their contraband brandy, and their wives danced in silks that had paid no duty in ballrooms across the county, Kit had seen the poor going hungry, so he'd kept up the smuggling even after he inherited his father's estate. To help his fellow Cornishmen, of course, but also for the excitement of it. Not to mention the fun of outwitting the revenue men.

Kit and Sam left their horses in the stables and went up to join the ladies in the morning room, where two of the footmen had just laid out a light meal of bread and butter and small cakes along with a tray of tea.

"Kit, darling," his mother exclaimed, her face alight with pleasure. "I wasn't expecting you and Sam for our little luncheon." She laid aside her sewing and nodded to the footman to withdraw.

"I was," Ysella said, sighing with obvious relief as she also set aside her sewing. "He's promised he'll help teach Morvoren to dance." She bestowed one of her best smiles on Sam, who colored to the roots of his hair. "And Sam has kindly said he would help too."

Morvoren, also blushing a little, closed the book she'd been holding. Was that an expression of relief on her face, as well? What dull and uplifting text could his mother have selected for her to read? Nothing Ysella would have chosen, that was for certain.

Kit and Sam made bows to the three ladies and Kit took a single seat close to his mother as she poured cups of tea for them all.

Sam perched at a distance on a hard-backed chair, looking uncomfortable. He rarely came into the drawing room to take tea with the family, but Kit had insisted as he was to be part of the dancing class.

"Teaching dancing?" Kit's mother asked, arching her eyebrows at him. "Morvoren doesn't know how to dance?"

Ysella butted in. "She has never learned, being from a corner of the country where dancing was not taught. So, as we are to go to the ball at Denby, I thought I had better instruct her. However…" she paused, "she cannot learn unless we have gentlemen to partner us." A naughty smile curved her lips. "So, Kit and Sam offered to assist me in my endeavors. We are to spend the afternoon in the music room. Dancing. It will be the greatest of fun, I'm sure."

Their mother pursed her lips for a moment but made no comment. Instead, she said, "I see you have been out riding across the estate, Kit," and passed him a delicate bone china cup and saucer. "The dust on your boots gives away your activities."

He nodded. "Sam and I did the rounds of the old folk—those who can no longer work or are widowed. We seem to have more of them than ever."

His mother nodded. "I rode out to visit them just over a week ago, by carriage, and took food Cook had prepared. The Widow Otley was sick in bed and we took her a good bone broth, enough for several days. Tell me, does she do better now?"

Kit nodded again. "I went specially to see her, Mother, as Sam told me of your visit. She does much better, you'll be pleased to hear. We found her in her garden, sitting in the sun, while her grandson, young Will, tended it for her. She asked me to tell you the bone broth was what cured her ills."

His mother smiled. "I doubt it very much, although good food is often the cure for some of what the poor suffer."

Ysella swallowed the bread and butter she'd been eating. "We are sending food to the young seamstresses who are stitching mine and Morvoren's gowns as a reward for their hard work." She smiled at Kit. "It was Morvoren's idea. She said they looked so thin and sad."

Kit glanced at Morvoren, who had remained silent during this exchange, delicately nibbling her bread and butter. Was that surprise in her eyes? Had she doubted that he ever did any good with his wealth? Not that he was rich by the standards of his neighbor at Denby. *There* was a man who could do more for his tenants if he tried… if he wanted to. But the old duke was a curmudgeonly fellow and whatever Kit suggested had always fallen on deaf ears.

At last, the food was finished and Kit rose to his feet, a tad nervous about what was to follow. "If you'll excuse me, Mother. I'm anxious to get this dancing practice done as Sam and I have other work to be about." He swept a bow to her and then turned to Morvoren as Sam and Ysella also rose to their feet.

"May I have the honor of leading you to the music room where I have happily secured the services of one of the servants who can play the fiddle?" How stuffy he sounded. But perhaps he only thought that because she was so unstuffy. Quite the unstuffiest girl he'd ever met.

Her blue eyes met his, twinkling with something he didn't quite understand, but she stood and took his proffered hand. He immediately wished he hadn't offered it as another sizzle of electricity ran up his arm, almost tangible in its intensity. Heat rushed up his neck making him turn his head away lest she should see. Why did her touch make him feel like this? She was a nobody, a well-bred nobody, and yet his whole body had been crying out to feel her hand in his... and more. Unable to release his hold on her for fear of offense, he led her out of the morning room and into the hall, followed by Sam and Ysella.

Old Jacko, one of the stable hands, who always played the fiddle for the servants' dances, was waiting in the music room, looking proud that he'd been asked to play for his lordship.

"Oh, you have found us an excellent musician!" Ysella gushed. "I don't know why I didn't think of asking Jacko. He's quite perfect." She released the hold she had on Sam's arm and bounced over to the old man. "This is all going to be quite splendid. What shall we start with?"

"Anythin' you likes, Miss Ysella," Jacko said, rheumy old eyes twinkling at her.

"Thank you." Ysella turned back to Morvoren. "There are several dances you're going to need to know for the ball. Mostly, we dance country dances in a long line, ladies on one side and gentlemen on the other, with lots of skipping up and down and twirling and some changing of partners, which is all great fun. They take a long time for everyone to go through, and if you and your partner stand well down the line, you'll be able to watch how everyone else dances the steps before it gets to your turn. So, I don't think we need to go through those just now. Maybe tomorrow or the next day."

She beamed at Kit. "I think we'll try 'Sir Roger de Coverley' first and put some chairs out to be the other couples. When Morvoren has seen what she has to do, you should dance with her and I'll dance with Sam." She turned her attention to Old Jacko. "Can you play 'Sir Roger' for us first, Jacko?"

Old Jacko touched his forelock with the hand that was holding the bow. "I can that all right, Miss Ysella." He struck up the tune with gusto.

Kit's foot began to tap. He'd always liked dancing.

Chapter Twenty
MORVOREN

Sir Roger de Coverley, which Morvoren had at least heard of, seemed very complicated indeed. She watched Ysella and Sam, the latter a little red-faced and self-conscious, as they skipped about pretending the chairs were three other couples. They had to do a lot of crossing over the center and swinging one another around, and Sam became more and more rosy cheeked as they went.

"And now they all skip around behind us," Ysella called breathlessly. "But you'll have to imagine that, because the chairs can't do it."

At last, she came to a halt and released Sam's hand. He took a diffident step back and hung his head. Not hard to see why. Here was a young man deeply smitten by Ysella's many youthful charms. A young man who, thanks to his station in life, would not be considered suitable to pay court to her. And he knew it.

"Now you two try, doing exactly as we did," Ysella instructed, a mischievous glint in her eyes. "Can you play more slowly do you think, Jacko? So Miss Morvoren doesn't need to dance as quickly as Sam and I did?"

Old Jacko touched his forelock again, his expression saying he could do anything if it were Miss Ysella asking.

So, Kit and Morvoren tried. Or rather, he danced and Morvoren tried. He was very elegant, which was just as well, as Morvoren had the horrible feeling she was anything but. How complicated it was remembering which way to go, which hand to put out, and to skip jauntily at the same time. She kept going wrong, despite Ysella's called instructions. It was worse than riding a dressage test.

Ysella clapped her hands and Old Jacko stopped his playing. "Perhaps you should just walk through the steps first, Kitto, for Morvoren to learn them. Both you and the music are going too fast and confusing her, I fear."

Too right. Morvoren bit her lip. "It's no good," she said on a sigh. "I'm never going to learn this in time for the ball. The steps are far too complicated. I'll have to be a wallflower." Not to mention the terrifying prospect at the back of her mind that she might have to dance these fancy steps with strangers.

Ysella shook her head in determination. "You don't need to worry about going wrong—lots of people make mistakes and nobody ever notices. And the more you practice, the better you'll get at it. I promise. Try again. Come on, Kit."

Under Ysella's garbled instruction, Morvoren walked through the movements slowly, with Kit but no music, repeating the steps until she had in her head what she needed to do. Every time his hand touched hers, though, that same flush of excitement shot through her. If only they were alone, and dancing the sort of dance where he could take her in his arms… Heat rose up her neck and cheeks at the thought of him doing that, and she had to concentrate hard on her steps to avoid tripping up.

A quick glance up at Kit's face told her that he, too, was blushing. Could he be experiencing the same feelings she was? If only. No. She was only here in his world temporarily. She'd surely be going back to her own time at some point and she couldn't allow herself to become involved with someone from 1811. No matter how handsome he was. And besides which, she wasn't even sure he liked her. The color in his cheeks could be due to exasperation at the length of time she was taking to learn these simple steps.

Old Jacko began to play again. Off they danced. As they came together, he smiled down at her in what could only be encouragement. "There. That's better now you're more familiar with the steps." A lock of his hair had fallen over his forehead making him even more devastatingly handsome than ever. How she'd like to reach up and brush it back for him.

She tripped over her feet.

No. She had to stop thinking about him like that. Concentrate. The more she did this, the easier it would become. Unfortunately, as the music sped up, she began to get lost, got in a panic and forgot which hand to take and which way she was supposed to go. She stopped, and Kit halted as well. "Don't keep thinking about it so much," he said, no doubt in an attempt to be helpful. "Just dance."

Morvoren forced a smile. "Easier said than done."

But Ysella seemed satisfied. "Now we'll all dance together," she declared, removing one pair of chairs. "We'll be the couples at either end and, this time, we have to be careful not to bump into each other as we twirl in the center. We need to take it in turns but stay as close together as possible. Off we go."

She must have been a born optimist.

Having two couples dancing at the same time turned out to be a nightmare. Ysella had made it sound so easy, but it was not. If only they could have danced more slowly, but Old Jacko seemed to have it in for Morvoren, and the tempo of the fiddle music was fast and bouncy as he kept up with the other three dancers. They had to skip through their steps at some speed, which meant, as Morvoren kept forgetting which way she was supposed to be going and what to do next, they kept on bumping into one another. And the more they did that, the more Ysella giggled, which made it even harder to concentrate.

"It's no good," Morvoren managed as they stopped for a rest, all of them breathing hard from the exertion. "I'm never going to get this right."

Ysella was fanning her pink face with her hand. "Of course you will. This is only the first day, don't forget. By the end of the week, you'll have every dance to perfection." She glanced at Kit and Sam who were taking off their jackets over by the window, which they'd opened. "And Kit is such a good dancer that he can disguise any mistakes you make." She frowned. "Although he'll only be able to dance with you once, of course. It's not done to dance with someone twice. Important to remember that."

What? Morvoren had been counting on the few dances she was able to do being with Kit. And now it seemed she could only dance one with him and would have to be partnered in any others by strangers. In that case, she'd just have her one dance with Kit and sit the others out.

"Do you never dance the waltz?" Morvoren asked. She'd gone to dance club at university for a term and it had been the only dance she'd mastered.

Ysella's eyes widened in shock. "Of course not. That would be too vulgar for words. We're not *allowed* to dance the waltz." Her eyes took on a naughty twinkle. "Although I can't deny it would be quite something to dance in a gentleman's arms." She sighed. "But terribly forward." She lowered her voice. "I have heard it said that ladies of ill repute will consent to dance the waltz with gentlemen."

Morvoren glanced again at Kit, wondering what it would be like to dance in his arms. A frisson ran down her back and settled south of her stomach. What would it be like to *lie* in his arms, preferably with both of them naked?

Ysella waved a hand at Old Jacko. "I think we'll do this all over again."

Distracted from her lustful thoughts, Morvoren turned back to the dance.

To start with, both Sam and Kit managed to keep straight-faced and stiff upper-lipped, trying to make up for the mistakes Morvoren was making and Ysella's rising laughter. But with Ysella reeling as though she were drunk every time Morvoren managed to bump into her, which was often, and Morvoren forgetting how many times they were supposed to swing one another around, which hand to offer up and which way to actually swing, very soon the faces of both their partners began to slip. And Old Jacko was openly chuckling to himself as he played.

Somewhere around the twentieth, or maybe the thirtieth, time Morvoren went wrong and trod on one of Kit's feet, everything went to pieces. This time they all managed to bump into one another in the middle and instead of just staggering, they collapsed in a giggling heap onto the polished wooden floor of the music room. Jacko stopped playing and hid his face behind his hands, his shoulders shaking. He probably didn't often see his master in such a situation.

Morvoren sat up and peeped at Kit. His normally serious face had broken into a wide grin which transformed his austere good looks into disturbingly dazzling handsomeness. He was chuckling to himself, as was Sam. Although Sam was also pink with embarrassment as Ysella had managed to collapse on top of him and was reclining almost in his lap with no indication that she intended to get up. Poor young man. He didn't know where to put his hands.

Kit sat up, the chuckle becoming a full-throated laugh. "Ysella, you are utterly incorrigible, and very bad at teaching dancing," he managed, shoulders shaking. "What will people think at the ball if we are all four of us taking part in Sir Roger de Coverley and this happens again?"

Ysella extracted herself from Sam's lap, levering herself up with a hand on his thigh that brought a richer scarlet to his cheeks. "Then we shall laugh just as we are laughing here." She giggled. "For I swear, brother, it is so good to see you can still do it. I was despairing of seeing you even smile these last few days. I thought you had forgotten how and would never again be the fun Kit I love so well."

Sam struggled to his feet, puce by now. "I am so sorry, Miss Ysella. So clumsy of me. Here, let me help you up." He pulled her upright.

Kit's eyes met Morvoren's, dancing with the same love of mischief as his sister's. "I declare," he said, "you might well be the worst dancer I've ever had the pleasure of meeting, Morvoren." But he wasn't angry.

Morvoren smiled back at him, her heart thundering in her chest far faster and louder than it should have been at such a backhanded compliment.

"I shall be perfectly fine," she managed, despite her suddenly dry throat, "so long as I'm not partnered with you, as clearly my two left feet do not match at all well with a perfect pair. I shall need to find a gentleman with two right feet for dancing and then I shall be well matched."

Kit laughed again. "I wish you good luck with that endeavor!"

Ysella reached a hand down to where they both still sat on the floor. "Nonsense," she said. "All you need is practice. Come, we have the Cotillion to try yet and then the Boulanger. No time to waste."

KIT

KIT COULDN'T BELIEVE he'd let his guard down like this. It must have been the influence of Ysella who never seemed to have her guard *up*. But there was no changing it now, and he didn't believe he wanted to. A warm flush of happiness had suffused his insides at the sight of Morvoren so plainly enjoying herself as she learned to dance, and when they'd fallen to the floor and her soft body had just for a moment rested against his, his whole being had flamed with a desire he hadn't felt for some time.

Not so much the carnal desire for a pretty girl, but a deep longing to take her in his arms and hold her close, pressing her pliant body against his, breathing in the scent of her hair and protecting her from the wicked world that surrounded her.

He quite surprised himself by his feelings, and they did make the rest of the dance session feel somewhat different now he'd acknowledged them. Each time he had to take her hand and she laughed up into his eyes, his heart swelled a little more. Each time he felt the warmth of her skin, even if it were just her fingertips on his, that same warm glow suffused his body from tip to toe, and he knew without a doubt that what he really wanted to do was press his lips to her delectably parted ones in a kiss.

But no. She was under his protection, and as such he couldn't take any advantage. That his mother would not approve of him harboring romantic feelings, the romantic feelings he'd already once denied, did not bother him in the least. He was his own man and this his own house, but there remained the dangerous life he led in Cornwall. Could he expose a gently bred young lady, a *wife*, to that life? If not, then he needed to hold himself in check.

Time raced past as they moved on to the Cotillion and had to start all over again with demonstrations and walking through the steps, until they were finally disturbed by a footman telling them her Ladyship requested their presence for tea in the library.

"Inform my mother we shall be with her in five minutes," Kit said.

"Oh pooh," Ysella complained, in a most unladylike manner. "Just when Morvoren was beginning to get the hang of this one."

"I wouldn't say I had the hang of any of them yet," Morvoren said, leaning against the pianoforte and breathing hard. A sheen of sweat sparkled on her forehead and her breasts rose rapidly from the exertion. Tantalizingly. What would it be like to rain kisses on them? Kit's breeches suddenly felt very uncomfortable and he had to turn away to the window for a moment in an attempt to get himself back under control.

"Nonsense," Sam put in. "You're doing better than some of the people I saw dancing here last year when Kit held his own ball."

"Did you attend it?" Morvoren asked, her gaze sharpening.

Sam nodded. "Because it was an Ormonde ball, Kit invited me." He shook his head ruefully. "I don't get invites from any of the local gentry though. A land agent is too lowly a creature."

"You're a very good dancer," Morvoren said. "I don't think you once put a foot wrong. I wish I could be as good as you."

"Many years of partnering young Carlyon ladies," Sam said, with a grin. "Derwa, Lady Monckton, is barely a year older than me. So when she was learning to dance, I made an ideal partner. And I repeated that task when Miss Meliora's turn came."

"And me," Ysella piped up. "He helped me learn as well. That's why I knew he'd be so helpful in teaching you, Morvoren."

Kit turned back from the window, hoping no one would notice his discomfiture. "We'd better not keep my mother waiting." To his relief, no one argued with his decision and he was able to lead the way from the room, the others following behind.

Chapter Twenty-One
MORVOREN

THE DAY OF the ball came around far sooner than Morvoren had expected. The Cornwall of Nanpean Cove felt far away, and her old world had receded into a distant memory, almost as though it were nothing but a half-remembered dream. This, even though it was in truth her past, was the world she inhabited now.

They'd spent the last few days at dancing practice every afternoon, and she'd improved enormously, at last being able to claim that instead of two left feet, she had a left and a right—most of the time. She'd also stopped causing chaos by forgetting which way she was meant to go at vital moments. Although, there being only the four of them and some chairs to take the place of the other dancers, this was no guarantee that she wouldn't go to pieces on a real dance floor populated by real people who might do unexpected things.

"You can just walk the dance steps if you're not sure of them on the night," Kit said by way of consolation, after she'd trodden on his foot for the umpteenth time. "A lot of people do that, you know."

His cheery mood persisted, and Morvoren had found herself looking forward to their afternoons all morning long, even when out riding first thing with Ysella, and definitely when she was sitting reading aloud while Lady Ormonde and a reluctant Ysella sewed. "I wish she'd let me read aloud instead of having to sew for that dratted baby,"

Ysella hissed when her mother's attention was elsewhere.

The new gowns arrived on the day before the ball, packed in tissue in large, flat boxes and delivered by a boy driving a small governess cart. The promised baskets of food were loaded onto this cart and dispatched back with the boy with strict instructions that they were to go to the three little seamstress's families, and not the Misses Sedgewick's shop. Ysella and Morvoren, who'd overseen the packing of the baskets themselves, also gave the boy the large package of sweetmeats and two bunches of hothouse flowers for the girls' employers.

"Don't forget to tell the girls' families that if they are in need of any further assistance they only have to ask," Morvoren said, deciding boldness was a good move. After all, Kit seemed predisposed to help those in need and had acquiesced to her earlier idea.

At the last minute, Ysella surprised Morvoren by bringing out three of her old china dolls, all beautifully clad in the silk gowns of a bygone era, and adding them to the baskets. "For their little sisters, who they are bound to have, that they may have as much joy from playing with them as I have had." She beamed. "These two I inherited from Derwa and Meliora, but this one, Agnes, was mine from new. Time for them all to have new homes now I'm a woman grown."

They spent the day of the ball quietly at home. "No riding or dancing practice for you girls today," Lady Ormonde decreed. "And a nap in the afternoon because balls can go on until dawn, even in the country. Can't have you hiding yawns behind your fans. That wouldn't be at all attractive to young gentlemen."

Morvoren had to press her lips together to prevent herself passing comment on this last remark.

Dinner at six was a simple affair, and as soon as it was over, everyone retired to their rooms to take their time over preparing for the ball.

"No need to rush," Ysella said as the girls parted in the corridor. "I doubt anything much will begin until after ten."

"Don't forget that Denby is ten miles distant," her mother, who had paused at her own bedroom door, put in. "It will take us over an hour to get there so we'll need to leave before nine. I shall expect you girls downstairs and ready to depart in good time."

"Yes, Mama," Ysella said with fake contrition.

Morvoren had better manners. "I won't be late, Lady Ormonde."

Kit poked his head out of his bedroom door. "I've no idea what you girls get up to in your rooms, but you'd better stop talking and get on with it. Because if you're not ready in time, then I shall leave without you." But he was laughing.

"Kit, you wouldn't!" Ysella exclaimed, but she was laughing as well.

Morvoren took a last glance at Kit, whose hair had somehow become tousled, and retreated inside her own room. If she had to look at him much longer, her heart was going to burst with longing. Would the ball be as fun as the dancing practice had been? She doubted it. What she really wanted to do was dance in his arms, with no one else around. A waltz, for sure, with all its lack of respectability. To feel his hands on her waist, to have him hold her close against his strong body and to rest her cheek against his. For his breath to mingle with hers, his lips to move to meet hers, and for him to press his hips against hers…

No. That was never going to happen. She could long for it as much as she wanted, but she was an interloper from another world, and he was a desperate smuggler with no interest in her.

Although that wasn't strictly true. Was it? But if he felt the way she suspected, why had he not acted on his feelings? Because she was a nobody, of course, and his mother wouldn't approve. That was why. In Lady Ormonde's eyes, her position was little better than Sam's. A bit of a charity case and not marriage material.

Loveday had hung the new gown on the outside of the wardrobe in its tissue paper covering and Morvoren's eyes kept going back to it as Loveday dressed her hair. "Sit still, Miss Morvoren, or it'll never come out the way Martha showed me," Loveday reprimanded. "I see you a-lookin' at your dress and it won't be goin' nowhere. Just let me get your hair pinned up and we can get it down."

Somehow, despite Morvoren's restless fidgeting, Loveday managed to draw up a bun on the back of her mistress's head and tease out a fine display of ringlets around her face. Then she set a couple of pretty, sparkling combs in Morvoren's hair and stood back to admire the effect with a harumph of satisfaction.

Morvoren peered into the small looking glass on her dressing table. "I look like someone out of a book." A Jane Austen book, of course.

"You look pretty as a picture," Loveday said. "And if I says so as shouldn't, it's thanks to how I done your hair."

Morvoren smiled. "Quite definitely it's thanks to your hairdressing skills that I shall look presentable this evening. Thank you very much for that, Loveday."

Loveday picked up a small jar. "And now for a touch of makeup."

Makeup? So far Morvoren had seen no hint that makeup was a thing in 1811. But she was wrong. With practiced fingers, Loveday carefully applied some cold cream, a touch of liquid rouge to her cheeks and lips, and darkened her carefully plucked eyebrows, with of all things, a clove she burnt in the candle flame. Fascinating. Not that afterwards Morvoren could even tell she had makeup on, although her lips did look a little redder than before. Subtle.

Next, a full-length petticoat went on over her slip and stays. The Misses Sedgewick had sent, among a lot of other fancy things, a brand new one for under the ball gown, of finest muslin. Feeling like the belle of the ball already, Morvoren rolled her white silk stockings up her legs and secured them with fetching new blue garters—not that anyone was likely to see them—and slipped her feet into the blue silk slippers that had come with her gown.

Time to unveil the gown.

With reverence, Loveday fetched it from where it was hanging and removed the tissue paper with care. Morvoren caught her breath. Exquisite. Quite the most beautiful dress she'd ever seen. A pale-blue, silk underskirt and a puff-sleeved sarsenet bodice embroidered with silver thread lay beneath a fine silk net overskirt, floaty as gossamer and embroidered with large delicately stitched silver flowers and swirls that matched the bodice.

How anyone could have sewn this net overskirt by hand, Morvoren had no idea, nor how this whole gown could have been completed in so short a time without even benefit of a sewing machine, but the tiny stitches of the little seamstress girls were almost invisible. She had a guilty feeling that a basket of food was small recompense to these girls for the work they'd done this week.

Perhaps she could do more for them while she was here?

She stepped into the dress with care, afraid she might tread on the lovely train and rip it, and Loveday fastened the tiny buttons down her back. This left her with a daringly plunging decolletage that made her glad of the support of her stays. The feeling of being part of a fairytale washed over her, and only the thought of how hard those little girls must have worked kept her feet on the ground.

"Just a dusting o' powder," Loveday opined, wielding a large furry thing that looked all too much like some creature's foot. "You have the clearest of skin and such a lovely complexion, 'twould be a shame to hide it." She wafted the foot across Morvoren's cheeks and made her sneeze.

She chuckled. "Why, bless you, Miss Morvoren. Does make me sneeze a bit too, but most ladies do like to cover up their blemishes with a touch o' powder." She paused. "Not that you got any to speak of." She set down the powder and the furry foot. "And what about a dab of perfume? Here, just behind your ears."

Morvoren had never been a girl who'd wanted, or, she liked to think, needed to wear a lot of makeup, being a more outdoor type, so she heartily agreed with her on this subject. Less was definitely more where makeup was concerned. But she'd take the perfume, with a delicate hint of the lavender that reminded her of her mother's garden at their old farm.

The long white gloves from the Sedgewick's little shop went on next, reaching to above her elbows. She'd have to be careful not to let them get dirty.

Clicking her tongue in approval, Loveday fastened a spray of delicate white flowers onto Morvoren's bodice as a corsage. Then, with a small, bejeweled reticule borrowed from Ysella, to keep her dance card and fan in, and a delicate silk shawl draped across her shoulders, Morvoren was as ready for a genuine Regency ball at a real duke's castle as she was ever going to be. A bundle of nerves, but ready.

Feeling a twinge of guilt about leaving Loveday to tidy up, Morvoren stepped into the corridor. Someone was waiting for her. Her heart leapt wildly. Kit, his brow furrowed in a frown, stopped striding up and down and made her a smart bow.

"Morvoren." His voice emerged deeper and huskier than she'd ever heard before. As though, perhaps, he'd just experienced the same sensations as she had. She certainly hoped so. "You look… stunning."

How handsome he looked in his black tailcoat and pale-cream silk breeches, silk stockings and buckled shoes. His gorgeous waistcoat was of the exact same blue as Morvoren's gown, embroidered with curlicues and twists just like her bodice. The suspicion that the Misses Sedgewick's little seamstresses had made it for him on purpose to match the gown warmed Morvoren's cheeks. Had he gone back specially to ask them?

"Lord Ormonde."

A warm feeling kindled in her stomach as she studied Kit's appearance for a brief moment, almost enough to replace her nervous agitation. Not a trace of stubble darkened his strong jawline, and his unruly hair had been artfully arranged into a tumble of Byronic curls. Morvoren had to fight an overwhelming urge to reach up and run her fingers through it. Would he have been shocked or would he have pulled her roughly into his arms and covered her in kisses? A shiver of glorious anticipation ran through her, and, with that warm feeling descending southwards, she had to give herself an unobtrusive shake to return to reality.

All she could do was gaze into his dark eyes as her heart skipped beat after beat. She could drown in those eyes if she looked into them for long enough. And was she mistaken in thinking he was gazing back with a longing similar to her own? Goodness. That hot feeling pooled somewhere well to the south of her stays and set her quivering with desire.

"Kit," she managed, although the word came out choked and croaky, making her cheeks flush with heat.

Did she want him to kiss her right now? Yes. She did. If she was honest, what she wanted him to do was to sweep her up in his arms and carry her back into the bedroom, to rip off their fine clothes and throw her on the bed and make passionate love to her until neither of them could stand up. She was a twenty-first-century girl, not an innocent Regency miss, and the two of them had been pussyfooting around each other all week in those dancing lessons, the sexual tension growing by the day. She couldn't have been the only one to feel it, could she?

He visibly pulled himself together. Did he have that same curling in his innards that had rendered her knees so weak they might perhaps deposit her on the long landing rug in a jellied heap of lust?

If he did, then he was hiding it well. He cleared his throat and from an inside pocket in his immaculate coat produced a slender, velvet box. Clearing his throat again, he held it out to her. "Er, I have something for you." He hesitated. "Something I would like you to wear tonight."

Yes, surely, he must have, for his voice had gone as croaky as hers.

"For me?" She took the box, her fingers just brushing his and a tremor of pure desire coursing through her. Swallowing, she stared down, forcing herself to concentrate on it and not think about how much she wanted him to take her right now. A jewelry box, long and flat. Was he giving her an actual piece of jewelry?

"Just to wear tonight," he said again, his words tumbling out in a hurry. "I thought it would match your eyes. Open it."

She opened the box and stared at the contents. A silver necklace of what looked like tiny diamonds glittered about a single, deep-blue sapphire on a velvet bed. Her eyes must have sprung open as wide as they could go. "I-I can't wear this," she managed to stutter. "It must be worth a fortune."

Kit reached over and took the necklace out of its velvet nest, managing not to touch her this time. "Yes, you can, because *I* am asking you to." He held up the sapphire close to her face. "And it is mine to give, inherited from my grandmother, who was a Cornish girl like you. I want you to wear it because you have eyes that exactly match the color of this stone, just as she did, and there's no one else could wear it quite so well." He smiled, an oddly serious smile after the fun they'd had dancing over these last few days. "I will brook no argument. If I am to escort you to the ball, then I would like you to wear my grandmother's necklace."

He moved behind her and put the necklace about her neck. His warm fingers on her skin as he fumbled a little with the clasp only served to renew her longing. He set his hands on her shoulders, his touch like fire, and turned her around. "There. This completes the picture I wish to hold in my mind."

Kiss me. I'm yours for the taking.

But he only held out his hand. "Let us go downstairs. Ysella and my mother are already waiting in the hallway and the carriage is in the drive."

So much for her vow not to allow herself to get involved with Kit, no matter how alluring he might be. Breathless with pent up desire, she let him take her hand and escort her down the stairs. More used now to not tripping over her gown with every untoward step, she made as elegant a descent as any she'd made this last week.

Ysella stood at the foot of the stairs looking radiant in her gold gown. Morvoren had already seen and admired it that afternoon, as Ysella had been too impatient to wait to rip the tissue from it in the evening and had bid her come and admire the intricate embroidery across the bodice. She had a silk shawl in a paler shade of gold draped about her shoulders and small golden flowers dotted her dark curls. A captivating beauty. Morvoren had a feeling she would be a great success with the local young men that night.

Kit's mother wore a deep aquamarine gown, and her hair was arranged formally in a less girlish style. But she was still a very beautiful woman, with a figure, aided of course by stays, many a younger woman would envy.

Lady Ormonde smiled with a new warmth, which surprised Morvoren. "I feel very proud of my two beautiful girls," she said, encompassing Morvoren along with Ysella. "How prettily Kit's necklace sets off the blue of your eyes, Morvoren. Really quite remarkable. Come along, girls. Let us get into the carriage."

The carriage waiting on the drive came equipped, this time, with not just the driver, James, whom they'd had before, now dressed in a livery worthy of the driver of Cinderella's coach, but now also two other liveried and bewigged worthies. Both of these were to perch on the back of the vehicle while it was in motion. One of these two was waiting with the step down and the door open.

Kit handed his ladies one at a time into the carriage then climbed in himself, settling on the backward facing seat beside his mother, who was already fanning herself with her prettily decorated chicken-skin fan. "I declare," she said. "It's too warm in here by far. The evening will be a hot one, I fear. I do hope there isn't a storm brewing."

Kit must have been as hot or hotter than they were, in his tight-fitting black silk coat and with his stock fastened up under his chin. However, at least he didn't have to wear stays underneath all that lot. Morvoren tried not to fidget, but she was feeling as hot as Lady Ormonde. Which reminded her that she, too, had a fan, so she took it from her borrowed reticule and employed it to waft some cooler air onto her face. It wouldn't do to arrive at the ball red-faced and sweaty.

The lackey closed the door and lifted the step, and the carriage rocked as he jumped up to join his fellow on the back. In a moment, they were underway, rattling over the graveled drive and swaying a little from side to side, but not sufficiently to give Morvoren the motion sickness she'd experienced in the mail coach. The horses seemed to be sticking to a steady trot, so it would take over an hour to get to the ball. With a refreshing breeze now wafting in through the open windows on either side, Morvoren settled back in her seat and stared out at the passing twilit countryside. All thoughts of lust evaporated to be replaced with the familiar knotting anxiety that she was destined to inevitably do something wrong and make a fool of herself that night.

Now she was more used to traveling by horsepower, the journey passed very quickly. All too soon, they were rolling up a wide driveway toward the looming shape of not a castle but a huge country house.

Morvoren peered out of the window to stare as the driveway curved around, affording an excellent view of the brightly illuminated edifice.

"Denby Castle," Kit said, his voice curt, as though this might be somewhere he wasn't fond of.

"It doesn't look much like a castle."

He nodded, his face now just a pale blur in the dark interior of the carriage. "There was a proper castle here once, but it's long gone now. If you were to take a walk in the grounds, you'd come across the bare bones that are all that remain of it now." He paused, and cleared his throat.

Why did she get the impression that those ruins held some bad memory for him? That Denby was not a place he was fond of?

He went on. "The house that stands here now is scarcely more than a hundred and fifty years old I believe. Nothing like as old as Ormonde."

The coach swung around in a wide arc and came to a halt on an expanse of pale gravel in front of the house. Lanterns, burning on tall poles every ten yards or so, liberally illuminated the whole front façade of the house, their flickering light sending shadows leaping in every direction across the driveway.

The carriage rocked as one of the lackeys jumped down to open the doors and let down the step.

Kit descended first, then handed his ladies down. It seemed they'd arrived at a popular time, for other carriages were disgorging sumptuously clad ladies and austere looking gentlemen. Fans fluttered, feathered headdresses bobbed, and laughter rose toward the dark sky.

Kit held out his arm to his mother and she took it, deploying her fan against the warmth of the evening. Ysella linked her arm through Morvoren's. "Come along," she whispered, suddenly sounding as nervous as Morvoren felt. "We must keep close to Mama, or she'll be angry. She'll want to keep a good eye on which gentlemen we dance with."

Even more lanterns lit the steps as brightly as if it were full daylight. As they climbed the steps, Morvoren took a closer look at some of the other guests: women like bright butterflies in their many-hued gowns, and among the somber black and navy coats of men like Kit, a few army officers, their rich, red military uniforms standing out like exotic birds of paradise.

She swallowed down her fears. She was at a real Regency ball. Her, a girl more used to listening to heavy metal, rhythm and blues, or maybe a bit of country and western. How scary was this? Would she manage to acquit herself without mishap? No. She mustn't think like that. She could do it. She had to. She couldn't let down Lady Ormonde, or Ysella, and certainly not Kit.

She looked at his upright, slim-hipped figure just in front and drew in a shaky breath. She could do it for him.

Ysella's arm linked through hers tightened. It was good to know she wasn't the only nervous one.

Chapter Twenty-Two
MORVOREN

MUSIC AND LIGHT spilled down the steps from Denby Castle's enormous double front doors. Both stood wide open to welcome in the chattering guests, a splendidly liveried footman in a powdered wig to either side.

Arm in arm with Ysella, Morvoren approached the haughty gaze of these footmen, trembling in her dainty silk shoes lest they spot her for an imposter. But they let her pass unchallenged, and, feeling very much like Cinderella, she found herself standing open-mouthed just inside an enormous hallway, staring at a wide staircase that rose to a galleried landing high above her head. Scores of imposing oil paintings that were probably by old masters hung on the walls of hall and staircase alike, all their carefully executed eyes fixed accusingly on her. Or so it felt.

"The Viscount Ormonde, Lady Ormonde, the Honorable Ysella Carlyon and Miss Morvoren Lucas," boomed another liveried man. Heads turned, and hot color suffused Morvoren's face. She hadn't been expecting a formal announcement like this, and now it felt as though every human eye in the wide hall, as well as those of the paintings, were on her, weighing and measuring, and finding her wanting.

For a house that possessed no electricity, the interior of Denby blazed with light from what might have been a thousand candles burning in chandeliers and on branched candelabras in wall alcoves, throwing a warm, golden glow over everything.

People milled everywhere, chattering gaily. Gentlemen of all ages and sizes, dressed for the most part like Kit, mingled with a few more soldiers in their bright red dress uniforms. Ladies stood about everywhere in the most gorgeous of gowns, either on the arm of one of the male guests, or in small groups with their heads together, fanning their pink cheeks and laughing. Some were old ladies with heavily powdered faces and long feathers waving from their elaborate hairstyles, others were of middle-years with the proportions of galleons in full sail, attended by slender young women like Ysella, under what must be strict chaperonage.

Ysella's hold on Morvoren's arm tightened again. "Oh, just look at all the beautiful gowns. And isn't that Henry Lockhart over there looking so handsome in his regimentals, standing with my dear Caroline?" She beamed at Morvoren. "I must introduce you to Caro. You'll adore her, just as I do, I'm sure."

So *that* was Caroline Fairfield, the young lady Kit's mother had lined up for him. Morvoren considered her with interest. A tall young woman with light brown hair and an intelligent face, she had been engaged in conversation with a young man in the red uniform of an officer, but right now seemed to have noticed the arrival of the party from Ormonde.

She neatly disengaged herself from young Henry Lockhart, and approached across the crowded hall. "Ysella! Kit! How lovely to see you here. And Lady Ormonde, how charming you look in that color. It so suits your complexion. My mother will be overjoyed to see you."

Her soft brown eyes moved on and settled on Morvoren, full of sparkling curiosity.

Morvoren returned her gaze, as curious about Miss Fairfield as she seemed to be about her.

Kit smiled, a genuine, friendly smile, and with a shock Morvoren realized that something existed between these two. Could it be love? How would she feel if it was?

Kit took Caroline's hand. "Caro, how lovely to see you. May I introduce Ysella's friend, Miss Morvoren Lucas?" He paused, looking at Morvoren. "And Miss Lucas, may I introduce Miss Caroline Fairfield, an old family friend."

But was that all she was? The green goblin of jealousy rose in Morvoren's heart, much to her surprise. And embarrassment.

"Miss Lucas, how lovely to meet you," Caroline said, and, releasing Kit, she held out her elegantly gloved hand.

After an infinitesimal pause, Morvoren took the offered hand in hers and shook it. "And you, Miss Fairchild."

"Oh, do please call me Caroline," Miss Fairchild said, her smile surprisingly friendly. "Everyone else does, and it feels so stuffy to be called Miss Fairchild—as though I were an old maid on the shelf."

Ysella's eyes twinkled. "I'm sure you will never be that."

Did she mean Caroline and Kit would soon be marrying? Morvoren looked up at Kit, but he was staring over their heads further into the hall toward where music was cascading through a pair of wide double doors.

"I see Rafe Huxley over there. I'll leave you ladies in Mama's safe hands. If you'll excuse me?" And he was gone.

Well, at least he didn't seem to have shown much interest in remaining by Caroline's side. That was a blessing.

Lady Ormonde shook her head in what looked like exasperation. Perhaps she too was wondering why Kit hadn't hung about near the young lady she'd selected for him as a bride. Morvoren couldn't help the smug feeling welling up inside her. Which was quite ridiculous as there was no way she could have Kit herself.

"This way, girls," Lady Ormonde said, wielding her fan. "We shall go into the ballroom and see which young men are present, and I shall find dear Diana."

"Caro's mama," Ysella hissed. "My mama's dearest friend."

Lady Ormonde shepherded all three of her charges into the ballroom, an enormous, gilt encrusted room with tables and chairs around the edges and dancers already prancing elegantly in the middle to the accompaniment of an ensemble of musicians. Wide-eyed at the spectacle, Morvoren allowed herself to be guided toward one side, where a redoubtable matron stood talking to an elderly gentleman.

They stopped talking as Lady Ormonde approached and both turned to face her, a wide smile on the lady's face and a slight frown on the old gentleman's, as though he were having trouble placing them all. Why did Morvoren get the impression the frown was directed at her?

"Diana, my dear," Lady Ormonde exclaimed, and was off into a flurry of introductions in explanation of why she had arrived with so attractive a stranger in her party. "And may I introduce Lord Russell, who is our member of Parliament and also a local magistrate."

Lord Russell, who must have been over seventy, eyed Morvoren through a single eyeglass, that one eye magnified alarmingly to look much larger than the other. "Well, demmit, you're a fine-looking young woman," he said. "If I were twenty years younger, I'd be takin' you out onto the dance floor right now, Miss Lucas. You mark my words."

This clearly required a reply. "Why thank you, sir," Morvoren managed, groping for polite words but very glad he wasn't twenty years younger as that would still have made him old enough to be her father. "I'm sure I would've enjoyed dancing with you very much." She was improving at polite banter.

He tapped his right foot with his silver-topped walking stick "Gout, m'dear, or by gum I'd still be makin' a try for you." And he winked at her.

"Ysella, Miss Lucas!"

Morvoren swung her head around and for once was glad to see

Captain Carlyon coming their way, clad also in the bright red of a soldier's dress uniform. And very handsome he looked in it as well. If she hadn't come across him previously and taken his measure, she might have been tempted into finding him attractive.

He bowed to Lady Ormonde and Mrs. Diana Fairfield, who gave the slightest of curtseys back. "Aunt Elestren, Mrs. Fairfield, you put the young ladies to shame. If only I were ten years older."

"You flatterer," Mrs. Fairfield said, batting her fan rapidly. "I know you're here to engage the girls in a dance, not us, so get on with it. You have no need to practice your fancy words on two old ladies."

Lady Ormonde chuckled. "Mind who you are classing as an old lady, Diana. I feel I could dance till dawn with any of the young men here tonight."

Before Captain Carlyon could continue though, another of the older ladies swept across the ballroom to them, the three-foot-long feathers perched in her hair waving in the breeze of her passage. "Elestren, my dear, thank you so much for coming. A ball at Denby would be nothing without you." She bestowed an indulgent smile on the Captain. "Fitz, my dear, as if I wouldn't know where to find you—dancing attendance on the prettiest girls in the room."

The captain bestowed a smart bow on this woman. "Mama."

So this was his mother, the flighty young thing who'd run off with a penniless army officer for love.

"Lady Elizabeth, you're looking very well," Lady Ormonde said with a genuine smile. "You must remember Ysella, although I believe the last time you saw her she was still in the schoolroom."

The newcomer, one of most galleon-in-full-sail of all the ladies present, and whose stays must have been working in overtime, bowed her head, making her feather headdress dance and bob. "My goodness. She's grown so extraordinarily pretty. But how could she not have, with you as her mother? She's the image of you as a girl. I could take you for sisters." Her gaze moved on to Morvoren, her delicate eyebrows slightly raised.

"May I introduce Miss Morvoren Lucas, a friend of Ysella's who is staying with us for a while." Lady Ormonde looked at Morvoren. "Lady Elizabeth Carlyon, my dear sister-in-law, the captain's mother."

Lady Elizabeth extended a plump, white-gloved hand, which Morvoren took. She bobbed a graceful, she hoped, curtsey, her brain cogs whirling. So, this was indeed the duke's daughter who'd run away with Kit's rakish uncle Robert. With her matronly figure and rather doughy face, she didn't look the sort to throw caution to the wind with a penniless younger brother and adventurer, but appearances could be deceiving. Perhaps he'd been as dazzlingly handsome as his nephew. Running off with Kit for a love tryst was an attractive proposition.

"Charmingly pretty," Lady Elizabeth said, as Morvoren rose from her curtsey to find her eyes fixed on the necklace Kit had lent her. "And such lovely eyes, brought out to perfection by your necklace, my dear. Do I not recall seeing that on the wife of the fifth viscount?"

Ysella had rehearsed Morvoren in how to reply to exalted people. "Thank you, Lady Elizabeth," she said, with all the demure manners of the Regency young lady she wasn't. "Lord Ormonde has loaned it to me just for the evening as I had nothing else to wear." Her secret felt as though it were written across her forehead in capital letters of fire. Imposter. Charlatan. Fraud.

But Lady Elizabeth's attention had moved on already and was back to Lady Ormonde. "Do come into the card room with me and let us play a hand of whist together. Jasper is in there and he can be such fun when he's in a good mood. He returned from London the moment he heard Papa was to hold a ball. He's here on the look out for a new wife who can give him sons, I've no doubt."

"Do excuse me, Diana," Lady Ormonde said, casting a reluctant glance at Ysella and Morvoren. "Would you be able to keep an eye on my girls for a while? You know how much I enjoy a hand of cards."

Mrs. Fairfield bowed her head to her friend. Presumably a duke's daughter took precedence over a mere Mrs. "Of course I will. Haven't you done the same for me enough times? The girls will be safe with me."

With no further look for any of them, Lady Elizabeth whisked her friend away, leaving Ysella, Caroline, and Morvoren standing beside Mrs. Fairchild.

Ysella turned back to her cousin Fitz. "You were about to ask us all to put your name in our dance cards, were you not, Cuz?"

Captain Carlyon, now his mother had departed, regained his voice. Who'd have thought him a man likely to be cowed by his own mother? But she had possessed the air of the sort of woman a man wouldn't want to cross. That no one would want to cross, really. Maybe it had been she who'd seduced the late Uncle Robert.

A cluster of other young men had joined Fitz by now, looking eager to have their names entered on the girls' dance cards. Could they possibly be keen to procure Morvoren's name as well, or were they all here for Ysella and Caroline, both of whom they must know?

Quite a crowd was gathering.

"Miss Carlyon, may I have the first dance with you?"

"Miss Fairchild, might you reserve the cotillion for me?"

"Could you introduce us to your lovely friend?"

Morvoren felt her cheeks start to glow again as their voices clamored over her head, all talking at once. Most confusing.

She took her dance card and tiny pencil out of her reticule and studied it, not wanting to look up into the sea of eager faces, and not really wanting to put down any of their names on the card. Both of her feet had definitely turned back into left ones again and she wouldn't be able to remember how to dance a single step if she had to dance with someone other than Kit.

A lean, tanned hand settled on hers, warm and reassuring.

She raised her eyes and gazed into Kit's face.

"Morvoren," he said, executing a smart bow. "I seem to remember that you promised *me* the first dance tonight." He glanced at the other young men. "I'm afraid you gentlemen will have to wait. The first dance is taken."

Morvoren took a sideways glance at Caroline, but she was busy writing down some young gentleman's name on her own dance card, and appeared not to have noticed Kit's knight in shining armor gesture.

"Of course I haven't forgotten," Morvoren said, as Kit took hold of her hand. "Thank you, Lord Ormonde." And he whirled her away onto the dance floor.

"Sir Roger de Coverley," Kit said, as they took their places. "Your forte, I believe."

Morvoren managed a nervous smile, but the fact that she was dancing for the first time in public with Kit as a partner made all the difference. She knew the way he danced, she knew he could hide her mistakes, she knew he would be tolerant of her treading on his toes. She smiled at him as they made their bows to one another.

The moment they were dancing, she forgot her fears. The music, louder and more elegantly played than Old Jacko's fiddle, soared, and Morvoren soared with it. On their last day of practice, she'd felt as though everything had come together, and now it did again.

"I told you you'd be fine," Kit said, as they came together again to make an archway for the other dancers to pass underneath. "Just think of everyone else as faceless chairs. And remember that no one ever notices if you make a mistake."

Morvoren dimpled, happier than she'd been all week. "Thank you so much for bringing me to this ball. It's-it's more than I could ever have hoped for. The lights, the room, the gowns the ladies are wearing. It's all like a fairytale."

His eyes twinkled. "You are an odd sort of girl, if you don't mind my saying so. Have you never been to any kind of dance in your entire life? Your upbringing must have been very sheltered." He frowned. "And very different to most young ladies. Riding astride, for a start." He was keeping his voice down low as the rest of the dancers skipped beneath the arch.

Morvoren couldn't answer, as the next part of the dance parted them.

In between their bouts of action, for this was a long dance, she faced Kit across the dance floor, which gave her a good opportunity to appreciate him.

He had to be the handsomest man in the ballroom. Tall, slim but strong, with delectably wide shoulders that had needed no padding from his tailor, and such a good dancer. Who'd have thought doing complicated steps in an old-fashioned dance would make a man seem so attractive?

He was unlike any other man she'd ever met. Perhaps it was the knowledge that under all the mannerisms of the gentleman, and that veneer of respectability he presented here at Ormonde, hid the soul of an adventurer engaged in smuggling in the home of his heart. The romance of his illusion had her snared, like a fish on a line, only one that didn't want to wriggle and escape.

At last, the dance came to an end, and, pink-faced with exertion, Morvoren allowed Kit to promenade her around the ballroom and procure glasses of lemonade for them both. As they passed along one side, cool night air came spilling in through tall French windows standing open onto a lamplit terrace, and several couples had already ventured out into the moonlight.

"You didn't yet tell me about your upbringing," Kit said, as they walked. "I'm curious as to why you're so different from any other girl I've met."

Morvoren bit her lip. What to tell him? Would she ever be brave enough to consider revealing the truth? No. Especially not here. He'd think she was making fun of him. "I had liberal parents," she tried.

"Eager to allow me all the freedom I wanted. Eager for me to have as good an education as possible." She paused. "For a girl."

His dark brows rose, and he looked as though he would have said something, but they were interrupted. By Captain Carlyon.

He came striding over, looking a little flushed in the face, with Ysella on his arm, also becomingly flushed. "Kit, you're hogging the prettiest girl in the room, apart, of course, from you, Ysella. Let someone else have a chance. Miss Lucas, Morvoren, if I may call you that as you are as good as a cousin, almost. I'd be enchanted if you'd allow me the pleasure of this next dance."

Morvoren couldn't miss Kit's face darkening, nor the stiffness in his arm as he relinquished his hold on her. "Of course," he snapped. "I bid you good evening." And he was gone.

Before she knew it, Kit's cousin had swept her out onto the ballroom floor again and they were dancing the cotillion.

Chapter Twenty-Three

KIT

DAMN FITZWILLIAM. DAMN, damn, damn him. But Kit couldn't keep Morvoren to himself. That just wasn't done. All the same, he'd so much rather have returned her to the safety of his mother or Mrs. Fairfield than allowed her to go off and dance with that rake.

Rafe Huxley, his old schoolfriend, materialized at Kit's side as he stood dithering. "Who was that dazzling creature you were just dancing with?" He paused. "Clearly one my mater hasn't spotted yet or she'd have her lined up waiting for me to procure an introduction and a dance."

Kit was watching Morvoren line up for the next dance with Fitzwilliam, a slight look of trepidation on her face. Good. He didn't want her falling for his cousin's dubious charms. What girls saw in him was beyond Kit. "A friend of my sister's whom we have staying at Ormonde at the moment," he said to Rafe, attempting to keep his tone offhand.

"Lucky you." Rafe grinned. "I only wish my sister had such lovely friends. She's such a bluestocking herself, the only girls she ever invites to stay are ones with the same interests as her. I told the pater it was a bad idea sending her away to school, and I was right, but the mater was insistent. She has it in her head that all my sisters should get what she calls a *good education*, and she has my father wrapped around her little finger. Who she thinks will marry them when all they can talk about is Latin and Greek, I don't know. A chap gets enough of that at Eton and Oxford. He doesn't want his wife spouting it." He rubbed his nose. "I think I might ask her for the next dance. Can't let your cousin keep her to himself, now can we?"

For some reason Rafe's words annoyed Kit immensely. He realized with a jolt that it wasn't only his cousin he didn't want dancing with Morvoren. He didn't want anyone at all dancing with her. Which was ridiculous. He had to keep himself under control or he was going to end up losing his temper and planting someone a facer and that would never do. Not in public, anyway.

Rafe wandered away, and for a full minute Kit stood brooding over the sight of Morvoren and his cousin. At least the lessons had paid off and she was making a creditable attempt at the Cotillion. Although dancing was not her forte. She was a girl more at home on the back of a horse, very much like his own mother.

"She's a lovely girl."

He swung around. Caroline was standing beside him, fanning herself in the heat of the ballroom, her cheeks a pretty shade of pink. She curtsied with an inborn grace and smiled up at him, looking almost beautiful, and for a moment Kit wondered if he'd been wise to spurn his mother's suggestion that she would make him the good and sensible wife she said he needed. One his mother would approve of, at any rate. Not that he wanted a good and sensible wife, or even a wife at all right now. Or did he? Then he remembered Ysella's declaration that Caro was in love with a soldier.

"Is he here?" he asked, following her gaze and staring across the room toward a group of three scarlet-clad officers laughing together.

Caroline gave herself a little shake. "I see Ysella has been giving away my secrets. I shall have to reprimand her."

"You should know better than to confide to her anything you want keeping quiet."

She smiled. "I should. You'd think I'd know her a sight better by now, wouldn't you?"

"I make it a policy never to tell her anything important."

Another smile. "Like the fact that you're in love with Miss Lucas?"

Color rose to Kit's cheeks. "I'm not."

Caroline's smile widened. "You underestimate your sister, my lord. She isn't the empty-headed chit you think her. She already told me this evening that you have fallen head over heels for Miss Lucas and that she has plans for you to be wed." She chuckled. "And now I've seen you both together, I can see it plainly written over both your faces."

"Since when have you stopped calling me Kit?" he blustered, aware of heat suffusing his entire body. If only they weren't standing in such a prominent position. He caught her elbow and steered her toward a more shadowy corner of the room on hurried feet.

She chuckled again as they came to a halt in a curtained alcove beside a bust of Lord Denby himself. "Don't let my mother see you secreting me in here or she'll get her hopes up again." She tapped him on the end of his nose with her folded fan. "I can see from your reaction that both Ysella and I are quite correct in our surmises. When do you plan to propose, Kit? She's uncommonly pretty."

He bit his lip. "She is indeed. But also uncommonly vexing at times." Telling Caroline about Morvoren would be like confiding in a priest in the confessional. She was not just his sister's oldest friend but also one of his. If just friendship were required to make a marriage, then he could have married Caroline in an instant. He might as well come clean about Morvoren and Ysella's escapade.

He recounted the story of the riding astride and the compromise they'd come to.

Caroline burst out laughing. "Oh Kit. You've been taken in by Ysella once again, I see. Can no one say no to that young lady? But it sounds as though she's found a kindred spirit in her friend." She narrowed her eyes at him. "And perhaps you have too?"

Damn the woman. She was far too perceptive. Another of the reasons he could never have married her—she'd have seen through him every time he tried to dissemble.

She frowned up at him. "Is there some problem? She seems a lovely girl—beautiful, one assumes well-bred, intelligent, and she dances moderately well." Her eyes crinkled as the smile returned. "Ysella tells me you helped teach her to dance and that there's some mystery about her. I'm intrigued."

Now he was in this quiet corner with her, Kit longed to escape. Longed to escape the ball itself, where he was going to have to watch Morvoren dance with gentleman after gentleman, see her escorted into supper by some lucky fellow, and promenade on the arms of men who were not him.

Perhaps honesty was the best policy. Well, some degree of honesty. Caro was a very old friend. "I cannot ask her to marry me," he said, aware of the bitterness in his voice. "I have reasons it would be impossible. And tomorrow," he paused, the idea formulating in his head even as he spoke. "Tomorrow, I have to leave Ormonde and return to Cornwall."

Caroline controlled a smile. "Tell yourself that if you wish, my Kitto, but you're telling yourself a lie. A wife has found you. It's as plain..." And here she reached out and tapped him on the nose again. "As the nose on your face. Mark my words. I'm never wrong."

Kit opened his mouth, thought better of it, and closed it again, unable to think of a reply.

Morvoren

Thank goodness Ysella had made her practice, because dancing with the captain was not nearly so relaxing as dancing with Kit had been.

She'd felt at one with Kit, safe in his hands, as though he could anticipate any move she made, but with the captain the sensation was much more dangerous, as though he were waiting for her to make a mistake and looking for the opportunity to exaggerate it.

They came together numerous times during the dance, amongst the twirling and swapping of partners and the "moulinet." However, Morvoren was concentrating so much, she had to pay attention to what was coming next and he seemed content to remain silent, his hot eyes devouring her as they danced.

Not so when the dance finally ended, though. He drew her arm through his, and they promenaded around the edge of the ballroom together. And now he had her full attention, or so he must have thought, although in fact she was searching for Kit amongst the crowd of happy, chattering people, hopeful of rescue. Although probably he'd be off dancing with some other lucky girl.

"Well, Miss Lucas," Captain Carlyon said, steering her toward the refreshment room. "At last, I have you to myself."

There wasn't much she could say to that, so she remained silent, still scanning the throng of strangers for a friendly face.

He either hadn't noticed her reluctance to go with him, or he didn't care. She suspected the latter. "I should like to introduce you to my grandfather, if that would please you."

"Thank you, Captain," she said, awkwardly conscious of her manners. What she really wanted to do was snatch her arm away from him and make off to look for Kit. Or Ysella. Or Lady Ormonde. Or Mrs. Fairfield or even Caroline, whom she thought she'd seen heading into an alcove with Kit. Any one of them would do as a haven of safety. But etiquette, as dictated by Ysella, insisted she should make small talk with the person who had just squired her onto the dance floor.

They approached a small group of elderly gentlemen, all knocking back glasses of golden liquid that might have been whisky. The captain cleared his throat, and the head of the nearest one, a corpulent old man who must have been eighty if he was a day, turned toward them.

"Grandfather," the Captain said. "May I present Miss Lucas, who is like a cousin to me as she is visiting Kit and Ysella at Ormonde. I told you I'd already met her on the coach up from Cornwall, did I not? And how charming she is."

The old gentleman, who had a head of bushy white hair, eyebrows to match and the ruddy-faced look of a heavy drinker about his portly self, furrowed his brows and leaned forward as if his sight were poor. "Miss Lucas, you say?" He made a smart, if stiff, bow. "A pleasure."

"Miss Lucas," the captain said. "May I present my grandfather, the Duke of Denby. Your host." He spoke with a mixture of pride and something else Morvoren didn't quite understand, that might have been bitterness, but by then she was too busy trying to make a perfect curtsey to the old man.

The duke held out his arm. "Come, walk with me a step and leave my grandson to find some other chit to dance with. Humor an old man who likes to be seen with a pretty girl on his arm."

Well, this was better than having to remain with the captain, so, with as sweet and innocent a smile as she could muster, she let go of the captain's arm and took the duke's. They set off around the edge of the dance floor at little more than a shuffle, hampered by the fact he had a decidedly stiff right leg.

"Tell me, Miss Lucas," he said as they walked. "Where do you come from?"

Morvoren wasn't about to fall into the trap of telling him she came from Reading again, so she opted for where she'd spent her childhood. Much better. "Oxfordshire. I'm a country girl at heart."

He harumphed a bit. "I'd like to introduce you to my son, if I may. Just came down from London in time for the ball, and I know he'd like to meet such a pretty and healthy-looking girl as you."

Healthy-looking? What was he talking about? Her warning antennae began to twitch.

They found his son in the card room, standing watching a game Morvoren didn't recognize. She had the briefest of moments to observe him as they approached. Easy to see he was his father's offspring. This silver fox of a man was burly rather than fat, with the look of a well-fed Hereford bull about him. A short neck sat on square shoulders and his thinning hair had been combed cleverly upwards into a peak on top of his head to hide his encroaching baldness.

He looked up as his father approached, and a broad smile lit his face, dropping the years away. The duke would himself have been a handsome man thirty years ago, just as this silver fox of a man was now.

"Jasper," the duke said, slapping his son on the back. "I'd like you to meet Miss Lucas, of the Oxfordshire Lucases. Miss Lucas, this is my son, the Marquess of Flint."

Morvoren made her curtsey and the marquess made his bow, his grey eyes appraising her and shining in what appeared to be appreciation. Not that she wanted that sort of appreciation from a man who must at best be in his early fifties. Where was Kit? She more and more needed rescuing, and although all the men were being polite, she couldn't get over the feeling that most of them were assessing her like a prize heifer. There was an obvious downside to a Regency ball.

"My," the marquess said, unable to tear his eyes away from Morvoren's decolletage, which she was now wishing wasn't so low. "You *are* a pretty girl. How have I not met you in London?"

Oh no. This was running into the sort of conversation she didn't want to be having, and that not even Ysella could have prepared her for. She glanced around the room, feeling hemmed in and hunted. If only Kit would appear and whisk her away to safety.

The next best thing happened. One of the young men who'd earlier pressed her to write their names on her dance card arrived, standing politely back and coughing into his hand, no doubt very much aware that he was facing his illustrious hosts. But thank goodness for his persistence.

Morvoren took out her dance card and pretended to study it. "Why Mr. Brunton, I'd quite forgotten I'd promised this next dance to you." She smiled up at the handsome letch who was still staring south of her face with a hungry look. "I'm so sorry, Lord Flint, but I'm afraid I must leave you."

"Before you go," the marquess said, the light of acquisition now shining in his eyes. "Perhaps I can have the pleasure of a later dance with you?"

How she wished she hadn't flashed her dance card about for him to see the gaps in it. The chance to tell him she was all booked up had vanished. With great reluctance she wrote his name down for a later dance, all the time vowing to hide herself away when it began. If she could.

More bows and curtseys all round, and she left on young Mr. Brunton's arm, the glow of success in combat emanating from him in tangible waves.

Goodness, dancing at a ball was more of a minefield than she'd expected it to be.

Chapter Twenty-Four

MORVOREN

THE BALL PASSED in a whirl of different dances and heady scents. All the younger guests bounded about the dance floor with seemingly endless enthusiasm, and some of the older ones, too. Morvoren found herself partnered by a different young man for every dance, returning in between dances to rejoin Lady Ormonde and Mrs. Fairfield who seemed determined to keep a close eye on their three girls.

To her relief, Kit turned out to be quite right. Not everyone was step-perfect with the dances, so it didn't matter if she occasionally went wrong. In fact, misstepping turned out to be the cause of great hilarity amongst the dancers.

Time ticked on. She managed to glimpse Kit from time to time, but never close enough to speak to. When supper was announced some time after midnight, the young man she'd had the last dance with led her through and took a seat beside her at the supper table.

Archibald Hatherleigh's skin boasted plentiful pimples, but his kind-hearted face radiated pride that it was he who could lead her into supper.

The light dinner at Ormonde felt a long time ago, so, what with all the dancing, Morvoren was feeling quite hungry by midnight, but she'd not expected such a spread. Platters of cold chicken and ham lay out on the long table beside whole poached salmon and glazed vegetables. There were salads and fruits fresh from Denby's hot houses, pies, trifles in individual dishes, biscuits, and cake, as well as an array of different cheeses and a tureen of pale soup. If only she weren't wearing these infernal stays, she could have done justice to such a banquet.

Her young escort, although a bit tongue-tied to begin with, soon relaxed after a couple of glasses of wine and at Morvoren's prompting recounted his life story. Although her interest in him as a suitor, which, by the look of adoration on his face he fancied himself as, was less than nil, she listened with interest to tales of his schooldays at Eton and the "japes" he seemed so proud of.

"Of course, when I was a senior boy, I had a fag of my own to run my errands, which was worth it after so long being one myself. It meant I could wield some power over the younger boys and go out into town whenever I wanted."

A fag? Oh, of course. She'd once read somewhere that the older boys at Eton all had younger boys as servants. Was that where Kit had been schooled? Was it anything like the Eton of the twenty-first century? She hoped not, for the sake of modern schoolboys. An awful lot of birching seemed to have gone on in Mr. Hatherleigh's day, some of it done by the older boys themselves. It all sounded a bit *Lord of the Flies*.

Despite her curiosity, it was hard to concentrate properly on his stories of days spent foxhunting, as part way through the meal she spotted Kit at the far end of the long dining table, bearing company to Lady Elizabeth Carlyon, the huge feather adorning her hairdo bobbing well above the table and interfering with the servants. She'd have made a good figurehead on a ship.

Narrowing her eyes, Morvoren took a better look at her. It was easy to see why Kit's uncle had seduced her, if he truly had. Beneath the veneer of pouchy middle age lurked the bone structure of a beautiful woman, a little faded around the edges by time, but nevertheless, still something worth staring at. Kit was laughing at something she'd said, so perhaps she was a wit as well.

After supper, Morvoren kept a weather eye on Jasper, who bestirred himself to seek her out and request the dance he'd earlier set his heart on. Then, to her consternation, he straightaway requested a second dance. Ysella had expressly warned her that she wasn't to dance with any young man more than once, but hadn't given her any advice as to what to do if a request for this came her way. So Morvoren, who had a gap in her dance card, had no defenses prepared when he asked.

And he was no young man but someone old enough to have been her father. His acquisitive eyes gave her the definite creeps as they roved over her body throughout the dance, and she'd never been gladder that none of the dances involved being taken in his arms. That would have been too awful for words. There was something to be said for the ban on dancing the waltz.

After that second dance, Morvoren finally managed to get a moment with Ysella, in between dances, who seemed agog with excitement. "Lord Flint has danced with you twice!" she gasped, drawing Morvoren into one of the curtained alcoves. "And you know what that means!"

Morvoren didn't. Kit and Ysella had neglected to inform her of every little nicety of dancing etiquette, or rather, of their possible consequences. Over by the refreshments the marquess himself was watching Morvoren over a glass of punch, his father by his side. She had the uneasy feeling they were talking about her, probably as though she were a brood mare they were considering purchasing.

"That I shouldn't have?" she asked. "You did tell me to only dance once with any man, but I couldn't think of an excuse the second time he asked me, and I had no other name on my card. What was I supposed to do? Doesn't *he* know the rules?"

"Why," Ysella exclaimed in a loud hiss that probably carried to the far side of the dance floor and set nearby heads turning. "Of course he does. Don't you *know* what it means?"

Double glass doors within the alcove opened onto a wide, flagstone terrace dotted with empty chairs and tables, the lights from the ballroom spilling through the windows the only thing illuminating it now the lanterns had gone out. Morvoren pulled Ysella through the doors to where they couldn't be overheard. "What *does* it mean?"

"If a gentleman should dance more than once with you, then you're as good as engaged." She frowned. "Although I *had* wanted you for Kit, I do think a marquess who will become a duke before too long is probably a better match, *if* a good match is what you would like. Mama would certainly think so, if it were for me. Even if he is so old… and fat."

Morvoren's eyes widened. "But I don't want to be a marquess's wife, whatever one of those is called, nor a duchess."

"I'm sure he must intend to propose to you," Ysella went on, unfazed by Morvoren's heartfelt declaration. "Or he would not have asked you to dance twice, as he did. The marquess is very proper, and he knows full well what dancing with you twice means, and that people here tonight will have remarked on it. He'll assume you know it as well, and that in accepting, you've virtually agreed to be his." Her brow furrowed. "Perhaps Mama would say that you have let yourself get into something of a pickle."

Morvoren scowled at her. "Well, I don't want to marry him at all. And if I'd known dancing with him twice would lead to this, then I'd have refused him on the spot. And if he asks me to marry him, which seems highly unlikely on the acquaintance of just two dances, then I shall turn him down. When I marry, it will be for love, and even if I'd known the marquess more than a few hours, I doubt very much that I could ever love him."

Ysella's face lit up. "Oh, I hoped you'd say that. In fact, I might have guessed you would, dear Morvoren. You are such an original, which is no doubt why the marquess is so attracted to you. All the young men have been clamoring to dance with you. I've been watching."

"And you," Morvoren said, her mood lightening a little now she was out of the marquess's line of vision. "You've been quite a success as well." The light shining from the ballroom windows showed Ysella blushing. "Has anyone asked to dance twice with you?"

She fanned herself looking coy.

Even out here the air remained warm, despite the hour. In the east, the sky was turning pink so it must surely be getting on for dawn. An overpowering longing for her bed swept over Morvoren and she sank down on one of the chairs.

Ysella sat beside her. "Several young gentlemen did ask, but luckily the dance they were after was already taken. I'm not such a ninny as to allow any of them to get the upper hand." She tilted her head to one side. "Not that I mean *you're* a ninny. You just didn't know. You need to learn the ways of politely refusing, such as claiming to be too faint or tired to dance, perhaps mentioning that your foot is too sore because the last gentleman you danced with trod on it so many times. That sort of thing."

She giggled. "There are so many ways a girl can say no without actually saying the word when an outright refusal is tantamount to saying you will not dance at all, with anyone. And wouldn't that be a shame when dancing is such delightful fun?"

Nice to be told now, after the fact. Another wave of tiredness drenched Morvoren. "I think I shall remain out here in the quiet and cool for a while," she said. "It's so hot in the ballroom and I'm feeling exhausted by all that dancing." she patted Ysella's hand. "You can safely leave me sitting here, as I can see you're desperate to get back inside to your young admirers."

Ysella threw a longing glance over her shoulder at the open doors, through which the sound of joyful music still cascaded, clearly torn.

"Well, I'm not sure you *should* be out here on your own, but it would be worse if you were with a gentleman, so perhaps I *shall* go back inside. You should have some peace to rest out here. No one else comes outside, usually, at this time of the morning. Don't go to sleep, will you?" She giggled. "I'll come and find you when they serve breakfast. It can't be long now."

Morvoren shook her head. "Don't worry. I won't fall asleep. But my feet are truly sore, although I trod on more feet than trod on mine, and my legs are aching. And on top of that, I need this cooler air to refresh me. You go back inside, Ysella. I'm used to being on my own where I come from. I'll be fine."

With only one slightly guilty backward glance, Ysella slipped back through the open glass doors leaving Morvoren to her own company.

Oh, the bliss of the cooler air across her skin, of the scent of roses from the gardens below the terrace and the muting of the incessant dance music. She must be feeble indeed if she couldn't dance the night away like an eighteen-year-old. Perhaps twenty-three was over the hill.

Despite her promise not to fall asleep, she put her arms on the table and rested her head on them. She just needed to close her eyes for a few minutes.

The clearing of a throat disturbed her reverie. Blinking in confusion, she pushed herself upright and stared at the figure before her. Jasper, Marquess of Flint, stood on the opposite side of the table. Even in her sleepy state, Morvoren recognized the look of lust in his eyes. Uh oh.

KIT

THE BALL DRAGGED past after that glorious first dance with Morvoren, and Kit deeply regretted having claimed it so early. By doing so he'd precluded himself from requesting a second dance without raising the eyebrows of all the stately mamas gathered in the seats about the perimeter of the ballroom. The mamas who wanted him for their own insipid daughters.

If only he were bold enough to laugh in their faces and write his name down for every dance on her card, so no other man could partner her. But he couldn't. No matter how much his heart ached for her, he couldn't subject her to the dangers of the life he lived. And besides which, he'd now decided to return to Cornwall in just a few hours time, so it would be unfair and ungentlemanly to let her think him interested. Even if his heart cried out to do so.

He'd aimed at least to seek Morvoren out to lead her into supper, but his plans were thwarted by his mother's request that he should escort Lady Elizabeth in while she herself went in on the arm of Lady Elizabeth's despicable brother, Jasper.

Then, after supper, to Kit's utter horror, Jasper begged two dances one after another from Morvoren, who accepted with a polite smile on her face as though she were encouraging his suit. Was the girl mad, or out to snare herself a duke's heir? In the eyes of most girls, a prospective duke must be a far better catch than a lowly viscount, but he'd not thought her that calculating.

Damn and blast it. Jasper had just returned from London where he'd been on the search for a new young bride to give him his longed for son. Did he think Morvoren, with her healthy glow and strong build, would fit the bill? Her beauty would be the icing on the cake for a man like that. After marrying for money to bolster his father's ailing estate the first time, it seemed Jasper was out to please himself this time around. And it looked as though Morvoren had set her cap at him.

He glared at her from afar as she whirled around in Jasper's hold, her face alight with a pleasure that twisted his heart.

Unable to tear his eyes away, he brooded, a heavy frown settling on his brow. Did he have the right to be this angry? He hadn't, after all, declared his intentions in any way, so she would not feel bound to him. In fact, he'd done his best to steer well clear of showing any preference for her this week, treating her much as he treated his sister. She still puzzled him, and he'd been telling himself, repeatedly as though to convince himself, that his fascination for her was just his need to untangle her mystery.

But he'd been a fool. Right from the moment he'd pulled her from the water he'd felt something drawing him to her. Wasn't that the reason he'd offered her the hospitality of Ormonde? And yet he'd kept her at arm's length as long as he could, telling himself that with his dangerous double-life he couldn't afford to become embroiled in a love affair. Only that minx Ysella insisting that he should help teach their guest to dance had brought down the barriers he'd erected between them.

She was such fun, so full of laughter, but so sensible in many ways. Good for Ysella, despite the affair of the riding astride, which, in all honesty, he could quite understand. And even his mother had come around to liking her, a difficult obstacle for any girl to overcome.

He shook his head. He'd missed his chance now though. A marquess had turned her head. If only Denby had not invited them to this ball…

He went into the card room and played a few hands of five card loo, losing moderately but breaking even in the end.

It was some time before he emerged into the ballroom again.

A promenade around the exterior with his eyes on the dance floor did not reveal Morvoren anywhere. Ysella was dancing with a young army officer, his mother was sitting chattering to his aunt, and his cousin Fitzwilliam was leading a rosy-cheeked young lady over to the refreshments. So where had Morvoren got to?

Automatically he sought out Jasper, who had been noticeably absent from his favorite haunt of the gaming room, but did not find him. A prickle of misgiving slid down his back. Had Flint sequestered

Morvoren somewhere private, as so often happened at balls? If so, was it a meeting by mutual consent? He nearly didn't continue with his search, and would not have, had he not felt that misgiving grow.

He strode onto the dance floor where Ysella and the officer were standing still while another couple danced, and leaned in close to her ear. "Where is Morvoren?"

She peeked up at him. "Outside. I left her resting on the terrace. She's quite safe. No one else is there."

He flashed an angry glare at her. "You should know better than to have abandoned her alone outside. How long ago did you do that?"

Ysella had the grace to look guilty. "Barely a quarter of an hour, Kit. She said she would be all right on her own, and Mr. Hartnell had the next dance with me. I'm sure she's fine."

"I'll deal with you later, young lady," Kit snapped. "And if you're not careful this will be the last ball you ever go to."

Leaving Ysella open-mouthed, he forged his way with long strides across the dance floor and found the open doors onto the terrace. The sun was rising in the east but the tall trees that grew around one end of the terrace had left a pool of deep shadow. For a moment Kit struggled to accustom his eyes to the lack of light.

Then he saw her.

She was standing in a corner beside a table and chairs and she was not alone. A man towered over her and she had her back pressed up against the hard stone of the terrace balustrade. The man had one hand on her shoulder and the other about her waist. The man was Jasper.

Had he come upon an arranged rendezvous between two people intent on love? Upon a young woman determined to make the catch of the year? For a moment, Kit stood rooted to the spot, unable to move as he stared at the tableau before him. And then Morvoren's hand reached up and slapped Jasper across the face, her voice ringing out across the cool air. "Leave me alone."

Kit was across the terrace in a trice. He seized Jasper's shoulder and swung him around before he could think about what he was doing. His right hand balled into a fist as he drew it back and planted it on Jasper's nose.

Jasper staggered back, releasing his hold on Morvoren, his hand going to where dark blood ran down his upper lip. His handsome, overblown face contorted in a sneer. "I'd call you out for that, you pup, were it not for the sake of my father."

Was the man a coward? Kit's blood boiled and he longed for the excuse to take Jasper on in a fight. Swords, not pistols. He was an accomplished swordsman himself and much preferred the cut and thrust of a good blade to the random behavior of a musket ball. But no, Jasper, the craven, no doubt remembering that he had no male heir as yet, was dabbing at his nose with his handkerchief and retreating hurriedly.

Kit turned back to where Morvoren still stood, leaning against the balustrade, her mouth a perfect *o* of surprise. She closed it as he turned, and a shaky smile lit her face. "I've never had a man do that for me before," she said.

Absurd woman. Kit swallowed. "Any gentleman would have done the same," he managed, then, to cover his own confusion about the way she was looking at him, "Did he... hurt you?"

She shook her head. "I may have a bruise where he grabbed my shoulder, but I have to say that I was about to knee him hard somewhere that would have hurt him far more than the blow you planted on his nose." She chuckled. "I've met worse predators than him where I come from."

So maybe her smile hadn't been so shaky.

Kit felt himself return her smile. "You are a conundrum, Morvoren," he said before he could stop himself. "I never know how to take you. Here you stand, moments after being almost dishonored, for I'm certain that was what Jasper had in mind out here alone with you, and yet you laugh as though nothing untoward has happened."

She moved away from the balustrade to the nearby table and chairs, but instead of taking a seat, she put her hands on the table and hoisted herself onto it in a most unladylike way, legs a little apart and slippered feet dangling, the early morning sunshine catching her eyes. "I am a product of my upbringing. And where I come from, ladies know how to look after themselves." She dimpled. "And we *all* ride astride."

"A veritable amazon."

She nodded, gazing up into his eyes. "You could say that, although we don't forsake all men as those legendary women did."

Was she laughing at him? Could she hear his heart thundering? The sound of it filled his ears, so surely, she could. How could she make him feel this way with just a few offhand words? Or were they? He longed to reach out to her, to take her in his arms and kiss those lips and maybe do more than that. But he couldn't, or he'd be as bad as Jasper, from whom he'd just rescued her. A sudden awareness swept over him of how alone on the terrace they were and of the pressing need to go back inside before someone caught them in a position that might look compromising. That definitely *would* be compromising.

He swallowed, unwilling to break the spell that had descended with the freshness of the new morning. One short step would bring him close enough to kiss her…

No, they had to go back inside. Breakfast would be served shortly. His mother would notice Morvoren's absence, and worse, his as well. Ysella needed watching lest she did something silly.

He gazed down into Morvoren's eyes, so like the color of the sapphire in her necklace, every part of him longing to take her in his arms and fighting with the knowledge that he mustn't.

Morvoren had no such reservations. She reached out and caught hold of the lapels of his coat. For a moment, he stood staring down at her hands, longing rising through his body in a wave of heat, and his desire pushing at his tight breeches.

Then, with a forceful tug, she pulled him forward that step he'd been so afraid to take. He was up against the table, standing improperly between her legs. His mouth went paper dry and the restriction in his breeches increased.

Her lips, so plump and kissable, parted slightly and the tip of her tongue darted around them. His knees went weak, his breeches became tighter still, and sweat prickled down his back and across his forehead. Why was he reacting like a green boy? Yes, he'd felt lust before, many times, and this was definitely lust, but it was also something else. A yearning for her to be his in every possible way.

She tugged on his lapels again, and he let his head bow forward as her mouth moved up to meet his.

Her lips were velvety soft on his, slightly apart, her tongue teasingly tickling. He gave in. He'd have had to have been a monk not to. He opened his mouth against hers and their tongues met, dancing over one another in a way he could only have dreamed of.

God! Kissing a girl for the first time had never been like this. Not even the very first girl he'd kissed when he'd still been at school. Nor the first bit o' muslin he'd been to at Oxford. Girls like that didn't want to kiss at all, just to get down to the act being paid for. He'd kissed a good few girls since—none of them young ladies of the *ton*, of course—but none had kissed him back like this. As though they wanted him and only him in every single way.

He didn't want this to end. His arms went around Morvoren pressing her close, her hands left his lapels and her fingers ran through his hair, pressing his face to hers, as though she wanted him to melt into her body. Oh, for this to never end, and for him not to have to forget her and go back to Cornwall in a scant few hours.

Chapter Twenty-Five

MORVOREN

MORVOREN LAY IN bed, unable to sleep thanks to the thoughts about last night tumbling over themselves in her head. And enjoying the tumultuous feeling of unrest that was knotting her stomach. They'd arrived home late, or was that early? Whatever it was, it had been full daylight, and, after hot chocolate and toast, Lady Ormonde had decreed, with a benevolent smile, that "her girls" should retire to their rooms to sleep.

Loveday, fresh as a daisy after a good night's sleep, had removed Morvoren's finery and tucked her up in bed with the heavy curtains in her room firmly drawn against the light. Whether Ysella was asleep or not, Morvoren had no idea, but if she'd had half as good a night as she had, then probably not.

She glanced at the light around the edges of the curtains. It was no use. She couldn't sleep. Not after what had happened on the terrace. Yes, she'd made the first move, as any twenty-first-century girl would have done. If she'd waited for gentleman Kit to kiss her, she'd be an old maid, for sure. He wasn't like Lord Flint, grasping and lecherous and desperate to snatch a kiss, or something more. Kit's diffidence had been pulsing out of him in alternate waves with his desire—an odd combination. It had been up to Morvoren to jump in.

And oh, what an experience it had been. She hugged herself at the memory. Yes, she'd naughtily moved her legs apart and pulled him close like that on purpose. And yes, she'd relished the feel of his arousal where it had pressed against her stomach even through the confines of her stays. That he was a young man who wanted her could not have been clearer. And once she'd kissed him, it was as though a dam had been released. Who'd have thought an upright, in more than one way at that particular moment, Regency gentleman capable of such passionate kisses. Not at all restrained Mr. Darcy.

It had been as though once kickstarted, he wanted to eat her up. Not that she didn't want to eat him up too, but she'd resisted the temptation to slide her hands down and casually brush his arousal. She didn't want to embarrass him. That could all too easily put a damper on what she was beginning to hope might be a relationship. Who'd want a fat old marquess when they could have a dashing young viscount with a bent for smuggling? What could be more romantic for a girl brought up on romantic novels and films?

Morvoren wriggled at the thought of seeing him again today. Of him kissing her again. Of his hands running over her body, even if over those horrid stays. Desire for him rose like a tidal wave and she shivered with excitement.

He was definitely not the cold fish she'd first thought him. Not that she'd thought that for some time now. Not since they'd begun her dancing lessons and they'd fallen laughing to the floor. A good ice breaker.

She lay on her back staring up at the four-poster bed's canopy, imagining what it would be like if he were to sneak into her bedroom right now, maybe wearing a silk dressing gown and nothing else, and slide into her bed. Another shiver ran through her body at that delectable thought. It had certainly felt like he had something down his trousers that would satisfy a girl, as long as he knew what to do with it.

Which set her mind off in another direction. What did men do for sex in this era? Did they make love to the society women they knew? Without having to marry them? Did they have affairs with safely married women? Or did they go to sex workers? Or keep a mistress? Did he, heaven forbid, have a mistress somewhere right now? A rather scary thought.

She wriggled again to get more comfortable, the feeling bubbling in her groin refusing to allow her to sleep. Never had she wanted a man as much as she wanted this one, and never had one been so inaccessible, hedged about by the social mores of his society. Or was he? Certainly, fat old Jasper had seemed to think he could steal more than a kiss. Maybe these people weren't so moralistic as she'd been led to believe. Maybe they all went about having sex with whomever they wanted? She certainly wanted sex with Kit. And soon.

Sunlight slanted across the floor of her room from between the curtains, and from outside came the sound of voices in the gardens. Servants, by the sound of them. How much easier it must be for them. No class etiquette to confine them, or not as much as the nobility appeared to have. Or maybe she was wrong on that one too. If only she'd done a history degree instead of an animal science one.

It was no good. She'd have to get up. Perhaps Kit hadn't retired to bed as the women had. He always seemed to have work to do. He was probably with Sam in the estate office right now. The urge to go to him and have him take her in his arms again blossomed in her heart, and elsewhere. She jumped out of bed and rang the bell for Loveday.

"But I thought you was havin' a rest in bed till this afternoon?" Loveday protested when she arrived, looking annoyed, as no doubt she'd been enjoying some time off without having to run around after Morvoren.

"I'm not tired," Morvoren said, taking off her nightgown and throwing it onto the bed. "I need to be up and dressed and doing something. Where are my clothes?"

Loveday hurriedly fetched her underslip and helped her into her stays. Before very long, Morvoren was dressed for the day in a blue-patterned muslin day gown, with Loveday fussing over her hair. The need for urgency pressed in on Morvoren for some reason, and she fidgeted under her maid's ministrations, impatient about the length of time it took a Regency young lady to do her toilette. Or rather, the length of time it took her lady's maid to do it.

"You can't be seen not properly dressed," Loveday chided.

At last, though, she was ready. On nervous feet, she descended the stairs into the hall and headed for the estate office at the back of the house near the servants' area. Outside the large oak door, she paused and tapped smartly on the silvery wood with her knuckles.

"Come in," called Sam's deep voice. Her breath catching in her throat at the prospect of seeing Kit again, Morvoren pushed open the door and went inside.

Sam was sitting alone at the large desk, the ledgers open in front of him.

She halted on the threshold, nonplused.

He smiled. "Can I help you, Miss Morvoren?"

She bit her lip. "I'd hoped to find Kit here with you."

His face fell. "Ah, well, I am afraid, as you see, that I must disappoint you. He's not here."

She stepped into the room, and the door swung shut behind her. "I can see that. Do you know where I might find him?"

Sam set down his pen. "Not here, I'm afraid. He set off for Cornwall no sooner was he back from the ball at Denby. He should be on the mail coach heading west even now."

What?

Morvoren's world swayed about her and, in a flash, Sam was up and fetching her a seat. "Lower your head if you're feeling faint," he suggested. "I'll fetch you a glass of water."

She didn't want the water, but she sipped it obediently when it came, her mind in a turmoil. And not because the man she fancied herself in love with had abandoned her. Oh no. The reason for her spinning head was the memory of that old fisherman's story of the smugglers who'd died and the painting in the tiny museum in Penzance of one of the victims who'd died on the beach at Nanpean. The painting of Kit. If only she knew the date of the attack.

"What ails you?" Sam was asking, his words finally breaking through the whirl of fears churning inside Morvoren's head. "I don't think you should have risen from your bed until this afternoon. You must be overtired."

She shook her head and put the glass of water on his desk. "I'm not tired at all. I have to go. Thank you, Sam, for your help."

She rose unsteadily to her feet and, despite Sam's worried frown, hurried out of the room. As soon as she was away from him, she ran, across the hall, up the stairs and into Ysella's room. The heavy curtains were drawn tighter than hers had been, and the room was in darkness. Without hesitation, she hastened across the thick rugs and snatched the curtains apart, letting the late morning light come spilling in.

Then she turned to the bed and, grabbing Ysella by the shoulders, gave her a good shake.

Ysella woke up straightaway, turning bleary eyes on her attacker. "Whatever is it, Morvoren? Goodness, is it afternoon already?" She pushed herself upright in bed, looking very pretty with her fluffed up dark hair and sleep befuddled face.

"It's Kit," Morvoren said, desperation edging her voice. "He's gone back to Cornwall."

Ysella rubbed her eyes and frowned. "Does that matter? He's more often there than he is here. I think in truth, he's only stayed here over a week because of your presence." A smile chased the frown away. "Are you certain he's gone back to Cornwall?"

Morvoren nodded. "Sam told me. We have to go after him."

"What?" Now she was really awake. "Why ever do we have to do that? He'll be perfectly fine in Cornwall. He doesn't need us down there. And it's such a long way." Her cheeks flushed pink. "And Lieutenant William Beaumont who was at the ball has promised to call on me, I mean on Mama, tomorrow. We can't go haring off after Kit just like that for no reason." She narrowed her eyes. "Even if you are more than half in love with him."

"Yes, he does need us," Morvoren snapped, ignoring the last part of her speech. The terror rose that if she told Ysella the truth, her friend would only think her mad and perhaps call her mother and have her confined in a madhouse from where she'd never be able to save Kit.

"How so?" She drew her knees up and put her arms around them. "You'd best tell me why you think that."

At least she was prepared to listen. Morvoren drew a deep breath. Her heart thundered with fear. She could think of no reason why Ysella wouldn't think her mad and run and tell her mother. However, in for a penny... "The reason I'm not like you is because I wasn't born in this world. I'm from the future."

Ysella stared, the frown returning and deepening. "The future? Do you mean from next week? How funny you are. I said you were an original and I was quite right. I generally am."

Morvoren shook her head. "No, not from next week. From over two hundred years in the future. That's why I've been to university and can ride astride and couldn't dance. That's the absolute truth."

Ysella drew in her bottom lip, studying Morvoren's face, perhaps for signs of madness. Once or twice she opened her mouth, perhaps to put a thought into words, but then closed it again. Eventually, she reached out a hand and laid it on Morvoren's. "For some reason I don't understand, I think I believe you. I have no idea why. I must be as mad as you. Tell me everything."

Thank goodness she at least wasn't laughing at this revelation. But that didn't mean she was going to believe everything Morvoren had to tell her. She would just have to take the risk, because she couldn't get down to Cornwall to save Kit without the help of someone else, and by far the best person to ask was his excitable sister.

So she told her. Starting with the dreadful holiday with Josh, whom she'd not spared a thought for in over a week, and describing the abortive fishing trip and her dip in the sea. Clasping her hands to prevent them shaking, she recounted her theory that there'd been a doorway into Ysella and Kit's world beneath the waves and how Kit had saved her life.

"But the day before I fell into the sea," she said, coming to the crux of her story, "I went to the museum in Penzance. There was a display about the revenue men's raids on the local bands of smugglers—"

"You mean the free traders," Ysella put in.

"All right, the free traders. One of the raids was on Nanpean Cove, in 1811. That's this year. All the smugglers—the free traders—were captured. Three were killed, shot I suppose, down on the beach, and the rest were tried then hanged at Bodmin jail." Morvoren paused, fixing Ysella's rapt face with a hard stare. "There was a copy of a painting of one of the smu—free traders. It was Kit. A copy of the portrait that hangs in the great hall here. Kit was—*is* one of the free traders who'll be killed on the beach. There's a traitor in their midst who's going to betray them to the revenue men and the soldiers. Who might already have done so."

When Morvoren finished, Ysella sucked in her lips and stared, her hands tight on Morvoren's still, her breasts heaving. Did she believe this? Morvoren had thought she did, but now she wasn't so sure.

"Are you certain Kit will be killed?" Ysella asked at last.

Morvoren nodded. "His name was mentioned in the information. At the time, I didn't know how important it was going to be for me to remember the details. I saw he was a free trader, but I didn't realize the man who rescued me was the person who was going to be killed on the beach. Not until I saw his picture in your great hall. But I do now."

Ysella's hand went to her mouth as she swung her legs out of bed. "The Lawrence portrait in the great hall? You saw that in… in the future? In a museum in Cornwall?"

Morvoren nodded. "I recognized it as soon as I saw it. It just reinforced my conclusion that Kit would be in danger if he were to return to Cornwall."

"Did you warn him?"

Morvoren shook her head. "You're the only one I've been able to tell. I didn't know he was going to go back to Cornwall so soon. I thought he was staying here." She didn't say she'd been more than convinced he would stay after what had happened between them last night. Ysella didn't need to know that. "I thought I had plenty of time to tell him later. I… I thought that if I told him he'd just think me completely mad." She looked down at her hands. "I see now that I should have been braver."

Ysella's turn to shake her head. "He wouldn't have listened. Despite the sometimes-stuffy way he behaves, Kit's always been one to laugh in the face of danger. And you're quite right—he probably wouldn't have believed you. I'm not at all sure why I do. Maybe it's because you've never told me an untruth, and… you taught me to ride astride. I see that in the future, ladies must have a *lot* more freedom."

"And no stays." Morvoren chewed her lower lip. "I just wish I'd taken in everything the display said about the revenue men and the smugglers. For all we know, Kit will be quite safe now because the raids won't be for months. If only I asked the captain of the fishing boat a few questions. But I didn't, because I was feeling too frightened being on his boat, and just thinking of myself. And when I was in the museum, I was cross with Josh for leaving me and going off fishing on the harbor wall. I didn't pay proper attention as I should have. All I can remember is that it was some time in 1811."

Ysella rang the bell for Martha. "So, you think it could be any time this year?"

Morvoren pressed her lips together. "It could, but I don't think it is. I think I must have fallen through the door at the right time to save his life. What other reason could there be? It couldn't have been random, could it? I have to be here for a reason."

But did she? Or was she falling into the trap of reading purpose in the random happenings of the universe? Was there no such thing as fate?

"Well," Ysella said, beaming. "We shall just have to get down there as fast as we can and save his sorry soul. Even if it isn't quite yet in need of saving. If both of us tell him the same thing, he'll have to believe us, and he can catch the traitor before he commits the betrayal."

At that moment, Martha arrived and, with as disapproving an expression as Loveday and protesting that Ysella should be staying in bed, helped her mistress dress. Morvoren sat and watched, itching at the delay as Martha did Ysella's hair. She couldn't hurry her as they'd both decided to take no chances and not involve any of the servants if they could avoid it.

As soon as Martha departed, Ysella ran to her wardrobe and fetched out a sizeable bag. "Go and pack a valise," she said. "And best to put in our boys' clothes, just in case. This is going to be a wonderful adventure, but we should leave for Cornwall before Mama wakes, which means we only have a few hours. Hurry!"

Chapter Twenty-Six

KIT

THE MAIL COACH and all its discomforts, barely more than a week after his last journey, was not pleasing Kit greatly. Neither was having to share the return journey to Cornwall with his cousin, who had appeared at the inn just as the coach arrived, heavy eyed and hungover from the night before. And especially not as the other two inside seats were occupied by an enormously fat parson and his sour faced daughter who appeared to be going all the way to Exeter.

"What a surprise to find you also on your way to Cornwall," the captain said, raising his elegant eyebrows at Kit. "You seem unable to keep away from it, even with the temptations of Miss Lucas to keep you at Ormonde." His knowing smile, as though perhaps he'd been spying on Kit when he'd been alone on the terrace with Morvoren, brought heat to Kit's cheeks. "But you were always like that as a boy, if I remember rightly. Cornwall, Cornwall, Cornwall. All you'd ever talk about at school. So very dull."

Kit grunted a reply and settled back in his seat with his eyes firmly closed. If sleep wouldn't come, he'd pretend it had.

At every stop for a change of horses, Kit availed himself of the chance to get out and stretch his legs, glad to breathe in some air not tainted with the strong odor of hot bodies that pervaded in the coach. Only the fact that he could try to sleep off his own exhaustion prevented him from opting to ride on the top of the vehicle in the fresh air with the two gentlemen already seated with the guard and driver.

The captain made no further attempts to involve him in conversation but settled back in his own corner, legs outstretched, annoyingly able to sleep like the proverbial baby. But then, he probably wasn't troubled by thoughts of Morvoren the way Kit was. Thoughts that every time he began to doze off resurfaced in alluring images that danced before his eyes.

At last, however, the coach rumbled into Exeter and drew up in the square outside the same inn Kit had caught it from just over a week ago. With mixed feelings, he descended from the coach and joined the captain and the fat parson and his daughter in walking into the inn.

It being evening, and with the driver of the Penzance coach already ensconced in the room the coaching company commanded for him, he had a room of his own to book. The coach would be heading west first thing in the morning.

Luckily, the landlord had rooms enough for all the travelers.

"And make sure the bed has been properly aired," Kit said, fixing the landlord with a fierce glare. "And that the sheets were clean on today." He paid out some coin. "And I'll take supper in my room."

Two hours later, he was in his room taking off his clothes to get into a bed that had indeed been fully aired by the landlord's buxom daughter with a warming pan. She'd also brought him his supper and a bottle of brandy that he doubted any excise duty had been paid on, and given him a come-to-bed wink he'd ignored.

Good thing too. The brandy, not the come-to-bed wink. He liked to believe that the little he was doing on the tip of Cornwall was generating extra income for his local villagers, who regularly risked their lives to bring in the contraband goods and distribute them. And if contraband brandy, whoever had brought it in and wherever it had come ashore, was getting as far east as Exeter, that could only be of profit for the people of Nanpean.

He sighed. He liked to tell himself that the reason he took part in Jago's smuggling activities was to help the poverty he'd been seeing since he was a boy. However, a sneaking part of him might just be forced to admit that he also did it for the adventure. That he liked from time to time to sail over to France or the Channel Islands and select goods himself, or to bring back someone escaping Boney's bloody regime.

In his time, Jago had brought back a fair few Frenchies, and as a boy, Kit had accompanied him on many trips. Although some time had now passed since either of them had been called upon to repeat their rescue missions. Kit had more than an inkling that his mother suspected him of clandestine activities. After all, she'd grown up in the household of smugglers. Had his father known? Most likely. But he couldn't ask him now, and he certainly wasn't going to ask his mother.

Kicking off his boots, and still in his shirt and breeches, he threw himself down on his bed, which set his candle guttering, and put his hands behind his head. And, of course, the first thing that jumped into his mind was the one thing he didn't want to think of. Morvoren.

Despite a battle to exclude her, she'd been haunting his thoughts throughout every waking moment of the journey, and her face had populated what dreams he'd snatched. Her face, her lips, her hands in his hair. Her tongue on his, the way she'd pulled him against her, making it impossible for him to hide his body's reaction to hers. How it hadn't shocked her at all. How she'd slid her hands inside his coat, the touch of her fingers through the thin linen of his shirt like tendrils of fire.

And now, with those disturbing memories, his breeches were uncomfortable again. He made an unhelpful effort to readjust himself and closed his eyes. He needed to rest. In the last thirty-six hours he'd had about three hours of sleep and none of it had been more than a half-hour nap at a time. He was exhausted, but Morvoren refused to leave him. What wouldn't he give to have her open the door right now and come into his room? She'd sit on the edge of his bed and bend over and…

This was no good, he'd never get to sleep this way. He had to put her out of his mind. She wasn't for him. With what he was doing so regularly now, and the dangers it entailed, he couldn't afford to get involved with any woman. It was too much to ask of a young lady to accept a man like him, a man who was breaking the laws of the land on a regular basis. Who risked execution if caught. He had to forget about her and pray she'd forget about him.

He rolled onto his side and blew out his candle, but the darkness didn't dispel his disquiet. Oh, how he wanted that girl, with a longing that refused to be ignored. His body ached for her, and so did his heart. She was so refreshingly different—unlike any other girl he'd ever met. And *that* only made him want her all the more.

No. He had to put her out of his mind and leave his mother and Ysella to take care of her. He'd left a note for his mother explaining that he'd needed to go back and deal with business he'd had to leave unfinished at Carlyon Court when he'd brought Morvoren to Ormonde. He'd written that he'd be away at least another month, and asked her to take care of Morvoren and see if she could locate some family or friends for her.

Or a husband.

It had been painful to write that. So much so, his hand had shaken, and he'd badly blotted the paper. With any luck she'd be gone by the time he returned to Ormonde. Only that thought didn't make him happy either.

With an angry huff, he rolled onto his front. Big mistake. Even more uncomfortable. He returned to lying on his back again and did some more breeches readjustment. Better.

And now he really did need to get to sleep. If she'd let him…

Morvoren

Ysella and Morvoren tiptoed downstairs carrying their valises. A moment of inspiration on Ysella's part had been to inform their two maids that they would be staying with Miss Caroline Fairchild whose own maid would be taking care of them, so neither Loveday nor Martha was needed. They'd already dispatched Martha to order four horses to be harnessed to the carriage they'd travelled to the ball in. It was only when they reached the foot of the stairs that something important dawned on Morvoren. "We don't have any money."

Ysella turned wide eyes on her, one hand to her mouth. "You're right. We don't. And we're going to need some, I'm certain. What are we going to do?"

Morvoren had stopped dead. "We won't get far if we can't buy food along the way. It's going to be a long journey, and we'll need changes of horses just like the mail coach does. That won't be free."

"And for tollgates and things like that," Ysella said with a groan. "Why didn't I think of that before now?" She gazed around the hallway as though one of the paintings on the walls might give her inspiration.

"We'll have to ask Sam," Morvoren said. "He was in the office earlier, and he'll have access to money. We'll get him to give us some. How much do you think we'll need?"

Ysella shrugged, and hefting her valise set off toward the office without another word.

Sam was still there, head bent over the ledgers, but he looked up when they came in and, rising to his feet, bowed first to Ysella and then to Morvoren. "Good morning, Miss Ysella, Miss Morvoren." A very formal young man.

Ysella didn't beat about the bush. "We need money, Sam. How much have you got?"

Sam blinked a couple of times, no doubt at the abruptness of her question. "I do have money in the strong box," he said, sounding cautious, "for the staff wages next week. I can advance you a pound or two of pin money from that if you wish to drive into Marlborough for some shopping." He didn't sound all that confident. Had he guessed they had an ulterior motive?

"That won't be enough," Ysella said. "And we don't want it for shopping."

Morvoren kicked her.

She flashed a scowl. "We're going to Caroline Fairchild's for a few days and will need to…" she hesitated, "…to tip her servants and buy her some presents. And… and go to the theatre." She must be trawling for the most expensive activities she could think of.

How unlikely did that sound, though?

Sam clearly thought so as well. "I'm afraid I can't let you have more than a pound or two. Not with Kit away. He's very exacting about the allowance he gives you, Miss Ysella, and I'm not allowed to give you more than a pound or two in excess of it. Plus, there'd be mutiny below stairs if I were to let you spend the staff's wages on fripperies."

"Don't tell him," Morvoren whispered to Ysella.

Ysella ignored her. "It's a matter of life and death. We're not really going to Caro's. We have to follow Kit down to Cornwall immediately, or he'll be in the worst possible deadly danger. The worst you can imagine. It's up to us to rescue him."

Sam's sandy brows shot up. "I don't understand. What deadly danger can Kit be in? He's only gone down to Carlyon Court. There's nothing dangerous there."

Luckily, he hadn't yet latched onto the fact that they were planning a journey by themselves in pursuit of his employer.

Ysella sighed and glanced at Morvoren. "I'll have to tell him," she said, with a martyred air. "He won't help us unless I do, and we can't go alone with no money."

"He won't believe us," Morvoren hissed, turning away in the faint hope that Sam wouldn't hear her. "He'll think I'm mad. He'll have me locked up."

"What won't I believe?" Sam asked.

Ysella ignored him and shook her head. "Nonsense. *I* don't think you're mad, so *he* won't. We have to tell him, Morvoren. Or who knows what's going to happen to Kit."

Morvoren sighed. "All right, but it's against my better judgement and if he locks us in our rooms afterwards and sends for the doctor, don't be surprised."

So they told him. Coming from both of them at the same time, the tale took a lot longer to tell than when Morvoren had recounted it to Ysella. With that young lady's constant tangential contributions to the story, poor Sam had a job getting the facts straight in his head. She would keep interrupting, usually at the wrong point with something irrelevant. But at last, Sam had the full story.

He looked Morvoren up and down, an incredulous expression on his face, then back at Ysella. "You want me to *believe* this fairy story?"

"I told you so," Morvoren snapped at Ysella. What were they going to do now? Any second he'd be sending for the doctor who'd prescribe bleeding and something to cool their nerves.

"It's all perfectly true," Ysella pleaded. "And the painting of Kit proves it. Morvoren saw it in the museum before she came here. She recognized Kit from it and then the painting itself when she saw it in the hall. How could she have done that if it weren't true?"

"Lots of ways," Sam said, brow furrowing. "She could have made it up, for a start." He shook his head. "And how ridiculous is it to accuse Kit, Lord Ormonde, of being hand in glove with a bunch of smugglers. That in itself proves this is a faradiddle."

"It's *not* a faradiddle," Morvoren said, having decided that now they'd told Sam it was up to her to convince him. No going back. She couldn't sit in a straitjacket while Kit was in danger, which was where she'd be if she didn't find a way to win Sam to their side. "Because I've *seen* the smugglers at Nanpean, at Jago's farm. The night I had to spend there, strange noises woke me up. I looked out of the window and saw a column of pack ponies coming up from the beach. They came right into the farmyard and were met by Kit and Jago. They were expecting them, I think. Either that or they both came up from the beach along with the smugglers. I couldn't tell."

"Your imagination. A dream." Sam shook his head and put a hand to one of his temples. "You hallucinated. You're a hysterical woman."

Morvoren put her hands on her hips. "I did *not*, and I am *not*." Although she would be in a minute if he didn't see reason. "Kit was out there with them as were Jenifry and Loveday. While I was peering out, he glanced up at my window. I thought he'd seen me. I ran back to bed and pretended to be asleep. Just as well, because he came upstairs and opened my bedroom door. I was terrified. But he just stood for a while looking down at me." She paused for effect. "I thought he was going to kill me."

Ysella let out a gasp, as she well might, because Morvoren hadn't told her this part of the story and was only telling Sam in an effort to convince him.

Sam bit his lip.

Had she succeeded? She waited.

He heaved a heartfelt sigh, his shoulders sagging. "You can't go alone."

"Of course we can," retorted Ysella. "We'll have our driver and we'll take another of the servants with us, armed with muskets or pistols or some such from the gun room. We'll be quite safe, but we do need some money or we won't be able to pay the tollgates, nor buy food, nor if we have to stop, acquire a room for the night. We could trade on Kit's good name and offer to leave a promissory note, but I fear not all innkeepers will be willing to accept one."

"No, you can't." Sam folded his arms across his chest. "Not two women on your own. I'll have to come with you. As your escort. Are you taking your maids?"

Morvoren and Ysella shook their heads in unison. "We're going to be maids for each other," Morvoren said. "We didn't want to involve too many servants."

"And besides, Martha's such a tattletale, she would've gone straight to tell Mama," Ysella put in. "I'm leaving a note to say we've gone to Caro's. Just as we told you we were doing. A fib, I know, but one made out of necessity as Mama would undoubtedly not believe us and refuse to allow us to go."

"Your brother is quite correct when he calls you a minx," Sam said. "Is the carriage being prepared?"

Morvoren nodded. "We just need the money for the journey—and you, as you've so kindly said you'd accompany us."

He got up from the table, closing the ledger as he did. "Very well. Go down to the stable courtyard and load your valises onto the carriage and I'll throw a few things into a bag—including the money—and meet you down there in ten minutes. Quickly now. If Miss Morvoren is correct, we may have no time to lose."

Heaving a heartfelt sigh, Morvoren grabbed Ysella's hand and together they hurried to the stable yard to see if James the coachman had the carriage ready. He and another two lads were busy harnessing the horses.

Ysella pulled James to one side. "We are not going to Miss Fairchild's," she hissed. "We're following Kit to Cornwall, so make sure you have your travelling things with you. And send one of those lads to the gunroom to fetch Mr. Beauchamp some pistols. Loaded ones. We shall need to be able to defend ourselves. And we'll take one of the grooms with us, so tell whichever you choose to arm you and himself as well."

At precisely two o'clock, the striking of the stable yard clock marked their departure, as the carriage bearing Ysella, Morvoren, and a still dubious Sam rolled out through the stable archway. High on the driver's seat, James, the coachman, sat resplendent in his livery, with an armed guard, not nearly so smartly outfitted, beside him. They were off at last.

Oh, for a fast car. Or a motorbike. Or a train. Their progress was from the start annoyingly slow. They might have good horses, but that didn't mean they would make as good progress as the mail coach, which Sam said could manage a lightning ten miles per hour. What speed. Not.

And they were handicapped by a driver who cared about his horses. Unlike the mail coach drivers, who knew they would be getting replacements every ten miles and were driven by the need to get from A to B inside a certain time. Not so their driver, no matter how much Ysella exhorted him to go faster.

In the end, when they stopped at an inn for their first drop of sustenance, James took the opportunity to point out the facts to Ysella. "These're good horses, Miss Ysella, belonging to his lordship. I won't hammer 'em. He wouldn't thank me for doin' it, an' he'd be mad with you for makin' me. You want to get there, don't you? Well, let me drive 'em at a pace they can keep to. We'll have to get a change of horses at some point, but the longer these can keep going, the better, because they're good horses. Anythin' we change 'em for won't be near such good quality."

So, Morvoren and Ysella had to control their impatience and sit back inside the carriage as first the Wiltshire, and then at last the Somerset, countryside crawled past.

As the evening sun sank toward the hills, Morvoren could only worry about how much faster Kit's mail coach must be going. By now, he must already be in Exeter and perhaps even on the coach back to Penzance. It might at this moment be carrying him inexorably on to Nanpean and the looming threat of danger. Maybe Ysella and Sam had the same thoughts, but they didn't share them. A frustrated silence fell between the passengers.

Night had fallen by the time they trotted into a little town Sam said was Yeovil. The Yeovil of 1811 was tiny, although in possession of a fine coaching inn. With all of them, including the horses, exhausted, Sam insisted they should stop for the night.

"You ladies had no sleep last night and barely any rest this morning," he pointed out. "And neither of you has managed to sleep in the carriage, so don't tell me you're able to keep going because you're not. And neither are our horses. Everyone needs a night's rest."

Against her better judgement, but barely able to keep her eyes open, Morvoren agreed. For all she knew, no smuggling was planned until the next moonless night, and Kit was safer than they were. Surely a night's sleep would do no harm? So, after a meal of boiled beef and over-cooked vegetables that she could barely nibble, Ysella and Morvoren stripped each other to their shifts, dabbed cold water on their hot bits and flopped into the narrow and lumpy double bed that had been provided. Morvoren was asleep as soon as her head hit the pillow.

Chapter Twenty-Seven

KIT

PROMPTLY AT NINE o'clock the next morning, after a breakfast of cold beef and ale, Kit caught the coach that would be heading via Falmouth to Penzance and beyond. Glad to find his cousin no longer among the passengers, he settled himself down into the shabby interior as it rumbled over the cobbles and out of Exeter.

This time, although all the outside spaces were taken, no one but he had paid to sit inside, and he had the malodorous interior to himself. Thankful for small mercies, he stretched out his legs, closed his eyes and, wedging himself into one of the corners, prepared to snatch some more much-needed shuteye for the next few hours.

Surprisingly, he managed to fall asleep and was only awoken as the coach rumbled up the steep hill into Launceston and the round castle keep on its high motte hoved into view. He yawned and stretched. Why was it every time you slept during the day you woke up bleary-eyed and unrefreshed with all your muscles aching? His neck and back were stiff, and his mouth felt paper dry. He'd get down here and find some refreshment.

His pocket watch told him it had gone one o'clock, not that this was any guarantee it would match the time they kept here in the west. He strode into the inn's taproom while the horses were being changed and ordered a mug of good Cornish cider and a plate of bread and cheese. No time to wait for roast beef to be fetched, which probably wouldn't be good anyway. Not even a miserly innkeeper could go too wrong with bread and cheese, although this bread's bitter taste indicated the addition of alum by the baker. The rogue.

He was just washing the crumbs down with the last of the cider, which was of far better quality than the bread, when a heavy hand thumped down on his shoulder. He swung around.

"Why, if 'tain't Mr. Kitto himself!" A huge, broad-shouldered, and pot-bellied man stood before him, grinning from ear to ear across a face burnt brown by the Cornish sun and wind.

"Aleck!" Kit stood up and took the offered paw, only to have his arm so vigorously shaken it felt as though it might come loose in its socket. "Aleck Tregothnan. I never expected to see you so far away from your lair at Nanpean. What brings you up country?"

Tregothnan released Kit's hand and stood back, his good-humored gaze traveling from Kit's ruffled hair down to his dusty boots. "Business," he said, tapping the side of his nose. "Parson's business."

Kit grinned. Parson's business meant smuggling business, so presumably that was what had brought his old friend, the landlord of the Ship Inn, a small hostelry situated between Nanpean and St Just, so far east. It either meant a new shipment was imminent or Aleck was seeing to the sale of the last of the previous one, which could take as long as several weeks.

"Aye," Tregothnan went on, hitching his bulk onto a seat opposite Kit. "I've been away from home two nights and I'll be right glad to be back. These eastern folks ain't what we're used to on the tip." He gave a great guffaw of laughter, but his merriment didn't hide a touch of worry in his eyes.

Was his old friend in trouble of some kind? Kit opened his mouth to ask, but Tregothnan interrupted. "When I seed him t'other day, Jago did say as you'd gone back up east to your big house." A small frown furrowed his broad brow. "What's brung you down here agin so soon? From what he said, I'd thought you'd be up England a good long time."

Again, that hint of something in his friend's voice that wasn't quite right, as though he were worried about some problem. As though for some reason he wasn't pleased to see Kit back in Cornwall.

But Kit had other things on his mind. "Women," he said, then laughed, a tad bitterly. "One particular woman, I should say. I had to leave because I was…" he hesitated. "I was in danger of becoming too involved." He shook his head. "And I can't do that to any woman. Not with the life I lead. It wouldn't be fair."

A touch of something that might have been annoyance flashed across Tregothnan's face to be quickly replaced by more bonhomie. "And glad I am to see you again." He leaned forward and dropped his voice to a whisper. "Wouldn't be the same without our Mr. Kitto. We've another consignment due in the next coupla days. Depends on the wind from France. I've all the men on standby." He glanced over his shoulder at the tap room's few customers as though they might be king's spies. "I've been up here arranging to sell it on. But I'll not say anymore. Walls has ears."

Kit nodded. "Are you taking the coach back west?"

His friend inclined his head. "Got to get back to the inn. Can't leave it too long in Bessie's hands or she'll drink the barrels dry."

Kit chuckled. Bessie, Aleck's wife, had never been known to finish a day upright, such was her capacity for drink. Aleck must have been desperate for business if he'd left her in charge. "I hope you locked your cellar door," he said as the shout came that the coach was ready. Together they walked out into the inn's stable yard. The few outside passengers climbed aboard and Kit climbed into the interior.

A little to his surprise, Tregothnan joined him inside. "Can't sit outside at my age," he said, by way of explanation. "Getting too old and fat for the scramble up. It's worth the extra money to me for a comfortable seat for my old bones."

All the same, for a country innkeeper it would be an expensive journey.

MORVOREN

MORVOREN WAS AWAKE just after dawn as she'd deliberately left the motheaten curtains in their room open to let the daylight in. The dirt on the windows didn't reduce the light by much, and as soon as she woke, she got up and forced them open to let in some much-needed fresh air.

On the bed, Ysella stirred and rolled over. "Oooh. Shut the curtains and let me sleep," she moaned. "I'm tired and it's too early."

Morvoren gave her a shake. "We have to get on the road again as quickly as possible and catch up with Kit."

The reminder served as a good wakeup call. Ysella sat up and rubbed her eyes. "Goodness. I thought myself at home in Ormonde. I'd quite forgotten the events of yesterday." She giggled, still, in Morvoren's opinion, not taking the mission seriously enough. "I do hope Mama doesn't go to call on Caro's mother, because she'll find out we're not there, and then she'll discover Sam gone as well, and put two and two together and make five and decide one of us has eloped with him and taken the other for moral support."

As that hadn't yet occurred to Morvoren as a conclusion Lady Ormonde might jump to, her blood ran cold for a minute. This was a world where if girls ran off with young men, they would be ruined if they didn't marry them. She definitely didn't want to marry Sam, dependable and sensible as he was, and she didn't think Ysella did either. Although strictly speaking, weren't they chaperoning each other?

Conscious of the need for speed, they struggled into their clothes and did each other's hair as best they could. However, they didn't end up looking nearly as spick and span as they would have done had Martha and Loveday had a hand in their toilettes. There was a lot to be said for a scrunchy for the hair and sensible jeans and T-shirts.

Morvoren was just deciding to go and knock on Sam's door, when a tentative tap came on their own. On invitation, Sam, fully dressed, came in. "I've ordered breakfast in the parlor downstairs," he said. "And James and John are preparing the horses. We've a long way to go today, so we need an early start."

Breakfast was bitter black coffee and yesterday's dry bread rolls. Morvoren's nerves, jangling in her head like warning bells, didn't allow her to eat more than one roll and that she had to force down, but the strong coffee jolted her into full action mode. As they walked out into the yard, she felt ready for anything.

With no further ado, the three of them climbed into the carriage, and James clicked to the horses as they set off out of the inn yard. The chase was on again.

"Where do you think Kit will be at the moment?" Morvoren asked Sam, as the horses, still the faithful four they'd brought from Ormonde, clattered out of Yeovil.

He rubbed his chin. "The mail coach will have reached Exeter last night, but he'll have had to stay the night there. The coach to Penzance goes back in the mornings, so passengers heading west have to wait for it." He glanced at his pocket watch. "He should be boarding in just over an hour."

He frowned. "It'll be back in Penzance this evening, but unfortunately, I can't see us catching up with him as yet. We won't reach Penzance today, no matter how many times we change horses." He patted Morvoren's hand with his large, suntanned one. "But I wouldn't worry yourself too much. If, as you said, they dealt with a consignment only about ten days ago, then another won't be coming yet. I've heard that free traders like to land their cargo in the darkness of a moonless night. We're heading for a full moon right now, so our journey isn't as urgent as you think."

His frown deepened. "But today we're going to have to pay for a few changes of horses. These won't last more than fifty miles after doing that and more yesterday. Unfortunately, it's more than their jobs are worth for the ostlers to give us the fast mail horses. They belong exclusively to the mail coach service. We'll be left with the dregs from the livery yard. And they won't be fast at all."

Ysella, who'd been looking out of the window, turned her head. "Will we have to leave our horses in some jobbing livery yard?" Her voice rose in panic. "Mama will be furious if we do that. You know how fussy she is about her horses, Sam." Her hand flew to her mouth. "I hadn't thought that having to pay for changes of horses would mean we'd leave ours at the mercy of some unscrupulous yard owner who might loan them out to any dreadful person who happens by."

Sam took her hand in his free one. "Don't worry yourself, Miss Ysella. I'll be telling whoever we leave them with that they belong to Viscount Ormonde and are not to be loaned out but returned to us when we pass this way again, hopefully in company with Kit himself. And I'll pay them well for taking care of them properly. Your mother will *not* be accusing you of abandoning them."

Ysella gazed up into his eyes and smiled her sweetest smile. "You *are* clever, Sam. You think of the smallest things while I just charge headlong into them without considering the problems I might encounter."

How unusually perceptive she was being.

Sam's eyes, full of hunger, drank her in, but she didn't appear to notice. Instead, she retrieved her hand and peered out of the window. "But I'm sure we can catch him if we try."

They might well have done, if they'd been able to maintain the speed they were travelling at. However, someone somewhere had it in for them. Late in the day, with the sun sinking into the west and the road just beginning to climb onto the heather-covered heights of

Bodmin Moor, the carriage gave an enormous lurch and toppled to one side. Ysella and Morvoren were thrown into a corner, both ending up in Sam's strong arms. It could definitely be said that they'd stopped.

James and John reacted quickly. They jumped down and, while John reassured the frightened horses, who at this point were no longer theirs but just rented nags, James hurried to the door on the upside of the coach and threw it open. Between them, Sam and James managed to help Ysella and Morvoren out onto the narrow, grassy verge. They stood in a row, surveying the damage to their vehicle in silence.

The right back wheel had come off and the back corner of the carriage had collapsed to one side. Morvoren glanced over her shoulder at the westering sun. It would be dark soon and they were nowhere near any kind of habitation.

She turned to Sam. "Can it be mended?"

He shook his head. "Not without help. See, the axle has broken. We're going to need a blacksmith and a carpenter."

She bit her lip, and Ysella gave a little mewl of frustration. Just when they might have been catching up with Kit, especially if they'd kept going all night. If she hadn't been keen to maintain her image as a sweet Regency lady, Morvoren would have sworn like a trooper. She did it in her head instead and held her tongue.

"What shall we do?" Ysella asked, shivering a little despite the warmth of the evening. "This all looks very remote." She peered down the road, if you could dignify it with that name. The amount of potholes in it qualified it in Morvoren's mind as only a track. "Might there be highwaymen out here? Cutthroats?" She shivered again. This girl had read too many romance novels. "Vagabonds?" She moved closer to Sam, as though doing so might add protection. Well, he did have two pistols in his possession.

"How far back to the last village we passed through?" Sam asked James, who was uncoupling the horses with John's help. At least the nags hadn't panicked when it happened. Not that they looked as though anything would disturb their somnolent natures. To prove the point, they were standing with their heads down as the two servants sorted out their tangled harnesses.

"Too far, Mr. Beaumont," James said. "But I do b'lieve there's an inn up here on the high moors. If we follow this road, then we'll reach it by sunset, if we're lucky."

Sam sighed. "We'll have to walk." He turned to John. "You stay here and guard the carriage, and we'll send back workmen from the inn to try and mend the wheel. We'll take the horses with us. There are bound to be stables at the inn."

Morvoren held up a hand. "We won't need to walk. We can ride the horses."

Sam shook his head. "We don't have any saddles."

She shook her head back. "What do we need them for? Have you never ridden bareback as a child?" She approached the likeliest looking beast, a chestnut—they were very mismatched for a team. "I'll have this one. Take off his heavy collar and fashion me something short enough for reins. I'll need a leg up."

The looks of shock on Sam, James and John's faces matched to perfection. "A lady can't ride bareback *on a horse*," Sam said, and James nodded vigorously, both of them a product of their time. John studied his feet, his ears puce.

"Of course a lady can," Morvoren snapped. "Doesn't she have legs? Now sort these horses out, and we'll get on them. We'll be at the inn a lot faster if we ride than if we walk."

Ysella leaned closer to Morvoren as James, galvanized by her firm voice, began to hurriedly divest the horses he was holding of their surplus harness. "I've never ridden bareback," she whispered. "Is it not slippery?"

Morvoren put her mouth to Ysella's ear. "If you can ride astride, you can ride bareback. It's just a question of balance. You'll be fine. And these are very quiet horses with nice broad backs. It'll be easy."

Sam looked as though he'd have liked to have protested at Morvoren's suggestion, but luckily, he could probably also see the sense in it and the danger of lingering on an isolated patch of moorland with two gently-bred young ladies. Soon, all four horses wore just their blinkered bridles to which rope reins had been attached.

Morvoren stood beside her chestnut and lifted her left leg. "Leg up, please?"

How diffident Sam was at touching a girl's leg. Morvoren would have laughed if their mission hadn't been so urgent. He touched her as though she were made of glass, or might burn his fingers.

"A good energetic lift."

He took her at her word and was strong as well. Morvoren sailed up into the air and landed on the chestnut's broad back, the skirts of her gown hitching up high enough to reveal the legs of her long knickers. She settled herself comfortably and rearranged her skirts for maximum modesty while Sam turned to Ysella with even more diffidence.

A minute later and she was up on her horse and gathering her reins, a grin of pure excitement on her face. She was certainly having a few unexpected adventures since she'd met Morvoren. Sam and James jumped up onto their respective horses without aid, and, leaving poor John with his pistols for protection, in the gathering dusk they set off up the road toward the inn.

Morvoren should have known which inn it would be. Jamaica Inn, of course, famous as a smugglers' haunt in Daphne du Maurier's book of the same name. It sat on the summit of the moors, and she'd been there once for a meal with her parents.

Already, a lantern shone brightly outside its door, guiding them the last few hundred meters as darkness fell. Thank goodness no one was outside to see their arrival, though. Ysella and Morvoren slid down from their horses and smoothed their skirts before they left James to find the stables and followed Sam inside.

It was a long time since Morvoren had read *Jamaica Inn*, and Daphne du Maurier's description wasn't vivid in her mind. However, in the flesh, it was every bit as gloomy, ill-lit and smoky as she'd imagined it would be.

A burly middle-aged man with an actual patch over one eye stood behind a wooden countertop, serving a motley selection of what must have been his locals. Difficult to make them out in the gloom, but they could all have stepped fully formed from the pages of the book.

"Good evening," Sam said, with a friendly smile. "Our carriage has lost a wheel and we're in need of food and beds for the night and stabling for our horses. I trust you can accommodate us?"

The innkeeper rubbed his bulbous nose, an unenthusiastic frown on his face. "I might be able to. I can't rightly say."

Not very welcoming.

Sam glanced at Ysella and took out his coin purse. "This is the Honorable Ysella Carlyon, sister of Lord Ormonde. We're traveling to Carlyon Court on urgent business. It's imperative Miss Carlyon and her companion have a bed for the night."

The innkeeper's attitude underwent a slight modification. "We-ell," he said, eyeing Ysella and Morvoren. "In that case, I has two rooms you c'n take, but they're not biguns. We don't get many ladies stoppin' here. Most fancy folk pass on by."

Thank goodness. Morvoren didn't fancy staying in this crowded taproom a moment too long. The eyes of every man present had fixed on them in something between curiosity and open hostility.

"And is there a blacksmith and a carpenter to be had locally?" Sam asked, presumably with his confidence bolstered by their host's apparent softening. "We shall need the axle mending on our carriage. If possible, tonight." He paused. "And a meal, too, for the ladies at least."

Morvoren didn't expect all of this to be doable, but to her surprise, it turned out it was. Perhaps the innkeeper was eager to be rid of his unwanted guests as quickly as possible. They soon found themselves in a small private parlor eating an unusually tasty beef stew with dumplings and drinking a fine claret. Morvoren had a strong suspicion the wine's quality probably had something to do with no revenue having been paid on it.

To their collective relief, the innkeeper dispatched several men with James and the horses to go back to the carriage and patch it up enough to get it back to the village smithy. Then, after the meal, a young girl showed them upstairs to two tiny rooms. Ysella and Morvoren had to share a narrow single bed, but Morvoren didn't care. After the stresses of the last few hours, she collapsed onto it as soon as she was out of her stays and was asleep in minutes.

Chapter Twenty-Eight

KIT

JUST AFTER SEVEN in the evening, Kit alighted from the coach in Penzance in Tregothnan's company. Having stowed his valise in a room at the inn, he and Aleck walked down to Penzance's little harbor to where Judd Kimbrell, Tregothnan's second in command, lived. They found him sitting on a wooden stool in front of his house mending a lobster pot, his strong brown fingers flying as he threaded new laths through the intricate network of basketry. A half-grown, barefoot boy sat cross-legged at his feet, working on a tangle of netting.

Judd gave the boy a poke with the toe of his boot. "Away inside and fetch us out a beaker o' cider each." The boy jumped up obediently and disappeared inside the house.

Judd got to his feet and held out a gnarled hand to Kit. "Mr. Kitto. Good to see yer. Tek a seat, tek a seat." He swiped a lobster pot off another stool and ran his sleeve over it in a cursory check of its cleanliness.

With a grin, Kit sat down, as at home here, or perhaps more so, as he'd been in his mother's parlor. "How's the fishing going?"

"Alright, me luvver." Judd set down the almost-repaired lobster pot. "Ketched m'self some fine crabs an' sold 'em up country fer a good price." He eyed Tregothnan. "C'd do with another passel o' goods comin' our way soon, though. Gotta put a bit by fer the winter with m'wife in the family way agin."

Kit nodded his agreement, sinking back into his place in the local community as though he'd never been away. No longer the up-country lord, but merely a friend of these two gruff Cornishmen—the fisherman and the innkeeper. He'd grown up here, and no one ever treated him as though he were anything more than one of them, something that Kit loved above all other things.

"Yer in luck then," Tregothnan said to Judd, sitting himself down on a coil of tarry rope. "I had word, when I were in Launceston, that there's a load comin' over either termorrow night or the one after, depending on the wind. I'll send a message when I knows. A big consignment o' good quality French brandy, fer the most part. Baccy an' tea too. Worth a lot o' money ter us. I'm goin' ter need all the men I can get, with all their ponies. So some from here, too."

Judd nodded. "I'll pass the word, an' you can do the ones in Nanpean village an' St Just."

Kit frowned. "I don't like the idea of the moon being so near to full. It's better for a consignment to come in the dark of the moon. Where's the stuff to be stored this time?"

Tregothnan rubbed his chin. "The old barn up at Carnwiddy Farm. Well away from the farmhouse. Nice'n'quiet. Not one we've used fer a long time."

Judd and Kit nodded. Both of them knew the tip of Cornwall's long toe as well as they knew the way to their own privies, and Carnwiddy Farm was a place all three of them had been to on a number of occasions.

Just then, the boy returned with three empty horn beakers in one hand and a jug of cider in the other. He put them on the ground beside his father and beat a hasty retreat. Boys around here knew when they were surplus to requirements.

Kit smiled. He'd been a boy like that once himself, and it had taken a lot of wheedling to persuade Jago to at last let him come on that first trip to Brittany. How exciting it had been to sail across the channel in the middle of the night in a little fishing boat, load up with a few kegs of brandy and then sail back again in full view of the revenue cutter, the brandy secreted under a catch of silver darlings.

Tregothnan knocked his beaker against Kit's and Judd's. "Yeghes da, then."

"Yeghes da," they rejoined, using the old Cornish salutation.

As Judd and Aleck took out their baccy pouches and began tamping tobacco down into their pipes for a companionable smoke, Kit looked past his two friends toward the little harbor.

A peaceful setting, and as typically Cornish as they came. Small fishermen's cottages like Judd's clustered the slope above the harbor, clinging on like limpets on a rock at low tide, as if they'd grown there rather than been built. Already, the women were setting empty baskets outside their doors in anticipation of their men returning with a good catch, and the smell of frying bacon and potatoes filled the air. At least some of these people were eating meat tonight thanks to him. If only he could help more of them.

Lost in his reverie, Tregothnan made him start when he suddenly slapped his knee. "Come along-a me then, Kitto. If we're to get somethin' ter eat tonight we'd best git along back ter the inn."

And within a minute or two, they were walking uphill toward the abbey ruins and the inn where they'd left their belongings.

MORVOREN

SHOUTS AND SCREAMS disturbed Morvoren's dreams. Pushing the covers of the narrow bed back, she sat up. The shouts continued... along with bangs. Whatever was going on? Moonlight streaming in through the small, curtainless window showed her Ysella sleepily rubbing her eyes, as confused as she was.

"What on earth's all that noise?" Ysella asked, sitting up. "Sounds like people fighting."

Morvoren reached for her shawl and pulled it around her shoulders. "I'll take a look out of the window."

Just at that moment a loud report, like a gunshot, went off, and both girls instinctively ducked, reaching out to grab hold of each other. "What the hell?" Morvoren managed.

Ysella snatched up her own shawl. "Are we safe? Is it the French invading?"

Disentangling herself from Ysella's hold, Morvoren went to the window. Wary of being spotted from outside, she peered out with caution. The moonlit front yard of the inn was full of soldiers, all in red jackets and carrying long guns of some kind.

"Oh my God," she whispered, glancing back at Ysella, whose face had blanched deathly pale. "I think it must be. There're armed soldiers outside the inn in the middle of the night. What else can it be?"

Ysella jumped out of bed and hurried to stand beside Morvoren. "They're not French soldiers. They're ours." She craned her neck around, trying to look along the front of the inn. "I don't see any French uniforms, and these just seem to be standing around looking fierce." She paused, head tilted to one side. "But there *are* an awful lot of them."

A hammering rattled the bedroom door so loudly it nearly sent Morvoren's heart leaping out of her mouth. "Who's there?" she called, clutching her shawl even more tightly, terrified they were about to be faced with burly soldiers thinking they were up to no good. Which of course they were, really. Although how could the soldiers know that?

"Sam," came the reply. "Are you all right? Can I come in?"

Ysella glanced at Morvoren, who nodded, conscious of the fact that they were only wearing their shifts and not their usual voluminous nightgowns and might be putting themselves in a compromising position. "Come in," Ysella called.

Sam was wearing only his breeches and shirt and carrying a candle, but his feet were bare. James the coachman was right behind him, similarly attired and also with a candle. No sign of John. Hopefully he was standing guard over the hired horses.

"Come away from the window," Sam ordered. "Shots have been fired and it's not safe."

Ysella and Morvoren stepped back, but neither sat down. "What's going on?" Morvoren asked. "Where have all those soldiers come from?"

The moonlight glinted on the pistol Sam was holding, which undoubtedly must have been loaded. Hopefully he'd be keeping his finger away from the trigger. "A raid," he said. "A midnight raid."

Morvoren's hand tightened on her shawl. "What on earth are they raiding this inn for? And why are we surrounded by soldiers in the middle of the night?"

"They're raiding in search o' free traders, Miss Lucas," James said. "It'll be a surprise raid to catch 'em unawares. There's a lot o' smugglin' goes on hereabouts."

Didn't she know it.

Ysella and Morvoren exchanged horrified glances. If they were carrying out a raid here, at Jamaica Inn, which was a long way inland, then might it be part of the county wide purge on smugglers described in the museum? Was Kit at this moment on the beach at Nanpean being shot by a soldier? Were they destined to be too late to save him?

"No need to be frightened," Sam said with seeming confidence. "James and I will station ourselves outside your door and prevent anyone from entering." But Morvoren could see he was as worried as she was that this might be a sign that they were going to be too late to save his employer… his childhood friend.

Footsteps sounded on the stairs outside the still open door, and the landlord's daughter came hurrying in, also dressed in only her shift and an enveloping knitted shawl that rendered her far more modest than either Ysella or Morvoren. "Ooh, Miss," she gasped as soon as she saw the girls. "They's arrestin' all the men wot's still in the taproom an' searchin' every room and outhouse." She looked at Ysella and Morvoren. "Best prepare yerselves fer bein' searched."

"Let them dare to lay a hand on Miss Carlyon and Miss Lucas and they'll have the nose of this pistol in their faces," Sam blustered, but Morvoren could see he was badly shaken.

She caught the girl's cold hand. "You'd best stay here with us as we have two men to keep us safe." A shiver ran through the girl's slender body, and Morvoren put a protective arm about her shoulders. The poor girl couldn't have been more than fourteen and was probably terrified for her safety. She shrank against Morvoren, her body trembling.

A few minutes only brought more footsteps on the stairs and a tall gentleman in a smart red uniform knocked on the open door.

"You might as well come in," Morvoren called. "Everyone else has."

He stepped inside with a diffident, somewhat apologetic air, a lantern swinging from one hand. "Please forgive me, Miss Carlyon." He made a bow aimed somewhere between Morvoren and Ysella as though he didn't know which of them was which. The name Carlyon clearly meant something to him.

Ysella let go of Morvoren's hand, which she'd grabbed when the landlord's daughter arrived, and stepped forward. "*I* am Miss Carlyon," she said with all the hauteur her breeding had instilled in her. "For what reason are we being disturbed in the middle of the night like this?"

"Captain Adderley at your service," the officer said, his heels clicking together as he performed a smart bow. "I must apologize to you ladies, but we are in the process of apprehending a parcel of smugglers who have made this inn their lair. I need to ask you if you have anyone hiding in your room."

"What?" Ysella's voice rose in angry disdain. "Are you accusing Miss Lucas and myself of harboring men in our *bedroom?*" She didn't frown but she could have slain him with her expression of disgust. "My brother is Viscount Ormonde and he will be furious to hear of your accusations. I shall be making a note of your name, Captain Adderley, and my brother will be reporting your outrageous behavior to your superior."

And now she did frown, the words spitting out of her mouth like bullets from a machine gun. "And no, we do not have any men hiding in our bedroom with us. The only men in here are yourself and Mr. Beauchamp the agent for my brother's estate and our coachman, James, who are here only to keep us safe. And they have nothing whatsoever to do with any smuggling going on here in this inn or in its whereabouts."

Sam stepped into action. "As you can see, Miss Carlyon and Miss Lucas's room has nowhere anyone could be hiding—unless you'd like to look under their bed. James and I will be standing guard over their door for the rest of the night, so kindly request your men to keep well away, as I am armed." His hand went to his belt where he'd slipped the pistol—not an act Morvoren felt to be all that safe as it was loaded.

"Sir." Captain Adderley's face suffused with an almost purple rush of blood, as he executed yet another bow, and withdrew, well and truly put in his place by Ysella and Sam. Morvoren wanted to high five them, but restrained herself. She was going to have to learn how to do putdowns like that if she was going to be staying here much longer.

"Ooh Miss," the landlord's daughter said, gazing at Ysella in admiration. "You was that good. Can I stay here with you? My pa told me to hide. He ses as soldiers ain't to be trusted with a woman."

"Of course you can stay," Morvoren said. "We don't want you going back out there with those awful soldiers." She nodded to the one chair in the room. "But you'll have to sleep on the chair—this bed is too small for three."

The child seemed very happy with this, and, with the officer gone, Ysella and Morvoren climbed back into their rumpled bed and lay down to try to get back to sleep. But Morvoren was wide awake now, with enough adrenaline rushing through her veins to run a marathon, and sleep wasn't going to come easily.

Their new guest curled up on the chair, and Sam and James set up guard outside the room, which was probably very uncomfortable for them. In fact, it was not at all a comfortable night for anyone, not helped by the fact that with the girl in the room, Morvoren couldn't talk privately to Ysella about what had happened nor plan what their next move would be if the carriage couldn't be repaired.

Instead, they had to lie in silence listening to what was still going on outside and downstairs, as heavy boots thundered through the rooms and more doors banged as a thorough search of the premises went on.

The sky was just lightening in the east when at last the noise died down and Morvoren managed to doze off for a short while. This was made shorter still by the landlord coming, looking for his daughter so she could start work. Ysella and Morvoren exchanged tired glances, and, as if by mutual consent, started to get dressed.

But once they were downstairs, they discovered good news awaited them. The local blacksmith and carpenter had both been to look at the carriage and were at present working on a lasting repair. They would, so Sam informed them, be on the road again by midday.

Midday? Did he not realize how important speed was? Did he not see the significance of last night's raid? Was Morvoren the only one with a burning sense of urgency?

Chapter Twenty-Nine

KIT

AFTER A LEISURELY breakfast, Kit and Tregothnan hired themselves a couple of nags from the livery yard beside the inn and rode back together. A gentle breeze barely stirred the leaves of the stunted hawthorn trees, and the sea reflected back the blue of the sky with scarce a white cap to be seen. With the weather so benign, Kit felt no need to hurry, and they took the low coastal road, letting their horses dictate the pace.

After a bit, their way branched inland over the higher moorland toward Nanpean village, where it lay tucked in a coastal fold beside the chimney of the old copper mine it had once served.

Kit and Tregothnan, keeper of the nearest inn to Nanpean, were greeted with subdued grunts and nods by the few villagers about. None of them were so unwise as to fall upon two of their benefactors as though welcoming Robin Hood to their homes.

Kit tipped his beaver hat to them, and Tregothnan nodded to the few old men, sitting smoking pipes filled with contraband tobacco in the warm sunshine. Some of the village women had moved their spinning wheels outside, presumably to keep an eye on small children playing in the dirt, and their hands worked the thin thread in graceful industry.

One of the old men rose stiffly to his feet and hobbled over to the horsemen, stowing his pipe in his waistcoat pocket as he came.

Kit leaned down as though examining his horse's shoulder. "Tomorrow night, Nanpean Cove. A consignment of brandy, baccy, and tea." And the man walked on by, as though nothing untoward had gone on between them. Kit straightened up and kept riding. Tregothnan's horse hadn't even paused.

"I'll leave you here," Tregothnan said as they reached a fork in their rough road. "I'm away back to St Just." He licked a finger and held it up. "You're right about it being tomorrow. I can't see as they'll get across tonight in this slack wind." He pointed downhill over the nearby cliffs toward the flat calm of the sea, still with barely a white crest to be seen. "So, we'll aim for midnight tomorrow, as normal, at your place with the ponies."

Kit nodded. "I'm more than a little worried about the moon though. Tonight's will be a gibbous moon, waxing, and tomorrow's will be more so. Unless we get cloud cover…" He waved his hand up at the cloudless sky. "Unless we get cloud cover, the night'll be near as light as day."

Tregothnan nodded. "Aye, lad, you're right, and it'll make a right nice change to be able to see what we're doing."

Was that a furtive look in the man's eyes? But it was gone before Kit had time to think, and Tregothnan was saying something else. "I'll get on down to my inn and organize the ponies and men from by me, and we'll be with you tomorrow night at eleven, as normal."

Kit nodded. "I'll see you tomorrow then, Aleck."

They parted company, and Kit headed his hired nag downhill toward Nanpean farm's little valley below the village, taking the track through the wind-stunted woodland.

By midday, he was dismounted and lifting the loop of rope from around the gate post to let himself into the farmyard.

Jago stumped out of the farmhouse as Kit led his sorry horse to the trough, its hooves clattering on the flagstones. His uncle lifted a hand in greeting. "You're back sooner'n I thought to see you." He raised his voice. "Jowan! Get out here now and deal with Master Kit's horse. Looks like it could do with a good feed."

Jowan emerged from the barn, for once looking as though he hadn't just been roused from sleep. Wonders would never cease. With a curmudgeonly grunt, and not a word in enquiry as to how his daughter was doing, he snatched the horse's reins and led him away into one of the barns, muttering what were probably complaints and insults under his breath.

Jago chuckled. "He's been in a bad mood since you took Loveday off with you and he's had to cook his own dinners. I don't think he's been doin' any washing of himself nor his clothes by the smell o' him."

Kit smiled. "Lazy old good-for-nothing. I don't know why you keep him on. You'd get better work out of one of the unemployed miners, and they'd be grateful for a job."

Jago slung an arm around Kit's shoulders. "Loyalty, boy. I won't see the old man thrown out. He might be lazy but he's always been loyal, and we was boys together." He chuckled. "Come inside, now. Jenifry's just taken some fine oggies out o' the oven. The smell must have hurried your feet."

The aroma in the kitchen of the freshly baked pies set Kit's mouth watering. Breakfast in Penzance felt a long time ago. After receiving a welcoming embrace from Jenifry, he sat down at the table. She slid a hot oggie onto his plate, then she and Jago joined him.

Kit slid his knife into his pie to let the fragrant hot air out, as his stomach rumbled in anticipation.

"So," Jago said, doing the same to his pie. "What's brought you back so soon? Aleck Tregothnan an' I were only talkin' about you the other day. I telled him we'd not see you for another fortnight, at least. Not till next dark o' the moon." He winked at Jenifry. "Next time we got a consignment due."

Kit took a bite of the potato and meat pie, a stalwart of the local miners. He swallowed the hot mouthful. "Chance has brought me back, and chance has put before us another consignment, coming tomorrow night." He took another hot bite and chewed.

"Halfway through the month?" Jago asked, bushy eyebrows rising. "How's that right wi' the moon the way it is right now, and how d'you even know this?"

"I met Tregothnan in Launceston. He said he'd had word another ship was coming over laden with French brandy. We traveled back together. I've not long left him. It could have been tonight, but by the look of the sea it won't be. By the smell in the air there's more wind coming. So, he and I think it'll be tomorrow night."

"Launceston you say? 'Tis odd he'd be that far from his inn," Jenifry put in as she cleared the table. "I've not knowed him go beyond the Tamar afore."

"Stop nitpicking, woman," Jago grunted. "Launceston's this side of the Tamar, anyways."

She gave a huff. "Only just." And stomped away to do the dishes, leaving Jago and Kit with a flagon of cider between them.

"Have you anything that needs doing this afternoon?" Kit asked. "After a week at Ormonde playing the idle viscount, I'd sooner do some proper work as sit here indoors and twiddle my thumbs while we wait for tomorrow night to come."

Jago banged his empty beaker down on the table. "Aye, I have that. A wall that's fallen down—pushed, more like, by them silly sheep climbing over it. We can walk down to the bottom meadow and get set on it, but not in them shiny new clothes o' yours."

Kit grinned. "I'll be off upstairs then and find something more suitable for a farm laborer to wear."

Morvoren

THE CARRIAGE DIDN'T get away from Jamaica Inn as early as Morvoren would have liked. The soldiers, under the command of Captain Adderley, would have let them go at first light had they been able to leave, but they couldn't, because the wheel on the carriage wasn't yet ready and there was no possible replacement vehicle to be had.

They took cold meat and bread at half past eleven, but the fear wouldn't leave Morvoren that they'd seen nothing but the tip of the iceberg of the crackdown on the free traders. A nasty gnawing emptiness seized her entrails, making it hard to swallow down the food provided. Half an hour later, James arrived to let them know the carriage repair had been done. He was about to harness up the horses and they could prepare to leave. Never had Morvoren been gladder to see the back of a place.

The not-so-good horses, harnessed again to the carriage but having had a night of rest and some oats in the morning, set off with renewed vigor. Barely two hours passed before they arrived in Bodmin, unfortunately, just in time for another nasty shock.

At the crossroads outside St Lawrence's church, a hanging had been taking place. Too late, James called a warning down to Sam, who leaned out of one of the windows to see what was happening. "I'm so sorry," he said, returning his head inside the carriage. "Try to avert your gazes. There's been a hanging. Luckily, it's over and the crowd is dispersing, but there may be trouble."

Of course, Morvoren had known that people in this time period were hanged for even petty crimes, but she'd never expected to see this for herself. Her stomach turned over with fear at the thought that even if she managed to save Kit this time, a hanging might be awaiting him some time in the future if he kept on with his free trading.

She couldn't help but stare out of the window, and so did Ysella, her face a shade paler than it had been.

But which would have been worse—the sight of the men still alive, awaiting their fate, or the view she got of half a dozen shapeless sacks that had once been men but now had shed all their humanity? Around each man's neck hung a placard on which someone barely literate had scrawled the word SMUGLA in shaky capitals.

She couldn't drag her eyes away as they rattled past, and it took Ysella's hands on hers to tear her attention back from the sobering, barbaric sight. Horrified, Morvoren stared from Ysella's face to Sam's haggard one. "They're attacking smugglers throughout the county." Her voice came out more querulous than she would have liked. "What if we're too late?"

From the look on Sam's face, he'd clearly had the same thought, because all he did was frown as though he couldn't think of anything to say.

Ysella was made of sterner stuff. "We won't be too late to save Kit. You mark my words. You're here because fate has put you here to save him, so save him you will."

Morvoren shook her head. "Suppose there is no fate, and all of this is just chance? Suppose it's impossible to change the past?"

"I don't believe *that*," Ysella retorted. "And this isn't the past, it's the present. Whatever you say."

"But for me it *is* the past," Morvoren protested, absurdly angry with Ysella at refusing to believe she lived in the past. Really, she should have seen Ysella's point of view, as after all, this was her own present now, as well as Ysella's. So surely, they could change it?

"In my old world, it's a fact recorded in a museum display," Morvoren said, struggling to explain something she didn't understand herself. "If I truly *can* change the past, won't the display in the museum have to change? And countless other things? Won't Kit live to have children and grandchildren and by my time lots of descendants? Won't I have changed my whole world by this one tiny act? That's why I'm so afraid I won't be able to change anything—because it's not just him, it's two hundred years of history by my time."

Sam looked up from studying his hands. "Maybe you don't know it, but some descendant of Kit's has to do something important—discover something—like a cure for consumption. Build something, invent something. I don't know. But what I'm saying is, perhaps Kit isn't the important one here but one of his descendants *is*."

He had a good point there. If she saved Kit and somehow returned to her own time, would she find it vastly different because of something one of his heirs had done? Could she leave some advice for Kit's descendants? Warn them to avert the two World Wars? To get rid of Hitler as a baby? To prevent the invention of the nuclear bomb? Now she was getting into the realms of fantasy.

"If he's caught," she whispered. "Will they hang him?"

"He won't get caught," Ysella said, determination in her voice. "I won't let them catch him and neither will you. We'll be in time. I know we will."

At this crucial point, one of the horses lost a shoe.

Was fate against them? Was time itself striking back at Morvoren to prevent her changing history?

"I'll have to let them walk until we reach the next village," James called down. "If I don't, on this road he'll go lame and we might not get a replacement."

"Will the carriage run with just two horses?" Morvoren asked, the cold sweat of fear trickling down her back at yet another delay. "Could we unhitch the lame one and its partner?"

Sam shook his head. "Our own horses could, but not these nags. The carriage would be too heavy. It runs well with two of our horses at home at Ormonde but only over short and well-maintained distances. On these hills, two hired nags would be struggling within a short time. It makes sense to get the shoe done."

It turned out, after an hour of walking to the next village, that the horse needed four new shoes or the others were going to come off as well.

"What about the other three horses?" Morvoren asked, scowling at where they stood munching a few oats in their nosebags. Supposing Sam said they needed doing as well?

"Luckily, their shoes are good," Sam answered, patting the scrawny quarters of the lead horse. "More than can be said for their condition. Poor old things. They look to me as though they're only a step or two from the knacker's yard."

The village blacksmith was old and bent-backed, and *not* a fast worker. He took his time with the horse and seemed disinclined to hurry, even when Sam waved money in front of his face.

"If I rushes, these shoes won't last," he grumbled, as Ysella, Morvoren and Sam stood in an impatient row willing him to speed up. "An' you'll be havin' the problem all over agin in less than twenty mile. Can't rush a craftsman."

At last, the horse's pedicure was done and Sam paid the blacksmith his extortionate price for emergency work. James and John reharnessed the horse with his patient fellows, and they were off again.

Luckily, Sam possessed some foresight. When he remounted the carriage, he carried with him a basket laden with bread, cheese, and fruit, all obtained from the inn opposite the forge, as well as a large earthenware bottle of cider. Once out of the village, he brought it all out and they half-heartedly nibbled on the food and drank a little too much of the cider.

If only willpower were able to drive the horses to greater speed. James and John changed them for fresh ones at an inn called The Indian Queen, a name, he told them in a transparent effort to distract them from their worries, that originated from a visit to the inn by none other than Princess Pocahontas. Then they were off again, bumping over the uneven high road. Until, as late evening fell, they reached Hayle on the north coast. Where the tide was in… of course… and there was no bridge.

"I'm sorry," James called down. "We're just too late for the tide.

There's no other way we can go. We'll have to wait until the tide goes out. The road crosses the estuary on the sands and it's not safe right now with the heavy flow."

Morvoren groaned in frustration, nausea welling in her stomach. Was everything against them?

As the next low tide was in the morning, they would have to wait for the water to drop before the road, if you could call it that, became safe to cross with the carriage.

"Could we not go south and find a bridge?" Morvoren asked Sam and James. "Surely there must be a bridge or even a ford upstream from here?"

Their shrugs were answer enough. Sam and Morvoren went to ask the landlord of the inn where they'd halted their carriage.

"You won't get that there smart carriage down they lanes," he said, his facial hair, which he had in abundance, vibrating as he spoke. "Too narrer and too bumpy. Yer'd do it on hossback, but yer haven't got no hosses to ride."

Morvoren eyed their newest set of replacements out of a grimy window. James and John were unhitching them from the carriage. She'd thought the ones they'd ridden up to Jamaica Inn had been bad, but these were a whole lot sorrier. She doubted very much if anyone had ever sat astride any of them. Plus, they didn't have saddles and Carlyon Court and Nanpean lay a long way off.

"We'll just have to stay here overnight," Sam said. "At least until the early hours. I'm sure everything will work out. We can't be more than a day behind Kit even with all the problems we've had." He gave Morvoren and Ysella a cheering smile. "And we don't even know whether he hasn't had any delays himself. We could have passed him on the road already, for all we know."

Morvoren smiled and pretended to agree with him, but her instinct was warning her that Kit was already far ahead and galloping headlong into danger.

Chapter Thirty

MORVOREN

THE NEXT MORNING, the earliest time they could safely make their crossing of the river was just after ten, so the landlord informed them. He even went so far as to show Morvoren the chart he kept in the tap room. "There ain't much of a safe time ter cross, Missy. On account o' the water bein' too deep most o' the time. We doan get too many carriages like yourn wantin' ter cross—most does like the mail coach and teks the longer road through Falmouth, away south o' here." He rubbed his bristly chin. "Be more than my life's worth ter let you an' your fine friends put yourselves in danger o' drownin' in the current."

It was with great impatience that she sat in the window of her and Ysella's small bedchamber, watching the all too gradual receding of the tide and exposure of the mud and sand banks. "We'll be there in time," Ysella said, taking Morvoren's clammy hand in hers. "Don't worry. I'm convinced we will."

Her conviction, however, was not enough to satisfy Morvoren. She sat, casting her mind back again and again, trying to remember the date of the attack on the smugglers and failing. Until it suddenly dawned on her that without knowing what today's date was, knowing the other date would have no meaning. She glanced across at Ysella, who was sitting on the bed, picking at her lace gloves and making a hole in them for want of anything else to do, clearly as impatient as she was. "Ysella? What day is it today?"

She looked up. "Why, I believe it's Wednesday, although I feel I've quite lost count."

Morvoren shook her head. "No. Not the day of the week. What is the *date* today?"

"Well, you already know it's 1811," she said with some asperity. "And let me see..." She counted on her fingers. "Today must be the seventh of July. I think... If today is Wednesday in truth."

The seventh day of the seventh month, 1811. Seven, seven, eleven. It rhymed. Of course. Now it all came rushing back. She'd read the date and laughed to herself at the inadvertent rhyme in the write up about the raid. But perhaps back then, well, *now*, they didn't think of the months by numbers and wouldn't have spotted the rhyme. And *today* was the seventh day of the seventh month. The day that rhymed with the year. It was today. Today, or more correctly tonight, was the night of the attack.

She grabbed Ysella's arm. "I remember," she cried, her fingers digging into her friend's flesh. "Seven, seven, 1811. The date rhymed. I noticed it when I was in the museum, and when you told me the date just now, I remembered. Today's the day of the attack. We only have today to get to Kit and warn him."

Ysella clutched Morvoren back. "The seventh of July? Today? We have to tell Sam. Come on."

They clattered down the stairs to find Sam in the tap room supping a brimming tankard of cider. Morvoren grabbed his arm, some of it spilled and both girls pulled him into the bay window away from the bar. "It's today," Ysella hissed. "Morvoren remembers. We have to get there as fast as we can to warn him. It's imp-imp..." Her voice trailed away.

"Imperative," Morvoren said, and she nodded.

To do him credit, Sam could move fast when he wanted to. He

sent James and John out to make sure the carriage was ready to go as soon as it was deemed safe to cross the estuary, whose waters still looked frighteningly high. What if the carriage was washed away by the outgoing tide? What if they couldn't get out of it and all drowned? What if she'd been meant to drown on that first fateful day in 1811, and time was waiting to exact its cruel punishment on her?

She didn't have time to dwell on this for long.

"Go and pack your things and have them down here to load on the carriage," Sam said. "It's after nine now, so we've not long to go." He smiled a hollow, desperate smile. "We can do it. I know we can."

If only they hadn't had one mishap after another. But at least they knew it hadn't happened already. How awful would it have been if today had been the eighth and for them to have been one day too late?

Just before ten, the man standing guard at the crossing point informed them it was at last safe to cross, and the carriage wheels rumbled off the stone slipway and onto the silent sand. Ahead, the river hadn't withdrawn entirely of course, and when they reached its banks, they were still going to have to negotiate what looked to Morvoren like very turbulent waters.

She hung onto Ysella's hand, and Ysella held onto Sam's. Morvoren forbore from saying, but her head filled up again with those frightening pictures of the carriage rolling over and over in the water with all of them stuck inside as it filled up and they were drowned. Of their horses thrashing in the water. Of the people on the bank standing staring but unable to save them.

No. She had to push images like that out of her head. She had to be brave. Perhaps Josh had been right and by facing up to her terror of water like this, for the sake of someone else, she could perhaps overcome it.

She gritted her teeth and clutched the balance strap, keeping her eyes averted from the watery prospect outside the carriage window, determined not to make a fool of herself. It took a lot of doing, and brought a whimper from Ysella, whose hand she had in a death grip.

But at last, after what felt like ages but was probably really only a couple of minutes at most, they rolled out of the water and onto the sand on the other side. Morvoren relaxed her grip on Ysella's hand and the strap, and heaved a deep, shuddering breath.

Ysella released Sam's hand and threw her arms around her, patting her back in encouragement. "I didn't realize you were so afraid of water, dear Morvoren."

Morvoren nodded, aware of her still thumping heart. "I can't help it. I've been like it since I was a small child. I don't know why. I know it's unreasonable, but nothing makes me more afraid than the feeling of being helpless in water." She sniffed. "Or the things I imagine might happen." No need to reveal what she'd been thinking, not now the ordeal was over.

Sam gave her an awkward pat on the arm. "Many of us have a morbid fear of something, Morvoren. I myself, despite being a man grown, cannot bear spiders. If one is in the office or at my home, I have to get someone to come in and deal with it or I cannot be in the room."

Whether that were true or not, Morvoren had no idea, but it had the effect of making her smile at the idea of big strong Sam having to get someone to rid a room of a spider before he'd go inside.

"That's better," Sam said, resuming his seat as the carriage jolted over some ruts in the road. "You were courageous to even contemplate the crossing. I admire your pluck after your experience under the sea."

"Well, I'm glad I did it," Morvoren said, now of the opinion that it hadn't been that bad. Memory can play false tricks, even short-term memory. "For Kit's sake at least." And she gave them both another watery smile. "How much further do we have to go?"

Sam leaned back in his seat. "Only about twenty miles to Carlyon Court, but that's as the crow flies. A good deal longer by these lanes and all their steep hills."

"Not Nanpean? Are we not going there?"

He shook his head. "Kit always goes to the Court. I've been with him once or twice and we've always stayed there. And besides which, we couldn't get the carriage down the track to Nanpean. You mark my words. We'll be there well before nightfall, in time to find Kit still at the Court." He gave Morvoren a reassuring smile. "We'll probably be there in time to dine with him. Smuggling goes on at night, or so I've been told, and it's not dark until late at the moment."

She leaned back against the upholstery as well, her heart refusing to steady. Twenty miles minimum, probably more like thirty, and it was already after ten and they had less than decent horses to negotiate the terrible roads. Could they do it?

The carriage rumbled on, James driving the horses hard, as despite him not knowing the true reason for the journey, they'd impressed upon him how speed was vital.

But fate was against them yet again. With evening drawing in and at least six miles still to go by Sam's reckoning, one of the horses went lame. Did someone up there not want them to arrive in time? Despite her constant anxiety, Morvoren had to feel sorry for the horses; they'd been finding the constant hills hard going even though there were four of them. Their speed had dropped to barely three or four miles per hour now—hardly above walking speed.

It wasn't the lead horse but the one on the right of the second pair that went lame. James brought the carriage to a halt and everyone climbed out while he took his knife from his pocket and dug a sharp stone from the sole of the horse's hoof. But it was too late. The stone had done its damage. The horse didn't want to put any weight on that foot.

They'd stopped at the bottom of a steep hill and no doubt the horses were reveling in not having to drag the heavy equipage up it. Just to the right sat a couple of poor cottages, with chickens scratching at the side of the road. A road whose uneven stoniness was to blame for their horse's lameness. Morvoren could have sworn. In fact, she did, but inside her head. What time was it now?

Sam provided an answer for that. As James ran his hand over the horse's front leg, he whipped his pocket watch out of his waistcoat and sighed. "Gone six. And now we're stuck with a lame horse. Can two of them pull the carriage up this hill, James?"

James shook his head. "Four of them can barely do it. They aren't good strong animals like we have at Ormonde. This lot're nothing better than farmyard cobs, and underfed farmyard cobs at that. The money they charged for them you'd expect better." He sighed. "But beggars can't be choosers."

"We could ride them again," Morvoren said. "Ride the three that aren't lame, that is. As we did on Bodmin Moor."

Sam shook his head. "That was nearly dark. This is broad daylight and people would see you ladies and be horrified. I can't let you do that."

Morvoren sucked her lips. "But we have to get to Carlyon Court, so we have to try everything we can."

Ysella tapped her foot on the road, such as it was. Suddenly, her face lit up. "But we have our riding clothes with us, don't we, Morvoren?" she exclaimed. "Why didn't I think of it before? If we put those on, no one will know any difference. Let us do that immediately. Sam, go and knock on the door of the nearest cottage and beg the use of a room so that Morvoren and I might change into our riding clothes." She turned to John who was still in place on the driving seat of the carriage, holding the reins. "Pass us down our valises immediately, John."

"Riding habits won't help any," Sam protested. "You'd still have to ride astride as there are no saddles and that's not at all ladylike. As I pointed out before."

"Well," Morvoren said, as John passed her valise. "Lucky we've brought our breeches with us then. You know we can both manage astride and bareback, so stop complaining. This is the only alternative we have and we're going to do it, whatever you say." She turned to Ysella. "Come along, and we'll do the knocking ourselves."

Holding her bag, Morvoren marched up to the door of the first cottage and rapped smartly on it. After a short pause, it opened a crack and a young girl in a white lacy bonnet peeked out. Her mouth fell open as she took in their smart appearance, even though by the standards of Ormonde they must look like a couple of gypsies by now. "Yes'm?" she whispered.

"We need the use of one of your rooms," Morvoren said, full of determination. "One of our horses has gone lame and my companion and I need to change our clothes. Can we come inside?"

The girl stood back to let them in. There wasn't much else she could have done, because if she hadn't, Morvoren was sure Ysella would have shouldered her way in uninvited. They found themselves in the cottage's spartan front room, where three more children were playing on a rag rug in front of a cold fireplace. They all looked clean and tidy, although a definite aroma of urine was coming from the baby, who was sitting playing with a wooden rattle. Goodness knows what they used for nappies, but this baby needed a change.

Morvoren forbore from saying so though, not wanting to offend her young hostess, who herself couldn't be more than eleven or twelve.

"Is your mother at home?" Ysella asked.

The girl shook her head. "She be at the farm, helpin' wi' the haymakin'. She do leave me to tek care o' the littluns, so they don't get in the way."

"We need a room," Morvoren said. "Can you show us where we can change our clothes?"

Three minutes later they were upstairs in a low-ceilinged bedroom. It must have belonged to the parents, as there was only one bed and a crib in the way of furniture. They stripped to their slips and hurriedly pulled on their shirts and breeches. Ysella was fairly crowing with excitement. "I knew these clothes and knowing how to ride astride would come in handy," she said as she slipped her feet into the buckled shoes that had once been Kit's.

Morvoren had some trouble with her breeches, but in a few more minutes they were finished and stuffing their gowns into their valises with no heed for how they were going to look when they took them out again. Who cared?

"Hair," Morvoren said, nodding at Ysella's. "No boy has a topknot like you've got. Let's undo our hair and tie it back behind. I've noticed a lot of older men still wear their hair like that so we can get away with it, as Cornwall's bound to be behind in the fashion for short hair."

They did each other's hair, confining it in low ponytails.

"I wish we'd brought hats," Ysella said, pulling on her waistcoat. "I'd feel more hidden if I had a hat."

An idea seized Morvoren. They descended the stairs in their boy's attire to be met with a row of horrified faces. The girl was only marginally less shocked than Sam, who must have come inside after them and now stood there with his mouth hanging open. Whether it was because they made such good boys or for some other reason, Morvoren didn't know.

"You can't ride anywhere looking like that," he said.

"Oh yes we can," Ysella said. "It's a matter of life and death, so we can. And you're not stopping us. Come, let's get the horses and set off."

Morvoren held up her hand and turned to the girl. "We need hats to hide the fact we're girls." She nodded to a row of hooks on the far side of the room where she could clearly see at least one hat, an old tricorn. "We'll pay you well if you can find us two hats." She turned to Sam. "How much do we have left?"

He shook a purse that still sounded satisfyingly full, not looking at all enthusiastic at having to part with some of it in order to get two ancient hats.

"A guinea," Morvoren said, poking about in his purse. "Give them a guinea per hat."

The girl was at the hooks in a flash and back with the tricorn and a sort of woolen beanie hat. She held out her hand for the money, her eyes alight with excitement. Clearly a guinea for an old hat was overpricing them, but Morvoren didn't care.

She put on the tricorn and Ysella jammed the wooly hat down over her ears. The hat turned her from a girl in boy's clothing into a real boy. Sam handed over the two guineas with some reluctance, and they hurried out of the house and back to James and John at the carriage.

The three men unhitched the sorry horses from the shafts and removed their harness, stacking it all beside the road, then Sam gave Morvoren a leg up onto one of the horses and Ysella onto a second. Luckily, despite Morvoren's doubts as to whether anyone had ever ridden them before, neither horse made any objection. Quite a relief.

"You two must stay here and guard the carriage and harness until we get back," Sam said to James and John. "The family in the first cottage appear helpful so here's another guinea so you can beg food and lodging for you and the lame horse. Ask them, too, for somewhere to stash the harness out of harm's way. We'll try not to be long. Good luck." He sprang up onto his own horse, a bony old nag, and they turned the beasts up the hill.

They were certainly not schooled as riding horses, nor even much as driving horses, but their responses to being kicked in the ribs did imply that they had at one point been ridden, and none of them made any attempt to dispose of their riders. Either that or they were just too tired to try it.

They couldn't push them hard though, or they'd have foundered like their fourth member. As they plodded westwards, Morvoren couldn't help but think that they might, in fact, have been faster if they'd been on foot themselves. A map would have been helpful too, but none of them had thought of that. They had to keep stopping to ask the way, and that, along with taking numerous wrong turns, slowed them down a lot. They didn't arrive at Carlyon Court until the sun was disappearing over the western horizon.

A pair of tall, iron gates opened onto a wide gravel drive in decidedly better condition than the roads they'd been traveling. An ornamental pond, on which the flowers of the decorative lilies had all folded up for the night, occupied the center of the drive and, beyond, an old Elizabethan brick and timber house stretched away to left and right, gilded by the last rays of the dying sun.

They'd made it so far. Surely they could make it the last bit?

Chapter Thirty-One

MORVOREN

Morvoren and Ysella remained mounted while Sam pushed open one side of the wrought iron gates and led his exhausted horse up the gravel drive. They passed the pond and came to a halt in front of the studded, silvery-grey, oak front door. As Morvoren and Ysella slithered to the ground, Sam rapped smartly on the door then pulled the bell rope hanging beside it for good measure.

They stood awkwardly in the evening twilight, Morvoren shifting from one foot to the other, hoping Kit would be here as Sam and Ysella expected. Somehow, she couldn't be sure they were correct. She'd only ever seen him at Nanpean, where he seemed to have a room and a supply of clothing. Was it his habit to stay here at Carlyon Court, as he had when he'd brought Sam? Or was he more likely to bunk down at Nanpean with his uncle for his solo visits to Cornwall? Which seemed more likely? If only she knew him better.

Sam was just reaching out to ring the bell again when the door creaked open and a wrinkled old face wearing a lace cap peeped out. "Yes?" a quavery voice snapped.

Sam stood up a little straighter. "Let us inside, if you please. We are here to see Lord Ormonde." He gestured at Ysella. "His sister, Miss Carlyon, has come to visit him."

Rheumy old eyes surveyed Ysella who, with the wooly hat on,

made a convincing if girlish boy. "Thass norra lady," the owner of the lace cap mumbled. "Thassa lad."

Ysella pulled off her hat letting her dark curls fall about her face. "I am most certainly a lady," she said with some asperity. "And this is my brother's house, so you will let us in straightaway or he'll hear about it." She gave the door a shove and it swung open revealing their interrogator to be a little old woman in a drab, homespun dress and an apron that might have been meant to be white.

"Where is my brother?" Ysella asked as she marched into a wide, flagstone hallway, gloomy and unlit as yet. "I need to see him now."

Sam and Morvoren abandoned their horses to their own devices and followed her inside.

"Ain't here," the old lady said, sucking toothless gums.

"Then kindly tell us where he is," Sam said. "It's imperative that we see him immediately."

"Dunno," the old lady mumbled. "Don't know why yer think I sh'd know. He ain't here, and I ain't his keeper."

Not a people person.

"Please," Morvoren said, grasping her hand. It felt like a bundle of old twigs wrapped in dry skin. "It's vital we find him. A matter of life and death. His life. We need you to help us."

She was so small and bent, she had to tilt her head back to look up, a difficult task as her back was bowed in a dowager's hump. But her corrugated face softened a little. "I do b'lieve," she said, her faded eyes fixed on Morvoren's. "I do b'lieve that when he come down here, he stays at Nanpean. He don't trouble us none here, 'cept when he have someone with him." She fixed her eyes on Sam, who perhaps she recognized. "House ain't bin opened up proper in quite a while. Not since Master Kit brung *you* down last." She nodded her head. "That'll be it. He'll be down Nanpean with his uncle. Thass where he'll be. Like he usually is."

Morvoren glared at Sam and Ysella, but managed not to say, "I told you so."

"How do we get there?" Sam asked, taking out his pocket watch. "It's just gone half past nine and it's nearly dark. How are we to get there from here?"

Morvoren swung round on Ysella. "Do you know the way?"

She shook her head, her face stricken. "Not at all. I've only ever been down here twice, and it was a long time ago. I barely remember anything. I've no idea even in which direction we should be going."

Morvoren turned back to the old lady. "Do you love your master?"

Her face split into a wide, gummy smile. "That I do." She smacked her lips. "Young master, he be one o' the best." She seemed about to say something else, but instead folded her lips over her bare gums and her arms across her scrawny chest.

Dared Morvoren risk it? This old woman might know nothing about the nighttime activities locally, about *Kit's* nighttime activities, but on the other hand, she looked as though she had something she wasn't prepared to share. "It's all right," Morvoren said, taking the plunge. "We know all about the smuggling."

The old lady's clawed hand shot out and grabbed her wrist. "Hush now, don't you shout about it then. Don't know who might be a-listenin'." She glanced around the shadowy hall as though quislings might be lurking in every corner, eavesdropping on their secrets.

So she did know. What a relief. "There's a traitor amongst the smugglers," Morvoren gabbled. "We found out about it, and we're here to warn them. It's tonight they'll be betrayed. We have to find Kit—Lord Ormonde—and warn him."

The old lady fastened on the one word that must have been most important to her. "A traitor?" Her clawed hand gripped harder. "A traitor 'mongst our men?"

Sam nodded. "We journeyed down via Bodmin moor. There was a raid on Jamaica Inn the night we were there, and in Bodmin they'd just hanged some smugglers in the square. We saw their bodies. It's going on across the whole county. We have to prevent it from happening here. Tonight."

Seemingly taking it in her stride that three strangers should turn up on her doorstep, two of them women dressed as boys, and start talking about smuggling, the old woman tightened her grip on Morvoren's wrist. "You come this way along-a me. Quick now."

Keeping her hold on Morvoren's wrist, she pulled her across the hallway and through a small door almost hidden beneath the rising staircase to the first floor. They were in the shabby servants' area of Carlyon Court.

After the silent and gloomy front hall with its shuttered windows, this part hummed with life. The aroma of food carried from the kitchen as she dragged Morvoren into it, Sam and Ysella right behind. Four people: two older men, a woman of about forty and a young boy in his early teens, were seated around a table built for twenty, dirty plates in front of them, and beakers of cider, or might that be contraband brandy, in their hands.

They set their beakers down as the old woman dragged Morvoren in, and the two men scrambled to their feet. In shirt sleeves and rough breeches, none of them looked like the sort of servants Kit had at Ormonde.

"What's this?" the elder of the two, a white-haired, portly man, asked, his tone gruff and even a little aggressive. "What you after?"

He was addressing Sam, but Morvoren answered. It was, after all, on her say-so that they were down here searching for Kit. "We need a guide to take us to Nanpean. Right away, even though it's nearly dark. It's a matter of life and death."

The man's face furrowed in a heavy frown. "An' who be you to go demandin' that we stir ourselves of an evenin' to do that?" he asked, the implication being that they were very rude to expect decent servants to bestir themselves out of working hours. Whatever their working hours might be in an empty house.

Ysella stepped forward. "I am Ysella Carlyon and I have the authority of my brother, your employer, to command you to do as I ask. If we don't get to Nanpean very shortly, Kit will die, and a lot of other good Cornishmen with him." She paused. "It's no use you all pretending you don't know about the smuggling, because we *know* you're lying. We know all about it." She waved a hand at Sam and Morvoren. "And we've ridden over two hundred miles from Ormonde to save Kit. He and the others are going to die tonight if you don't help us."

The woman, who must have been the cook, bestirred herself. "Master Kit and his men's in danger, ye say?"

Morvoren nodded, taking off her hat so they could see she was a girl like Ysella. "There's a traitor amongst the smugglers, only Kit doesn't know it. The revenue men and soldiers know there's to be a consignment tonight. We have to warn Kit and his men and stop them getting caught. We have to hurry."

"A traitor?" The white-haired man banged his beaker down on the table. "D'you have the name of the traitor?"

Morvoren shook her head. "I'm sorry. All I know is that they've been betrayed and the revenue men will be lying in wait for them with armed soldiers."

The second man, younger and less corpulent, glowered across the table. "I'll away over to Nanpean village to warn the wives." He paused. "Though one o' them'll know already, because I'll be bound the traitor won't be on the beach tonight. He'll be hidin' back home with some excuse for why he couldn't be there."

Morvoren glanced back at Sam, who hurriedly took out his watch and nodded to her. She turned her hat in her hands. "We've already wasted twenty minutes here. We have to get to Nanpean Farm to warn Jago and Kit, but we don't know the way."

The woman's wide-eyed stare went from the two men to the still seated boy. She bit her lip in evident indecision, then dropped her hand to the boy's shoulder. "Father can't go, not on his legs, but my boy

Jem do know the way to Nanpean like the back o' his hand, so to speak. He can show you the quickest way to get there all right, even in the dark. Can't you, Jem? Take them along the cliff path. 'Tis the quickest way."

Jem, a sandy-haired, slight boy, nodded vigorously, the light in his eyes betraying his excitement at what he must see as the coming adventure. Perhaps he already pictured himself as the savior of the day.

His mother tightened her grip on his shoulder. "A moment. You fine folks must remember my son's jest a boy. Don't you go lettin' him get in the way of any o' them musket balls." She looked down at him. "And Jem. Once you got Miss Carlyon and her friends to Nanpean, you come straight back here to me. No heroics. You're too young to join the gentlemen."

She had a faint hope of that, from the look on Jem's eager face.

"I'll make sure he goes back," Morvoren said, giving him a stern glare. "I promise I'll do my best to keep him out of danger."

Jem ducked his head and, shaking off his mother's hand, got to his feet, all long skinny limbs and big feet, like a newborn colt.

"Best put those hats back on," the old woman muttered. "So's you lads don't go out there lookin' too much like a pair o' girls." At least she wasn't disapproving of their disguises.

Ysella and Morvoren jammed their hats back on, and Jem, shoulders squared and with a proud step, led them out of the kitchen door into the back yard of the house. He seemed to be entering into the spirit of the evening extremely well. "This way," he hissed. "We has to keep quiet. Don't speak a word lessen I ses yer can."

They followed him out into the darkness.

KIT

IN THE FARMHOUSE at Nanpean, Kit pulled on one of Jago's tatty coats and his old tricorn hat, ready for the off. From outside the open door, in the moonlit darkness, came the muffled sounds of the men bringing their string of sturdy pack ponies into the yard: mutters and whispers from the men, the grate of hobnailed boots, and the shuffle of small unshod hooves on the flagstones.

Only a single oil lamp burned in the middle of the table as Kit loaded his pistols, mindful of Jago's motto to never go unprepared to a possible affray. Never assume the best, always expect the worst. Wise words, even though Kit had never yet needed to use a pistol. He glanced at the stairs as Jenifry clattered down them. She'd been in the box room setting up the only other lamp in its window. A signal to let the little French cutter know it was safe to bring the contraband goods ashore in its yawls.

Her face was flushed and her eyes alight with the excitement they all felt on the night a consignment was coming ashore.

"All done," she said.

Jago came stomping through the front door from the yard, bringing with him the cool night air and a whiff of pony. "Damn it," he said, the lamplight casting his features into frightening shadow. "Clemo's just come with a message from Aleck Tregothnan to say as he can't be with us tonight. He's down with a bad stomach and can't leave his bed nor his privy."

Kit raised his eyebrows. "Really? When I saw him yesterday, he seemed in good health." Why did a little nagging feeling of doubt bother him about this?

He had no time to dwell on Tregothnan's absence though. Jowan Curnow, who'd followed Jago in, shrugged. "Been eatin' wot he serves in his inn, I'll warrant. Last oggie I et over there were all gristle." He shook his head. "Since you took my Loveday away up England, I's had to find wot food I can, if'n I doan want ter cook fer meself."

Kit slapped him on the back, his worries about Tregothnan vanishing. "Time you learned how to bake an oggie for yourself. You're no true Cornishman if you can't."

Jowan spat on the flagstones. "Women's work, that be."

Jago laughed. "How d'you think other men on their own manage, then, you lazy old bugger?"

Jowan lifted a shoulder and huffed, turning toward the bottle of brandy sitting on the table beside the lamp. "I'll have me a glass o' somethin' fine an' strong as I've et no dinner ternight." Not bothering with a glass or beaker, he upended the bottle and took a long swig. He'd be swaying his way down to the beach if he wasn't careful.

Kit took the bottle back before Jowan drained it. He was a good worker if prevented from becoming pie-eyed, but that was becoming increasingly difficult, especially with the absence of Loveday's soothing influence. "That's enough, Jowan. We need you sober on the beach. We don't have enough ponies to be carrying you back up as well as the brandy barrels."

Jowan gave him a filthy look and stumped back out into the yard.

Kit followed, trying unsuccessfully to push away the vision of Morvoren his thoughts of Loveday had conjured. Had he done the right thing in leaving her? No, he had to think about tonight. He mustn't dwell on her face, her laugh, her eyes, her... He dragged himself back to reality with some difficulty.

A dozen men stood waiting in the yard in the all too well-lit darkness, a moon that was well on its way to being full shining down on them out of a frighteningly clear night sky. Not a good night for landing contraband, but at least Nanpean Cove was well out of the way and difficult to access. He could be fairly sure no one knew of their activities—no one that shouldn't, anyway.

Jago emerged from the house, Jenifry by his side, and all heads turned in his direction. He cleared his throat and stepped onto the mounting block. The block Morvoren had tried to use before Kit had given her a leg up onto Prinny such a long time ago now. His hand on her strangely clad foot… No. He had to stop this.

"Now, I'm afraid tonight you've only got me," Jago said, keeping his voice low. "Aleck's not able to come with us, thanks to his own cookin', so I'm told."

A ripple of quiet laughter rustled through the listening men. They all knew the food at the Ship Inn, as it was where most of them drank of a night. They were a motley crowd, at least one from each family in Nanpean village and the cottages up the valley, some from as far afield as Penzance thanks to family ties.

They shared one thing—they were all out to improve the lot of their poor families, even Jago, whose small farm wouldn't make a profit were it not for his smuggling activities.

On an impulse, Kit glanced over his shoulder and upward, at the curtains of his own bedroom window, still open tonight, and dark. Of course, no small pale face appeared there this time, to be briefly glimpsed, but recognized, nevertheless.

He smiled to himself. He'd had to go up and check on her that first night, not knowing what he'd do if he found her up and about. But she'd been lying in bed like one dead. Too still for real sleep. He'd stood in silence, watching her where she lay with her blonde hair spread on the pillows—his pillows—before deciding that perhaps he might just be able to trust her not to say anything. And deciding, as well, not to mention to Jago that he'd seen her watching.

His heart ached for the sight of her face up there, sending him out to help his villagers. But no, she was a lady of good breeding, and there was no way he could involve her in his smuggling. He couldn't be two things at once—an illegal smuggler on the one hand and a married man, possibly a family man, on the other. It was too much to expect of a gently bred young lady. He'd just have to forget about her.

Jago was still talking, telling the men what they had to do, cautioning them rather unnecessarily to silence, suggesting they blacked their faces with the soot Jenifry was passing around in the ash pan from the kitchen range.

Kit took some soot and smeared it across his face and hands—both areas that would show up on a moonlit night like this one, if they weren't careful. Ned Treloar was smearing soot onto the white blaze his pony had, and one or two other men were decorating their ponies' white socks. Best to choose ponies with no white markings at all, really, but they had to make do with what they had.

At last, they were ready. Tom Cardy, a lad of only nineteen who was the breadwinner for his widowed mother and her seven other children, came running from the end of the house where he'd been watching for a light at sea. "I seen it," he called, his whisper hissing around the farmyard over the silent heads of his colleagues and the ponies. "Out to the east an' headin' our way. One light burnin'. On her foredeck, I doan doubt."

Jago gave the nod, and Ned Treloar and his disguised pony took the lead out of the gate and onto the narrow path to the beach. The other ponies followed in a long, shuffling line, their muffled hooves nearly silent in the quiet darkness. Directly overhead now, the moon shone down mercilessly onto the column of men and ponies, illuminating them, it seemed to Kit, nigh on as brightly as if it were full daylight.

In silence, they wended their way down the twisting track, Kit with one hand on the nearest pony's back for support lest he tripped on stones he couldn't see. The brambles on either side loomed dark and somehow protective, and the sound of the surf drew ever closer.

Chapter Thirty-Two

MORVOREN

IF ANYONE HAD asked Morvoren to find the same tracks Jem led them down and take them back to Carlyon Court that night, she'd have been lost within minutes. It wasn't just that it was dark. The moon, heading toward being full, illuminated the countryside in a way she was sure would be alarming to the smugglers but a boon to their would-be attackers. It was more the roundabout route their youthful guide seemed to be taking.

They followed close behind him down narrow pathways between high, overgrown hedgerows that gave no idea of what lay beyond. He led them through at least two small, dark copses, before weaving his way with confidence across open moorland, the moon silvering the path ahead. Where the land dipped, they zigzagged their way into a deep and shadowy valley where they had to jump across a rushing stream on steppingstones then climb up the other side.

Sam had no trouble keeping up with Jem, but Morvoren and Ysella began to struggle before too long, both panting with the exertion and the steep inclines of the paths Jem had chosen. Morvoren's breath was rasping in her chest and sweat had stuck her shirt to her back long before they at last came in sight of the sea.

They heard it first. The roar of surf against the cliffs' feet rose up toward where they'd paused for breath amongst the fragrant gorse and heather.

"Lookee out there," Jem said, his skinny arm pointing. "There she be."

Sure enough, beyond the brow of the clifftop stretched the grey expanse of whitecapped waves that was the English Channel. On it, the dark outline of a little ship bobbed, a single light shining out, dimmed by the brightness of the moon.

"That'll be they Frenchies," Jem muttered, spitting a gob of phlegm onto the path, clearly a young man with a low opinion of his gallic neighbors. Maybe rightly so, as surely these were only delivering the contraband goods to line their own pockets. Morvoren chided herself at her uncharitable thoughts. Wasn't all smuggling for the same reason? Personal gain.

"We has to take the cliff path now," Jem said, keeping his voice low. "You'll be needin' to step careful, like. 'Tis a might close by the cliff edge, but the only way ter get to Nanpean Cove quick like."

He wasn't exaggerating. The path teetered right at the cliff edge over a steep drop down to those same wave-washed rocks Morvoren had first seen from the deck of a fishing boat. She did *not* want to see them again, close up. Mentally adding heights to her list of fears, she followed light-stepping Jem and Sam onto the cliff path.

Ysella reached out a trembling hand and grabbed hers. Perhaps she didn't much care for heights either.

The path sloped down as the cliffs grew lower, and in a few minutes, Morvoren caught a glimpse of the pale crescent of sand that marked Nanpean beach, still partly obscured by the cliffs. Deserted. Or was it? The revenue men and soldiers wouldn't be waiting in full view—they'd be hidden, waiting to catch the smugglers red-handed.

"It looks deserted," Ysella hissed.

Morvoren glanced back. "I hope you're right and I've been wrong all along." But somehow, she didn't think she was.

Ahead, Sam whispered to Jem, "Looks like no one's on the beach as yet. We should head to the farm to stop them." His voice carried above the rumble of surf. "Can you lead us right down into the valley? We'll need to hurry."

Jem nodded. "The path do foller the cliff edge most o' the way, like it do here. We can tek that un, but you leddies," he gave Morvoren and Ysella a hard stare, "had best watch yer footin'. They's narsty cliffs an' if'n you was to fall, yer'd not stop till yer hit the rocks at the foot of 'em."

Like that hadn't already occurred to Morvoren.

She swallowed. This might be dangerous, but they had to stop Kit and his friends walking into a trap. "Lead on," she said, struggling to conceal the tremble in her voice. What if Ysella were to slip and fall? She'd released Morvoren's hand once they'd had to go in single file and Morvoren wouldn't be quick enough to save her. What would Kit say to that? What would she say to him, more importantly? Especially if her memory proved faulty and tonight was *not* the night the excise men had chosen to strike.

With Jem slowing his pace as the path became steeper, she followed behind him with Ysella behind her and Sam taking up the rear. If she didn't look to her right, she wouldn't be afraid. Or so she told herself. Over and over again.

Who in their right mind would put a path right on the edge of a bloody cliff? Who wanted to walk this close to the edge, to court danger so openly? A madman, clearly.

She kept her eyes on where her feet were going and from time to time on Jem's narrow back. If only she had some kind of walking stick to lean on like a third leg, that would stop her overbalancing to her right, something she was horribly aware of and overcompensating for with a definite lean to the left.

The path became steeper still, with stunted bushes to their left, and the ground underfoot rougher, with the stones looser in their beds as the beach drew nearer. Jem slowed down. In fact, halfway down, he stopped altogether. He raised his hand again and pointed. "Look, now. See them's boats in the surf. They's bringin' the goods ashore already."

Morvoren strained her eyes through the darkness, which, even though you could have said the moon shone bright as day, was still pretty dark. It took her a moment to spot the boats. Three small rowing boats were coming in on the waves breaking on the beach like a trio of surfers.

By the cliff's foot, on the far side of the cove, which they could now see better than before, something moved. Was it Kit and his smugglers or the dreaded soldiers and revenue men? Small figures were hastening across the sand towards the edge of the surf. They must be Kit and his men.

A sudden idea seized Morvoren. She spun around so fast she nearly overbalanced, and only Jem grabbing her shoulders stopped her from falling.

"Doan go makin' any sudden moves like that," Jem hissed as he steadied her.

She ignored him. "Sam! Fire your gun!" Her whisper hissed through the night. "Kit's men will know it's a stranger firing and they'll straightaway think there's an ambush. Quick. Fire it now before the soldiers pounce!"

Ysella sat down hard on her bottom on the path. "Yes, fire it now, Sam! Before it's too late." Her voice rose in urgency. "Warn Kit's men."

Morvoren joined her, feeling far more secure once she was firmly anchored to the ground. Ysella's hand slid into hers, small and cold.

Sam drew out one of the two pistols he was carrying and pointed it toward the beach. With shaking fingers he cocked it and pulled the trigger. It went off with a report like a—well, like a gun firing. He staggered back a step and pulled the other one out of his belt.

Down on the beach, the tiny figures of the men who'd been heading toward the surf faltered, slowing their pace and looking around themselves in confusion as though perhaps wondering if they'd heard right. It must have been hard to hear the gunshot above the sound of the waves sucking at the sand.

"Fire the other one," Morvoren hissed.

Sam cocked the second pistol and fired again.

For a moment, the men on the beach stood immobile, before all hell broke loose. More shots rang out, the flare of them crackling in the darkness from the hillside not far below and on the beach near the cliffs. Were there revenue men hiding on the cliff path?

"Quick," Sam said. "We have to move before anyone comes up here to see who fired the warning shots. They're not far ahead." He turned to Jem. "Kit and Jago will be heading back to the farmhouse. Which way do we go?"

"If the revenue men are that close," Morvoren said, "then they might think one of their own got trigger happy."

"Not twice," Sam hissed. "Quickly. We have to move." He yanked Morvoren and Ysella to their feet.

On the beach, the smugglers had turned tail and were bolting back toward the dunes.

More gunshots rang out, the flare of them lighting the night. And shouts filled the air, some frighteningly close.

Sam turned to Jem, shoving the two empty pistols back into his belt. "Which way to the farmhouse?"

"Oh my goodness," Ysella gasped. "Look what we've done."

More gunshots, and more shouting. Were the smugglers armed, or was all this firing the revenue men and soldiers? The only thing in Morvoren's mind was the fear that she might not have been in time to save Kit from death on the beach.

Jem seemed transfixed by what was going on. Sam had to grab him by the shoulders and give him a shake. Maybe the reality wasn't so exciting as he'd expected. He wasn't much more than a child, after all.

"Jem. Pull yourself together," Sam hissed. "Point us in the right direction and then it's time for you to go back to Carlyon Court to your mother. You must take Ysella with you to safety. If the worst comes to the worst, she can't be found here at Nanpean. But I have to be there."

"But I want to come with you," Ysella protested, grabbing Sam's arm. "He's my brother."

"All the more reason for you *not* to be there," Morvoren said. "How would it look if the revenue men come to the house and find you there, dressed as a boy? How guilty does that make Kit look? Sam and I will go."

Sam looked from Morvoren's face to Ysella's and back again. "I think *you* should go back too," he ventured.

Morvoren shook her head. "It's because of me you're here, so I'm coming with you, whether you like it or not. Girls from my time don't take orders from men."

He shut up.

Jem, with great reluctance, showed them a narrow, sheep trod path down the hill, mercifully heading inland away from the cliffs but just as steep as the one they'd been negotiating. "Down there. Sh'd bring yer to the back o' Nanpean farmhouse, all righty." He cast his eyes once more over Morvoren. "You's a brave un for a girl, I guess. Good luck to yer."

Ysella threw herself into Morvoren's arms. "Be careful, Morvoren, and bring Kit back with you, please. Alive."

Morvoren hugged her back. "Let me go, or they'll be back at the farmhouse before we are."

Ysella released her hold, and with only a quick look back over her shoulder, Morvoren plunged after Sam down the rocky path toward where two tall trees marked the farmhouse.

KIT

THE SOUND OF the first pistol firing ricocheted around the amphitheater of the beach, echoing between the towering cliffs until it sounded like a myriad of shots had been fired.

Kit and Jago ground to a halt on the wet sand and their men slowed and stopped. Before them, the beach sloped down steeply toward the waves where three yawls were at this very moment struggling in the surf. A sharp wind was beating onshore and the waves were bigger than normal, and out to sea the light of the mother ship bobbed on the swell and went out. They, too, must have heard the shot.

A second shot rang out, the flash of its firing high on the cliffs to Kit's right.

"Revenue men," Jago shouted. "Scatter."

More shots went off, followed by angry shouts. From the telltale flare of each report there must be men both up on the cliff path and down on the beach, hiding amidst the rocky outcrops. Who had tipped them off?

No one needed telling twice. Without waiting to see what the men in the yawls would do, every man turned on the spot and headed back up the beach toward the deep, dry sand of the dunes.

Kit ran too, keeping to the rear of his men to make sure no one fell behind. Bullets thudded into the sand around his feet as he dodged sideways, his legs struggling as he reached the dry sand. To his right, a man fell in a spray of blood, his arms out-thrown as though pleading for help. Kit dropped to his knees and rolled him onto his front. Sightless eyes stared up at him as blood pooled under his head.

"Leave him," Jago shouted. "Save yourself."

Kit struggled upright and ran on. Nothing he could do for Clemo now. More bullets thudded into the dunes ahead as his men reached the path where they'd left the ponies waiting. Not waiting now. The sound of a hundred panicked hooves galloping up the path towards the farm echoed down the valley like distant thunder.

He was nearly there. Jago had already gained the solid ground of the track, the dunes left behind him. Kit's lungs were bursting with the effort of running on the deep sand.

A report went off, the echo of it almost in his right ear. Kit staggered and fell before he realized he'd been hit. He rolled across the sand, for a moment confused, his left hand reaching for his upper arm. It felt numb but his fingers found the warm wetness of blood.

A strong arm yanked him to his feet. "Are you hit, boy?" Jago must have seen him fall and come back. "Can you walk?"

More shouts. A few more bullets bit into the sand, far too close for comfort.

Kit nodded, not sure if that were true, the world receding into a blurry fuzz. "It's nothing. A flesh wound. It doesn't even hurt." His voice echoed in his head.

He let Jago drag him up the last bit of the dunes, the effort suddenly so enormous that his feet felt as though they were made of lead. He struggled for breath, and for a moment his head swam and he saw stars.

"Come on," Jago growled, urgency in his voice. "They mustn't catch you."

Another man materialized on Kit's right, his arm going around Kit's waist. "Come on, Mr. Kitto." Jowan.

The shots had died away. They must be reloading. Kit's feet scuffed on the solid gravel. He was on the path now, the abandoned ponies long vanished, and the going was easier. A second wind came to Kit and with it, clarity of thought. He shook off Jago's hold. "I'm all right now. It was the shock. I can walk by myself."

"Yer'll need ter run," Jowan grunted.

Kit ran, one hand fast over the wound. He needed to stop the bleeding or he was going to faint and be caught, and what a scandal that would make if the revenue men caught themselves a free-trading viscount. The path was steep, but it was a path he was used to taking several times a day when he was in Cornwall, and he was a fit young man. His arm throbbed with every jarring step he took, but he ignored it and concentrated on putting one foot in front of the other as fast as he could, willing himself not to stumble over the uneven surface.

How short a time ago he'd helped Morvoren up this very path. Not even a fortnight. Who'd have thought he'd so soon be running up it for his very life? His thoughts, befuddled by the wound, jangled in his head as he ran. All he was conscious of was Jago and Jowan by his side and a blurry shape in skirts that had to be Jenifry running up ahead.

It seemed forever until the pale bulk of the farmhouse loomed out of the night. The last of the men must be scattering across country up the valley, heading for their homes as fast as they could go. Not a pony in sight. Jowan unhooked the gate, closing it behind them, and Kit staggered across the farmyard to the front door of the house where a welcoming light was already burning. Who could have lit it when they were all down on the beach?

Jago shoved open the front door and Jenifry tumbled inside. A man was standing by the table, one hand on the lantern, a slip of a boy in a tricorn hat just behind him.

"Good God, Kit!" Sam's horrified voice rang out.

Kit slumped into the chair beside the range and closed his eyes, his arm on fire, all feeling returned.

Dimly, he heard footsteps as Jenifry ran to the door into the back kitchen and came running back with a pan of water which she set down with a thump on top of the range, the water slopping onto the fire with a hiss.

"They'll be coming up the hill behind us." Jago's voice echoed in Kit's head. "Get his dirty clothes off. Wash the soot off his face and hands. We have to hide that he's been shot, or they'll ha' proof we was down there."

Someone pulled Kit forward and took Jago's old coat off, left arm first. Fingers, gentle and soft, went to the buttons on his shirt. Was that Jenifry? A ripping sound as the shirt was torn. Then pain as water ran over his wound.

"Burn that shirt," someone said.

"It's gone right through. He was lucky." Whose anxious voice was that? He should recognize it, but try as he might, he couldn't.

He wanted to open his eyes and look, but the lids were leaden and, try as he might, they wouldn't obey him. Those gentle hands were dabbing at his arm again. Who was that? He'd had Jenifry's ministrations as a boy often enough and this didn't feel like her rough make do and mend.

"Bandages," someone said, lifting his throbbing arm a little. Those same gentle hands began to bind it, the tightness of the bandages fierce. He winced at the pain but kept silent.

"How long do we have?" came a voice he ought to know. Sam's voice. Yes, Sam was here. Sam? How so? Sam was at Ormonde, not here at Nanpean, and Sam knew nothing of his master's smuggling activities.

"Not long. Clean shirt and get him into his coat, then if the bandages leak no one'll see." Jago's voice, gruff and concerned.

What must have been a clean shirt went on, was tucked into his breeches with hasty fingers and then Sam and someone else, someone big and strong, got him into a coat that felt too tight and pressed on his wound. He bit his lip to prevent himself from crying out.

Quick fingers did up a scarf around his throat, and someone held a flask to his mouth. Liquid trickled in. He coughed on it, swallowed, and coughed again, the liquid running down his chin.

"Keep drinking," that same gentle voice he ought to know said in his ear. "You have to appear to be drunk. Drink a little more so you smell of it."

He did as he was told.

"They're a-comin'," came Jenifry's voice from afar. And someone bodily lifted him and set him at the table. His head flopped forward onto his left arm, his right arm hanging loose onto his lap, throbbing, his fingers fat sausages he couldn't move.

The grate of chairs on the flagstones, and he had the sense that other people had sat down at the table, the clink of glasses, the rustle of cards. Someone put a glass into the loose fingers of his left hand. What were they doing? He had to play the part they'd given him.

A hammering on the door. He wanted to get up and tell whoever it was to go away because his head hurt near as much as his arm, but he couldn't. His head swam at the thought, and if he had to stand up, surely he'd embarrass himself by casting up his accounts.

"You go, lad," Jago's voice grunted. "We's too busy at our card game, ain't we?"

The slap of cards on the table. Who was playing? Sam was here. What was Sam doing at Nanpean? Playing cards with Jago, whom he'd only met once before, of all people?

Kit managed to open an eye. A tall, slim boy, barely visible away from the one light in the kitchen, plodded to the door and lifted the latch. The door swung open and a moment later, half a dozen redcoat soldiers were standing in the kitchen.

Jago's voice, calm as if this were an everyday occurrence. "What're you about, this time o' the night when decent folks are shut up in their houses?"

"Are you Jago Tremaine?" A cultured voice—an officer. Another voice he ought to know.

The scrape as Jago pushed his chair back. "Aye, I am that. And you know well I am, Captain Carlyon."

Fitz. Here. At Nanpean. With the revenue men. Kit wanted to lift his head and tell his cousin to get out of the house, but he couldn't. His body wouldn't lift his head.

"Have you been out of this house tonight?" An edge of irritation in the voice. Fitz was more than a little angry. Frustrated probably. He'd thought to make arrests tonight and what had he got? One dead man on a beach and no contraband. Kit managed a chuckle from his position prone on the table. It turned into a snort.

"What's wrong with him?" Fitz demanded. A clump as he stepped closer.

Kit rolled his head onto one side and hiccupped. "C'n I help you, Cuz?" He chuckled again and blinked myopically up at his cousin. "C'n I offer you a drink?" He hiccupped and blinked again. The man would simply not come into focus.

"Kit!"

Fitz sounded astonished to see him.

"What the hell are you doing here?"

"Ignore him," Sam said with a sneer. "He's foxed. Again. Just as well because he cheats at cards."

"I do not," Kit mumbled, incensed by the foul calumny. This was taking realism too far. "I do not cheat…" but his words ran away with themselves and ended in a slur. Fresh blood was trickling down his right arm, tickling his skin. He lifted it with care and put it in his lap, burying his face in his other arm again so none might see him wince.

"There's horse droppings out in your farmyard, and there were ponies down on the beach to meet a ship from France," the captain said to Jago. "How do you account for that?"

Jago gave a snort of laughter that Kit wanted to join in with. "Horses did it," he said. "What did you think did it? Passing dolphins?"

The air shimmered with resentment that even Kit, inebriated as he was, could feel. Men like his cousin didn't take kindly to being mocked.

"There are a *lot* of droppings," the captain went on, his voice stiff and stilted, accusatory even. "And there were men down on the beach with the ponies, only someone warned them so they fled. You must have seen or heard something. They must have come right past this farm."

"I've got horses," Jago said. "Who ain't round here? An' I been out wi' them today, sev'ral times, so they bin in my yard on an' off all day. Want to see them? I c'n get the boy, there, to nip out and fetch 'em in for you." He paused and a bottle clinked against his glass as he topped it up. "And we been here at cards all evenin' an' not heard a thing."

The captain grunted. Kit closed his sausage fingers around the sleeve of his coat, blood running onto his hand and breeches. It was going to drip onto the floor in a minute.

"Well," Fitzwilliam's angry voice boomed out, echoing in Kit's head. "I'll leave you to your card game. But mark my words, we'll be keeping an eye on this little cove from now on. So, if you know of anyone who was down there tonight, you'd best let them know we're onto them. And next time, make no mistake, we'll get them."

A shuffling of feet as the soldiers crowded toward the front door.

Kit tried to lift his head but the room swam again. He gripped the table edge with his good hand, his breathing coming in shallow pants. Please let them go so he could give in to his pain.

The door banged open and the tramp of feet reverberated around the kitchen as the soldiers crowded out. Kit's grip on the table slackened, the world spun, and darkness swept up to envelop him as he slid sideways onto the flagstone floor.

Chapter Thirty-Three
MORVOREN

MORVOREN CLOSED THE door behind Kit's cousin Fitzwilliam and the redcoat soldiers just as Kit slid from his seat at the table into a crumpled heap on the floor.

"Put the bar across," Jago growled at her, and she didn't dare argue. With fumbling fingers, she lifted the heavy wooden bar and slid it into place. Only then could she run to where Jago and Jenifry were kneeling beside Kit on the flagstones. His right hand was wet with blood and his face had gone a dreadful shade of grey.

"Is he dead?" was all Morvoren could think of to say, her voice high with panic. Please let him not be dead. Please. She'd never been one for church going, but right now, she offered up a silent prayer.

Jago's fingers slid under Kit's stock to search for a pulse. Without looking back, he grunted, "No, he's not dead, you foolish girl. But he's bleedin' bad. We need to get him upstairs and into his bed." He looked up at Sam, the only one left standing, his face near as pale as Kit's. "C'n you take his legs if'n I takes his head end?"

Swallowing down what looked like nausea, Sam jumped into action. In a moment, he and Jago were struggling up the twisting staircase to the upper floor of the farmhouse with their precious load. Morvoren followed behind, fighting to overcome the panic surging through her. It was an arm wound, the bullet had gone right through, it didn't seem to have chipped the bone, he was young, he wasn't going to die. But the thought of what had been written in that museum exhibition wouldn't leave her. Had she averted the massacre and the hangings but not Kit's death?

Sam and Jago pulled Kit's coat off and laid him on his bed. Blood had soaked through the bandages and his sleeve was sodden to the wrist. She had to pull herself together. She was fine in operations on dogs and cats or farm animals. She could detach herself as they were nothing to do with her. But this was a person, a person she cared for. A person she loved.

"Let me see." She pushed them aside. "I'm a nurse. I know what I'm doing."

Something about her tone of voice must have told them she meant business, because they moved out of the way and let her bend over Kit where he lay, white-faced and unmoving, on the bed. She could do this.

"Scissors, some of that brandy you're so proud of, strong cotton and sharp needles." She looked up at Jenifry as the one able to source all this. "Clean cloths to make a pad, clean bandages, and honey. Hot water in a bowl. And light. Lots of light so I can see what I'm doing. Now."

Jenifry ran to do her bidding.

"I'll help you carry it all," Sam said and hurried after her, his face nearly as grey as Kit's. It looked like blood might be his phobia, not spiders.

When the scissors came, and with Sam standing well back by the door, his hand to his mouth, Morvoren carefully snipped the old dressing off Kit's wound. She'd slapped it on with haste to disguise his state, and it hadn't done its job. A jagged tear in his arm indicated where the bullet had ripped into his flesh from front to back. Blood still pumped sluggishly from it. Morvoren pulled the top sheet from the bed and applied pressure. That was what was needed. She had to stop the bleeding or he'd go into shock, and that could be fatal.

"Will he be all right?" Jago's voice came out so querulously Morvoren had to turn her head to look at him. His rugged face had lost its outdoor color and his eyes held a mix of fear and worry. Of course. Kit had jokingly called Jago his favorite uncle, and although the older man had tossed the praise away by saying he was his only uncle, there'd been real pride in his eyes back then. It hadn't occurred to Morvoren till now that Jago might love his nephew like a son.

If only she could say an unequivocal yes, but she couldn't. That museum exhibition wouldn't leave her mind. But she tried a nod. "I hope so."

Taking a deep breath, she relaxed the pressure on the wound and took a peek to see if the bleeding had stopped. It had. Thank goodness it wasn't arterial. He'd never have made it up from the beach if it had been.

Using some of the clean cloths Jenifry brought, Morvoren carefully cleaned the wound with the warm water and then doused it with the brandy as the next best thing to disinfectant. But what to do about the gaping wound? She'd have to stitch it carefully but leave somewhere for any infection to get out. And all she had for an antibiotic substitute was honey.

She peeked at Kit's unconscious face. How pale he was, his lashes dark on his cheek and beads of sweat on his brow. This was a time when you could die from the slightest wound or illness… or infection. *Please don't let that happen to Kit.*

She soaked the thread and needle in the brandy then, with careful hands, began to stitch the wound together, piecing the broken flesh in the hopes it wouldn't leave him with too terrible a scar. This took some time.

Over by the door, Sam, his hand over his mouth, finally succumbed to nausea and beat a hasty retreat down the stairs, but Jenifry and Jago maintained a threatening presence as they loomed over her every move.

At last, she was done, and ready to plaster honey onto what had been a gaping hole in Kit's arm but now looked like a particularly bad jigsaw of bloody flesh. She'd seen wounds like this before on horses, caused by barbed wire and fence posts, or the kick of another horse. But when she'd helped the vet treat them, they'd had modern medicines to fight infection. She applied a clean pad, wrapped his arm in bandages from shoulder to elbow and stepped back from the bloodied bed.

"He can't lie in all that blood," Jenifry said.

Morvoren nodded. "We should move him as little as possible in case we start the arm bleeding again. Slide him over to the clean side of the bed. That'll do."

Taking great care not to touch his arm, Jago and a returned Sam, still green about the gills, slid Kit to the clean side of his bed and Morvoren pulled the blankets up to cover him.

"Why's he not wakin' up?" Jenifry asked.

Morvoren sucked in her lips. "Shock and loss of blood. His body's shutting down in part to cope with the shock." She hesitated. "He could still die. Shock can kill you even if your wound is going to heal."

Oh, let the museum not be right.

"Can I do anything?" Sam asked, his eyes on Kit's face. "Do you need anything else to treat him? Anything I can fetch from Carlyon Court? Should I go for a doctor?"

"Best not involve a doctor," Jago said. "Captain Carlyon'll be checkin' doctors, I'll be bound, as they'll most likely know they wounded one of us."

Morvoren shook her head. "Only time will tell. You go downstairs and get the kettle on. I think we all need a hot toddy." She gave a half-hearted grin toward Jago. "I'll stay here with Kit in case he wakes. I'll call you if he does."

Grumbling to himself, Jago led the way out of the room and

Morvoren was at last left alone with Kit. She sat down on the chair by the bed, and reaching out, took his left hand in hers. The light of the one candle they'd left flickered over Kit's unconscious form. He lay so still only the shallow rise of his chest told her he lived.

She studied his hand where it lay slack in hers, the fingers cool. The hand that had hauled her from a watery grave, whose touch had sent shivers coursing through her body. The hand she'd held as he'd taught her to dance, that had slid around her waist in the dark garden at Denby and drawn her close. The hand that had gone to the nape of her neck and cradled her head as he kissed her.

She had a sudden overwhelming urge to burst into tears. This wasn't fair. She'd been somehow snatched back into the past and presented with the man of her dreams, a man she thought it her mission to save, and yet here he lay, barely breathing. She dropped her head onto her arms as the tears ran down her cheeks and cried herself to sleep as exhaustion swept over her.

She had no idea how much time had passed before something disturbed her fitful sleep and she blinked herself awake. Kit's hand had moved. It twitched in hers a second time. She jerked fully awake and lifted her head to gaze at him. His fingers curled around hers, warmer now than they had been.

Darkness surrounded her, and the candle on the bedside table, that had half burned down, threw only a pale light across the bed. Someone had draped a blanket over her shoulders as she slept, and a glass of brandy stood alongside the candle.

Kit's fingers tightened around hers, as though he needed something to hang onto. She studied his face. The pallor had lessened a little, and his eyelashes flickered on his cheeks as though his eyes were about to open. She squeezed his hand. "Kit?"

His eyes opened a crack.

"Kit, it's me. Morvoren."

His eyes opened wider, blinking as though she were something he'd never expected to see at Nanpean again. To be fair, he probably hadn't.

"Mor-voren?" The one word came out as a breathy croak.

"You think I'd let you ride into danger alone? You think I could forget you after the way you kissed me at Denby?"

His tongue darted around his dry lips. She only had the brandy, and water would have been better, but she dipped her finger in the glass anyway and ran it around his lips. They felt papery and cool. As she did so, the intimacy of the gesture overwhelmed her and hot color surged up her cheeks. Hopefully it was too dark and he too befuddled to notice.

He licked his lips again. "Morvoren." Stronger this time.

"Someone betrayed you to the revenue men and soldiers," she said. "They were waiting for you on the beach. Ysella and I persuaded Sam to bring us down to Carlyon Court to save you, but everything was against us and we were delayed and delayed time after time. It was awful. I thought we'd be too late." She finished on a gulp as she tried not to burst into tears again. Hysteria was very near the surface.

She squeezed his hand. "I thought we were going to be too late to save you because we were still on the headland when we saw you and your men were already on the beach. But Sam had pistols with him, so I told him to fire them to warn you."

His brow furrowed. "I-I heard the shots." He licked his lips again. "So, it was you and Sam. Well I never." His eyes roved past her. "Have you more of that brandy?"

She shook her head. "Not good after you've had such a nasty injury. What you need is water. I'll call Jenifry and get her to bring some up."

She went to pull away from him, but his hand tightened on hers, pulling her back. "No. Don't go. Stay."

She sat down again.

He managed a thin smile. "How—how did you know we'd been

betrayed?"

Well, Sam and Ysella both knew, so she might as well tell Kit. If he decided she was nuts then those two could defend her. Bending close to him so she could keep her voice low, just in case Jenifry or Jago was outside the door listening, she told him the truth, at last.

He didn't interrupt and at one point when she faltered, thinking he'd drifted off to sleep as his eyes had closed, he squeezed her hand. "Keep going. I'm listening."

It was a long story, not told this time in a feverish hurry, and Morvoren missed nothing out, finishing at last with how she and Sam had sent Ysella back to Carlyon Court and hurried down to Nanpean. They'd been there only in time to light the lantern when Jago had dragged a near fainting Kit in and dumped him on a chair at the table. "We need to get him drunk," was all he'd said, as he whipped Kit's clothes off to deal with his wound. "And you need to be a servant boy."

He'd tossed Morvoren a knitted hat to cover her hair. "Get that tricorn off—no one wears' em indoors for playin' cards."

"A good thing for you it was dark," Kit said, as she finished. "You make far too pretty a boy and Fitzwilliam could have recognized you."

She bridled. "Is that all you can say when I've told you I'm from two hundred years in the future?"

He sighed. "That's a lot for me to take in, even if I weren't addle-pated from the brandy Jago poured down me last night, and from this arm." He smiled, a soft, gentle smile. "But I do believe you, Morvoren. I think I knew from the moment I pulled you out of the sea that you were something different." He managed a light laugh, a sound Morvoren was glad to hear. "Maybe that's why I thought at first I'd caught me a mermaid. After all, your name does mean mermaid in Cornish."

They fell silent. A companionable silence where neither of them needed to speak. Morvoren's head began to nod and she thought Kit too had fallen asleep, when he spoke again. "Does your inside knowledge give you the name of the traitor in our midst?"

She jerked awake again, pulling herself together and yawning. "No. I'm sorry. The captain of our fishing boat said the traitor was thrown off the cliffs east of Nanpean, but he didn't say his name, and I don't remember what the museum said. It must be possible to find him." She paused. "Or her—I suppose it could be a woman just as much as a man. But I think you should stop your men from throwing him off a cliff. For a start, they might be accusing the wrong person."

Kit shook his head. "No. I think I know who did it, all right. Although I can scarce believe it of him. I need to speak with him before the others get there. Ask him why he did it." He made as if to rise, but Morvoren put her hand on his bare shoulder and held him down. Easy. He was still weak from loss of blood.

"No. You lie still. There's nothing you can do about it right now. You're going to have to leave it to Jago. And Sam. Whether you like it or not." She kept her hand on him, enjoying the warmth under her touch, the feel of his skin against her fingers. "That bullet's made a nasty mess of your arm and if the stitches don't hold, it'll be worse." Best not to hold back. "If you get an infection, you might at best lose your arm, at worst, your life."

He frowned. "I can't just lie here in bed like a baby while they're out after the man who betrayed us." His voice rose. "Clemo's lying dead on the beach because of what he's done. I could've been dead as well. We all could've been. Or destined to be transported. You as well. The man who did this to us has a debt to pay."

"Not tonight though," Morvoren said, pushing him down more firmly. "Although judging by the sky outside I'd say morning's approaching fast. You need to sleep and let your body mend. You need to appreciate how lucky you've been. And know that if you get up now, your luck won't hold."

He shifted as though uncomfortable. "I'm not used to lying idle."

"It'll only get worse if you try to do anything. You have to learn to delegate. I'm sure if you think you know the traitor then Jago will already be on to whoever it is. And he's got Sam to help him. Sam won't let them throw anyone off the cliffs."

But would he be able to stop them? The thought of someone, even the man whose actions had led to Kit lying here badly wounded, being hurled onto those unforgiving rocks left Morvoren's stomach queasy. If she'd changed the outcome of the raid, then surely she could prevent a kangaroo court trying and condemning the perpetrator of the betrayal?

Under her hand, Kit relaxed, his eyes closing as he lay back on the pillows. But not for long. A deep chuckle emerged and his eyes flicked open. "I can't believe you managed to get strait-laced, upright, law-abiding Sam involved in smuggling. You must have some good powers of persuasion." His face softened, his gaze suddenly serious, and his hand sought hers. "And you must have had good reason to come rushing down here the way you did."

He had her there. She pressed her lips together and nodded. "I did."

"To save my life."

She nodded again. "I had to."

He sighed. "And why did you have to?"

The early morning twilight of the room pressed in, her breathing loud in the silence. "I think you know the reason," she said, the blood pounding in her ears.

He smiled. "But I want to hear it from your own lips."

Morvoren's heart was going to come leaping out of her mouth if she opened it again. She'd have to take the risk. "Because I love you." Her stomach had knotted itself into something even Alexander with his sword would have found difficulty dealing with.

He gazed into her eyes for a long moment. "And I love you."

Her overactive heart did a great leap of joy and the knot untwisted itself.

He tugged her hand. "Can a nurse kiss her patient or is that not allowed?"

"She can." She bent forward and their lips met, his a little dry still and tasting of brandy. They didn't kiss long and hard and passionately, as they'd done on the terrace at Denby, but it was a kiss of understanding, of coming home, of pent-up promise.

Chapter Thirty-Four

KIT

BRIGHT SUNLIGHT STREAMING in through the open window woke Kit from a deep and dreamless sleep. And with dawning consciousness, the throbbing in his arm made itself known with a vengeance. For a moment he struggled, his brain a fog, before everything came rushing back. Morvoren. Where was she? Someone else was in the room, moving just out of his line of vision. With what felt like an immense effort, he turned his head. Jenifry.

She glanced his way. "I see you're awake then."

He didn't grace that with a reply. "Where's Morvoren?" The words came out as a croak, damn it.

Jenifry, who had been folding clothing—perhaps his own from last night—stomped over to the bed and stood looking down on him from what seemed a great height. "Asleep in bed, as she should be. After sittin' up all night wi' you."

He licked his lips. "She shouldn't have."

Jenifry picked up a beaker from the bedside table. "Couldn't stop her. She were that worried about you, she swore she'd sit up and watch you herself. Wouldn't let me nor Jago do it."

Was that begrudging praise?

She slid a strong arm under his shoulders and held the beaker to his lips.

He gulped a few long mouthfuls of water. That was better, although he felt weak as a kitten. "What time is it?"

Jenifry snorted as she laid him down again. "As if I'd have an answer for that. 'Tis nigh on time for dinner, thass what. You been asleep all day if thass what you want to know. Morvoren said as sleep was what you needed and we wasn't to disturb you."

Another thought shouldered its way to the front of his mind. "The traitor?"

She tutted her tongue against her teeth. "That be for Jago to tell you. I'll go fetch him."

As she bustled out of the room, Kit closed his eyes again, shifting his arm a little to tentatively feel how bad it was. Hot pain sending jagged lightning bolts to his brain confirmed his suspicions. Best to lie still. But where was Morvoren sleeping? Not in the box room, surely?

His lips twitched in the hint of a smile. How easily thoughts of her brought that change in him. He'd always thought of himself as immune to love, if not the temptations of the flesh. But this wasn't just lust he felt for her. This was an inner stirring of the heart, a longing to hold her in his arms and keep her safe. Yes, he wanted her physically, although maybe not right now. But another part of him craved her company, her laughter when she fell over her feet dancing, and her bravery astride a horse.

What would that bravery be like in bed? Despite his weakened state a stirring in his loins told him he wasn't immune to her physical charms. His previous conviction that he couldn't expose her to his lifestyle melted away. This raid had probably put a stop to his nighttime activities for quite some time to come. There'd be no more consignments from France coming to Nanpean Cove for some time after this, and he would have to revert to being Lord Ormonde at Carlyon Court and finding other ways to help his poor villagers. And as Lord Ormonde, he might need a lady by his side. A lady with a social conscience. Just as Morvoren had proved to have.

Footsteps clumped on the landing. Kit's eyes flicked open as Jago came into the room in his outdoor clothes, bringing with him the smell of fresh air and horses. He paused on the threshold before coming to drop into the seat by the bed. "Well, Kitto," he began. "That were a near thing."

Kit nodded. "And would've been nearer still for all of us had it not been for Morvoren."

Jago's face scrunched up. "Aye. You're right there. I were wrong about her, an' I'm not ashamed to admit it. She's a girl wi' plenty o' pluck. Despite them clothes she were wearin' when you fished her out the sea." He grunted. "An' what she be wearin' right now."

Kit couldn't help the chuckle. If only his uncle knew the truth. He wasn't sure he believed it himself, except for the fact it seemed more likely than that she was a mermaid. He'd been addlepated when she'd told him, and it had seemed a good explanation of how she'd come to know he'd been betrayed and driven post haste all the way from Ormonde in his pursuit. But now? Was it really true? Would he ever have the courage to share the story with Jago?

He licked his lips again. What he needed was a flagon of sweet cider to wet his whistle. "Is she all right?"

Jago nodded. "She's a good little nurse. Stitched up your arm an' made a proper job of it. But she's exhausted. Been on the road for days, Sam says, an' rid the last ten miles on a hired carriage horse without a saddle." He chuckled. "She'll be a mite stiff when she wakes up, I'd wager."

Jago might as well be the first to hear. "I'm going to ask her to marry me," Kit said.

No surprise showed on Jago's face. "Thought you might. She's a girl to be grateful for, like your mother. A girl as brave as Elestren always were. A girl not afraid to get her hands dirty and help the Gentlemen when needed." His eyes took on a faraway expression as he stared toward the open window. "I remember her in my old britches up on that pernickety mare Father had. Slipper, her name were. A wild girl, your mother was, but your father tamed her." He laughed. "Well, he tamed her a bit."

His attention returned to Kit. "When're you plannin' on having the weddin' then?"

Kit grinned. "As soon as my arm's up to it and the banns can be called. As long as she says yes, that is."

Jago nodded. "I thought as much. No point in waitin', I'd say."

But another thing tugged Kit's mind back to the present. "Aleck Tregothnan. What's been done about him?" That his friend Aleck had betrayed them horrified him, but it could have been no one else. Now Tregothnan's shiftiness on being caught in Launceston made sense: his worried looks, his disquiet at finding Kit in Cornwall rather than in Wiltshire. Perhaps, and this was to give him the benefit of the doubt, he'd never meant to betray Kit but just the villagers and Jago. Which, in its way, was worse. The man needed punishment to suit the crime.

Jago's face darkened with anger. "We have him fast. I went by his inn at first light but the men'd been there before me. He weren't a pretty sight to behold, I can tell 'ee."

"Have they thrown him off the cliff?"

His uncle's bushy eyebrows rose. "How did 'ee know that was what they wanted to do wi' him?"

"Just a suspicion." Could he avert Aleck's fate now Morvoren had averted his own? But Aleck's actions had led to the death of one of their men. Would the rest of them be ready to spare him? What other punishment than death was possible? If Aleck had done it because he needed the money, then the same could be said of all of them, and no one else had peached on them.

Jago shook his head. "I wouldn't let 'em. They was all up in arms about Clemo. The soldiers've tooken his body so his widow's not got him to bury. 'Twas hard to hold 'em back from draggin' Tregothnan straight up to they cliffs, I can tell 'ee." He shook his head. "But I did. I thought as you'd best deal wi' him when you're up agin. We've got him locked in the cellar here. Seemed as good a place as any. None o' they soldiers'll think o' searchin' for him here."

"I'll get up," Kit said. "We'll deal with him right now."

Jago shook his head. "He'll still be here tomorrow and the next day. Let him stew in his own shit for a while. Won't do him no harm. He could do wi' reflecting on what he done wrong and how he betrayed the men what drink in his inn and pays his wage."

Kit sank back into his pillows. Perhaps that was a good idea. "Can you ask Morvoren to come to me? I've a question I need to put to her."

MORVOREN

YSELLA ARRIVED IN the evening, on horseback, just as Morvoren was returning from Kit's room a newly engaged young lady. Ysella was dressed once more as a girl and riding sidesaddle. And she brought with her a sizeable bag with all the things required to transform Morvoren into something similar. However, it was with resignation that Morvoren submitted to Jenifry and Ysella helping her back into a pretty, muslin gown and soft slippers. Clothes that made her feel incapable of any action, or even of independent thought. If she was to marry Kit, she would need a little more freedom than these clothes gave her.

The thought that in agreeing to this marriage she'd never be going back to her old time washed over her. Would she miss it? Was loving Kit enough to expunge all she'd had there from her heart? She had to hope it was, because if it wasn't... No. She wouldn't think about it. This was her home now. Here with Kit.

Once she was dressed and her hair arranged in a sort of messy updo by Ysella, they went together to Kit's bedroom to see him.

He was sitting up in bed, propped against a sizeable pile of pillows, his face a little less pale than it had been that morning. Sleep had wrought a change for the better in both him and Morvoren.

"Kit!" Ysella ran to the bed and almost flung herself on him, only a restraining hand from him preventing her landing squarely on his injured arm.

"Steady on, Yzzie," he said, reprovingly. "Don't squash me flat."

She retreated a few inches, and Morvoren drew up a stool as Ysella lowered herself onto the chair beside his bed. Ysella's small hand found Kit's and hung on tightly. "I'm so glad you're not dead." Tears sparkled in her eyes. "Because if you were, who would take me to Town next year for my coming out?" She gave a nervous giggle and glanced at Morvoren. "And what would I do without Morvoren for a sister-in-law?"

"She's told you?" Kit asked.

Ysella and Morvoren nodded together, and Ysella wiped away her tears with the back of her hand. "I couldn't be happier for you. I told you, didn't I? Right back when you first brought dear Morvoren to Ormonde. That you were meant for one another." She paused, a small frown furrowing her brow. "But you must promise me—no, promise us both—that your days as a free trader are done."

Morvoren's gaze moved to Kit's face. Would he do that? For his sister and for her?

He sucked in his lips and sighed, silent for a moment. Then, "I fear our activities down here will be severely curtailed by Captain Carlyon and his redcoats for some time to come. So, although I can't promise never to be tempted that way again, I suppose I can say that at least for the foreseeable future, I will be steering clear of free trading."

Morvoren narrowed her eyes. A good way of not promising but placating them at the same time. Sneaky. But if she was to be his wife, then she could make sure he never again got the opportunity to put his life in danger.

She patted Ysella's hand where it still clung onto Kit's. "Don't worry. I shall find some other ways for Kit to help the poor. He won't be needing to be a free trader any longer."

Ysella beamed, more tears in her eyes and running down her cheeks.

Morvoren

A Month Later

"ALONE AT LAST," Kit said, with a wicked laugh as he closed the bedroom door with his foot, a little awkwardly as he'd just carried Morvoren across the threshold. "I thought we'd never be allowed to retire."

"Well," she said, giving him a demure smile. "It was our wedding breakfast and those were our guests." Although she had to admit it hadn't been quite as she'd envisioned getting married would be. No white dress, no crowded church, no dancing afterwards, at least, not the sort she'd have expected in the twenty-first century. And somehow this had made the ceremony more intimate, instilling a glow of contentment in her heart.

The decision had been made; she was a nineteenth-century girl now, and intended to stay that way. With Kit's proposal a month ago, she'd accepted that she'd never be going back to her old world. Not that the door was in any way accessible, being under the sea. No way was she overcoming her fear of water and learning to swim, especially not underwater, and going off looking for that hidden doorway. And besides which, she loved Kit. No, she'd be staying here in his world.

And now, in the early evening of a warm August day, she was finally upstairs at Carlyon Court with Kit, on their own, married. Her whole body tingled with anticipation of what was to come.

She wriggled in his arms. "You can put me down now, if you like."

He shook his head and instead carried her across the room to the large four-poster bed. Someone, Ysella perhaps, had scattered rose petals across the counterpane. He set her down and remained bending over her, his face close to hers.

"Aren't you going to kiss me?" she asked.

"I was just examining my wife's face, and thinking how beautiful it is, and how lucky I am she chose to remain here with me."

"But you're going to kiss me now?"

For answer, he lowered his head and his lips met hers, at first gentle and exploring, then growing hotter and more demanding. Morvoren's own lips parted and their tongues met, dancing over one another. Her insides tightened with excitement and her arms went round him, pulling him closer.

When they came up for air, both were panting, and in unison they both laughed.

"Phew," Morvoren gasped. "You can do that again."

He did. This time even longer passed before their second break for fresh air.

She let her fingers run through his hair, just as she'd longed to do on the night they'd met in the corridor on their way to Denby's ball. He was hers and she was his, at last. The thought brought tears of happiness.

He must have seen. "Don't cry. I don't want to make you cry. You've no need to be afraid."

She shook her head. "I'm not afraid. I'm happy. Kiss me again before you dissolve to nothing and I realize this is just a beautiful dream."

A puzzled frown furrowed his brow, but he did as she bid. His lips came down on hers, hotter and more demanding than ever, his body pressed hard against hers and his arousal evident through the thin layers of fabric that separated them.

Time for some less ladylike behavior. She slid her hand down and brushed him with her fingertips through the fabric of his breeches.

He stopped kissing her and gave a sharp gasp. "My God, Morvoren. You tease."

She grinned. "I know. Teasing is such fun. But we're both wearing far too many clothes for *proper* teasing."

He pushed himself into a sitting position, his face flushed. "Your fault. Normally a married couple are prepared for bed by their servants. It was you who made me dispense with that service."

She put a hand up to his cravat. "Because I wanted to undress you, and for you to undress me. That's why. Far more fun."

And so it was.

She pushed his coat off his shoulders and slid her hands inside his shirt, feeling the taut muscles under her fingertips and the trembling of his body that so perfectly matched hers. He gave a deep groan that settled the longing in her body into a glorious ache between her legs.

"Get this dratted gown off," he muttered, his hands fumbling with the buttons down her back. "I can never understand why girls wear so many layers of clothing with so many fastenings to undo."

The gown slipped off Morvoren's shoulders to pool gently around her, leaving her in just her thin muslin petticoat.

That came off next, along with her lemon slippers.

"Stays," Kit said, the tension in his voice palpable. "I also don't know why you girls wear stays, other than to keep us men at a distance. I can't undo all this. I'm cutting those ties. You'll have to get new ones tomorrow."

Her stays sprang away from her body and his hands sought out her breasts through the thin fabric of her slip. Her back arched at his touch and her own hands went to his breeches. "And you need to get these off. I can't wait." A hot sensation had flooded her body and she was aching for him as much as he evidently was for her.

He wrenched off his shirt, a small bandage still evident over his damaged right arm. The dark hairs on his chest, that until now she'd glimpsed only at his neck, curled across his muscled torso.

Reaching out to unbutton the drop on his breeches, her fingers brushed his arousal again, eliciting yet another groan.

He kicked his breeches away, naked now and more of a man than she'd ever expected or dreamed of as he snatched the slip from her body and threw her back onto the bed.

Finding her breasts, he groaned again, his lips coming down on an erect nipple and making her back arch as he sucked it in. His arousal pushed at her stomach, and she parted her legs, eager to take him in, more ready than she'd ever been.

His lips found hers, his tongue delving into her mouth as he entered her and shivers of exquisite pleasure rocked her body. He filled her to capacity, his long, strong strokes shimmering through her as she locked her still stockinged legs about his back and held him to her.

Her fingers dug into his naked back, the muscles quivering under her touch. Thrust after thrust drove a matching quivering through her own body, deeper, deeper into her molten core. That core overflowed, sending rivulets of fire from her toes to the top of her head, throbbing through her veins as his cries matched hers and he filled her to the brim in an explosion of heat.

Kit's weight sagged against her.

She realized she'd had her eyes screwed tight shut when she opened them to the sight of the four poster's canopy above her head.

"Whew," she managed, her voice just a breath of ecstasy still, the aftershock still skittering through her.

"I'm sorry," he said, all apologetic. "That was far too quick."

Morvoren shook her head as he shifted his weight. "Not for me. And anyway, it's not even dark yet. We've got all night ahead of us to practice."

He grinned. "Not just tonight. We've got the rest of our lives."

THE END

About the Author

After a varied life that's included working with horses where Downton Abbey is filmed, riding racehorses, running her own riding school, owning a sheep farm and running a holiday business in France, Fil now lives on a widebeam canal boat on the Kennet and Avon Canal in Southern England.

She has a long-suffering husband, a rescue dog from Romania called Bella, a cat she found as a kitten abandoned in a gorse bush, five children and six grandchildren.

She once saw a ghost in a churchyard, and when she lived in Wales there was a panther living near her farm that ate some of her sheep. In England there are no indigenous big cats.

She has Asperger's Syndrome and her obsessions include horses and King Arthur. Her historical romantic fiction and children's fantasy adventures centre around Arthurian legends, and her pony stories about her other love. She speaks fluent French after living there for ten years, and in her spare time looks after her allotment, makes clothes and dolls for her granddaughters, embroiders and knits. In between visiting the settings for her books.

Social Media links:
Website – filreid.com
Faccbook   facebook.com/Fil-Reid-Author-101905545548054
Twitter – @FJReidauthor

Made in the USA
Columbia, SC
22 June 2024